Love and Consequences

To order additional copies, please contact us.
BookSurge, LLC
www.booksurge.com
1-866-308-6235
orders@booksurge.com

Love and Consequences

A NOVEL

LaTanya Whitmore

2004

Love and Consequences

In Loving Memory Of My Mother, Edna Earl Williams And My Big Brother, Harold Dean Kirby- You Both Live On In My Heart Daily. And To My Daughter, Tyana, Who Made Me Believe That Dreams Really Can Come True.

PART ONE:

Reasons

ANTHONY

I

I smelled smoke and where there is smoke there is fire. And the way I see it, there can't be a fire without me. I placed my ear against the girl's bathroom door. After a moment, I recognized the two voices. I eased my way in, took a look around and saw two pair of tennis shoes behind one stall. Girls. They don't know how to do nothing right. I knocked on the door. Dee Dee tried to curse under her breath as a cigarette butt hit the floor. I held my laugh and spoke in my highest pitch voice. "Come out of there you two. I know what you're doing."

Just as the door opened, I stepped into the stall next to them and partially closed the door. I could see them looking around and then, suddenly, I opened my stall and they both screamed.

"Boy! Anthony, you scared the mess out of us," Melonie said aloud.

I put a finger to my mouth just as Dee Dee bent down to get the cigarette butt and flushed it down the toilet. "Girl, do you want a real teacher to come in here? Be quiet. Damn, don't you know anything?"

I walked over to the window and push it open. "You can't smoke in here without opening the windows. It goes all in the hallway. And what good is it to hide in the stall if your feet are showing. Stand on the damn seat. That way, if someone was to come in here and do a quick check they wouldn't see anything."

Melonie rolled her eyes at me and lit up another cigarette. "Well, of course you would know all the tricks in the book since you hardly ever go to a class."

I slowly walked closer to her. "That's not the only trick I could teach you, Mel."

"Pleeeeease, you are seventh grader okay? I am two years older than you. There's not much you can teach me."

"No?"

"N.O."

I rubbed Bad through my jeans. "You know what to do with this?"

Melonie's eyes widened, her mouth opened, and she let out a loud squeal, "Oh my God!"

"You are so nasty. Get out of here," Dee Dee joined in even though her pimple face was broke out in a smile.

I smiled and continued to rub Bad as I made my way closer to Melonie. "You know you like it."

3

Melonie backed up as I moved closer. "Get away from me, Anthony."

"Come on, Mel, " I moved closer, cornered her between the sink and the paper towel dispenser. She had nowhere to go. I smiled down into her face. "I've seen the way you been looking at me in the hallways. I'm just giving you what you want."

Melonie eyes became wider as she dropped the cigarette into the sink. "You don't know what you talking about. You are twelve for Pete's sake. What on earth do I want with you?"

"Well actually I'm thirteen but I know you're not going to hold my age against me. I know about the letter you wrote Dee Dee."

She lowered her eyes and then quickly looked back into my face. "I...I...I didn't write any letter,"

"You didn't?"

"No."

I moved closer to her and lowered my face into hers. I looked into her eyes and stared down at her shaking lips. "So, you didn't write that you want to know what it's like to kiss me?"

Dee Dee gasped behind me as Melonie grabbed the sink next to her with this dazed look on her face. She was watching my every move and I could see her shaking. I moved closer staring at her mouth like I have seen the cool guys do in the movies. Cause shit, I was cold as ice. Hell, I should be in the movies. I coolly licked my lips. Melonie's mouth opened as she stared at my mouth. "I don't know what you're talking about."

"You don't?"

"No."

"So you don't want to kiss me?"

"I...I ..."

I reached for her hand, took it into mine then moved my mouth slowly and whispered so only she could hear me. "You know I like you a lot, a whole lot. And I would be lying if I were to stand here and tell you that I'm not dying to kiss you." I took my free hand and ran a finger across her lips as I stared into her eyes. I had her just where I wanted. I eased my hand to the front of her blouse, copped a feel as I smiled down in her face. She didn't move. "All you have to do is ask," I whispered before I lowered my face to hers and kissed her. I slid my tongue in her mouth. She let go of my hand and both of her arms came around my neck. I kept kissing her as I slowly moved us to a stall, closing the door, and she never let me go. I copped another feel then took her hand and placed it on the crotch of my pants, letting her feel Bad. For a split second she kept her hand right where I wanted and then started screaming her head off as she almost broke the door trying to run out of the stall.

I stepped out of the stall but before I could laugh the bathroom door came flying open and the vice principal was right behind me. I quickly turned around.

"What is going on in here?" Ms. Robinson asked as she stood with her hands on her hips looking first at Melonie and then to Dee Dee waiting on an answer but neither one said anything. She focused her attention on me. "Mr. Washington, what are you doing in the girls bathroom?"

I hunched my shoulders up and threw up my hands. She glared at me and gave me that look that mama gave me when I done got on her last nerve. *Shit!* I said the first thing off the top of my head, "I smelled smoke."

Ms. Robinson screeches, "You WHAT?"

"I said I smelled smoke."

"Mr. Washington you march yourself into the office and wait until I get there."

"But I didn't do anything."

"Go, Now!" She pointed her hand toward the door. I slowly moved toward the exit, rolling my eyes and then, when I got close to Melonie, I wink at her, blew her a kiss, grabbed Bad and headed out the door.

"Anthony Washington, what are we going to do with you?" Ms. Robinson asked taking a sit behind her big old brown desk.

"Ms. Robinson I didn't do anything wrong."

Ms. Robinson leaned across her desk with her hands folded neatly in front of her. "Why weren't you in your fourth period, Anthony?"

I sat up straight in the seat across from her. "See, actually I was feeling kind of sick. That lunch we had today made my stomach turn and I was actually headed into the boy's bathroom but I saw the girl's bathroom first and so I went in there because I didn't want to throw up in the hallway. And I didn't think anybody would be in there because I heard the last bell ring already. But when I went in, Melonie and Dee Dee were already in there. Then, I scared them and they scared me and that's when you came in."

"You said you smelled smoke."

Shit, I forgot about that. "I did."

"What kind of smoke? Cigarette, marijuana or did you think the building was on fire?"

I slid back in my seat. I didn't want to rat anybody out. And besides if I mentioned the word cigarette, I probably would be suspended my damn self. "I don't know."

"You don't know."

"No, ma'am."

Ms. Robinson looked at me and I could tell she was trying to decide if she believed me or not. I sat still and looked as pitiful as I could as I stared down at my new red Converse tennis shoes. I looked back up when I heard Ms. Robinson scribbling on a piece of paper. "Here. Take this and go to what's left of your fourth period class."

I held my stomach. "Well, actually I still don't feel too good. I tell you that lunch it..."

"Very well go see the nurse," she said handing me the excused note.

"Okay," I slowly eased out the chair like I was in pain. When I reach the door, Ms. Robinson calls out my name.

I turned around slowly. "Yes, ma'am?"

"Make this your last time in this office, you understand me? We just came off of Christmas break and I would like to get through the rest of the school year without seeing you. I hope you get to feeling better."

Out in the hallway I leaned into the wall and let out a deep breath. That was close. I walked toward the nurse's office and then quickly turned and took the stairs up to the second floor heading toward my locker instead. I had no plans of staying cooped up in this stinking building.

I eased down the upstairs corridors and duck down low as I passed each classroom door. I just needed to get my coat. It was cold and I was headed straight to the park to play some b ball. I turned the last corner and peeked down the hall. Damn, there was a girl standing by my locker. I stood up straight and walked like I was supposed to be in the hallway while I was trying to recognize her from the back but I didn't think I knew her. Which was odd, 'cause even though this is my first year at Sharples Junior High, I knew everybody and everybody that needs to know me, know me. She has to be new, a transfer or something.

She stooped down and turned slightly toward me as she reached inside her locker. I stopped only a couple of feet from her and stretched my long arms over her head and slowly enter the combination to my locker that was above hers.

She stood straight up just as I opened my locker but didn't look at me. I reached in my locker and got my jacket and out of the corner of my eye I could tell she was looking at me. I began to ramble in my locker like I was looking for something just so I could have a chance to scope her out and let her scope me too, 'cause she look like one of the people who needed to know me. I picked up my history book, my notebook, and then reached way in the back of my locker like I was digging for gold, feeling her eyes on me the whole time. She kneeled back down in front of her locker and tried to get in it, but I, so innocently move to the right and blocked her.

"Are you going to be all day or what?" I heard this little voice say. I smiled and put my notebook and history book back down, turned and looked down into the most beautiful pair of brown eyes that I have ever seen in my life. She was beautiful! And just like that, I lost it. My entire well-tuned rap was gone and I couldn't say a word. For the first time in my life, I was speechless.

But now Bad, was reacting big time. I stood there staring at her for about twenty or so seconds and I got so hard, I thought I was going to explode. Her eyes went to the bulge that was growing in my pants.

Shit, shit, shit! Now what! If I were some pimple faced white boy I would be turning all kinds of shades of red and running down the hall. But, because I am who I am, I can't let her think I was no punk. I had to do something, but what? I couldn't move! She had me trapped. I couldn't breathe and was at a total lost for words. She brought her eyes back to mine. Started shaking her head as a small smile formed on her face. I slammed my locker and practically ran out of the school and didn't stop running 'til I got home.

I didn't understand it. What the hell just happened? I'm the man! I'm the boy that every girl wants, and the boy that every boy fears. I'm the troublemaker, school bully, the class clown and I have my young world in the palm of my hand. Everyone caters to me. I am and have always been the coolest, cutest, tallest, toughest, funniest, cruelest kid around. It is my world. So why in the hell did I just run away from my school like some punk? And all because of some girl! I just froze! What if someone saw us in the hall? What if someone saw me running away, hell, what if she tells the whole school! There goes my rep.

I walked in the kitchen, grabbed a strawberry soda from the fridge and then went and sat on our back porch. I had to think of something. My rep was at stake. I'm the Badman. I get whatever I want, period! What I don't have, I take. What I think I need, I take. I towered over most of the ninth graders at school and there ain't too many who have had the courage to try me. Although some tried to say that my mouth is tougher than I was, a few people knew better. That's my rep. And I had to protect that.

I looked through the screen door and squinted to see the clock. It was ten 'til one. Any minute now, the mailman would be coming and our nosey neighbor Ms. Louise Lonely Jenkins would be stepping out hanging out her laundry. I swear that woman had to only have one pair of draws or something. 'Cause every-day she hung a pair of big bloomers out for all to see. I guess women got a thing about their underwear cause my four sisters always have their pantyhose thrown over the shower or their bras drip drying somewhere in the bathroom.

I went back into the house, closed the back door and stretched out on the couch in the living room. Maybe I could get some sleep before Angela and Anita came home from school around three thirty. My sisters, Ashley and April would probably be looking for me after school. But hey, they know not to wait. I told them I don't need them walking me home anyway. I'm a man. Well, almost any-way, so I don't need them always babying me even though it is mostly my fault that they do.

I learned how to get next to my mother and my older sisters a long time ago. I am, after all, their baby. And my father no problem. He could be stern some-times and really put his foot down. But most of the time, I'm his boy, his only son! And he is damn proud of it. My favorite story to tell is how proud my dad was when he first saw me in the hospital nursery. He and my mom already had four girls, and he was so happy that I had been a boy. Dad saw me laying there kicking and screaming my head off, with my bad sitting on my thigh; he smiled and told everyone. "That's my boy!" It's a little story that I'm sure years ago, my father told somebody, because fact is fact.

I remember when I was about six and was looking through some girlie magazines that my dad kept in the garage, I got my first hard on and then and there knew that my bad was meant for better things. And thanks to Big Brenda things got better.

She was a tenth grader who was after me last summer. She was a friend of my sister Angela and sometimes came over to do whatever it was that they did. Anyway, she was around the same height as me but outweighed me by a good twenty-five pounds. I was tall and lanky, while Brenda was plump and curvy with big breasts and a huge butt that wiggled when she walked.

One day, Brenda came over when I knew she knew that I would be the only one at home. She knew that my parents were working at our barbecue restaurant and that all of my sisters helped out in the restaurant in the summer. But there she was standing at our back door trying to knock softly.

"Angela's not here yet, " I had told her as I peeked out at her from the kitchen screen door. I was holding a glass of milk in one hand and about three chocolate chip cookies in the other.

"I know she's not here yet," Brenda said placing one of her hands on her wide hips. "I wanted to wait for her, if that's okay with you."

I looked at her as I took another bite of my cookie, chewing it slowly as I thought it over. "Come on in," I said shrugging my shoulders stepping back so she could get inside.

I then went back and leaned on the counter and started back watching the small television set that sat on it. Speed Racer was on. I'm a cartoon freak, but I could hardly concentrate on it with Brenda staring at me as she sat at the table. Finally I asked, "You want something?"

"Yeah."

"A cookie?" I asked, reaching across the counter to get the cookie jar.

"No, thank you," Brenda answered in a different but sweet voice.

"Some milk?" I asked looking at her again.

"No, thank you," Brenda answered in that same sweet voice.

"You want a glass of water," I said, now becoming annoyed.

"No, thank you,"

"Well, what the hell do you want?" I asked more than a little annoyed. She was making me miss Speed Racer.

"You," she said and quickly stood up and planted a wet kiss on me.

8

LOVE AND CONSEQUENCES

Her tongue darted in and out of my mouth as her hand found the crotch of my pants. At first, I just stood there unable to move. But then, the more Brenda rubbed her hands on me through my jeans the more Bad responded.

Before I knew what I was doing, I had both of my hands pressed against Brenda's behind pushing her closer to me. She began to moan under her breath and started unbuttoning my shirt. Suddenly, I came back to earth and pulled away but still remained inches in front of her.

"Shit, Brenda, you know what you doing?" I asked breathing heavy.

"Yeah, I know. Question is do *you* know?"

"Hell yeah," I answered nervously. Brenda smiled as she looked at me.

"No, you don't. You know you have never been with a girl, boy. But it's okay. I heard about what you got down there," she said as hers eyes roamed down to Bad. I felt the color drain from my face.

"If you want," Brenda said as she stepped closer to me and put her hands on me again. "Brenda will teach you what to do with all of that," she concluded and pulled out a rubber.

I was outdone. Suddenly, I didn't care that Brenda was slightly fat and had zits all on her face and a head full of nappy hair. I was dying to feel her big breast and get between her legs. I held out my hand and she took it. To hell with Speed Racer, I led her upstairs to my bedroom.

Maybe I needed to do to that new girl what Brenda taught me. Yeah, that would certainly put my rep back intact. Shoot! Just thinking about her brown eyes made Bad wake up.

NICOLE

2

I walked into the big blue two-story house that had been my home for just under four months. It wasn't at all what I thought it would be. I had expected to see a big red brick building behind a black wrought iron gate. But instead was this blue house nestled in Southeast Seattle, not too far from where I grew up, in a neighborhood with other houses and look like any other house yet it was different. It was a house for homeless girls such as myself.

Every day that I have walked up the walkway toward the door and tried to feel as cheerful as this house looked I couldn't help but think what had I had done wrong to deserve this. I didn't understand how on what was supposed to be the happiest day of my life, turned out to be the worst.

I walked into the house and went straight to the room that I shared with two other girls. Lisa, who had been abandoned when she was eight years old by her teenage mother and Crystal, who was practically born here. Ms. Haywood, the fifty-three year old director of the home of twenty years, had found her in a trashcan when she was an infant.

Grateful to be alone I went and laid on the bed and let the flood of tears fall from my eyes and I prayed for sleep as the memory of that horrible day replayed in my mind.

From my bed, I had looked out at the sunrise that was shining through my bedroom window. I got up and went toward the big bay window. I could see snow-capped Mount Rainier dominating the city's horizon and tall green trees and forever green grass that was in front of pretty colored houses. To the left, was Lechi Park where my family went on bicycle rides almost every Sunday. Down further, beneath the steep hill streets, was the Mercer Island Bridge that floated across the sky-blue waters of Lake Washington carrying cars to and from Seattle.

I loved my house and my room with the pretty view from the second floor and the pretty yellow floral tieback curtains that matched the floral bedspread on my white canopy bed. My room had bright yellow walls and all white furniture including a white desk where I like to sit reading or writing short stories.

I wanted to be a writer and would spend hours writing about my adventures with my make believe brothers and sisters. In my stories, I always had a big family because I thought they were much more exciting than being an only child. I often wondered why my parents only had me. When I asked, my mother would simply say that God blessed them with one beautiful child and didn't feel that they needed any more.

There was a tap on my door and I turned around to see my mother coming toward me with open arms. Mama's sandy colored hair was in one big braid in the middle of her head, with bangs in the front. She wasn't a tall lady, only five-five and looking at her, one could hardly tell that she was thirty-six. She had smooth, rich, honey-colored skin and Daddy always called her his yellow hamma. "Happy Birthday, baby."

I hugged her tight as mama smiled at me with a huge smile. "Thank you."

"I can't believe you're getting so big. You're not my baby anymore."

"Ah, mama," I said pulling away from her embrace. "I'm going to always be your baby. Because you make the best chocolate cakes."

"Speaking of...drum roll please!"

I went to my desk and started a drumbeat while mama went outside my door and came back in seconds later with a double fudge chocolate cake. She placed the cake down on my desk, lit the candle and sang happy birthday to me. I quickly made a wish the same wish I always did, which was for love and peace and blew out the candle. I was ready to eat my cake. Ever since I was five years old mama has made me a chocolate cake that we eat first thing on my birthday.

I looked at her as she pulled out two forks, plates and a knife and I got down to cutting a huge chunk and licking my fingers clean before I took my first bite.

"Slow down, girl. Look at your face. You are a chocolate mess."

"Ah, mama," I said, licking my fork clean.

"You know, next year I'm going to have to make you something else. You're getting too old for this."

"How can I get too old for chocolate cake?"

"Because after thirteen, Nicole, everything you eat stays with you. Remember, a moment on the lips equals a lifetime on the hips."

"What's wrong with having hips?" I asked twirling around my room and taking a glance at my reflection in the mirror at my string bean image. I could use some hips since my breasts seemed to be taking their time about getting here. I was still in a training bra while some girls I knew where in a B cup.

"I'm going to remind you of that statement twenty years from now, okay."

"Okay. Say, what time is daddy coming home?"

"He won't be in until late tonight, Nicki. So it looks like you and I are going to have to celebrate your birthday today and then have another celebration tomorrow with daddy," Mama said walking toward the door. "Are you ready for your surprise?"

"Of course."

"Follow me."

Mama went into the living room of our small three-bedroom house that had wall-to-wall carpet, and nice furniture that I helped pick out just last year at Levitz. In the closet, she pulled out a huge box with pretty blue shiny wrapping paper and a big satin red bow.

"Oh, Mama, what can it be?" I asked since it looked like it was too heavy for mama to even carry it. I quickly helped her carry it into the kitchen and put it on the table.

"There you go. Hope you like it."

I quickly attacked the box, tearing it open. My eyes opened wide when I saw an electric typewriter inside.

"Your father and I thought you were getting too big for another fancy doll. Also, we know how important your writing is, so we thought you could use a typewriter," Mama said over my shoulder. I ran to her and hugged her as tightly as I could.

"Mama, it is exactly what I need. Thank you so much. Now I know I'm going to be a good writer. Let's take it upstairs to my room and put in on my desk."

The two of us lifted it up and carried it carefully upstairs and placed it in the middle of my desk. I quickly found some paper and as soon as Mama plugged it in I went to pecking away. I was so happy that I didn't know what to do. Mama came over and hugged me and then went back downstairs. I pecked, pecked until I heard the phone ringing and went down the hall to answer it. Before I could say anything, I heard my mother's voice on the phone downstairs saying hello.

"Hi baby, it's me," My daddy said on the line. I covered the receiver with my hand and tried not to laugh. I loved to listen to my mother and father talk on the phone.

"Me. Me who?" Mama said and I could tell she was smiling.

"How many people you know that call you with a voice as sexy as mine and a heart filled with as much love as I got for you."

"Ooh, don't talk like that when you two hundred miles away from me."

"How's my sugar doing?"

"Missing you."

"I miss you too, baby. I promise I won't take anymore clients that will require me to go out of town."

"I've heard that before."

"Well I mean it now. I can't stand being away from you."

"You miss me much?"

"Of course I do."

"How much?"

"Enough to walk two hundred miles home if I thought I could get to your loving any sooner than nine o'clock."

"Ooh daddy," I said giggling on the phone.

"Hush that talk Nick, your other woman is on the extension."

"Hey, princess. Happy birthday."

"Hi daddy, thank you for my present."

"What present?"

"The typewriter."

"Typewriter, what typewriter? What is she talking about Chantel?"

"Oh, I found this beat up old typewriter in the dumpster behind Kmart, put it in a box and gave it to her. Nothing special," Mama said.

"Ha, ha funny, mama," I said.

"Oh, I thought you gave her the real present," Daddy said.

"What real present?"

"No, Nick I thought I would wait for you," Mama said ignoring me.

"What real present?" I asked again pulling the phone and stretching it down the stairs to look at mama as she was leaning against the sink smiling into the phone. I couldn't go any further so I had to sit on a step.

"No, baby, I think you should give it to her. Otherwise she would have to wait half the night until I get home."

"Oh, but Nick she can wait. She's not a little..."

"Hello mother, father, will you two please stop ignoring me and tell me what you are talking about?"

Mama turned around and walked toward me. "What we are talking about is this," Mama said and held a small blue velvet box in front of me. I took the box and slowly opened and, for the second time that day, I was totally surprised. Inside was a small diamond heart shaped necklace.

"Oh, this is so pretty!"

"You like it baby girl?" Daddy asked.

"Oh yes, daddy. It is beautiful. Put it on me mama, put it on me."

"Okay, okay hold on little lady."

She came over and placed the necklace on me as she balanced the phone between her shoulder and neck. "There you go."

"It is so pretty. Thank you daddy, thank you mama."

"You welcome, princess. When you look at it, always remember you are loved," Daddy said.

"I know, daddy. I have the best parents in the whole wide world."

"Well, we think you are pretty special too. Even if you are a girl," Daddy joked.

"I miss you."

"I miss you too, princess. I'll be home tonight though and we'll celebrate your birthday all over again tomorrow."

"Can we go to the Center?"

"Sure, baby girl. Now you have a good day with your mama today and I'll see you tonight."

"O.K. daddy, I love you."

"I love you too, baby. Hugs and kisses."

"Hugs and kisses, daddy."

"So, I'll see you later Nick," Mama spoke into the phone.

"Yeah, baby. And don't worry; I'll catch a cab from the airport. You stay there and keep it warm for me."

"I love you, baby."

"I love you Chantel. Hugs and kisses."

"Hugs and kisses, Nick."

I watched Mama slowly put the phone down in its cradle and could see the sadness in her eyes. I didn't know a lot in this world but I knew one thing. My parents really loved each other. I went and hung up the phone and then came back to the kitchen where Mama was staring out the window.

"Mama, you want me to wash the plates?"

"No, I'll take care of that later. Let's get some clothes on and go downtown. We could go shopping, have a nice lunch and maybe go down to the waterfront. What do you say?"

"I'll be dressed in ten minutes."

We left the house around ten thirty and decided to ride the bus downtown since on most Saturdays trying to find a parking spot could be a major job, as mama would say. Mama wanted to find me a nice dress. She said, now that I was thirteen, I needed to dress like a lady all the time and not just on Sundays when we go to church. I didn't see what was wrong with my Levi jeans and my favorite blue shirt.

We went to Frederick's and Nelson, The Bon Marche', and finally, Nordstrom's where we found just the right dress that was white with pink flowers. Then, we hoped on the monorail and rode to Woolworth's and looked around in there but didn't buy anything. I was getting hungry. Mama said she had seen a hot dog stand on the corner and we both started running toward it before he moved on down the block. I got a hot dog with mustard and sauerkraut, while Mama got a chilidog with lots of onions.

After we ate, we walked back to catch the monorail and then, on foot, headed down the steep hills to go to the Public Market. There, fresh fish was placed on heaps of ice along with crabs, oysters, shrimp, and other seafood. One stand even sold octopus. Sometimes, the smell reminded me of being right in the middle of the Pacific Ocean on a fishing boat.

Further down, there were fruit and vegetable stands. These were the stands that I loved the best. Almost everywhere we looked there were apples, plums, cherries and blackberries. I loved blackberries. I would spend almost an entire Saturday picking blackberries and bringing them home so Mama would make pies and preserves with them.

Then, there were the stands that sold pretty Indian jewelry and handmade belts. Seattle was rich with Indian culture. The name of the city itself derived from an Indian chief named Chief Sealth. Most people would go to up to the Indian reservations near the mountains and bring back turquoise rings, bracelets, and other handmade items to sell at the market. These items were very popular in Seattle. Mama bought us matching rings and I picked out a belt for Daddy to wear with his blue jeans.

We left the market and headed down several steep flights of stairs that led to the waterfront. For about a mile and a half, there were piers that stretch along Elliot Bay. Once, this was Seattle's working waterfront from which freighters and passenger liners departed for trips to Alaska, the Orient and down the Pacific coast. Now the piers have been converted to restaurants, shops and attractions like the Seattle Aquarium, which had a viewing dome beneath Elliot bay.

I talked Mama into going on a ferry ride to Bainbridge Island. Once there we went to a store and bought all the makings to have a nice picnic lunch on the beach. I loved the beach. It was my favorite place in the whole world. I wanted to take off my tennis shoes and put my feet in the cool sand, but Mama wasn't hearing it. The October breeze was too cool.

"Nicki, we need to head back now," Mama said after she glanced at her watch. I really wasn't ready to go. I could stay out at the beach forever.

On the way home, I thanked Mama for a nice birthday and my nice presents. I told her again that I had the best parents in the whole world.

"Well, you just remember that when some pinhead boy comes to calling on you and your father and I don't like him."

"Oh, mama, I don't like boys."

"Famous last words, Nicole Chantel."

We entered the house just in time to hear the phone ringing. put all the packages down and Mama answered the phone.

"Hello, Nick baby is that you? What's wrong?" Mama said. I leaned in on her ear so I could hear.

"Hi baby. No, I just missed my plane. There's another one though and I should get home around midnight."

"Oh Nick, I was hoping for you to be here in the next thirty minutes."

"I know baby, so was I. I just got caught up in a few last minute things with Mr. Lee. But I promise I won't miss the next one. I'm already at the airport waiting on my departure."

There was a silence between them.

"Well, hurry home Nick. I love you."

"I love you."

"Hugs and kisses."

"Hugs and kisses, Nick." Mama hung up the phone and once again I could tell she was thinking about Daddy. I leaned in and kissed on the cheek. "I'm going to go take my bath Mama, I'm beat."

"Yeah Nicki, I'm pretty tired myself. Your birthday has worn me out."

After my bath, I went in my room and lay down. I was so tired all of a sudden. Mama came in gave me a kiss good night and said she was going to wait up for Daddy. I gave her a hug and teased her about missing her man. She laughed and then closed my door. I was asleep before my head hit the pillow.

"Nicki, Nicki, baby get up. Come on baby, there's a fire," Daddy was shaking me. Shaking me real hard. I opened my eyes just as he lifted me up.

"What is it, daddy?"

"Nicki, there is a fire," he said carrying me toward my bedroom door. Suddenly I was wide-awake, fully understanding the urgency in his voice and in his eyes. I squeezed him tight around the neck. He ran out in the hallway and saw the flames at the end of the stairwell. Tears began to flow from my eyes. Our house was burning up.

Daddy went back in my room and opened the window with one hand while he held me tightly with the other. He looked down at me and then kissed my forehead. "Princess, I need you to jump. It's the only way out of here."

I held onto his neck with all of my might. I couldn't let go. "No, Daddy no!" I cried.

He looked at me and patted my hair and then kissed me again. "Nicki, you're going to be all right. Please baby, I need you to be brave O.K? I'm going to go get your Mama and we will meet you outside."

"Where's mama?"

"I think she's in our room. Go on now jump! You're going to be alright."

I nodded my head and Daddy helped me out of the window. I slid down the drainpipe that ran down the outside of my room. I looked back and saw Daddy watching me. My feet reached the ground. When I looked up at my window, Daddy was gone. Soon, I heard sirens and saw firemen rush to my now inflamed house. Then I heard screams. My father's screams! My heart dropped to my stomach and my tears drown me.

More sirens and more firemen came and tried to put out the flames. But it was too late, much too late. The left side of the house crumbled. Crumbling all that I knew with it. And then everything was quiet. Dead quiet. Firemen walked by, their faces covered with smoke, their eyes covered with despair. A hand touched my shoulder and through blinding tears I looked up into the eyes of a stranger. He had found my parents together, wrapped in each other's arms, burned to their death. I was now alone.

I was screaming. "No, No, NO!"

"Nicole. Nicole, wake up!"

I opened my eyes and saw Lisa standing over me. "Are you okay? She asked, with her thick Filipino accent. I looked at Lisa trying to remember where I was. Lisa sat on the edge of the bed, her black hair hanging way past her waist.

"I'm okay."

"Are you sure?" Crystal asked, coming to sit next to Lisa. "You still having nightmares?"

I nodded my head and Lisa reached over and gave me a hug. "I feel so bad for you."

I looked into her eyes and saw that she had tears in them and I felt my own tears falling down my cheeks. "I try so hard not to get sad but I can't help it."

"One day it's going to be easier. You'll see. One day." Lisa said with all her thirteen-year old wisdom.

Crystal patted me on the shoulder. " How was it at school today? I was hoping we had some classes together."

"Girl, let me tell you about this boy I met." I said sitting up on the bed and then told them briefly of meeting that boy at my locker. They both shook their head smiling and laughing.

"What?" I asked.

"The Badman has struck again." Lisa said and then proceeded to give me the low down on the Badman.

ANTHONY

3

It was lunchtime and I stood out on the football field throwing the football up in the air while me and Brian picked teams. Some of the guys out here were on the basketball team with me and it didn't matter that after school we had basketball practice, we still liked to play football and played it every chance we got.

I looked over the group of guys and picked Russell, who I nicknamed Wally, cause I swear he looked goofy like Wally Cleaver. Brian was in the middle of picking from the lot of losers when out nowhere comes this familiar little voice. " Hey, what about me?"

I turned around slowly and couldn't believe it. Standing before me, with one hand on her hip and the other one blocking the sun from her eyes, was the girl that had sent my ass running from school two weeks ago! The girl that I had been trying to ignore every since, but kept running into every time I turned around. The girl that had the prettiest eyes I had ever seen.

It turned out she was in my sixth period study hall. A class I used to enjoy going to but now found it hard because when she saw me she would break out laughing. As far as I knew, she hadn't told anyone about what happened so my rep was still intact. But, still, she loved to laugh at me every time she saw me.

Brian stepped over to me. "You know her?"

"Yeah," I answered, staring at her then walking over to her. I stood a few feet away from her and let me tall frame tower over her. "What about you? You want to know who to cheer for?"

"Cheer?" Heck no! I heard you say you need another man."

"Well, go find me one and tell him to bring his butt on. We don't have all day."

"What about me? she asked again, stepping up on me. Now, by this time, several of the guys had come to see what was going on. I glared at her with one of my infamous mean looks. No way was I going to let her punk me in front of the guys.

"Excuse me, football is a man's game. Now why don't you just run on," I said then turned to face Brain again.

"Looks like to me that you don't have any men playing yet. So why can't I play?"

I couldn't believe it! No she wasn't *still* standing there and trying me. Ooh, she was on it. If she had been a guy she would already be laid out, period! I turned back around and looked at her with my meanest look. The look that said I wasn't to be messed with. "Have you lost your mind? Do you know who you're talking to? I asked getting up in her face.

"Yeah, I know who you are Badman, " she said with a grin that said she was about to put my business in the street. I stood there waiting on her to say what I know she bet not say and glared at her as hard as I could. She didn't flinch! "Do you know who you're talking to? I don't believe you do. But no matter let's line up. As you say, we don't have all day." She reached and took the ball from me.

"Say girl," I said, trying to retrieve the ball, but she started to run with it and then turned around with a smile on her face.

"The name is Nicole. Nicole Williams. But you can call me Nicki."

I ran up on her and she stood there smiling at me. I didn't think nothing was funny. "Look, Nicole, Nicki or whoever it is you're trying to be, we're not playing flag football today. This is tackle," I said taking my ball from her and began to walk away from her.

Then she snuck me. Pushed me right on the ground. Everyone went into shock, especially me! I was so stunned I almost went against my mother's one request to not hit girls and pounce on her with the quickness. But, before I could react, she walked over to me, looked at me with those big brown eyes and smiled as she held out her hand. "I don't have a problem with that," she said. I took her hand and she helped me up. "Let's kick some butt, Badman."

"Alright. Let me see what you got." I said. We played the remainder of our lunch period and when it was all said and done we won. Turns out Nicki could catch a football pretty good, and when she ran she could damn near fly. I was impressed. She was all right for a girl.

Brian dared me to pull the fire alarm. Bet me twenty dollars that I wouldn't do it. And hey, I couldn't turn down a dare or twenty dollars. I decided to do it on Tuesday right before the end of the second period.

At a quarter 'til ten, I asked for a pass to go to the bathroom. I eased down the hall on the second floor ducking and dodging the other classrooms until I reached the middle of the corridor where the fire alarm was located. I eased up my right hand and pulled down the alarm as hard as I could. Instantly, the bells went off and I made a mad dash down the hallway. I had to get downstairs before anybody came out of the classrooms. Before I reached the staircase, a door opened and, before I could stop my feet, I hit something. Hit it hard. Knocked it down and fell down with it. I rolled across the hallway floor and landed against the lockers. My back and my knees ached, as I turned around still prepared to run and make my getaway. When I looked back to see what I hit, I stared down into the crowd that was in the middle of the hallway. Somebody was lying on the hard cement floor. I slowly stepped into the crowd to see who it was. It was Nicole. And her eyes were closed.

I sat in the nurse's office holding my head down with my hands covering my face. Never in my life have I felt so bad. How could I have been so stupid? Why didn't I think? I looked over at Nicole who still lay lifeless on the nurse's bed. It seemed like it had been hours since Coach Richardson carried her down here and still she hadn't moved. The nurse came over and looked at Nicole whispering that the ambulance was on the way.

Technically I was suspended. I wasn't supposed to be here but I begged them to let me stay until I knew she was okay. I didn't care what happened to me, I just wanted her to be all right. I was scared out of my mind.

I looked up when I heard the sirens of the ambulance approaching. It seemed like within seconds the paramedics were in the nurse's office and crowded around her and I couldn't see what was happening. Soon after a woman came in saying she was Nicole's legal guardian and asked the nurse what happened. Nicole made a sound and I tried to see her face but the nurse asked me to step outside. I stood up just as my mother came into the small room. I wanted to find a hole to crawl into. My mother's arms came around me and for the first time in my life I felt undeserving of her love. Didn't she know? Didn't she understand? I messed up big time.

"Anthony, listen to me son. She's going to be okay," I heard my mother's voice speak but I didn't understand. She didn't understand. Nothing was okay. I stood up and backed away from my mother. I was so sorry. So sorry for all the stupid pranks I have pulled over the years. So sorry for causing her so much grief and for all the times she had to leave work and come see what I had gotten myself into.

The paramedics placed Nicole on the stretcher and rolled her past me and down the hall. I stood motionless as my mother went and briefly spoke to the nurse and then came back over to me.

"I tell you what, let's go to the hospital okay? You can see for yourself. Come on." My mother spoke in a calming voice. I saw her head toward the door and then she stopped to wait on me. Slowly, I moved my feet forward. I don't know how, but somehow, I followed her to the hospital. Once there, my mother left me in the waiting room and said she was going to look for the head nurse. I sat down in a chair and once again held my head down. I don't know how long I sat there like that. I don't know how long my mother was gone, but soon, I felt someone's hand on my shoulder and I looked up into the eyes of the woman that had said she was Nicole's guardian. She introduced herself as Mrs. Haywood. I looked into her face and noted the sadness in her eyes. I swallowed hard and braced myself for the bad news. She then smiled into my eyes and told me to follow her because Nicole wanted to see me. I nodded my head and followed her down the hall. We reached the room Nicole was in with two other people. Mrs. Haywood pointed to the bed by the window behind the half-drawn curtain. I eased behind the curtain. Nicole lay in the bed with a tube in her nose and her eyes were still closed. I stepped closer to the bed, my head pounding with each step. I didn't care what Mrs. Haywood, my mama or the doctors said. Until I saw her open her eyes, I couldn't believe she was okay.

Nicole began to blink and gradually her brown eyes opened and she was looking at mine. She crooked her finger toward me telling me to come closer. I leaned over her, my face in her face. She grabbed me by the collar of my shirt.

"I'm kicking your butt on the football field next week," she said.

I looked down into her eyes and saw her smile. I let out a deep breath, felt my heart slow down and a smile crept across my face. "You got to catch me first," I told her.

"Don't worry, I will."

On Monday, I was allowed to return to school. I arrived extra early and waited on the east side of the building where I knew Nicole came in. I stood against the building away from the smoking section. Finally I saw her coming down the sidewalk with two other girls, one Filipino and one black. I walked and met them half way. "Hey."

"Hey Badman," Nicole said to me.

"Look, you can call me Anthony all right?"

"Okay, A.M.," she said and I looked at her strangely. "Your mother told me you full name when she came to see me in the hospital, Anthony Marcus."

"Oh."

"These are my friends Lisa and Crystal."

"Hi," they both said together.

"Hi," I said and then looked back at Nicole. "Look, is it okay if I walk you to class?"

"Why would you want to do that?"

"I just want to make sure you get there okay."

"Why wouldn't I get there okay?"

"I don't know. Stupid things happen in this school," I said looking down at my feet and then looked back at her. "I just want to say I'm sorry. I really am."

"It's okay A.M.. I know it was just a stupid prank, right?"

"And I guarantee, my last. I'm never doing anything like that again."

"Famous last words," she said smiling into my eyes. I laughed just as the first bell rung. Lisa and Crystal headed for the school and Nicole started to move in step with me telling me of her brief stay in the hospital.

"Well, I guess I'll see you at lunch," Nicole said when we reached her first period class.

"Yeah?'"

"Yeah, I owe you, remember? See you on the field, badman."

"Yeah, all right Lil'Bit."

From that day on, Nicole and I hung out every chance we got. After she royally kicked my butt in football, I made sure she didn't play against me again. Instead, we were together picking the losers to play with us. Then sometimes, we played basketball, which she was not to good at. But, baseball was another story. She could play a mean shortstop and hand no problem hitting a home run.

In between sports, we talked a lot. I met her at her classroom door at the end of each period, sat next to her in study hall and walked home with her, Lisa and Crystal. It was in those walks that I learned how she became so good at sports as she told me how her father would spend almost all of his time off with her outside throwing a football or baseball at her.

Then one day she told me how she lost her parents and how she came to live at the Haywood House with Lisa and Crystal and then talked about her night-mares of that night. Then, Lisa told me her story, and then Crystal. I had never known anybody who hadn't at least had a mom at home and for the first time in my life I felt bad for someone else. I couldn't imagine how they could go on with-out some kind of family. I complained a lot about my family and Lord knows my older sisters sometimes be on my nerves but I couldn't see my life without them.

On weekends, I often found myself at the Haywood House, picking up my girls to go bike riding at Seward Park. The four of us would spend hours at the park riding through all the bike trails and then on the way home stopping at Seven-Eleven to stock up on junk food. Nicole loved Snicker bars and strawberry soda. On some Saturdays, I took the three of them to one of my parent's restau-rant where my father would give them the special, a barbecue beef sandwich, and fries and of course, strawberry soda just for Nicole.

By the end of May, the four of us were really close. So close, that I hardly hung out with the guys from my neighborhood or at school. It wasn't that I didn't want to be with my boys, it was just that I think, without realizing, I got comfortable without always thinking about what other people thought of me. Around Nicole, I didn't constantly have to prove that I was tough or cool. Around her, I felt okay to laugh for real when I thought something was funny and it felt okay to raise my hand in class when I knew the answer to a problem. Hell, I found it cool to be smart.

On the morning of the last day of school, I waited for my girls at our usual spot before school started. Yesterday, we had all agreed to head out to Seward Park after school and go for our first swim of the summer. Lisa and Crystal reached me first and then finally Nicole came up and right away I noticed some-thing wasn't right.

"What's happening," I said as cheerful as I could as I looked at Nicole and could tell she had been crying. Lisa whispered hello but Crystal and Nicole said nothing.

"What's going on?" I asked Lisa. She looked at Nicole who still had said nothing and then mumbled something and walked away and soon Crystal followed her. I stepped closer to Nicole pushed her on the shoulder like I always did but she didn't react, at least not the way that I expected. She suddenly looked at me with tears in her eyes.

"I'm leaving the Haywood House," she said softly.

I didn't understand. "You're what?"

"I'm leaving the house. I've been placed in a foster home."

"Why?"

"Because it's best for me."

"What do you mean?"

"Nobody is supposed to stay in a orphanage forever, Anthony Marcus."

"I know that Nicki, I just...what does this mean? Where is the foster home?"

"I don't' know. I didn't ask."

"Well, when do you leave?"

"Tomorrow."

"Tomorrow, why so soon?"

"They want me to have the summer to adjust to my new surroundings and my new life.

"What about school? Will you be coming back here next year?"

"I don't know yet."

Damn, this wasn't right. None of this was right. "So, is this the last day, the last time that we will see each other?"

Nicole's eyes looked sadly into mine. "It's the last day that I will see anybody. You, Lisa, Crystal, everybody."

Shit, I couldn't believe this. Just like that she was leaving. I'd never known anybody to just leave, disappear, go away and never come back. Everyone I have ever known in my whole life was still around. The first bell rang and I looked down at Nicole who stood so still it was scary.

"I got to get to class," she said looking down but didn't move. I looked at her looking at the ground and suddenly I felt sad. I didn't want her to go. She was my friend. My best friend and now she was leaving. It just didn't seem right. I reached and pulled her in my arms. Her body started trembling and in moments the front of my shirt was wet with her tears. I held her. I couldn't believe this was happening. And I couldn't do anything as she cried.

NICOLE

4

"Well, look at you," Emily Nelson boomed out the moment I walked downstairs. "Aren't you a pretty thing? Girl, come over here and give me a hug."

She held out her arms and I couldn't help but stare. She was the biggest woman that I had ever seen. She had a big black Afro with very black skin. She stood around six feet and had mountains of breasts that seemed to have no end as they blended into her stomach.

"Come here, child!"

I went to her and the woman squeezed my breath away making me feel lost in those never ending breasts. "Are you all ready to go to your new home?" she asked smiling as she released me.

I nodded yes and then went to get the small suitcase that Mrs. Haywood had given me. Without looking, I knew Lisa and Crystal were on the staircase looking down. We had cried and said our goodbyes already this morning. I couldn't turn around and face them now.

"Just you wait and see how much fun were going to have living together. I'm going to take good care of you," Emily rambled on as she reached for my suitcase and then headed out the door with me behind her.

The moment I saw Emily Nelson's house, I silently wished for the pretty blue house of the orphanage. The small gray frame house was definitely a sad sight and in need of paint as it seemed to lean on 29th Street with its two green rocking chairs on the creaky front porch.

I followed Ms. Emily inside and I swear I could see the whole house from the front door. The living room consisted of a brown sleeper sofa that was placed in front of the window with dingy beige curtains. There were two brown plaid chairs that sat on the other side of a small brown coffee table. In the corner, was the matching end table that held the only lamp in the room and a small clock radio. The one wall was black with dirt and had only one picture on it of Jesus.

In front of the living room to the left was the kitchen that had a sink full of dishes that had food stuck to them. A big black roach scrambled across the dirty linoleum floor from under a small metal table that had two metal yellow plastic chairs, said hi, and then went to hide under the refrigerator. What I think was a white stove had grease on it at least three inches thick and even the door of the refrigerator was filthy. To the right of the living room, was a bedroom that had clothes and magazines thrown about it. The bed was unmade, and the hardwood floors were full of dust.

Then I saw the bathroom and almost gasped in horror. The white porcelain bathtub had a nasty black ring around it and the toilet was even worse. I tried not to, but I had to frown up my face as I tried to hold my breath from the stink of the whole house. Why am I here? How could anybody live here? My mother would just scream.

"I know it doesn't look like much but it's home," Emily said almost proudly to me.

She has got to be kidding.

"Over here is your bedroom," she said pointing to what looked like a large closet that had a bed that was at least made up and a small dresser and one window. Emily ventured off into the cluttered bedroom and proceeded to take her dress off with the door wide open. I turned my head just as she was about to unleash her big breasts.

"If you need to, you can put some of your things in the closet in the living room," she yelled from the bedroom.

I looked behind the front door and saw a closet. I was scared to open it.

"I'm hungry, what about you?"

Emily came out wearing a loose blue housecoat that did nothing to hide her huge breasts that sat on her stomach like watermelons.

"You want me to fix you something to eat, sugar?"

I didn't trust myself to speak. I didn't know how to answer her. I felt shocked and I realized I hadn't moved an inch since we walked in the door. Emily was staring down at me waiting on an answer. All I could do was shake my head. Food was the last thing I wanted in a place like this.

"Are you all right?"

I quickly looked away from the woman who was nothing like my mother and suddenly I missed her terribly. I missed our house, the smell of mama's food cooking in the kitchen and the smell of my daddy's cologne when I hugged him. I reached around my neck and touched the diamond heart that I never took off and suddenly tears started flowing from my eyes. I just wanted my daddy's hugs and kisses. That's all I wanted right now. That's all.

I felt Emily arms come around me and she began to rock me back and forth. "It's gonna be all right, you'll see," she half whispered in my ear.

No it wasn't. I know that now. Just seeing this place made it all too real that I was never going home again. I would never see my mother's face or hear my daddy's voice. I twisted the heart around in my hand. It was all I had of my past. Everything else was gone.

"Listen, put your bag in the room and then go lay down in my room, while I fix us something to eat."

"I'm not hungry," I finally was able to say.

"Well, I've got to eat something," Emily said going into the kitchen.

I placed my suitcase down in the middle of the floor and followed her into the kitchen. As she looked in the refrigerator for some food, I looked under the sink and found the Ajax, dishwashing liquid and the bleach.

I pushed the sleeves of my sweater up and took the dishes out of the sink and stacked them on the counter and began to clean the sink with the Ajax and bleach like I had seen my mother do.

Emily turned and faced me and then quietly put the package of meat she had in her hand back in the refrigerator. Next thing I knew, she was in the living room picking up the scattered newspaper and magazines lying around and then gave the table a good dusting.

By the time I was actually washing the dishes, Emily had come in the kitchen and got the broom and mop and started on the hardwood floor of the living room. I continued to clean the kitchen from top to bottom. I scrubbed the stove and cleaned out the refrigerator, throwing away old food that had been long ago forgotten. By the time I was cleaning the countertops and table, Emily was in the bathroom giving it a good scrubbing, leaving it shining and smelling like bleach.

I went to ask her for the broom and found her on her hands and knees scrubbing the floor of the bathroom. Emily looked up at me letting out a long whistle.

"I'm sure glad you came girl," she said. "This place needed a good cleaning."

She rose up her big body slowly, first on one leg then the other, pushing against the wall and looked down at me and then started to laugh. I mean really laugh. And every time she tried to stop she would laugh some more. She was laughing so hard that soon I heard myself laughing with her.

"Look at you," she was finally able to say. "You look like my kitchen did about two hours ago, all greasy and grimy. You better go take a bath before one of those big roaches think you are the kitchen and crawl all over you."

I looked down at myself. I was a mess. I caught a glimpse of myself in the bathroom mirror. My hair was all over my head; my face was covered in grease, dirt and Ajax. To top it off, I reeked of bleach. Between the two of us, I think we had almost used the whole gallon jug. I briefly smiled up at Emily and then looked at the tub so shiny and white. This is a tub I could get into. Emily reached down and began to run some bath water.

"Here, you bathe and I'll finish the house and then I'll fix us something to eat."

She closed the door behind her and I exhaustedly got into the warm water.

The smell of hamburger meat cooking woke me out of my sleep. I found myself with one of Emily's big dresses on asleep on the couch. The floors had been mopped and even Emily's bedroom had everything put away nice and neatly. I had to admit that the little gray house did look homey now that it was clean. I walked into the kitchen and sat down at the table and watched her cook like I used to do with mama. Emily looked at me, smiled and continued to fix the hamburger that she had cooking in a skillet and looking over at the potatoes she had frying in another.

"You know how to cook?" Emily suddenly asked.

"Nope."

"Well, how you expect to keep a man if you can't cook?"

"A man!"

"You do like boys don't you child?"

"No!"

"No? How old you say you are?"

"Almost fourteen."

"Well, I guess," Emily, said chuckling. "I wasn't too crazy about them when I was thirteen either. Come to think about it, I didn't start paying boys much mind until I was about fourteen and half," she said winking her eye at me. What was I going to do with this woman!

Emily wanted to know everything about me. For two weeks straight, she asked me everything from what my favorite color was to if I had ever kissed a boy. She wanted to know how tall I was, when was my birthday, who my friends were, did I get good grades. She asked if I ever had a boyfriend, did I know how to fish, what was my daddy like, what was my mama like, had I started my period, what did I dream about. On and on, it seemed like a brand new question popped in her head every few seconds of every day. I was exhausted from all of her questions. Seemed like I was taking a pop quiz every day.

And laugh! The big woman with the big afro would laugh so hard that tears would come out of her eyes and she would hold her stomach and say she was about to pee on herself. We spent hours talking except between twelve and three, when her soap operas were on. She sat down on that couch glued to the set only to get up when a commercial came on to go the bathroom or get something else to eat. After about three days, I caught on to who Erica Kane was and found myself glued to the television trying to figure out her problems.

On Saturday mornings, we got up early and went to the market downtown, just like mama and I use to do. The first time we went, I thought about my birthday and how Mama and me had shopped and bought blackberries and plums. We were supposed to make pies the next day and mama was going to make

Daddy's favorite, some plum preserves. Emily arms came up around me and her big hands wiped at my eyes. I didn't even know I was crying.

Saturday's also meant fried fish. Emily loved fish, but only fresh fish. She would pick out the biggest fish at the market that was swimming in the tank and wait for the man to clean and wrap it.

"This will do for now, but soon you and I are going to go fishing," she informed me.

After watching that man at the market cut up and take all the insides out of the fish, I don't think I want to go fishing. They looked too slimy and nasty.

For the past six days all she has talked about is the fourth of July. I sat at the kitchen table and listen to her talk about going to see her sister Nora and how she couldn't wait to eat some good barbecue. I thought about A.M. then. Wondered what he was doing. Wondered if he forgot all about me. I realize I missed him and Lisa and Crystal and our weekend rides to the park and our plans for the summer. I wondered if Lisa and Crystal saw A.M. and if they were still at the Haywood House.

"Ms. Emily is okay if I call my old friends?" I asked as she coated the fish.

She turned around and faced me. "Well sure child give them a call. Invite them over. Just because you're living here doesn't mean everything has to change. You can still see your friends. We've been cooped up with each other for almost four weeks now. Lord knows you probably sick of looking at my big self all the time."

I could have hugged her. I jumped from the table and ran to call Lisa. Mrs. Haywood answered the phone.

"Hi, Mrs. Haywood, this is Nicki."

"Nicole, how are you?"

"I'm fine. I was wondering if I could talk to Lisa."

For a second Mrs. Haywood didn't say anything. "Lisa's not here baby."

"She's not?"

"No she got placed about a week after you did."

"Oh. Well is Crystal still there?"

"Yeah she's still here but she gone to the park today?"

"Can you tell her to call me. Ms. Emily said it was alright."

"Well of course she can. I'll tell her to call you when she comes in."

"Okay, and if Lisa calls will you tell her too."

"I sure will."

I left her the number and hung up. Then I called the Badman. A sleepy voice answered the phone. I knew it was A.M.

"Hello."

"A.M," I said smiling from ear to ear.

"Who is this?"

"Oh you forgot me already," I said pouting.

"Lil' Bit is this you," he said his voice perking up.

"Well who else calls you A.M.?"

"Hey, what's happenin'! Where are you?"

"At my foster home."

"Are you doing all right?"

"Why don't you come see for yourself?"

"For real?"

"No for play. Do you know where 29th Street is by Jackson Street?"

"Yeah."

"I'm at 119 29th Street."

"I'm on my way."

We hung up and I couldn't help myself I was smiling so hard. Emily still stood over the stove placing the fish in the skillet. She turned around and winked at me. I just smiled. Then I ran to the closet and pulled out a pair of Levi's and my green and white Super Sonics tee shirt and ran to the bathroom. I couldn't believe he was coming.

The doorbell rang and Emily answered it. I was standing by the kitchen table. She showed him in and I walked into the living room.

"Hey Lil' Bit," A.M. said

I walked closer to him looking up. "Say, you grew."

"I have to. You know I'm going to be playing for the Sonics one day."

"Well it's a good thing you can play basketball, cause you stink at football."

A.M. pushed me on the shoulder. I pushed him back.

"Ms. Emily this is Anthony Marcus."

"How are you doing, Anthony Marcus?"

"I'm fine, ma'am, thank you."

"Well you two run on now before it gets late."

I grabbed my sweater from the closet while A.M. waited on the porch. I headed out toward the door turned around and went and hugged Emily. She squeezed me hard as she smiled down at me.

We headed down Lake Washington Blvd so we could ride to Seward Park but stop by a Seven Eleven on the way. Where I lived now was further from my favorite park and we had a long way to go, so A.M. said we better stock up on supplies. I waited outside and watched our bikes while he went in. After awhile, A.M. came running out the door telling me to hurry up and let's go. He jumped on his bike and started peddling real fast. I looked in the store and saw an old man coming to the door. I jumped on my bike and quickly caught up with him. He didn't stop peddling until we were three blocks away. I was tired and felt like I couldn't breathe. I got off my bike and sat down on the curb.

"A.M. did you steal that stuff?" I asked trying to catch my breath. He came and sat next to me.

"No, I didn't steal it. I just didn't have enough money," he said opening the bag. He had four Snicker bars, two big bags of barbecue potato chips, two strawberry sodas and some Now 'n Later candy.

"Well, how much did you have?"

"Almost a dollar in change."

"How much did that stuff cost?"

"More than two dollars."

I popped him on the back of his head. "Boy, that's stealing!"

"Hey, what was that for?"

"Because you are a thief!"

"No I'm not. I'll pay him back next time."

"You bet not never go back in that store. He'll probably have the police waiting on you."

"Don't worry bout it, Lil' Bit. Here, have a candy bar. How you like your step mom?"

"She's not my step mom she's my foster mother," I said, biting into the candy he gave me.

"Well okay, how is she?"

"She's okay. She's a teacher."

"Where?"

"At Garfield,"

"For real. Well, is she nice?"

"I told you yeah."

"Did you know Lisa is gone too?"

"I know. I just found out today. Has anybody talked to her?"

"I don't think so."

"You talk to Crystal?" I asked finishing my candy bar.

"Yeah, I saw her at the park yesterday."

"Mrs. Haywood said she was at the park today."

"Well, come on hurry up if you want to see her."

We finally made it to Seward Park and rode around all the bike trails but didn't see Crystal anywhere so we stopped by the lake and I started feeding the ducks some potato chips while A.M. went to the bathroom. Seward Park sat in the middle of Lake Washington. One side of the lake was the swim area. I wanted to get in, but I didn't bring a change of clothes. Past the swim area was where the hydroplane boats would race all the way to the floating bridge. A.M. and I hung out on the other side of the park where the bike trail started. I kept feeding the ducks and looking to see if I could find the Haywood House up in the hills that faced me. Before, all I had to do was go down a long trail to get here.

I got tired of staring at the hill of houses and turned around to look for A.M. He was standing over by the swim area talking to a girl who was almost as tall as he was. All of sudden she leaned over and kissed him. And I could tell she was sticking her tongue in his mouth and she even touched his private area. I couldn't believe it! Then she let A.M. touch her breasts.

They stopped kissing and she was just standing there smiling. A.M. started heading toward me. I turned around and started feeding the ducks. Within seconds he was behind me.

"Hey."

"Hey," I said unable to look in his eyes.

"Why are you giving the ducks all of our food?"

"We still got another bag," I answered.

"What's the matter?"

"Nothing."

"You ready to ride again?"

"Sure," I said closing the bag of chips and leading the way back to our bikes.

"Hey, there goes Crystal!" A.M. said suddenly.

"Where?"

"She just went into the bathroom."

"Stay here, I'll go get her," I said and ran into the bathroom and looked under the stalls until I found her navy blue tennis shoes. I looked around we were the only two in here. I beat on the door.

"Hey, come out of there!" I yelled in an angry voice.

"Nicki, is that you?" Crystal yelled back.

"No, it's the police," I said trying not to laugh. The toilet flushed and suddenly the door flew open.

"Hey girl!" Crystal said excitedly and went to hug me then thought about it and went to wash her hands first. I looked in the dirty mirror at her reflection. She had more pimples on her face than the last time I saw her. She quickly washed and dried her hands and came and hugged me. I squeezed her as tight as Emily squeezed me.

"What are you doing here?"

"Looking for you. I called Mrs. Haywood and she told me you were down here. So who you come with?"

"This girl named Monique. Did Mrs. Haywood tell you Lisa is gone?"

"Yeah. Have you talked to her?"

"No, not yet. Say, who you come down to the park with?"

"Guess."

"Badman! Where is he? I saw him yesterday. He is so cute! You see how tall he is?"

"Yeah, he's gotten taller. You wouldn't believe what he just did."

"What?' Crystal said leaning on me.

I told her what I saw just moments ago.

"Girl you lying," she said her eyes big as saucers.

"If I'm lying, I'm flying."

"Dang, I bet he kiss good too."

"Crystal!"

"What? You know Badman is too fine. And I just know he can kiss."

"Crystal, I can't believe you would want to kiss him."

"And I can't believe you don't."

I didn't know what to say to that, so I just shook my head. "Come on girl, let's go." I pulled her dreamy eyed self out the bathroom.

A.M. was standing right where I left him. I looked at him as Crystal and I walked toward him. He had on Levi's and a tee shirt that showed the outline of the muscles in his long brown arms. His short wavy hair was covered with a baseball cap that hid his light brown eyes. Okay, yeah I admit he was cute. But I still didn't want to stick my tongue down his mouth.

The four of us hung out awhile until it got late and then we jumped on our bikes and rode with Crystal and Monique back to the Haywood House, promising to get together soon. I looked at the house and felt strange standing there. Just as I was about to leave I saw Mrs. Haywood on the porch. She waved and I waved back.

In about an hour we made it back to 29th Street. I was tired. My legs hurt as I jumped off my bike. I sat on the porch and started rubbing my legs. I hadn't ridden in a long time. A.M. came and sat on the step below me.

"What's wrong, those little legs hurt?'

"Yeah, I think we went too far."

"Come here," A.M. said grabbing my right leg and started rubbing my calf muscle. I started to tell him to stop but he was rubbing the soreness right out of it. He worked on it awhile, took off his hat, laid it next to him and then started to work on my left leg.

"A.M. can I ask you something?"

"What," he said still rubbing my leg.

"Who was that girl?"

"What girl?"

"The one you kissed at the park."

For a second he stopped rubbing my leg and then started back again without looking at me. "That was Brenda."

"Is she your girlfriend?"

"I don't have a girlfriend."

I was confused. "Then why were you kissing her like that?"

"She kissed me."

"That's not all she did either," I said.

A.M. stopped rubbing my leg and we sat there quietly for a second. I was trying not to be nosey but I had to know. "Do you be doing it with her?"

"Doing what?"

"Doing it!"

"What you know about doing it?"

"I know what everybody else knows."

"What does everybody else know?" he asked looking at me.

"That you do it with girls."

He looked away and put back on his baseball cap.

"Is that true?"

"Nicki, why are you asking me all these questions? We can't talk about this stuff."

"Why?"

"Because you're a girl."

I hit him on the head. I hated when he said that. "I thought we were friends."

"We are, Nicki. Best friends okay."

"I thought best friends could talk about everything."

"Well, we can."

"So are you?"

"What?"

"Doing it with that girl."

"Yeah."

"You like her?"

"Why?"

"She looks old."

"She's in high school."

"You done it with her a lot?"

"A couple of times."

"Ain't you scared that she's going to get pregnant?"

"I use a rubber every time."

I didn't know what that was. I heard of them but I wasn't sure and I didn't want him to know that I didn't know so I didn't ask. "So, are you going to marry her?"

"Why would I want to marry her?"

"Because you doing it with her!"

A.M. took his hat off again, grabbed my shoulders with his hands and started shaking me. "Nicki get this through your head. She is not my girlfriend, I don't even like her and I am not marrying her, period. Okay?"

He let go of my shoulders and grabbed his hat again. What was wrong with him?

"Well what's it like?"

"What?"

"Doing it."

"I'm not telling you that!"

"Why?"

"Will you stop with all the questions?" he said standing up. I wasn't sure but I think he was mad at me.

"Well, can I ask you one more question?"

"What?"

"If you don't like her then why do you do it with her? Don't you want to do it with somebody you like?"

He stared down at me for a long time before answering. "What difference would it make?"

"I don't know."

"Ms. Nicole is that you out there," Emily's voice came from inside the house.

"Yes, Ms. Emily."

She opened the door and stepped out on the porch. "You two have fun today?"

"Yes ma'am," A.M. answered. I stood up from the porch slowly.

"Did you tell your friend about the big barbecue we're going to on the Fourth of July."

"No, I didn't tell him," I said smiling up at her. She was so excited about the Fourth of July.

"Well, why don't you invite him? Have you ever been to the mountains, Mr. Marcus?"

"Oh, my last name is Washington, she just likes to call me by my first and middle name like my mom does. But no ma'am I have never been to the mountains."

"Well check with your folks and if you can, meet us here on Monday around seven o'clock in the morning."

"Okay, I will," A.M. said to Emily and then looked at me. "See you later, Lil' Bit."

"Bye. A.M."

He jumped on his bike and headed down the street. Emily's hand was on my shoulder. "He seems like a nice kid."

"Yeah, he's all right for a boy."

She laughed and we turned toward the front door. We both headed for the kitchen. I was hungry with a capital h.

"Yeah, that A.M. seems like a nice young man," Emily said taking a glass out the cabinet. "I say he's kind of stuck on you too."

I almost dropped my plate.

NICOLE

5

On Monday, Emily woke me up at five o'clock in the morning talking about it was time to pack the car down so we can head out to the mountains by seven. I peeled my eyes opened and looked out the window for the sun. It, like everybody else, had some sense and was still sleep. I slowly rolled off my bed and went to the bathroom while Emily was in the kitchen just a singing away. It was just too early.

At a quarter 'til seven, A.M. was knocking on the door. I answered it and was greeted by his cheery face hidden under his favorite hat. I moved back so he could come in and then I sat down on the couch. Emily had had me going back and forth to the car for over an hour and I was already tired and ready for a nap.

"Well, hey there Mr. A.M.," Emily said to him all smiling.

"Good morning," A.M. said smiling back at her.

"You all ready to go?"

"I'm ready to roll," A.M. answered.

"Well, come on. Get up Miss Nicki, time waits for no man."

I don't know how far up in the mountains we were going but I know one thing it seemed like we had been driving for days. Emily and A.M. sat in the front seat and I tried to stretch out in the back to go back to sleep. But, unfortunately, Emily had A.M. singing song after song with her in a high-pitched singing voice. They sang Row, Row, Row your Boat so many times that when I closed my eyes I could see the three of us on that river in that dinky boat. A.M. turned around and looked at me, giving me wide smile. He was just too happy.

Around eight o'clock the car stopped, finally. I sat up and looked out the window and saw a big sign that said Snoqualamie Falls Park.

"Is this it? Are we here?" I asked.

"Nope, we still got an about an hour of driving time to go," Emily answered and then opened her door. I opened mine and so did A.M. Boy, it felt good to stretch.

"Let's go get us some breakfast. Have you two ever seen the falls?"

I shook my head and so did A.M.

"Oh, well you two are in for a treat."

We went into a tiny restaurant and had biscuits and sausage and orange juice. Then Emily led the way to the waterfalls. I leaned against the railing and looked down. They were beautiful. I never saw anything like it.

"There's a trail that leads to the bottom of the falls and you feel like you right under it," Emily said.

"Really?" A.M. said.

"Sure is."

"Can we go?" he asked.

"You two young folks go right ahead. I'll be right here when you get back. But try to hurry I want to get to my sister before eleven."

A.M. grabbed my hand.

The trail was real wooded and there seemed to be so many different birds in each tree. There were several people walking with us but nobody was saying anything. We were all listening to nature, the birds, the frogs and the sound of the waterfalls gushing down. At one point, we had to climb over rocks and A.M. had to hold my hand cause I just couldn't seem to keep my balance. Every time I thought I could stand up I would slip. I looked at A.M.'s shoes and then at mine. He had on his Converse and I had just plain old girl tennis shoes. I'm going to have to ask Emily to buy me some Converse if I'm going to have to be climbing rocks.

We finally made it to the bottom of the waterfall. It was amazing. The sound was so loud, but so pretty. Like a soft roar if that was anyway possible. People were sitting on the rocks at the bottom of the river that the falls ran into, taking pictures and playing in the water. A.M. took my hand again and led me as close to waterfall as he dared. I reached out and touched the water and so did A.M. He then cupped some in his mouth and drank it.

"How is it?" I asked.

"It's cold," he said and the cupped some more in his hands and put his hands in front of my face so I could get some. I looked down at his hands and then slowly put my mouth to them and tasted the water.

"It's good," I said surprised. I didn't expect it to be good for some reason. I wanted some more and looked up at A.M. to tell him to get me some more but he was looking strangely. First at me, then back at the falls. I looked around tried to see what he was seeing.

"What's the matter?" I asked.

"What," he asked looking back at me.

"Why are you staring?"

"I like it here. It's nice."

"Yeah, it is."

We turned in all directions looking around at the falls and the rocks. "We should have brought a camera," I said looking at everyone take pictures. There was a couple in front of us that was under a waterfall. The man was holding the lady's face in his hand and then he bent down and kissed her. I wondered what that felt like. Wondered if anybody was ever going to kiss me like that. Wondered if A.M. ever would.

A.M. reached for my hand. "What you thinking about?"

"Uh," I said looking up at him. He looked down at me for a long time and then took his other hand and pushed my bangs out of my face. I stared in his eyes. I liked the way the sun bounced off them and I like his long eyelashes but mostly I liked the way they looked into mine.

"Come on, we better head back," he said and then led the way back in the direction we came from. He stopped on the way up the trail looked back then looked down at me. "We didn't need a camera. I don't think I will ever forget this place."

I didn't think I would either.

We left the falls with Emily and A.M. up front singing 100 Bottles of Beer on the Wall and with me in the back seat thinking about waterfalls and kisses in the backseat as we headed further up north. We drove and drove and at one point we seemed to be driving straight up. And the road seemed more like a bike trail then a road. It was very narrow, bumpy and seemed to curve up. I bumped my head I don't know how many times as I kept thinking what were we going to do if someone was coming down.

Finally, we were on level land and I looked out the window and saw a cabin house and a small barn sitting with nothing but sky around. I couldn't believe this. Emily started blowing the horn like crazy. All of a sudden the front door of the cabin came open and this woman came running out to the car just as soon as Emily stopped it and jumped out.

The two hugged each other like they hadn't seen each other in ten years. Then Emily turned toward the car and told A.M. and me to get out. I opened my door and was headed toward the house when all of a sudden something was all around my feet. I started screaming and practically knocked A.M. down as I jumped on top of the car. A scrawny man wearing overalls came out of the house wanting to know what all the noise was about.

"Get those things away from me," I yelled looking down.

"What, the chickens?" the man asked.

"Yes!" I screamed.

"Lil' Bit, you have never seen chickens?" A.M. asked me.

"Only floured down and deep fried in a skillet."

The four of them looked at me and laughed like crazy. I didn't know what was funny.

"A.M. get that girl off the car like that," Emily said.

"Yes, ma'am," A.M. said and then came and put me on his back.

"Don't try nothing funny Anthony Marcus," I said with my arms squeezed around his neck. I kept looking out on the ground as he made our way to the house.

"Jessie, go on and find the boys so they can put these chickens back in the coop 'for this child have a heart attack," Emily sister said behind us.

"Jessie, Jr., where ya'll at?" The man yelled and I swear his echo was heard way back in Seattle.

A.M. put me down in the middle of the front room. I was surprised at how big it was. It even had an upstairs, which I couldn't tell from the outside.

"Come here girl let me get a good look at you," Emily's sister said. I walked over to the slender woman who looked nothing like Emily except for the loose dress she wore. Emily had told me she was her big sister so I guess she was probably around forty something since Emily was thirty-five. Her hair, which was braided in two big braids, was slightly gray but otherwise she looked young.

"So you're Miss Nicki, huh," she said squeezing me in her arms. These sisters sure loved to hug tight.

"Well, I'm Nora and that man hollering around the mountain is my husband, Jessie and we got us three hard head boys, Jessie Jr, Skillet and Pete."

"Did you say Skillet?"

She smiled down at me. "Honey it's a long story. Tell Emily over there to tell you one day."

She let go of me and then looked over A.M. "And who is this good looking young man. This your beau?"

"My what?"

"Are you two courtin'?"

I looked at Emily. I didn't have the slightest idea what she was talking about.

"Nora, that's her good friend Mr. A.M., uh, Anthony Marcus. They go to school together."

"Well it's nice to meet you A.M."

"You too ma'am."

"Ya'll have a sit down over there. Anybody wants some lemonade?"

We all answered yes and just then the door opened up and Jessie came in with his three sons running behind them.

"Stop that running, boys," Nora said.

"We put the chickens up mama," the smallest one said.

Nora went over to him and popped him on the back of the head. "Where's your manners boy. Ms. Nicki, A.M. this is Pete."

"Hi." A.M. and I said at the same time.

"The middle one here is Skillet and the tall one is Jessie Jr."

I nodded at both of them while Jessie Jr. came over and slapped five with A.M. I didn't know they did that up here.

"What's happenin'?" A.M. said.

"Why don't you boys go unload the car for Emily," Nora said. They left and Nora went into the kitchen and came back with three big glasses of lemonade. It sure was good and cold.

Emily and Nora sat and talked while Jessie went outside to check on the barbecue. I had to admit that smoke sure did smell good coming from his pit. The boys finished unloading the car and Nora and Emily started fixing the food in the kitchen.

"Jessie Jr., why don't you take them two outside and show them around. I know they didn't come all the way up here just to look at the inside of this old house," Nora said from the kitchen.

"Come on ya'll," Jessie Jr. said.

A.M. and I got up and followed him outside with me checking to make sure the chickens were gone. For as I far as I could see there was nothing but green grass, trees and blue sky. No streets, no cars, no schools, nothing.

"Where do you go to school?" I asked Jessie Jr. as we headed out through the grass.

"Mama takes us into town on the other side of the mountain. It's about an hour away."

"How old are you?"

"Fifteen. How old are you?"

"I'll be fourteen in October."

"October what?" A.M. asked suddenly.

"The second."

"For real?"

"No, for play. Why?"

"My birthday is on the first."

We both shook our head. Never would have thought it.

"How old are your brothers?" I asked Jessie Jr.

"Skillet is eleven and Pete is six."

We all walked a little longer without saying anything.

"How long have you been living with Aunt Emily?" Jessie Jr. asked.

"Since June."

"You like staying with her?"

"So far."

"How come you don't live with your own mama and daddy?"

I took a deep breath and looked up at the sky as I tried to stop the tears I felt forming in my eyes. A.M. pulled my hand in his and then pushed my shoulder. I looked into his eyes. He was smiling at me.

"Say man, any wild animals live up here?" A.M. asked.

"You mean like bears?"

A.M. and I both looked at each other. "I was talking about like deer or maybe wild rabbits," A.M. said.

"Oh yeah, they up here all the time."

"What about bears?" I asked.

"We haven't seen one in a couple of months."

"A couple of months!"

"Girl, I'm just pulling your leg."

"Ha, ha."

"We really hadn't seen one in about two years."

I let go of A.M.'s hand turned around and started walking the other way. Jessie Jr. came and turned me back around.

"I'm just pulling you leg again. Ain't no bears up here. It's not cold enough. At least that's what my daddy says."

"Why do you live on this mountain anyway?" A.M. asked.

"Compromise."

Okay, I didn't get it. I asked, "What do you mean?"

"Daddy was raised on a farm in Tennessee and Mama's from Canada and wanted to be by her sister. This mountain is compromise."

"I think I would have settled in Utah, uh Nic," A.M. said.

"Definitely. Aren't you afraid you're going to fall off this mountain?"

"Naw, girl."

"Look! Nic, there's a rabbit," A.M. said pointing to the right. A brown rabbit with a pretty white tail stood still only a few yards away from us moving its mouth real fast as its nose twitched.

"She's beautiful."

"How you know it's a girl Lil' Bit?"

"Cause I'm a girl."

"It's a good thing Skillet it's not here," Jessie Jr. said.

"Why you call him Skillet?" I asked.

"Everything he shoots goes in a skillet."

"Jessie Jr., Jessie Jr.!" Someone was screaming loud.

"What is it, Pete?"

"Come see what we got! Come see!"

Jessie Jr. took off and so A.M. and I had to follow. We walked a few yards and soon little Pete was in front of us dragging something behind him with the help of his older brother.

"What on earth is that?" I asked walking slowly behind the two boys.

"I think it's a deer," A.M. said.

"Naw, that's a goat," Jessie Jr. said.

I jumped on A.M.'s back and closed my eyes. I didn't want to see a dead goat.

"Come on Nicki, let's check it out," A.M. said holding my legs piggyback style on his back and running toward them. I peeked under my eyes just a little bit.

"Papa, come quick!" Pete yelled and his daddy appeared out of nowhere and walked over to us.

"How'd ya catch em?"

"Skillet shot 'em with his B. B. Gun and then I threw a big rock at it," Pete answered proudly.

"Well, it looks like we are going to have to put some more coal on that barbecue pit. Jessie Jr. get the fire hot," Jessie said and then picked the goat up and threw it over his shoulders. The next thing we knew he strung it up between two trees, cut its throat, and began to strip its skin.

I closed my eyes shut. I couldn't take it anymore. I wished real hard that I was Dorothy in the Wizard of Oz. I wanted to go home. A.M. carried me in the house. I stayed inside for the rest of the day and evening and only ate potato salad for my Fourth of July meal.

ANTHONY

6

The phone was ringing loud, waking me from my dreams. I jumped, hitting my head on the wall, before finding the cord and pulling the phone toward me, as I glanced at my clock. It was six thirty. Who on earth was calling here this early in the morning anyway? "Hello."

"A.M."

"Nicki?"

"Yeah."

"What is it?" I said trying to wake up. I know it had to be an emergency otherwise she wouldn't be calling here this early on a Sunday morning.

"Guess where I'm going tomorrow."

"What are you talking about Nicki?"

"Guess what school I'm going to?"

"Where?"

"Franklin High School," she screamed so loud that I had to take the phone away from my ear. I could hear her smiling in the phone and damn if I wasn't smiling too. My girl was back. Back big time.

"Do you know what time it is?" I asked smiling.

"Six thirty."

"Oh, so it's normal for you to call people this early in the morning?"

"Boy what's your name?"

"A.M."

"And who is my best friend?"

"A.M."

"And what does A.M. stand for?

"Anthony Marcus."

"It stands for you. It stands for morning. It stands for the first person I want to talk to when I got something important to say. Is that a problem, my best friend?"

"Not at all, Lil' Bit."

"Good, go back to sleep. See you tomorrow at school! Bye."

I hung up the phone, thinking of the person that had been on my mind every night before I went to sleep, since our trip to the mountains two and a half years ago. I had said I would never forget that day and I haven't. I never forgot how she looked under those falls and how close I came to kissing her.

Her transfer to McMillan Jr. High made me realize a lot of things. I didn't realized before how much time we had spent together until she was gone. I didn't know I was going to miss seeing her in between classes, at lunchtime, and our walks home. For the past two years, our time had been limited. We tried to get together for Friday night football and basketball games; Saturday's at the park and occasionally went to the same party. It seemed like every time I would see her, I would notice something different about her. And I often wondered if she noticed the difference in me.

I was hot again. More popular than I ever been. Anthony Washington was my name and basketball was my game. We won two straight championships in a row and the basketball coach at Franklin High promised me I was going to be starting on the varsity team.

Everybody said I had good chance to make it to the pros. Especially, if I kept growing. With just a month shy of turning sixteen, I was six- two and growing like a weed, let my mama tell it. Yeah, I was destined to play basketball, but I still loved to play football. The basketball coach doesn't want me to play football at Franklin but I don't know if I can keep that promise. He's going to have to understand I'm the Badman and I cannot be limited. I never have to choose. I can do it all.

Yeah, my rep was back, and going strong. Girls, girls, girls, what am I going to do with all those girls? Sex was a drug for me. A high I can't even explain. And I can't have enough. The more I get, the more I want. Brenda was gone but believe me others took her place. By the eight grade, I was getting some meat on my bones and wasn't as lanky. By ninth grade, that meat was turning into muscle as I played more sports. Girls were all over me, waiting to get a taste of Bad, and hey, I did not deny them. Well there were some girls that I just could not get with it no matter how many joints I smoked. I mean I did have a rep to protect.

Yeah, I smoked. Marijuana was crazy. Made me feel bigger than I was. And to have sex when I was high was a double high for me. But I didn't smoke too much. Not like most of the guys I knew who smoked before school, after school and even in school. Most of my smoking was done when I was alone. Alone thinking about Nicki and all the things I was trying not to feel. Now she was coming back. Back big time.

Bright and early Monday morning, I saw her. She stood there wearing a blue dress. Not Levi's jeans, a tee shirt and tennis shoes but a dress! Complete with stockings and platform shoes. The legs that used to out run me on the football field were shapely. The small body that used to jump on my back was slightly taller and curved in all the right places. Her hair was longer, her bangs combed away from her face showing her smooth skin with a little makeup on. I noticed

LOVE AND CONSEQUENCES

the lip-gloss on the lips I dreamed about almost every night and the eye shadow on the eyes that made me lose my train of thought.

She stepped on the bus, saw me and headed in my direction with a smile. I slid over to let her sit down. I leaned over and hugged her. Bad was dancing in my pants, my heart was pounding in my chest and my stomach was flip-flopping my mom's flapjacks from this morning. I felt her breath against my neck, my ear. I inhaled and smelled her fresh breeze scent and wrapped my long arms totally around her. The bus took off and we were pulled apart. For about thirty seconds, I knew what heaven felt like.

"What's happenin' A.M," she said pulling her purse in her lap. I couldn't find my voice. All I could do was look at her.

"A.M. Are you okay?"

"Yeah, it's just you look..."

"I know girlie. This was all Ms. Emily's..."

"Nice," I said meeting her eyes. "Very nice."

A slow smile came across her lips. "Thank you."

We rode for a couple of minutes without saying anything. I felt like I was meeting her for the first time again.

"So how was California," she asked.

I hadn't even thought about my trip. My parents had decided to take the last three weeks of the summer off and we headed for California. "Great! I saw my grandmother, my cousin, Michael and his parents. He took me to every beach. You would love the beaches, Nicki. They are so beautiful."

"Did you bring me something back?"

"Yeah."

"What?"

"Me."

"Well, I guess I should be happy."

"You guess? Do you know how many girls I had to fight off me?"

"Hundreds."

"Thousands. They loved me in L.A."

"A.M., are you ever going to change?"

"Why mess with perfection?" I asked pushing her on the shoulder. She pushed me back.

"Where is my present?"

"Baby, I'm sitting right next to you."

"If you didn't bring me anything back I'm going to make you go back and get me something."

I turned away and reached down into my blue jeans pocket. "Well, I did bring this back with me. You might want it," I said holding a silver bracelet in front of her. She took it out of my hand, held it up and then tried to put it on. I turned my body toward her and clasped the hook around her arm. She shook her arm, jingled the silver charms.

"Thank you, A.M. It's pretty."

She smiled and pushed my shoulder. I pushed her back. Like the person wearing it, I thought to myself.

We were going fishing. My dad had bought a big trailer and wanted the whole family to go up to Pacific Shores on Labor Day weekend. And I didn't know how to tell him I didn't want to go.

We have been in school for only four days and Nicki and I had two classes together, we were back to eating lunch together, and had wanted to spend our three-day weekend together. And now this trip! I didn't like to fish that much anyway. Well, I did, but I just didn't want to go. Not this time.

"Dad?" I called out looking in the garage for him. He poked his head from under the hood of our old Impala. I don't know why he didn't get rid of that car when we got the new Cutlass. It seemed like he spent more time under the hood of the Impala than behind the wheel of the Cutlass. And the Cutlass was sharp, boy. My dad walked over to the toolbox and got a wrench.

"What's on your mind, Junior?" he asked and then leaned back under the hood.

I leaned against the side of the car so that I wasn't really facing him but still close enough that we could hear each other. "Are Ricky and the baby coming with Anita?"

"Yep. And your sister Angela is coming in from college first thing in the morning. It will be the whole family."

"We're not going to ride in the Winebago are we?"

"No it's against the law to be in it while it's hitched to the back of the car. Ricky is going to drive his car. That way, we'll have plenty of room for everybody."

"It's still going to be kind of cramped."

"We'll manage, you'll see."

I took a deep breath. Yeah, I'm sure we would. "What if I don't go?" I asked after a moment.

Dad poked his head from under the hood, grabbed a rag and began to wipe his hands on it. "Why wouldn't you want to go?" he asked standing in front of me.

I stopped leaning against the car so I didn't have to look so far up at his six-four-frame and took another deep breath.

"What is it, Junior?"

"Nothing. I was just thinking..."

"Thinking what son? That you don't want to be with your family?"

"No, of course not."

"Family is everything, Junior."

"I know sir," I said looking into eyes that looked like mine.

"You know I'm getting old son. I got one daughter in college, one married, two more to do whatever it is they're going to do and you. I worry a lot about my girls. I got to always watch out for them, got to. But, maybe I don't worry enough about you. Maybe I've left you out on your own too much."

"I can take care of myself dad."

"I know you can Junior. But you got a wild hair up your nose."

I looked at him but didn't say anything wondering how much he really knew about the things I did.

He came over and put an arm around me and leaned in real close to me. "See, I know you're at that age where you want to scratch that itch, but you need to watch yourself, Junior. Making a hasty decision for a moment of satisfaction can affect the rest of your life. You understand?"

"I understand."

"Do you?"

"Yes sir."

"Good, good. Now, tell me why don't you want to go on this trip."

"It's not that I don't want to go Dad, it just Nicki...sometimes holidays get to her since, you know, her parents. She won't even celebrate her birthday."

"Well, what she's been through is hard son."

"I know. It's just she tries to be so tough on the outside but every now and then she gets this look in her eye and you can just see it."

"Sounds like somebody else I know. Tough on the outside."

"Who me? Shi... I mean I'm tough through and through."

My dad laughed. "Yeah, Junior I see you out there on the football field throwing those long passes and then on the basketball court slam dunking on everybody. And I tell you I sit with my chest stuck out yelling and screaming telling everybody that's my boy. I'm proud of you son. You've never been in a run-in with the law. You get pretty decent grades when you apply yourself and you keep your nose clean. Yeah, I'm real proud of you. But nothing makes me more proud than to see you be a true friend to Nicki the way you have."

"Oh yeah?"

"Oh yeah. She doesn't have a lot and you're somebody she can turn to and that's a good thing. But every now and then, Junior, you get this look in your eye. You got it bad for her don't you?"

I took a deep breath, swallowed real hard, and stepped across from the car and leaned my head against the wall. "Dad, she's my best friend. We've been hanging together for three years now. We share everything. She tells me everything. Things I don't want to know. She asks me things I don't want to tell her. But I find myself doing it anyway. For the past year or so I can't get her off of my mind. I think about her twenty-four hours a day. I think about her when I'm on the football field, at basketball practice, or in class. And when I'm not thinking about her, I dream about her, constantly. And my dreams, God, they're getting stronger and stronger. And I'm scared. I'm scared that when I'm with her I'm going to do something that is going to scare her away. But I'm more scared when she's not with me cause it's like she's...I don't know. I just can't..."

"Son, son. Slow down. Have you told her how you feel?"

"No!"

"Why not?"

"Dad, she's knows everything about me. Everything!"

"And that's good Junior. She knows everything about you and you know everything about her. You two don't have any secrets and that's what makes this work."

"Makes what work?"

"Do I need to spell it for you son?"

I didn't answer.

"If she means that much to you, you need to leave all the rest of those girls alone and tell her how you feel or you're going to lose her. But Junior, don't ever forget the way she makes you feel right now. Remember how special she is to you right now. Hold on to it everyday that you're with her. Hold on to it, so that you won't forget how to treat her. You can't treat somebody special the same way you treat everybody else. You understand? Now go call her and invite her to go fishing with us this weekend. It's some big perches out there in that ocean and I sure would hate for you to miss them." He turned around and went back to the toolbox.

"Dad?"

"Yeah, Junior."

"You're alright for an old man."

He walked back toward me and looked me square in the eye. "I love you too, son."

I stood speechless for several seconds. I didn't know how to say the same. But I know he understands. He understands so much. I hugged my father.

The sound of my parents voice woke me as we rode in the car. I opened my eyes and looked out the window. It was still black outside. I shifted in my seat. Nicki was lying on my shoulder with April on the other side of her, both of them were knocked out. My dad was driving and mama was sitting only inches away from him talking to him as he drove. She has this thing about long trips. She never sleeps. She always stays up and talks to him since that time he was driving us to Portland and she said that when we were crossing a bridge, she woke up and so did he. I placed Nicole's hand in mine, and closed my eyes and tried to go back to my dream with the sound of my parent's voices drifting from the front seat.

"Anthony?"

"Yeah, baby?"

"You notice how close Anthony Marcus and Nicki are getting? I mean they've always been close, but I think things are a little different now."

"You think so, Ann?"

"Yeah, have you noticed the way he looks at her now."

"Kind of like the way I look at you."

"It's amazing."

"What's amazing? The apple never falls too far from the tree."

"I'm not talking about that. It's amazing to watch your kids grow up and fall in love and be us all over again."

"Guess I never thought about it like that."

"Have you talked to him? I mean talked to him about girls, about Nicole?"

"Oh yeah. Junior knows what to do about Ms. Nicole."

I opened my eyes and saw my father wink at me in the rearview mirror as Mama's head rested on his shoulder. My parents have been married for twenty-six years and to me they're just parents, mom and dad. But, looking at them now in the front seat sitting close like they are, I just see them—a couple. They got a house full of kids and one grandchild, but it all started with just them two. And after all of us are gone, it will be just them two. That was a trip. I looked at my father and then closed my eyes again.

An hour later I hunched Nicole with my arm. "Wake up, sleepy head," I said to Nicole, who had rested her head on my shoulder so long it was sleep.

"Are we here?" She asked yawning.

"Kind of."

"What do you mean?"

"We're at a camp site. My dad's hitching up the trailer so we can have some electricity. We're going to spend the night here and then go to the ocean first thing in the morning."

"What time is it?"

"Almost midnight."

"All right, everybody, the trailer's ready. Let's go in and pick our sleeping spot," my dad said coming back to the car.

I stepped out and then helped Nicki out of the car. We both stood and took a long stretch. My sister April slowly got out of the car and came around to our side. "Look at the moon," she said.

Nicki and I both looked up at the sky. It was clear with a full moon and a blanket of stars.

"I've never seen so many stars," Nicki said yawning again and walking toward the trailer. She stepped in behind Ashley and my mom.

51

"This is a little house," Nicki was saying when April and I stepped in. She was looking around in the small kitchen area that had a small sink and a minia-ture stove and refrigerator under a small counter with two cabinets. Across from that, was a table that had two long seats in front of it. In the back of the trailer, there was a couch and a bed above it and in the front, there next to the bathroom, there was another couch and bed above it. The three of us sat at the table while my mom and Ashley were sitting on the back couch when Dad came in with Ricky, Anita, Angela and little Ricky.

"Okay, this place is supposed to sleep twelve and it's, let's see, nine and half of us. Ricky, Anita, you and the baby can sleep on one of the front bottom couch-es. Ann baby, I guess you and I better take the back bottom couch. And let's see, April and Ashley can take a top bunk. Angela, you're still young enough to hop up on a top bunk right? You and Nicole can take the other top bunk. Now, that just leaves Junior. Well boy, I guess you're just going to have to sleep outside."

"What there's no more room at the inn?" I asked jokingly pushing Nicole's shoulder and she very weakly pushed mine back.

"Anthony, you can't have my baby sleeping outside," My mom said behind me.

I smiled at dad, knowing I had pure advantage being a mama's boy.

"Well, I guess I don't want the bears to get you. Push that table up and those two benches make a bed."

Everybody started moving around except for Nicole and me and, for a while, the trailer seemed to be rocking. When April got up, I moved to the other bench and sat across from Nicki. Suddenly, I was wide awake and wasn't ready to crash. I looked at Nicki who was busy watching everybody else get situated. One by one, everybody was crashing and we were the only two up.

"Are you sleepy?" I whispered.

"Not really," Nicki whispered back.

"Let's go for a walk."

"Out there?"

"There are not any bears out there."

"But it's so dark and you don't know what's out there."

"You scared?"

"No."

"Then come on," I said, standing up and holding out my hand to her.

"A.M., are you crazy?"

"I'm not crazy, but you're scared, huh?"

Nicki sat there a few seconds without saying anything and then grabbed my hand. I slowly opened the door and she followed me out.

"See, there's nothing to be scared of out here. Come on."

I led her out on a small trail that went through the campsite. We walked past several trailers that were parked for the night. There was a park area that had a merry- go-round, swings, and a couple of benches. I held Nicki's fingers tighter and half ran to the merry-go-round. She jumped on and I ran and pushed it until it was spinning as fast I thought it could go and then jumped on behind her. She was standing in the middle of it with her legs against a bar and her hands up in the air. I tried to walk closer to her as the merry-go-round was spinning and kept getting further away from her. Finally, I was able to stand across from her and held onto the bar in front of me.

"You better hold on," I said to her.

"Now, who's scared," she said looking at me and making a face with her nose all crinkled up.

"I'm not scared, I'm just cautious."

"The Badman cautious?"

"Okay, I'll say I'm careful then."

"Careful at not getting caught at whatever you doing."

"What do you think I be doing?"

"You tell me."

"What have you heard?"

"That you had to jump out of Cheryl Stephens' window with your pants halfway down."

"Who told you that?"

"Cheryl Stephens."

"That girl is lying. She wished I would climb in her window. I don't even like her."

"Oh, so now you like the girls you do it with?"

"I didn't say that."

"You don't like them."

"No. I mean I like them but I don't like, like them, you know. I can't explain it."

"Don't bother."

"Why? I thought you always wanted to know everything."

Nicki didn't say anything. Something was up.

The merry go round was slowing down. I grabbed her hand and led her to the swings. "You want me to push you?" I asked when she sat down.

"That's okay."

I sat in the swing next to her and looked over at her and she was staring off into the sky. I looked at the ground and then back at her. She looked at me then back at the sky and then at me again.

"Okay, what is it?" I asked.

"What?"

"Nicki, I've known you for three years. You got something on your mind just say it."

She turned away from me.

"Nicki?"

"What?"

"Spit it out."

She turned to face me again looking at me with her deep brown eyes and blurted out, "Do you think I'm pretty?"

I was blown over. She had to be kidding, right? This was the same girl that sent me running home from school when I first laid eyes on her. The girl whose face I dream about every single night! Nicki was more than pretty! She was everything. I liked everything about her. Her face her smile, her hair, her laugh, her mouth, her eyes, everything!

"You don't do you?" she asked.

"What? No, are you crazy."

Nicki flew off the swing and started walking toward the trailers. Man, what did I say? I jumped down and then ran to catch up with her.

"Thanks for your honesty A.M.," she said her eyes shining with tears. I grabbed her and turned her toward me. She looked down at the ground and I watched her tears fall. Something inside me hurt.

"Nicki, I didn't mean what I said back there, I mean what I wanted to say was..."

She looked up. Her eyes looked into mine and I forgot what I was trying to say. I looked down at her mouth. Big mistake, cause now all I could think about was kissing it. She turned and walked away.

I quickly searched for words. "I think you're beautiful."

She stopped walking and I walked closer to her and stood behind her. "I think you're very beautiful and I think it's crazy that you don't recognize how pretty you are."

"Why don't boys like me?" she asked with her back still turned to me.

"Who?"

"Boys, guys. I mean they like me. But they don't like, like me." She turned round and faced me. "Nobody has ever asked me out on date. Everybody goes out on dates but me! What is wrong me? I'm not too short, I'm not tall, I'm not fat, I'm not real skinny. I'm just me. But what's wrong with me? Is it because I like sports, or is because of where I live or that I don't have parents or because I like to wear blue jeans. What is it A.M.?"

"What it is Nicki, is that you're special. You're not like any other girl I know. You're not like any other girl period. You're pretty, you're bold, you're smart, you got style and I think a lot of girls look up to you. As to why guys don't ask you out well it is because of me."

"You?"

"Have you forgotten who I am? I'm the Badman. And every guy in Seattle knows I'll mess them up if they mess over you."

"So I guess the only way I'm going to get a date is to find me a new best friend, huh?"

"You just try it." I said pushing her shoulder. She pushed mine back and then we headed for the trailer.

NICOLE

7

Today is A.M.'s birthday and tomorrow is mine. It's been three years. Three years since my life was turned upside down and I can't forget it. Every year on my birthday, I see mama and me eating chocolate cake, shopping downtown, riding the ferryboat. Every year I smell fire, see flames and I hear my daddy's scream. I twisted the heart around my throat, heard my daddy's voice. 'Always remember you are loved.' I try to be happy. I swear I do. I mean I know things can be worse than they are. I just miss them so much.

"Ms. Nicki, you're home from school already?" Emily called from inside the house. She came and sat in one of the green rocking chairs that were on the porch. I wiped away my tears and picked at the bush that was next to me. She reached down at patted me on the shoulder.

"It's getting cool now."

I looked up at the sky. It was full of rain clouds. All of our neighbors had a yard full of brown leaves. I couldn't see Mt. Rainier.

Ms. Emily looked over at me. "Soon, fall's going to be over and it's going to be winter. Say, what do you think about going to the mountains and spending Thanksgiving with my sister Nora this year?"

"Ms. Emily I want turkey for Thanksgiving."

She patted my back again and laughed. "Oh, Ms. Nicki you need to live a little. There's nothing wrong with a little wild meat every now and then. Speaking of wild, where's that A.M.?"

"He's at football practice. He should be here any minute. I got to give him his birthday present."

"You get him something special?"

"An autograph basketball of the Super Sonics?"

"Well, that is nice. Any idea what he got you?"

"Not a clue." I said turning and leaning against the pole.

We sat in silence for a while. It was getting cooler but I didn't feel like going to get my sweater.

"Well, it's Friday night and I got me a date," Emily said cheerfully.

"That's good."

"What about you, you have any plans?"

"Nope. I've seen all the Bruce Lee movies already, so I really don't have nothing to do."

"Well, what do you want to eat? I can fix you something before I leave."

"That's okay. A.M. had said something about going to Wendy's for a burger. So I'll just wait on him.

She stood up, stretched and pulled the screen door open. "Well, let me know if you need something," Emily called out going inside. I rubbed my shoulders. It was getting colder. Emily put on Al Green's, 'Let's Get Married Today', and I could hear her singing.

She loved music, especially Al Green and Bobby Womack. Almost everyday, as soon as she gets home, she sticks in an eight track and sings all over the house as she cooks or grades papers. She even liked the stuff I liked, like the Jackson Five, the Ohio Players, Commodores, Earth Wind and Fire, and the Emotions.

I stood up and stepped back and looked up at the little house with the green rocking chairs that leaned more to the right than it did two and a half years ago. I listened to the woman singing that everyday made sure I had something to eat, clothes to wear and spending money in my pockets and who understood about why I couldn't celebrate my birthday. Emily was a special woman. And this little house was home.

"Boo!"

I turned around jumping. "A.M. you almost made me jump out of my skin."

"Ah, quit sounding like an old woman."

"No, you're the one old."

"Ah, we'll see what you got to say about that tomorrow," he said sticking his tongue out at me.

"How did you get here, where's your bike?"

A.M. leaned back and pointed his head toward the street. I looked around him.

"Your dad let you drive the Impala?"

"Not let me drive," he said pulling keys from his pocket grinning from ear to ear. "The Impala is mine! And I just left the DMV and you are looking at Seattle's newest motor king."

"I thought you were at football practice," I said pushing him.

"Ah, Nic, I thought you would catch on. We never have football practice on Fridays."

"You lied to me?"

"Yeah, I did. Only because I wasn't sure I would pass the test. But I aced it. So, where's my present?"

"I didn't get you anything."

"Say what!"

"You heard me. I am going to wait until tomorrow to see if you got me something then I'll go get something for you."

"Uh, uh Nicki. That's not how this works. My birthday comes first, so my present comes first. Your birthday comes second, your present comes second," A.M. said.

I looked at him as he stood there with that grin of his stretching from ear to ear. "You are just too happy."

"Haven't you heard, it's great being sixteen? Oh, but I guess you won't know that until about five and a half more hours?"

"Get on in this house before my neighbors call the cops on you."

"Is my present in there?"

"Come on in here, Anthony Marcus," I said going up the porch steps and into the house.

Emily was standing in the middle of the living room wearing a black pants suit putting on lipstick.

"Ooh wee, Ms. Emily, do you know what you're doing to me!" A.M. said and then let out a long whistle. Emily posed turned in a circle and posed again.

"Oh stop, Mr. A.M., stop," she said waving her hand like she was a Hollywood star.

"Ms. Emily you do look pretty," I said smiling.

"Well, thank you Ms. Nicole. I got to go girl. Time waits for no man and no man likes to be kept waiting. You two lock up the house when you leave."

"We will. Have fun."

"You too, baby. Bye now."

She turned and headed out the door. I went and locked the door and A.M. was standing right behind me. I ignored him, went into the kitchen, pulled opened the refrigerator, and just stood there looking. A.M. cleared his throat. I stuck my head deeper in the refrigerator like I was looking for something way in the back. He cleared his throat again. I kept looking. I finally pulled out a strawberry soda, struggled with the top and then took a long drink looking at A.M. out the corner of my eye. He was glaring at me now. I started laughing and spit soda everywhere.

"So, you're trying to be funny," A.M. said from the living room.

"What are you talking about?" I asked in my innocent voice as I reached for a paper towel and cleaned up my mess.

"Well, you heard Ms. Emily. No man likes to be kept waiting."

"I don't see no man in here," I said coming into the living room and looking around like I was looking for somebody.

A.M. stepped closer to me. I eased my eyes up to meet his. "Where's my birthday present?"

"I don't know. It could be behind door number two or door number three."

"What if I picked door number one?"

"You might be disappointed."

"I want door number one."

"Okay, you asked for it."

I went to the closet and pulled out the basketball. "Happy Birthday." I said handing it to him. His eyes lit up. He rolled the basketball over looking at all the signatures.

"I don't believe it," he said still examining the ball.

"I always wanted see what a real championship ball looked like. Next time I get one, your name is going to be on it."

"You believe I'll make it to the pros?"

"Hell, yeah!"

A.M.'s light brown eyes looked into mine and then he walked closer to me and hugged me.

"This means a lot to me. Thank you."

"You're welcome."

We stood there silently for a moment. I watched as A.M. kept twirling the ball in his hands.

"Nic?"

"Yeah?"

"Will you help me celebrate my birthday tonight?"

I took a deep breath and didn't answer. A.M. placed his hand on my chin, making me look him in the eye. "Let's make tonight special. Let's celebrate," he said smiling at me.

I stepped away and didn't answer.

"Come on, what ya say?"

"A.M. I..."

"Okay ,listen. How about we just go for a ride?" He dangled the keys in my face. "Just to my house and back."

I stood there a second longer silently thinking. It wasn't that I didn't want to be with him, it was just the birthday. On our last two birthdays we have only exchanged presents, nothing else no big deal. That's the way I liked it. I can't help it. Just the word birthday makes me sad. I didn't want it to be like this. I swear I didn't, but I didn't know how to stop. I didn't know if I ever could.

I looked back at A.M., my best friend. He stood in his jeans and leather coat waiting on me to say something. Suddenly, I was mad at myself. It seemed like I was always asking him to do something for me but I can't ever remember him asking me to do something for him. I walked closer, stood up on my tiptoes and looked him dead in the eye.

"To the car, Batman!"

"That's Badman, Robin." He said grinning.

"The name is Lil' Bit!"

"Surprise!" Several voices yelled out as soon as I walked into A.M.'s house. I smiled into smiling faces. Faces of people I knew; A.M.'s mom and dad, his sisters, Crystal, and some kids from school. Soon, they all started singing, Happy Birthday. I turned around and looked at A.M. to see if he was surprised as I was. He stood there smiling and singing with them, which baffled me. I mean it was his party, wasn't it?

I turned back around, faced the singing voices, and out of the kitchen Emily came holding a huge german chocolate cake with enough candles to light up Detroit. Behind her, was Lisa trying to hide. Lisa, who I hadn't seen since I left the Haywood House! I can't believe it. Tears sprang to my eyes, just as everyone said, "Happy Birthday, dear Anthony and Nicole".

A.M. slid next to me and grabbed my hand. Everyone was suddenly quiet. Emily, Lisa and Crystal moved through the crowd and stood at my side as Mr. and Mrs. Washington stood close by. I looked around at all the people I knew. The people who have for the last three years, made my life bearable; the people, who were my friends and who have somehow become my new family. I couldn't stop tears from falling from my eyes. This was the nicest thing.

"I know how you feel about birthdays Ms. Nicki, but this is the most important birthday in a girl's life," Emily said looking at me with teary eyes.

"And in a guy's life too, Ms. Emily," A.M. added.

"You two need to blow out all these candles before they melt the cake," Crystal said.

A.M. and I stepped closer to the cake and blew and blew until all thirty-two candles were out. This was so nice. I just couldn't believe they did all of this. Couldn't believe they went to all of this trouble.

"Happy birthday, Nicole."

I turned at the sound of Mrs. Haywood's voice. She stepped closer and gave me a hug. I let go of A.M.'s hand and held her tightly. When she let go, Emily came over and gave me a big hug. Then Mrs. Washington did and soon everyone was taking turns hugging me and telling me happy birthday.

"Girl, you know, you're sixteen now, hey now!" Lisa said in her thick accent as she hugged me. I missed her. She looked so different and had the nerve to grow a little.

"Yeah, sweet sixteen and ain't never..." Crystal whispered under her breath.

I cut my eyes at her and dared her to say another word. She smiled into my eyes and then hugged me too.

"Hey, what about me? I thought it was my birthday too, alright." A.M. said suddenly. Lisa, Crystal and I all turned and faced him. He stood there trying to look sad but that big grin of his crept out anyway. The three of us went to him and hugged him at the same time. His long arms wrapped around all of us and then we all took a turn giving him a kiss on the cheek.

"Now, that's more like it," he said smiling still holding onto us. "Well, is everyone going to stand around here all night or are we going to have a party!"

"I'm ready to party," Lisa said bumping me. I bumped her back.

"Let's get it on then," A.M. said leading us past the dining room to the stairs that led to the basement.

Soon, the crowd of people that had been standing in the living room followed us, leaving the grown-ups to have their own party. The staircase was decorated with streamers and a birthday banner and there were more streamers hanging over the wash area. We passed a table that had platters of chips and dips, sandwiches, and a punch bowl and cups.

To the left of it was the pool table that A.M. had taught me how to play pool on two years ago and now I was good enough to whip his butt. Two guys from school quickly rushed over to it and started playing.

The rest of us went into the den where music was already flowing and where a red light set the party scene. Brian was working the stereo and trying to figure which song to play next. Right now, the Commodores were playing Brick House and couples quickly went to the middle of the floor with A.M. and me right in the midst. Before I knew it, we had danced three songs in a row! And I can't lie; I was having a funky good time.

We carried on for hours. On the dance floor, we all did the hustle and then opened up and did a serious soul train line. Couples were bumping, doing the robot, the pop lock, the freak, and everything old and new. Lisa and her boyfriend Timothy came down doing the funky chicken. And then, I swear Crystal was doing the mashed potato with her date, Joe. It was too funny.

Soon after, everyone left the dance floor. We were too pooped to pop. And, just like most parties, the guys went to their side of the room and the girls to the other. Lisa, Crystal and I went to get some punch with Lisa telling us about her foster home and her high school. She said she was really happy living with a nice couple that could never have children and I could tell she was.

"Girl, I can't believe you, Crystal. You and Joe went too far doing the mashed potato," Lisa said.

"Girl, I know. But ain't he fine," Crystal laughed.

"Fine as wine. Where did you meet him?" Lisa asked drinking her punch. I poured me some more as I listened in.

"At the Money Tree."

"Isn't that that club in Renton?" Lisa asked.

"Yeah, it is so cool. They got three dance floors. Two upstairs and one downstairs."

"That does sound cool. I'm going tell Timothy about it."

"Speaking of Timothy, where did you meet that fine brother?" Crystal asked with a raised eyebrow.

"He goes to my school. I see him every single day. He walks me to class, buys my lunch and even drives me home everyday," Lisa said proudly.

"Sounds to me like you two really got it going on," I said to Lisa.

She glanced over at me with dreamy eyes and smiled. "In more ways than one," she said and then started speaking Filipino.

Crystal pushed her. "Um, whatever you just said sounded nasty."

"I only said that he is the love of my life."

"You're in love with him, Lisa?" I asked.

"Definitely. I want to marry him and have a whole bunch of babies with him."

Crystal laughed, "I'm scared of you two. But, I got to hand it to you girl; they would be some cute babies. What is he mixed with?"

"He's Samoan and black."

"See, Nicki, I knew she liked black guys."

"Uh, I never said I didn't. Shoot, look at Badman. He is too, too, too fine."

"Alright now, Lisa. Lay off the Badman," Crystal laughed.

"Why?" Lisa asked and then looked at me. "Nicki, are you and the Badman..."

"What?"

"You know."

I looked at her moment making sure I was hearing what she was asking. "No, we're just friends."

"Still?"

I didn't see what was wrong with that. "What do you mean, still? A.M.'s my best friend. That's never going to change."

Lisa looked at me like I was crazy and started talking with one hand on her hip. "Well, hell it needs to. Are you blind? I mean don't you see what the rest of us see when we see him?"

"Yeah, I see the tall, beautiful, brown-skinned, bowlegged brother with the light eyes, muscular arms, dimples and a smile that the sun can't justify. But I also see more."

Lisa and Crystal both stared at me with their mouths wide opened but with no words coming out.

Lisa finally spoke, "Damn girl, what else have you seen?"

Crystal leaned in closer to us. "Well, you know, what he tried to show her at her locker that time when he was thirteen."

The three of us started laughing hard when A.M. crept into our circle.

"What are you three over here laughing at?" He asked.

Crystal laughed harder and then so did Lisa and I. We couldn't help it. Crystal was laughing so hard she said she had to leave before she peed her pants.

A.M. looked at me smiling. I looked back into his light eyes and smiled back. Lisa said something about Timothy and walked off. A.M. headed back toward the red-lit den with me right behind him. He reached and pulled my hand in his.

Ohio Player's "Sweet Sticky Thing" was playing. He pulled me to him and we started doing the Cha-Cha. He stepped back. I stepped forward. He turned. I turned. He dipped. I dipped. His hands were on my waist, mine on his shoulders. Then he intertwined his fingers with mine, pulled both of our hands over our heads, and he spun me out. Then he leaned back, pushed forward, and my body rested against his. We swayed slowly. For seconds, his eyes locked down on my mine. He moved his lips like he was going to speak but didn't. The song ended. But he didn't let go. And I can't lie. I was glad he didn't.

Another song was soon on. "Easy" by the Commodores. We changed our sway to the beat of the music. A.M. held me closer. I rested my head against his shoulder, closed my eyes, and replayed the conversation I just had with Lisa and Crystal.

I couldn't believe I said what I said about him. But honestly a girl would have to be blind not to notice how handsome A.M. was. All I did was state the obvious. But what they don't know, what I didn't say, is what I've been trying not to say to myself for over a year. I really like him. I like him a lot. Like him so much that my heart skips a beat every time he smiles at me.

I don't exactly remember at what moment it hit me. I mean, two and half years ago as we stood under those waterfalls, I remember wondering what it would it be like to kiss him but nothing more. I was just wondering for the sake of wondering. I didn't take it seriously. And when I changed schools, I was so busy trying to fit in that I didn't let myself wonder about kissing A.M. or anybody else for that matter. Until I would see him!

It seemed each time we got together, he was a little bit different in a good way. His wore his hair differently; cut close while others wore Afros. A pencil line mustache was above his lips, sideburns on his cheeks, broader shoulders, muscular arms, and stronger and longer legs. But that's not all that was different.

He treated me differently. Almost every time he would see me, and no matter who was around, he would take my hand into his, hug me or kiss me on the forehead or cheek. And I don't know when it all started. I just knew that it made me feel special. And when he looked at me, looked at me with half closed eyes, a look that I swear was just for me, I couldn't concentrate!

I wanted to tell A.M. on Labor Day how I felt about him. I wanted to tell him that I daydream about him constantly! I wanted to tell him that I have put our names together and played the true love, hate friendship marriage game and we come out love and marriage one hundred percent! I wanted to tell him that I've practiced writing Mrs. Nicole Washington and Mrs. Anthony Washington at least a thousand times and I have already decided that we should have three kids and live close to Seward Park.

But none of this came out. I couldn't say it. I mean as close as we are, as easy as it is to talk to him, I can't tell him how I feel. I could tell him about me being scared when every girl I knew had started her period and I didn't. And when it did start, I had cramps so bad I could hardly walk. Or, I could tell him about how when my breasts finally came in, one was bigger than the other one. I had no problem talking to him about what was happening to me in that way. But the things that were happing to me inside, the feelings and daydreams I couldn't tell him about. What I was supposed to do? Just walk up and tell him! Go to my best friend and just say A.M. I think I am in love with you!

The song was coming to end and I could already feel him letting me go. I raised my head from his shoulder. I looked into his eyes and he was looking at me with my look! His face came closer to my face and then he lifted my chin up with his finger. I couldn't believe what was happening. He was so close that I was breathing his breath. My heart stopped beating. I stared at his lips and then back into his eyes, at his lips and then back at his eyes again.

The music stopped.

He looked around and then slid his arms from me and stepped several steps away from me. Every part of me was in shock. I couldn't move. His hand took mine and I watched him take in deep breaths as I wondered if he was feeling what I was feeling. He had to be. He almost kissed me! My hand was shaking inside his. Or was his shaking inside mine? He turned and looked behind him and my eyes followed. Brian was trying to decide what record to put on next while everyone was standing around talking or going to get something to eat or drink.

A.M. turned back toward me still looking at me with my look. His tongue ran across his lips before he spoke. "So...are you having a good time?"

"Yes," I said in a voice I hardly recognize.

"Do you want me to get you anything?"

"No I'm fine."

"You sure? It won't take but a sec," he said pulling away but I pulled him back.

"A.M. I don't want anything," I said leaving out 'except you kissing me'.

He stepped closer to me. "Are you okay, Nicki?"

I took a deep breath hoping to find that courage that was hiding inside of me to say what I really wanted to say. "I was just thinking how nice all of this is, the party everybody that's here. This is the nicest thing anyone has ever done for me and I know you had a lot to do with it and I just wanted to say thanks. You always know... I'll never forget tonight."

He stepped even closer to me. "Neither will I," he whispered.

A drumbeat started followed by the slow moan of Phillip Bailey as he started singing Reasons. With one arm A.M. pulled me in arms and his eyes looked down at me. With my look! I placed my arms around his neck waiting on him to lead me. He didn't move. His other arm came around my waist. His head lowered as he kept looking at me and this time there was no hesitation. He kissed me. Touched me like a bee touches a flower. And I can't lie I melted.

Maybe it was because it was my first kiss. Maybe it was because I wanted it so bad. I don't know. I just know that, at this point in my life, it was the best thing that had ever happened to me.

I closed my eyes and let his lips take control of mine and instantly I responded to his every move. His tongue slipped in and out of my mouth and I never felt anything so good. I followed his lead. Let my tongue slip in his mouth. He squeezed me tighter and I held on for dear life. I heard him moan under his breath as I was screaming under mine.

We kissed, we kissed, we kissed!

Slowly, softly, passionately, hungrily, deeper, all of it! I wanted to kiss him for the rest of my life. I knew that as well as I knew my own name.

Our lips slipped apart. I opened my eyes. He was watching me. His fingers brushed across my lips before he softly touched them again with his. He leaned his head against mine with his eyes staring directly into mine. His mouth started moving but if he was saying something I couldn't hear him. He suddenly grabbed my hand and led me out the den and didn't stop until we were outside in the backyard. He let go of my hand and walked over and leaned against the garage. I stood in front of him catching the breath that I had lost inside.

I looked at him wondering what was next. Wondering if that was it. Wondering if he like the way I kissed him as much as I liked the way he kissed me. He grabbed my hand and pulled me closer to him and then for a second looked down at the ground.

"I um, I don't know what you're thinking right now, Nicki," he started raising his eyes back to mine. "About what just happened in there. I mean, I don't know what I was thinking. I just felt..." his words faded off.

He looked around the backyard and then at me again. I watched as his adams apple moved up and down in his throat then looked into his eyes.

"I liked what happened in there," I heard myself saying aloud and then watched the surprised look in his eyes.

"You did?"

"Yes."

A quick smile set on his face. He licked his lips and then shyly looked away from me. I couldn't believe it. I think I was embarrassing him.

"Nicki," he said looking back at me turning my hand inside his. His eyes were more serious than I have ever seen them.

"Yeah."

"I um... I think...no I want...I was just wondering if..."

I stood there waiting on him to finish but seconds ticked off with me waiting.

"If what?" I whispered.

"If you...man, this is hard."

"What's hard?"

"Talking to you like this."

"Then shut up and kiss me again," I said without thinking.

For seconds he stared at me as if he couldn't believe what I just said. Well, I got news for him, neither could I! But suddenly, I felt a boldness I never felt before. I moved and stood inches away from him and watched with anticipation as he lowered his face to mine, opened his mouth to mine and touched me with a softness that I was already craving. His arms wrapped around me and mine around him as our kiss deepened. I never wanted him to stop holding me the way he was holding me now.

"Nicki," he whispered still kissing me.

"Yes." I answered kissing him back.

"I need to give you your birthday present."

"Now?"

"Yes," he said kissing me again. I didn't want him to stop.

"It can wait. It's not even my birthday yet."

"Yes it is. It after midnight."

"But I wasn't born until nine fifteen." I kissed him again.

"A.M. or P.M.," he laughed.

"A.M.," I laughed back.

He moved his arms from around me stepped back but didn't let go of my hands. The smile on his face faded and his eyes changed. He let go of my left hand and slid his hand into his pants pocket and pulled out a small white envelope.

"Here, happy birthday," he said handing the envelope to me.

I let go of his other hand and reached for the envelope and slowly opened it up and pulled out two tickets of some kind. I squinted and moved toward the moonlight to read then. "Are these concert tickets to see the Commodores?" I asked looking back at A.M.

"Yeah."

"Oh my God! Thank you. I've always wanted to see them."

"Well, now you can. You even have two tickets so you can take a date."

"A date?" I laughed.

"Yeah, I'm sure your boyfriend would love to take you."

I stood there looking at him as A.M. looked at me with my look and I felt my knees turn to water. "But, I don't have a boyfriend."

"You do now. That is, if you want one."

"What are you saying?"

"That I *like*, like you. I'm crazy about you. I think about you every single day and I wish I could be with you every single second. I'm saying that I want you to be my girl."

For seconds, I stood and just stared at him, totally speechless. It seemed like everything around me this very moment was changing. I have never felt so happy. I have never felt my heart pound so hard.

A.M. brought his hand to the side of my face as he stepped so close to me. "So beautiful, are you going to give me an answer? Are you going to be my girl?"

I looked into those light eyes that I loved to look in. The ones that made me feel warm from my head down to my toes. "Yeah."

A.M.'s fingers came across my face and lifted my chin. He kissed me again and it felt so good that I could have cried. From now on, on my birthday I'm going to think of this night.

ANTHONY

8

I wasn't dreaming anymore. Not like I used to. Cause ever since our party, I don't have to. It's real, all so real. Nicole and I are Nicole and I. Like peanut butter and jelly. Like cookies and milk. Like cake and ice cream. We go together like ABC.

It's funny when I think about it. Three years ago, I was going around trying to get with anything that wore a skirt. Now, I don't even notice them. When I open my eyes, all I see is Nicki. But they're noticing me. I don't know what was said at school about the party but everybody that is anybody is talking about us. And now, every time we are together, I hear sniggling and laughter and see pointing fingers. Before, when we walked the halls together nobody paid us attention, but now, everybody does. Brian said that since the party, I been walking around with my head in the clouds. And he was right. For three solid weeks I've been on cloud nine.

I'm sixteen years old, the starting quarterback on the varsity football team, and the starting point guard on the varsity basketball team. But the thing that makes me the happiest is having Nicki as my lady.

I reached into the closet and pulled out a pair of jeans and grabbed my Nike's smiling and thinking about the party. It was hard but we pulled it off. My mom and Ms. Emily and my sisters did most of the work, but I was in charge of getting her there and I didn't have a clue how knowing how she feels about birthday celebrations. But when my dad surprised me by giving me the keys to the Impala, I knew exactly what to do.

On the way over there, I kept thinking about what my dad had said about telling her how I feel. Basically, telling me that if I want something to happen then I'm going to have to make the move. But I was scared. Nicki knows me inside out and upside down. And it's what she knows that scares me. I kept thinking she would think that to me she was like every other girl I've been with. And it is the furthest thing from the truth. She is like nobody else, period.

All night, at the party, I kept thinking of ways to just come out and say what I needed to say. But I couldn't. We were having so much fun dancing and clowning around. She was actually singing and partying and laughing and I didn't want to do anything to change that. So I held on. Held on as long as I could to what was burning inside to get out.

For a split second, I thought about my rep. I needed to keep that intact and I couldn't let anybody see me weak behind a girl. But when we slow danced and I was holding her so close to me, I became too aware that I didn't want to let her go. And one look into her dark brown eyes reminded me of the way they made me lose my mind from the very first time I looked into them. To hell with my rep. Nicki was what I wanted, what I needed. And somehow, someway I was going to tell her how I felt. I didn't know how I was going to get the words out. Couldn't think of the right words to come out. But she was going to know.

So, I kissed her. And then waited. But there was nothing to wait for cause she was kissing me back. And slowly and surely I eased up to cloud nine.

I can't say what happened after that cause honestly I don't remember. I have kissed dozens of girls before but I never heard my heart beat inside me the way it did when our lips touched. I never felt that pull in my chest or that light feeling in my stomach. I tuned out everyone around us, forgot that we were in the middle of the dance floor in my basement with a room full of people. All my senses came alive and were boldly going where they had never been before. I touched, smelled, tasted, saw and heard nothing but Nicole Chantel Williams.

I hurriedly laced up my shoes, grabbed my leather jacket and headed down the stairs two at a time. I went into the kitchen. It smelled good. My mom, and Ashley and April were in there cooking for tomorrow. I glanced over my mom's shoulder as she was cleaning greens at the kitchen sink. I gave her a kiss on the cheek, went to the refrigerator, got two sodas out, and began to make my exit.

"Anthony Marcus, where are you headed in such a hurry?" my mom asked not even looking up from the sink.

"Don't know yet, mama. I'll see when I get there."

"You sure do stink! What you do, waste a whole bottle of cologne on you?" Ashley said, frowning up at me.

"Don't worry about it," I said laughing and bumping her out of my way.

"Anthony Marcus, don't you stay out too late."

"I won't," I said easing out the kitchen.

"Hey?"

I stopped in the dining room and turned around as my mom came toward me. She walked slowly drying off her hands on her apron. She folded her hands across her chest and looked up at me. "I know you think you're too big to listen to me, but you better do it anyway. Are you putting moves on Nicole?"

"Mama, come on now." I said like I was shocked. What did she know about moves anyway?

She looked at me with that face that said I better answer her and I better know what to say.

I took a deep breath and gave her my mama's boy smile. "Now, mama you know I am always a gentleman," I said hugging her.

She shooed me away and gave me a look that said she was not impressed. "The only thing I know is, that you are a sixteen year old boy with raging hormones. And Nicole is a nice girl. A nice girl, Anthony Marcus! And I don't want you pressuring her to do something you think you need for the moment."

"I wouldn't do that."

"Nicki's my friend mama and has been for a long time. I'm not going to do anything to mess that up."

"Son, your mama's no fool. I see the way you look at her. She's got your nose wide open. I just want you to be careful. She's been through a lot in her life. She don't need you playing games and running lines on her."

"I don't. What we got is real to me. Real real," I said honestly looking her directly in the eye.

She reached and patted me on the face. "Have a good time tonight."

I kissed her cheek and left.

Seven minutes later, I was getting out of the car in front of Nicki's house. Ms. Emily was sitting on the porch snapping green beans. I greeted her with a kiss on her cheek like I did my mom. Over the years, we have become close and I always felt like she was rooting for Nicki and I to get together. Looking back, I guess she knew before either of us knew.

She said hello and asked where we going tonight. I told her wherever my baby wanted to go. That made her laugh as she snapped the green beans. I looked up at the house just as Nicki peeked out the window. I winked my eye. She smiled and held up a finger to let me know she'll be out in a minute and closed the curtain.

I sat down in the other chair and reached over into the big barrel of beans and started snapping them like I had seen my grandmother, mother and sisters do.

"What you know about snapping beans, Mr. A.M.?" Emily asked, looking over at me.

"Ms. Emily, I like to eat. I got a big family and a lot of times I got to get in there and help if I want to eat anytime soon. And plus, I got to do my share at the restaurants."

"Is that right."

"Sure is."

"Well, that Miss Nicki acts like she scared of a kitchen. She only comes in there to eat, sit and talk, or clean it. But believe me, she can't even boil water," Emily laughed.

"You mean she can't cook?" I asked surprised at this information.

"Not a lick. She's always been too busy hanging out with you to learn her way around a kitchen."

"Oh well, I guess I'll forgive her then."

"Um, um. I bet you will."

"Hey, A.M." Nicki said from behind the screen door.

I put the beans down, stood up, and opened the door. Nicki stepped out on the porch. She was wearing black corduroy pants, a white sweater and my old leather jacket that I grew out of last year.

"Hey," I said and then gave her quick kiss on the mouth. Something I wouldn't dream of doing in front of my parents but Emily didn't mind. Like I said, she's our number one fan.

Nicki reached and wiped her lip-gloss off of my lips. "Crystal and Lisa called. They heard about the scary house at the Center and said it was supposed to be pretty good. I know how you like all that fake blood and gory stuff so I thought we could go."

"Sounds cool."

"They want to know if they can tag."

"Who?"

"Crystal and Lisa and Timothy and Joe."

"Plus us makes six."

"Yeah."

"In the Impala?"

"Well, it would be cool if we all rode together instead going in two cars."

I hesitated for a moment like I wasn't going to go for it. But shoot, Nicki knew me better and just pushed me down the steps of the porch.

"Goodnight, Ms. Emily," she said over her shoulder.

"See you two later, have fun."

I grabbed Nicki's hand and led her to the passenger side and let her in and then walked back to my side. When I got in she was going through my music. My 1968 Impala had an eight-track player in it and my dad gave me a bunch of old music. I bought four new Realistic speakers and now my baby girl was jamming eight tracks like it was nobody's business.

Nicki reached for EWF, That's The Way Of The World eight-track and stuck in it as I started the car and immediately fast-forwarded it to Reasons. It wasn't the live version that we played at the party, but it was still the song. The song we shared our first to. The song I sing the most when I think of her. I looked over at her as she sung softly, trying not to look at me by keeping her eyes straight ahead. I handed her a soda, smiled and kept driving. *Sing baby.*

I approached the intersection of Empire Way and 23rd and slowed down so I could catch the red light. I pressed my foot firmly on the brake took one hand off the steering wheel leaned over and kissed her like I been wanting to since I picked her up. Slipped my tongue in and out of her mouth and felt hers in my mine. She placed her hand around my neck pulling us closer together as we continued to kiss.

LOVE AND CONSEQUENCES

I don't understand why kissing her makes me feel so good in places I didn't know could feel good. Somebody needs to explain it to me cause I swear my toes curl up when this girl kisses me. The hair on the back of my neck stands up and my knees feel like water. And, with all of this going on, Bad is going into overdrive.

I don't think about sex as much as I used to. Okay, I do, but not in the same way. Since our first kiss, I know there's a difference in what I did with all those other girls and in what I do with Nicki. When I kiss Nicki, all of me is in that kiss, not just Bad. When I kiss her, I'm thinking waterfalls cause that's what I feel like. One minute I'm caught up in a rushing stream and then the next I'm slowly falling off a cliff over and over again.

I can think all of this and feel all of this but I can't say it. At least not out loud and especially not to her. I know she knows me, I know she understands me, but I'm scared of showing her what she really does to me. I'm scared of seeing it myself.

A car horn forced me out of my thoughts and out of my baby's arms and away from her lips. She reached over, touched my lips with her fingers, and then slid back closer to her door, smiling at me with her dark brown eyes looking into mine. I shifted my weight in my seat so she couldn't see how Bad was acting up.

"So, who am I picking up first?" I asked trying to think of something to take my mind off of the softness of her lips.

"We're supposed to meet everybody at Lisa's."

"Cool. At least I don't have to drive all over Seattle."

"Baby, you know I'm not going to have you doing all that driving. We got a curfew to keep."

"Yeah, you right," I said thinking about her two o'clock curfew. Emily was cool but she didn't play with that curfew. If I had Nicki home one minute after, she was practically standing in the street watching for my car to ease down their street. And Nicki always had to tell her where we going. I think that was because Emily wanted the right to come and drag her home if needed.

In ten minutes, we were in front of Lisa's house. She lived by Sunset High School. All the houses over here seemed to be too close together and hardly didn't have a front yard because the city came through and widened the street. The four of them were standing outside talking by Timothy's car. They quickly piled into the Impala. Crystal squeezed in the front seat next to Nicki putting her closer to me. I stretched my arm across the seat hugged my girl and stole another kiss as everybody got settled.

Before long, we were downtown. We decided to ride the monorail, so I parked at the station and we hopped on the train. It was crowded with people dressed up for Halloween. There were only three seats, so all the guys sat down with our girls in our laps. I started nibbling on Nicki's neck as she sat on my legs. She starting laughing and then turned and gave me a quick kiss. I pulled her face back toward me and placed my mouth on hers and kissed like I like it. Her hands came up around my face and she began caressing my neck and my ears as we kissed.

Big mistake! Big, big, mistake. Bad woke up and I couldn't hide it. I continued to kiss her with my hands wrapped around her body and pressing it against mine. I don't want to let her go. Ever! I was losing control!

I forced myself to stop kissing her and to try to stop the thoughts that were going through my head, the thoughts of holding her, kissing her and loving her all over. For the rest of the six-minute ride, I looked into her eyes. Trying to tell her with my eyes what I couldn't say with my mouth. 'Baby I want you, I need you and hell yes, I love you.'

Yeah, I said it. Said it to myself anyway cause no matter how I keep trying to run away from those three words they keep slapping me in the face. Like I told my mom, what we have is *real* real.

"Come on you two, let's go," Lisa said as the train stopped at the Center. Nicki stood up and then I stood and we all headed off the train.

The Center was packed. Especially with little kids dressed in their scary costumes. The six of us decided to ride some rides before heading for the scary house.

We headed for the roller coaster first. Nicki was running and telling me to hurry up because she wanted to sit up front. I didn't like roller coaster, and she knew this, but always forced me on it every time we came, talking about I need to toughen up. I want to see whose going to be so tough when we get in the scary house.

We got on the ride and Nicki screamed in my ear as soon as we took off and headed for the top.

"Oh so you're trying to be funny," I said

"What?" she asked, looking innocent.

"Like this part is so scary."

"I always scream when I ride roller coasters."

"On the way up?"

"Well, I got other things to do on the way down."

"Like what, jump?"

"Like this," she said and then just as I felt the car going down hill, her mouth was covering mine, her hands were rubbing my ears and then she was kissing my neck. I let out a sound that came from somewhere deep inside me. It wasn't fear. It was nowhere near fear. It was that want thing that desire thing, that thing that had me going crazy.

I let go of the bar in front of me and pulled her closer to me and then kissed her with everything that was inside of me. Nicki held my heart. Every time our lips touched, she held my heart and there wasn't a damn thing I could do about it.

In the scary house, I was in control. I didn't like roller coasters because I didn't like heights. But a scary house was another story. We had to walk through darkness just to get to the cars. Passing by all types of gory monsters, spiders, and walking hands. Nicki was holding my arm so tight she was cutting off my circulation.

We got inside our car and I insisted that we sit in the front like we did on the roller coaster. She moaned and then sat so close to me that she was practically in my lap again. Lisa and Timothy were behind us and Joe and Crystal behind them.

The three girls instantly started screaming as soon as we took off into the semi dark cave. It was almost deafening. I put my arm around Nicki, kissed her and then sat back to enjoy the show.

Soon, a headless figure jumped out in front of us and reached for Nicki. She quickly covered her face screaming for me to take her out of here.

"Tough it up baby," I laughed.

"Anthony Marcus Washington, Jr., you just wait until we get out of here," she said glaring at me with that look she used to give me on the football field.

I kissed her cheek, laughed and stared into those brown eyes. "I love you, baby."

The words flowed off my tongue so quick I didn't even feel them coming. It was like somebody else was saying what I was thinking. What I was feeling. I kept looking at Nicki who was sitting next to me with a face I couldn't read. She sat straight up. Her mouth was slightly open. Her eyes were staring straight into mine and not blinking.

"How could you," she said suddenly throwing me way off.

"What?"

"Tell me you love me in a scary house," she said so seriously.

I didn't know what to say to that. What did she want me to do, take it back? I couldn't do that. "Because I do."

She leaned in and kissed me. Kissed me over and over and held me so close. We didn't see the rest of the scary house. I don't know what else was flying around or jumping out at us. I just know that Nicki was kissing me and whispering that she loves me back.

It was one o'clock. I had just dropped off Lisa, Timothy, Crystal and Joe. Nicki and I were easing into Seward Park. I parked the car, facing the floating bridge, turned off the lights and turned off the motor. I looked over at Nicki as she was going through my tracks.

"Oh, I see you got Rick James," she said.

"Yeah."

"I like that song, You and I."

"I like Dream Maker."

"I don't know that one. Play it."

I stuck the track in. The song started. "Come here."

I shifted in my seat so that I was leaning against the door and so my legs could stretch out in the seat. Nicki slid inside my arms and leaned her back against my front. I kissed her neck and then looked out at the water. This felt so perfect. For moments, we sat in silence as the song played. All of a sudden she started laughing.

"What are laughing at?" I asked.

"You."

"What?"

"On that roller coaster. Your eyes got so big!"

"That's because you surprised me when you kissed me."

"Oh, you lie. You know you were scared. Fess up."

"Okay. But, I must admit, I like the way you distract me. Nice trick."

"So is that why you said what you said in the scary house, you wanted to distract me?"

"No, actually I didn't mean to say what I said."

I felt Nicki's body tense up and she slowly sat up and turned so she could face me. "You didn't?"

I rubbed her face with my hand to calm the sudden fear she had in her eyes. "I meant what I said it's just that... I've been feeling that way for so long that I didn't know how to say it."

Nicki closed her eyes and her mouth started trembling. Almost instantly, a tear was sliding down her face. I sat up and reached and turned off the music. "What is it, baby?"

She opened her eyes and looked into mine. "People always say to me when they find out that I lost both of my parents, that they feel so sorry for me. I have no other family, they died on my thirteenth birthday and I lived in an orphanage and now a foster home.

"But what they don't understand is what I hated the most is the fact that I didn't die in that fire. I used to ask myself why did I survive. Why did I have to live without them? And for three years I've been trying to figure out what my parents used to say, about how every thing happens for a reason. Everything! And I didn't get it. But now I do.

"If I hadn't survive, I wouldn't have been placed in the Haywood home. I wouldn't have gone to a new school and I wouldn't have met you. And, I wouldn't be feeling the way you make me feel."

"Come here," I said, reaching for her and pulling her in my arms, holding her tightly and kissing her over and over. I looked at her and placed her beautiful face in my hands. "I'm always going to love you Nicki. I'm always going to protect you. There's nothing I won't do for you. Nothing!"

"I know A.M. You are my morning. My new life started with you. I love every part of you with every part of me. I don't ever want to lose what we have."

I kissed her. "You won't. You're my forever."

ANTHONY

9

I dream often
of us being together-daily
and I can't tell you
how often in a course
of twenty-four hours
that you enter my mind so much
that a part of me is with you.
I know it sounds crazy
believe me
I find myself wondering
how is it
that you've gotten inside of my
mind and changed my thoughts
and in my heart and changed it's beat

I looked down at the paper in front of me filled with the words I just wrote and seeing Nicki's face between every line. I heard a car door close and looked out my bedroom window. Emily was reaching for the backseat as Nicki got out and closed her door.

She glanced my way and then went to Emily's side of the car and began to help her pull out bags from the back seat. I placed the sheet of paper in my pocket and headed downstairs. I'll have to finish it later.

In no time, I was outside taking the bags from her hand as my dad came out and helped Emily with her bags. With no words we spoke and then headed into the house.

"Come on in and make yourself comfortable," my mom said coming from the kitchen.

"Oh, girl I'm sure glad you invited us over for Thanksgiving," Emily said taking off her coat. "I hate to miss spending the holiday with my sister and her family but you know they're talking about snow and I didn't think Ms. Nicki and I should chance going up that mountain this year."

"Well, you know you and Nicki are welcome here anytime," my mom said, hugging Emily and then Nicole. I went and placed my bag of food in the kitchen and then came back into the living room.

"Anthony Marcus, take their coats. You two come warm up by the fire," my dad said.

I went and helped Nicki off with her coat. She was wearing a navy knit sweater with a matching long skirt and black knee length boots. I looked down into my favorite brown eyes. "Hey," I whispered.

"Hi, Morning."

I love it when she calls me Morning. I looked deeper into her eyes. Got totally lost inside them, just stood there staring. Wanting to kiss her.

"Junior, put those coats up and come help me with the fire," my dad spoke from somewhere behind me.

I slowly walked away and headed for my parent's bedroom and placed the coats on their bed. When I came back into the living room, Nicki and Emily were standing by the fireplace. My father was handing Emily a cup of tea and then gave one to Nicki.

"Here's a little something to warm up your insides," he said and then turned to the fireplace. He began to sift through the fire with the iron poker. I picked up two logs and placed them on top of the one that was almost burned out. Dad worked his magic with the poker and the lighter sticks and soon the room was a warm glow. The four of us stood there awhile looking into the blue and orange flames.

"That takes care of that. Now, let's go see what we can do in that kitchen to speed up things. The game comes on at five and I want to be good and full and in my chair in front of the television," my father said and led the way as we followed.

One thing I can say about my family is that we go all out for holidays, especially Thanksgiving and Christmas. It seems like as soon as November rolls around there is a mood shift in this house.

My sisters and I don't argue as much. My mom and dad are hugged up and whispering more than usual and are always smiling and happy. And don't let it be real cold and snowing. When the weather forces us to be more in than out, we're all up under each other. Playing games in front of the fireplace, watching old movies on television, and sometimes even breaking out some old eight tracks and dancing around all crazy.

And then there are days we do nothing together but everybody's together all in the living room, doing our own thing. My mom might be reading, while my dad is sitting in his favorite chair with the television watching him snore off and on. Ashley will sit on the love seat looking out the window and sketching. April crochets and I sit on the floor with my headphones on low listening to my music while watching the football game that my dad is supposed to be watching.

Then the phone will ring and it will be Anita or Angela calling. Sometimes each of us will talk to them and I can tell that they wish they were home doing nothing with us.

"Baby, something sure smells good in here," my dad said, leaning over my mom and giving her a quick kiss on the cheek.

"Anything I can help with?" Emily asked, looking around our busy kitchen. We're a restaurant family and sometimes our kitchen looks like a kitchen restaurant. Everybody is busy and in charge of something.

Anita and Angela were putting the finishing touches on a chocolate cake. April was working on some potato salad. My mom was checking on the big pan of dressing. Dad stuck his head in the oven and looked in on the turkey. Ashley was mixing an apple salad in a bowl. Which meant I needed to start on the dishes.

"Emily, you just take a seat. You've done enough with all that food you brought over. Besides, we got it all under control," my mom stated with a smile.

Emily sat down and I headed toward the sink and started making some dishwater. We had a dishwasher but hardly ever used it.

"You want some help?" Nicki asked, standing a few feet from me. I looked down into her eyes. I know she said something, but what? I couldn't focus.

All I could think of was the piece of paper in my pocket. I wanted to give it to her even though it wasn't finished. I wanted to see her face while she read it. Then hold her in my arms.

For seconds, I stood staring at her and thinking about the paper in my pocket, thinking about her eyes and about kissing her. Without thinking, I took one of her hands inside mine and pulled her closer to me and then reached to touch her face.

Suddenly, my dad squeezed by me and poked his hand inside the drawer to my left. My mom put a bowl in the soapy water that was filing the sink and then turned back toward the stove. I glanced around the kitchen. All of my sisters and Emily were looking like they were trying not to look at me. Angela and Anita were whispering and practically laughing as they continued to frost the cake. What was so funny?

I turned my attention back to Nicki, trying to remember what it was she had asked me. Oh yeah, the dishes. I turned off the water.

"You sure you don't mind?" I asked.

"It's the least I could do."

"She's means the most," Emily said with a small laugh.

Nicki turned and smiled at Emily.

"Come on Emily, Ann, let's let the kids finish up. They need all the practice they can get," my dad said. Then him, my mom and Emily headed out the kitchen. I began gathering up the dishes on the counter tops and tables. We hadn't even eaten yet and already there was a sink full of dishes.

I started washing the dishes and handing them to Nicki as she stood beside me rinsing them off. For minutes, we stood side by side not saying a word as my sisters all came over giving me more dishes to clean. Then, one by one, they all were finally gone and Nicki and I were alone.

I glanced in the dining room. Nobody was in there. They were all in the living room talking and laughing. I looked back at Nicki. She had started to dry the clean dishes off. I took a bowl from her hand and leaned over her and placed in the cabinet above her head. When I closed the door, I realized that I was standing only inches away from her.

I took her hand and led her over near the stove that was out of sight from the living room.

Nicole smiled up at me. "What are you doing?"

"I wanted to...show you our stove."

"Your stove?"

"Yeah."

"Why?"

I pulled her closer to me then brushed her hair from her eyes so I could see them better. "Because Ms. Emily told me you don't know how to cook."

"So."

"Well, I do."

"And?"

"And, I could show you how."

"How to cook?"

"Yes."

"You think so?"

"I know so," I said glancing down at her lips wanting to feel them on mine so bad. She formed them in a slow smile.

"What if I don't want to cook? What else could you show me?"

I brought my eyes back to her eyes and then slowly leaned my face closer to hers. For seconds, I looked into her eyes, as our lips were only inches apart. I hadn't touched them but I could already feel them, already taste them.

"Does anybody else want anything while I'm in the kitchen?"

Nicki stepped back.

I dropped my head down.

Damn, Angela!

She came into the kitchen with a glass and then went to the refrigerator. It took her two years and six months to fill her glass with ice and then pour some Pepsi in it. She glanced our way sipping her drink. Nicki had another bowl in her hand drying it off. I grabbed a cake pan and started washing it.

Angela walked over to the stove and peeked into the pots and turned the fire down lower.

"Junior, you're watching the food, right?"

"Yeah," I said in a voice to let her know she was not wanted in here.

"No need to get hostile, little brother. Just checking," she said and then slowly walked out snickering under breath.

Nicole placed the bowl down and stepped closer to me. "Now, why did you get all mad at your sister?"

"I'm not mad at her," I said facing her.

"Then what's the matter?"

"Nothing."

"Nothing?"

"No. I'm cool," I answered shaking my hands out of the water.

"Okay, if you say so."

I found a towel and dried my hands off. "Nicki?"

"Yeah?"

"I have something for you."

A look of surprise came over her face. "What is it?"

"But I'm not finished with it yet."

"A.M. you made something for me?"

"No, I wrote something."

I looked into her eyes. They became watery, shining, and dreamy. I can't explain how that made me feel. So connected, so close. She hadn't even read the words and she was already feeling what I was feeling. All those damn feelings that not so long ago I would have sworn guys don't feel.

Those damn feelings that make you want to sing, want to laugh, and tell whoever is listening or watching that you're on top of the world because you have someone that makes you feel things you never thought you could feel. And I swear, just the look on her face, the look in her eyes as she looks at me is why I wrote those words on the piece of paper that was in my pocket.

I reached into my pocket and pulled out the sheet of paper and handed it to her. I watched as she slowly unfolded the paper. I watched as her eyes and lips moved simultaneously as she read each line. My heart was beating so loud I was sure she could hear it.

Seconds ticked off.

She kept reading.

My words.

My thoughts.

My feelings.

My love.

All of me.

She lifted her face toward mine, her eyes already showing me what she hadn't yet said. She came into my arms. I squeezed her. Held her close to me. Closed my eyes and just felt her.

"Dad said it's time to come into the living room."

I eased my arms down then watched Nicki's eyes as she stepped away from me. I kept her hand inside mine then turned and looked at April standing in the doorway waiting. "Here we come."

We have a tradition. A tradition that was originated by my mother when we were younger and used to fight over whose going to sit where, whose going to get a turkey leg and who had the most food. We all have to line up and tell each other that we are blessed to have them in our lives and that we love them and then give them a hug, a kiss or hand shake.

As crazy as it sounds, my mother was dead serious. She hated for us to argue over anything, especially during the holidays. She insisted that we do this in order to show us the value of being a family. But we were kids. And we were hungry. So we did what all kids do when they're forced to do something. We made a game of it.

Instead of all five of us going around saying words that should have meant something to us, we would make faces at one another trying to distract each other. Soon everyone would be cracking up and forgetting about fighting over anything and then we prayed and had a peaceful dinner. It works and we've been doing it ever since.

Nicki and I went into the living room where my family was already in a straight line. I led her to stand next to my dad so that I was on the end. This was a strategically planned spot. Everybody had to come to me and I didn't have to move.

Angela begins turning first to April and makes her way down the line. Like always, all of my sisters make faces, laugh, hug and say the required words to each other. By the time they reach my parents, my mom's in tears and my dad is look-ing at them like he wished they were all upstairs fighting over doll clothes instead of leaving the house one by one.

As each one of them makes their way down the line to me I give them my grossest look, the one with one eyelid flipped inside out and the other one looking at it. Angela hits me, April doesn't want to touch me, Ashley breaks out laughing and Anita hugs me anyway. I hug them all, tell them I love them and how the older we get, the more I'm glad they have me as they're brother.

Ricky's next. He's my brother in law, been in the family for three years, but I swear I never know what to say to him. He's so quiet. He comes down holding little Ricky. I un-flip my eyelid and we kind of just look at each other. No words come from my mouth and none from his. I look at my nephew and give him a pinch on the cheek. He breaks into a grin. Big Ricky smiles, shakes my hand and then moves on.

Emily, my mom, dad, Nicki and me are still in the line. Emily comes next, really into this sentimental notion. She's all in tears as she hugs my mom telling her that the next time she sees her sister, Nora, they're going to have to start this tradition. Then when she hugs Nicki, she practically picks her off the floor, goes into Hallelujah praise to God for bringing her into her life. And then to me she says, I'm good people and that she loves what I do for Nicki.

For seconds, she stood looking almost eye-to-eye with me and I didn't know what to say. She reached and hugged me, pulling me into her large arms, and let out a loud laugh. When I caught my breath, I told her I was glad she's in Nicki's life too.

It suddenly becomes quiet. My mom faces my dad. They stand there looking at each other for a while, a long while. Then finally she speaks first, telling him more than the required words and he does the same. It is quite clear that my folks are still crazy about each other. They hold hands they hug and then kiss. And not just some quick kiss, they kiss! Like no one is even in the room.

When I was younger, I used to moan and groan watching them carry on. But now, even though it is a little embarrassing, it amazes me. And as I glance into Nicki's eyes and see the tears for the parents I know she wishes she still had, I feel damn lucky that my parents are still alive, still together, and still in love.

Soon, my mom leaves my dad's side and goes to Nicki telling her that she considers her family and if she ever gets sick of me to come see her anyway. Nicki smiles, thanks her through teary eyes and hugs her.

Standing in front me, my mom looks up at me and then pulls me in her arms. She tells me how much she loves me and I hug her tighter than I have in a long time. Don't know why but I just did. She squeezed me tight and then let go and for a moment just looked at me. I bent down and kissed her cheek and told her how blessed I was to be her son.

My dad turns to Nicki. She's looking down and has her hand on her diamond heart as tears stream down her face. My dad pulls her into his arms and hugs her. Softly she cries on his shoulder. I watch as her body trembles in his arms as he holds her, pats her back and whispers soothing words in her ear.

She slowly calms down and lets go of my dad and I can tell she's a little embarrassed. I look at her without saying a word. Letting her know with my eyes I am never going to leave her side. Never.

In front of me my dad is standing. Towering over me is the man I most respect, admire, the head of this house. The one who has always taught me to be strong, a leader and to always protect and take care of those I care about.

He looked down into my face and I was trying hard to look like I was all that he wanted me to be. But the only thing crossing my mind was the girl standing next to me. When I looked into her eyes, I became weak. If she asked me to, I would follow her around the world.

His brought his arms around me, hugged me, let me go, and said three words, "Go to her."

I held her like the first time I held her. I kissed her like the first time I kissed her. In a room full of people, it did not even faze me not to.

I looked down into her eyes as I held her face in my hands. Without hesitation, I said to her what I've been taught to say to someone I care about. "I love you and I am so blessed to have you in my life."

NICOLE

10

I don't know how, but time just keeps on moving. Already, it's March. It seems like only yesterday that A.M. and me were racing in the snow, having snowball fights, and sliding down Graham Hill on box tops and now Spring is just around the corner. It's just so unreal. Everything is. Except for what I feel for A.M.

If someone had told me last year that I would be this happy, I would have not believed it. But it's oh, so true. A.M., my Morning, makes me totally happy. For the past five months, we have spent every second we can together discovering and exploring each other and I can't lie, I don't want it to end and if I weren't so scared I would go further. I would tell him to keep on holding me, keep on kissing me, and to just keep on. But I'm scared. Scared of what will happen next and scared of what won't.

I turned and looked at the picture that sat on the nightstand next to my bed of us that we took at South Center Mall with Santa when we were on Christmas break. I had told A.M. how I hadn't seen Santa since I was five and he insisted that we take a picture. We both had sat on Santa's lap and had to hold on to the man real tight so we wouldn't fall. We were squeezing him so hard that in the picture all that is seen is A.M. and me and a piece of Santa's little red hat and white beard sticking out between us. A.M. has the biggest smile on his face as he leans into my own smiling one. As Ms. Emily would say, we are definitely a pair. I squeezed the picture close to my heart and then jumped when the phone ringed. I let it ring one more time so I could catch my breath and then picked it up.

"Hey, Morning."

"Morning? Girl, what time zone are you on?"

"Oh, hey Lisa. What's going on?"

"Nothing. You're still coming over tonight, right?"

"Yeah, I'm coming."

"Well, you don't sound too happy about it. What's wrong, you're going to miss your Badman?" Lisa asked teasing me in a baby voice.

"Maybe."

"Maybe, my foot. You know you're going to miss your baby."

"Yeah, whatever Lisa, okay. Just shut up."

"Oh, I know you ain't trying to get mad."

"Lisa, what did you call me for?"

"Shoot, to mess with your head. Psyche! I was calling to see if you were going to need a ride over cause my mom said she would come and pick you up."

"Oh, isn't that cute. You said your mom," I said in my own baby voice.

"Nicki, quit tripping."

"That is so sweet."

"Yeah, yeah I know. Now do you need a ride or what?" Lisa asked hurriedly with her thick accent changing the subject. Never can take what she dishes out.

"No, my mom's going to bring me over as soon as she gets back from the store," I said in my Jan Brady voice.

"Fine."

"Fine."

"Well, I'll see you when you get here, square," Lisa said laughing and then hung up the phone before I could respond. She knows I'm going to get her when I get over there.

I looked at the picture I was still holding and then placed it back on the nightstand and then finished packing my bag to take over Lisa's. Lisa, Crystal and I were getting together for a long overdue sleep over. We both have been wrapped up in our significant others for months and haven't spent any time together.

I went to the closet and got my favorite leather coat out and threw it on the bed. My private line that I got for Christmas rang again. This time, I jumped across the bed and picked it up after the first ring.

"Hello."

"Hey, baby."

"Hey, Morning," I said smiling into the phone. I was hoping he would call me before I left. I lay across the bed and closed my eyes. "A.M. are you still there."

"I'm here. Although I wish I was there with you."

"Yeah."

"You know I do," he said in his sexy voice. I covered the phone with my hand so he couldn't hear me squeal loudly under my breath. I love his voice especially early in the morning. It gets so deep.

"Nic, are you there?"

"Always."

"Yeah?"

"Yeah."

"Then, what would you say if I asked you not to go to Lisa's tonight?"

I took a deep breath before answering. "What would you say if I asked you not to ask me that?"

"Oh, okay, yeah that's cool. That's cool," A.M. answered and I could hear him smiling so I smiled too. "Crystal is coming too, right?"

"Yeah."

"Then I should be there too. It could be like junior high all over again. You know, the four of us."

"Oh, I don't think so. Crystal had it bad for you in junior high."

"Oh she did?"

"Please, you know she did."

"Well hey, what can a player do?"

"A player?"

"You know back in my day baby, before you. I'm a changed man now."

"All right Mr. Man."

"Are you questioning my manhood now?"

"No way, *hombre*."

"Cause, if you have any questions or any doubts about me being the man that I am, you know, I can be there in about six, seven seconds tops just to..." his voice stopped and then floated into that laugh of his that says more than any words can. "Let me stop."

"No, don't."

"Baby, don't say that to me. I really will be there in six seconds. I will break the sound barrier girl."

"You are so crazy. That's why I love you."

"That's why you love me?"

"Yeah."

"I thought it was because of my good looks."

"Not even close."

"Say what? Oh, all right. Then it's the car."

"You drive a '68 Impala with an eight track."

"You're ragging on my car baby. That's cold. That's real cold."

"I'm not ragging your car. I like your car. I just don't love you because of it."

"Oh, so it must be my money. Cause you know I'm a working man."

"I can't tell you have money cause you're always stealing."

"Nic, I haven't stolen anything in about two or three years."

"What about the money you stole out the cash register at your father's restaurant to pay for the Earth Wind and Fire concert tickets last week?"

"That was a loan."

"Oh, so you put it back?"

"No, my dad took it out of my paycheck."

"See, you're crazy, that's why I love you."

"Well, you better."

"No, you better be glad I do."

"Hell, I am! I'm most grateful."

"How grateful are you?"

"Enough to drive over there in six seconds and give you the biggest kiss you ever had."

"How would you know it was the biggest kiss that I ever had?"

"Cause it would be the biggest kiss that I ever gave you."

"How do you know somebody else has never given me a big kiss?"

"Cause I was the first."

"Are you sure?"

"What? Hell yeah. I've known you since you were buck-toothed and had a flat chest. I know I was the first."

I jumped off the bed. "I know you didn't..."

"Baby, I'm sorry."

"Too late, sorry don't have anything to do with it."

Marcus laughed into the phone. "I was just joking."

"That was personal."

"Baby, come on, your ragged my car."

"You just called me buck-toothed and said I had a flat chest."

"Baby, now you know you had a flat chest."

"Take it back."

"Baby."

"Take it back."

"Nic, why are you going to be like that?"

"Take it back"

"Okay, okay. You weren't buck-toothed. And you chest was only flat on one side."

"Bye, A.M."

"Nic, come on baby. We can't talk now?"

"I got to go. Ms. Emily's here and she out there blowing her horn."

"Okay, wait a minute baby. I love you."

"Yeah, all right."

"I'm going to miss you."

"Um huh."

"I want you."

"Shoot. Why can't you let me stay mad at you?"

"Because you love me and you're going to miss me. And you want me just as bad as I want you. See you tomorrow."

"Good night."

I hung up the phone, grabbed my bag and coat, and floated to the car.

Mrs. Lewis opened the door holding a bowl of chips, a platter of sandwiches, and bowl of popcorn. She shoved the chips in my hand and led me to Lisa's room. Crystal was already there and the two of them were sitting on the floor going through Lisa's albums. 'Easy', by the Commodores, was playing on Lisa's component set and instantly my mind went to A.M. and our birthday party.

Mrs. Lewis put the food on the dresser and then quietly left, closing the door behind her. I threw my bag on Lisa's bed and took off my coat and sat down next to Crystal who started eating the chips soon after I placed them down.

"What's kicking chicken," Crystal asked.

"Not a thang chicken wang," I answered.

"Well, what took you so long to get here?" Lisa asked.

"Hey, I got things to do, places to go and people to see. So, don't worry about it," I said rolling my eyes at her trying to still be mad at her for calling me a square on the phone.

"Well, since you're trying to be funny I ain't going to tell you my secret."

"What secret?" I asked looking at her suspiciously.

"Don't worry about it. I'll just tell Crystal."

"Tell me what?" Crystal turned to face us.

"That I'm thinking about doing it."

"Doing what?" I asked reaching for some popcorn.

"Man, Nicole. You're really a square or what?"

"I'm not a square. I just want you to clarify what you're saying, 'cause I know you're not saying what I think you're saying."

"Well, I got news for you honey. I am saying exactly what you think I'm saying," Lisa said proudly.

"Lisa! I don't believe you."

"What, Nicole? I love Timothy and he loves me. And we are going to do what comes naturally. Hey! I'm a poet and didn't know it," Lisa said pushing Crystal and laughing with her silly self.

"Crystal, can you believe this girl," I said but Crystal gave no response.

"Believe it, honey," Lisa said standing up and going to her bed where she reached under her mattress and then came back with a small pink container that she opened up slowly showing us the small pink, green and white pills. Her eyes got as big as saucers. "I got these. Now, do you believe me?"

"Where did you get those?" I asked.

"At the free clinic on Jackson."

"Does your mom know that you have those?"

"If she did they wouldn't be under the mattress."

"You're serious, huh?"

"As a heart attack," Lisa said closing the pills and putting them back under her mattress.

"So, what do you think?"

"Think about what?"

"Me and Tim."

"Nothing," I answered. My mind was already on A.M. There were so many times that we could have done it but something inside makes me stop. I don't know why. I mean I love him with everything inside of me and I believe he loves me back. But I can't think about knowing him that way yet. Okay, I can think about it. Shoot, I dream about it constantly. But I can't do it. Not yet. I don't think.

"Why are you two so quiet?" Lisa said after a moment.

"I'm in shock. I just can't believe somebody wants to be with you in that way," I said throwing a pillow at Lisa's head. She dived on me hitting me with a pillow and the two of us wrestled and threw pillows for the next five minutes. I finally got the best of her by climbing on her and hitting her repeatedly in the head until she begged me to stop. I rose off of her and went and sat near the bed on the floor.

"Don't call me a square no more."

"Alright, alright, man, some people are so touchy."

"I'm not the touchy one."

"Whatever. Can I ask you a personal question?"

I held my breath. I knew it was coming. "What?"

"You and Badman haven't done it?"

"No," I said looking at the floor.

"Why?"

"Shoot! Lisa I don't know. I'm not ready. I mean, I'm not saying I'm going to save myself for marriage or whatever, I just know I'm not ready. I'm just scared. I mean, what if it hurts?"

"It won't hurt," Crystal said quietly. Lisa and I both looked at her.

"What did you say, Chris?" I asked.

"You don't even think about it. You just know that you want to be with him because you love him and he...he loves you."

Lisa hit Crystal in the head with a pillow. "Crystal Denise Ashton you've been holding back on us! Sitting over here acting like you're some L7 square and you have already done it!"

Crystal didn't' respond and Lisa and I looked at each other puzzled.

"Chris, what's wrong?" I asked sliding next to her on the floor. Instantly, tears were in her eyes. She looked at me and then at Lisa and started to cry hard sobs. I went to her and hugged her. "What is it?"

"I think I'm pregnant."

"What?" Lisa and I both said at the same time. Crystal started crying even harder and then ran out of the room into the bathroom.

Lisa and I looked at each other all of five seconds and then ran to the bathroom and found the door locked. Lisa pulled a hairpin out of her hair, expertly picked the lock, and opened the door. Crystal was sitting on the edge of the bathtub crying her eyes out. I went in and pulled her back toward Lisa's room and we closed the door behind us. For a good five minutes, Crystal cried as a thousand questions entered my mind but I dared not to ask. But Lisa, on the other hand, went on like she was Perry Mason or somebody.

"Where did you guys do it?"

"At some stup...id motel," Crystal got out between sobs.

"When?" Lisa asked.

"Over two months ago. "

"And you haven't had your period."

Crystal shook her head.

"You told Joe?"

Cyrstal nodded yes with tears steaming down her face.

"What did he say?" Lisa probed.

"That it wasn't his and that he didn't want to see me anymore."

"Damn," I said aloud without realizing it. Tears sprang in my own eyes for Crystal. I reached for her and squeezed her tight and cried tears on top of her tears. I couldn't believe this. I held Crystal a little longer as we both cried and then let her go as I realized that Lisa was going on a rampage in Filipino. Her little head was swinging back and forth as she paced the room and I knew that whatever she was saying wasn't nice. If looks could kill and if Joe was in this room he would be six feet under some concrete!

I stood up and grabbed Lisa by the arm and told her to be still and to be quiet. We didn't want her foster mother to come in here. She looked at me strangely and then hit the floor in front of Crystal.

"What school does that no good dog go to? Let me know so I can go there and cut his ass up!"

Crystal looked at her strangely. "Joe's out of school. He's nineteen."

"What?" Lisa and I again said at the same time.

"Look, you guys, I know it's bad okay? I'm stupid. It's just that nobody's ever loved me. You guys know where I come from. Nobody's ever wanted me. You two got out but not me. Joe came along and said everything I wanted to hear all of my life! And I fell for it. Stupid me. And now I'm going to pay for it and I don't know what to do. I can't stay on my own and take care of a baby. And how is it going to look for Mrs. Haywood with the authorities if I'm sitting around there big, fat, and pregnant. What if she loses her license? I can't let that happen."

"Oh, Crystal," Lisa said, taking her in arms and rocking her. Just then her phone rang and I went over to pick it up.

"Hello."

"Hey, can I speak to Lis."

"Timothy?"

"Tell him I'll call him later," Lisa said over her shoulder.

Timothy heard, said okay and I hung up the phone. Lisa went to the bathroom, got some more tissue for Crystal and handed it to her. She then went to her mattress, pulled out the pills, and went back into the bathroom. She came back with the empty container. Crystal and I both looked at her.

"I'm not ready for this," she said throwing the container in the trashcan.

NICOLE

II

It turns out Crystal wasn't pregnant but she was never the same. And I can't lie, neither was I. I was so upset about the whole ordeal that I refused to see A.M. for three days. Ms. Emily, who was never one to miss a beat, finally had to pry it out of me. I told her everything; everything about Crystal and Joe and about me and A.M. About how I wanted to be with him and how I believed he loved me just as Crystal had believed Joe.

"Child, you can't figure out men, young or old. 'Cause they can't figure out themselves. They always talking about what they want and what they need but love, I think that's something that a lot of them are really scared of. It's that whole macho ego thing of theirs. They have to be so tough. But there's no room for tough in love and they don't get that. Love requires a gentleness and patience cause it ain't always going to be smooth sailing. But, I guarantee, it's the best thing that can ever happen to you."

"Then why does it have to hurt?" I asked.

"Love doesn't hurt. People do."

"Why?"

"Because they don't how to spell love."

"What do you mean spell it?"

"R-E-S-P-E-C-T"

***

I watched the clock slowly make its way to two-thirty. Finally, the bell rang. Everyone rushed out of the classroom and out into the hall. Instantly, my eyes searched for A.M. After my talk with Ms. Emily, I felt much better about him, me and us and soon afterwards I was back on love street thinking about him twenty four hours a day and being with him whenever I could, which was hard because of his schedule. He was having basketball practice Monday through Thursday after school, had games on Friday and then working at his family restaurant on most Saturdays.

We still talk on the phone every night, have three classes together, and have the same lunch period. Plus, on some days, he surprises me and picks me up for school in the mornings. And then, on the Saturdays he works, I hang out at the restaurant with him and watch him burn, as he would say.

I walked toward my locker. I was going to throw this old book bag in there and run out of here. I was grateful that none of my teachers assigned any homework. It was spring break and I couldn't wait to run out of these doors and not come back for a week. Especially since Ms. Emily and I were going with A.M. and his family up to Whidby Island.

I spotted A.M. walking down the hall. He was smiling and walking like he owned the world with his cool self. A couple guys spoke to him as he glided toward me. He stopped, said something that made them laugh and then he moved on. I smiled inside out as he eyes met mine. He moved his eyebrows up and down playfully as he headed toward me. Then, out of nowhere, a hand grabbed him and pulled him into a corridor. I made my way down the hall just in time to see Traci Smith all in his face with her hands all over his body. A.M. was smiling down at her as his hands were pushing her away but it was obvious that Traci didn't want to be pushed away.

"Now Traci, what's your boyfriend going to think if he sees you all over me like this," I heard A.M. say.

"That I don't want a boy, that I want a real man. You know what I'm saying. Just like you want a real woman. Everybody knows Miss Goody Two Shoes Nicole is not taking care of you like she should. And I think that's just a shame."

"And I think you need to get out of my face Traci," A.M. said pushing her aside and then stepping past her. His eyes met mine and I saw an anger I had never seen before.

"Let's go," he said to me grabbing my hand.

"Oh, hell no! Hold up, man. Don't think I didn't see what just went down." Glen Hall said before we could walk away. A.M. let go of my hand and turned around. Glen was a senior who some said had flunked at least twice which made him more close to twenty than anything else. He lived two streets over from me, was mean and ugly as all get out, and nobody in their right mind understood what Traci saw in him.

"Look, I don't know what you think you saw, but believe me it wasn't real," A.M. said calmly.

"I said, ain't nobody going nowhere until Traci tells me what the hell she was doing putting her hands all over your punk ass."

"Glen, baby, that ain't what happened. He was trying to rap to me," Traci said walking over to Glen and putting her hands on his chest. "But I told him I was your woman."

Glen pushed her so hard her face hit the lockers and blood was instantly oozing out her nose as she slid down the lockers. I went over to her and held out my hand and helped her up. Kids everywhere were circling around us but at a safe distant away. I looked down the hall. Where the hell was a teacher, the principal, somebody!

"That was messed up and you know it Glen," A.M. said stepping closer to Glen who stood at least an inch shorter but thirty pounds heavier. But something inside told me that A.M. didn't even notice and if he did he certainly didn't care. I was coming unglued. I have never seen A.M. this way. In junior high, I heard all the rumors about how mean he was but I never seen this side of him that I was seeing now.

"A.M. can we go, please?" I reached for his arm. He looked down at me and I hoped he saw the fear in my eyes, cause I was indeed scared and ready to get out of here.

"Go on and mind your business before I have to take that little fine bitch off your hands," Glen said and began to laugh but was cut off by the swing of A.M.'s right hook. Over and over A.M. hit him until he was no longer standing. I was too shocked to move.

Kids were circling around us closer and closer, yelling and screaming for blood. Glen somehow got back on his feet and was swinging like crazy at A.M. Next, someone passed him a knife and I screamed in horror as my heart raced inside my chest. A.M. kicked the knife out of his hand and kicked him in the mouth at the same time knocking him down again. Finally, I saw a group of teachers come inside the crowd and pull everyone away. It took three teachers to hold Glen down who was cursing everybody.

A.M. stood there breathing heavily, his knuckles bleeding, his shirt torn. His eyes slowly found mine in the crowd, and I can't lie, every part of me, hurt for him. He continued to breathe heavily as one of the teachers took him toward the office. Just before they turned the corner he looked back at me and I ran to his side.

Ms. Emily and I got up early, finished packing and were at A.M.'s house by seven in the morning. I knocked softly on the door. April opened the door and instantly we noticed the hustle and bustle of everyone moving about the house. A.M. came downstairs, kissed me and greeted Ms. Emily before going off into the kitchen where he returned with a big box of food and headed out to the Winebago.

"Hey there, ya'll ready?" Mr. Washington asked coming from the kitchen.

"Ready as rain," Ms. Emily answered.

"Hey, Ms. Nicki," he said to me and kissed my forehead.

"Hey, Mr. Washington."

"Is that Nicole and Emily," A.M.'s mother's voiced rang from somewhere in the house.

"Yeah, and they're ready Ann, so come on. You're holding up the party."

"What you talking about old man. I am ready to go," A.M.'s mother said coming into the living room wearing jeans and a Washington Huskies sweat-shirt.

"Nice shirt," I said

"Catchy name don't you think," she said, smiling and then hugging me and turning to Ms. Emily.

"Say, Em, you ready to go out there and catch us a whale?"

"Shoot, at my age that's the only thing I can catch," Ms. Emily said.

"Girl, if you're still breathing, there's still hope."

"Watch what you say now," Ms. Emily said laughing.

"Well, I know one thing, that Ms. Nicki ain't the best fishing partner. On the last trip, she had us putting on the bait, taking off the fish. She didn't want to touch nothing. Just got too much city in her," Mrs. Washington said.

"Girl, you should have seen her when I took her to see my sister Nora in the mountains. The girl saw real chickens and liked to have had a cow. Now, I ask you, how citified is that," Emily said.

"I think I'm going to see if A.M. needs any help outside," I said to no one in particular and headed out the front door in search of my man.

I reached the Winnebago and didn't see him outside so I stepped inside. The minute I did, he came out of nowhere and pulled me inside his arms. I watched as he licked his lips and then lowered his head to kiss me, and everything inside of me melted. I returned his kiss breathlessly as he held me closer. My arms came up around his neck and I wished that I could hold onto him forever. Like a butterfly he kissed me over and over and I can't lie he felt so good that I never wanted him to stop.

I opened my eyes and found him staring down into mine and for seconds I felt spellbound. A.M. knew how to get to me. He knew how to push every single button to make me weak. And I hated and loved him for it.

"I missed you," he said looking into my eyes with my look.

"You just saw me yesterday," I said smiling into his eyes.

"I know but everything about yesterday was so crazy."

I nodded my head. "I'm so glad you didn't get suspended. Everything is okay now."

"Is it Nic? I mean I find myself wanting to be you with more and more and I just can't get close enough. Sometimes I feel like the whole universe is against us."

"Well, I got news for you, Anthony Marcus. The whole universe can't keep me away from you," I said kissing him.

"Alright, you two. Here comes the family," Ashley said entering the door. I slowly slipped out his arms but not before I read his lips as they said I love you.

The drive to Whidby Island was short and sweet. A.M. drove his Impala with me in the front and April and Ashley in the back, while his dad drove the Cutlass with his mom, Ms. Emily and Angela. Anita, Ricky and little Ricky were supposed to meet us up there.

A.M. had just recently put in a cassette player in the Impala and since all the old people were in the Cutlass, we jammed to Prince, Rick James, Parliament and EWF all the way. The sun was shining brightly and we rode with windows partly down taking in the cool April breeze. I took off my shoes and socks and propped my feet out the corner of the window so they could breathe, leaned back into the seat with my shades on and sang off key with EWF.

Shortly after we left, April got hungry and started making sandwiches and had my stomach growling. We pulled into a gas station. A.M. went to get the gas and I helped April make sandwiches for everyone while Ashley ran to the bathroom.

I looked into the other car. Ms. Emily and Mrs. Washington were laughing hard about something while A.M.'s dad pump the gas and Angela slept. Soon, we were off on the road again. I ate a sandwich, fed A.M. while he drove and then soon found myself dozing off.

When I awoke to the sound of a loud horn, I sat up and looked around and saw nothing but cars.

"Where are we?" I asked A.M. sitting up, yawning, and wiping my eyes.

"We have to take the ferry to the Island."

I looked up at the beautiful blue sky at the seagulls flying over my head. April and Ashley were already out of the car and A.M waited on me to put on my shoes.

We headed out toward the front of the ferry. Tree-lined mountains were everywhere surrounding the water with little houses nestled up on them. It seemed so peaceful here despite the noisy boat. I looked up the to the upper deck and Ms. Emily and Angela waved down to us both holding a can of soda.

"What are they doing up there?" I asked.

"Knowing them two, they're trying to catch," A.M. said laughing. I pushed him on the shoulder.

"Alright now," I said turning back around at the sound of the boat's horn. We stood there and watched as the boat came into the wooden docks, hitting both sides until it was steady. Then a long plank came out and we headed back to the car so that we could drive off the boat.

In less than fifteen minutes, we were driving down to a small, secluded beach area. There was a long pier, that A.M. explained to me, is where we would do most of the fishing. We followed his dad up a few miles more and he stopped and unhitched the trailer. Soon, the whole family got out and got the trailer ready and running with electricity and water like they did before when we went to Pacific Shores, while Ms. Emily and I put away the food.

A.M. soon came inside to see if we needed any help.

"No, Mr. A.M. I'm about ready to put my fishing pole in that water out there and catch me a bucket of fish," Ms. Emily told him and stepped out in search of his parents. We followed, but in search of Ashley, April and Angela. I wasn't in the mood for no fishing and hopefully they weren't either.

"Hey, Junior are you ready to take Nicki hiking?" April asked when we found his sisters.

"Hiking?" I asked."

"Yeah, they got two trails," Angela informed me. "One up and one down. We hit the up one in the daylight and the down one at night."

"Is that right," I said looking around, thinking maybe I should go fishing with the old folks.

"Come on Nicki, you'll be all right," Ashley said. "Little brother won't let anything happen to you."

"Okay," I said looking around the mountainside, remembering our trip to the waterfalls three years ago. How bad could it be?

A.M. grabbed some canteens of water and his camera and we headed up. And up and up and up with Angela and Ashley leading the way. It seemed like hours would pass before we would stop and take a one-second break. I would barely have enough time to drink a swallow of water before they were saying it was time to be off again.

I fell in step behind April and tried to keep up as best as I could but it seemed the harder I tried the more they kept ahead of me.

"Say you guys, slow down. My legs are shorter than yours, I can't climb as fast," I yelled over my head.

"Let me go past you and I will help pull you up," A.M. said going by me with ease. I stayed in my position and rested as he went by. I took a deep breath and for some unknown reason looked down and behind me and saw nothing but rocks and the ocean below us.

"Whoa!" I yelled.

"What is it Nic?" A.M. asked looking down at me.

"How in the world did we get way up here?"

A.M. rolled in laughter as I tried to reach for the next tree branch in front of me but couldn't get to it. The only thing I could reach was an ugly looking weed sticking out of the mountainside.

"Baby, get that branch," A.M. said.

"I can't get the branch my arms are too short!" I yelled under my breath.

"Well put your leg over here on this rock so you can come up."

I moved my right leg but couldn't reach the rock either just like I knew I wouldn't. Why did I let them talk me into this? "I thought you were going to pull me up."

"I can't from here, you're going to have to come up a little higher so I can reach you."

"Anthony Marcus Washington, Jr., you get back down here and get me or I am never talking to you again!" I screamed.

"Baby, I can't. There's only one way down and that's on the other side. You have to come up," he said smiling at me. I knew he was lying. I knew it, knew it, knew it! So help me when I get a hold of him he's going to wish...

"What's all the ruckus?" Angela asked. I looked up and she was standing above A.M.

"He won't help me!" I yelled.

"Nicki, climb up," Angela said.

"I can't. Why can't you two understand that," I said looking at them as I held onto the earth, with my fingers wrapped around a weed. My legs were aching and I was extremely thirsty and these two wanted to play twenty questions.

"Where are April and Ashley?"

"They are already gone over," Angela said. "Come on Nicki, you can make it."

I looked down and back up. I was so mad and scared I didn't know what to do. This nature mess was for the birds. From now on I'm staying in the confines of the city limits. Never, never, never again. I don't care what Ms. Emily or A.M. says. It's to the Center and back. Give me a roller coaster any day.

I looked up just as A.M. pulled out his camera. My mouth dropped opened and he snapped the button.

"You know you're dead now," I said trying to pull myself up again, but went nowhere.

"Give me your hand," he said stretching his hand out in front of me. I wanted to grab it and pull him over if I didn't think I would go over with him. I reached for his wrist and in one big thrust he pulled me up and over. I sat still for a long time and was happy to see flat land in front of me. I took a long swallow of water, wiped my mouth and just sat and sat.

"You alright?" A.M. asked kneeling in front of me smiling.

I looked at him a long moment without saying a word. Then I pounced on him like a tiger knocking him straight over.

It was nightfall and the moon was shining bright in the sky amongst a blanket of stars. Anita, Ricky and Little Ricky arrived about an hour ago. We all ate the fish and fries that Mr. Washington had cooked and now A.M.'s parents, Ms. Emily and Angela were at the card table set up outside the trailer playing bid whist while Ashley and April were inside watching the portable television. I didn't know where A.M. was and I frankly didn't care. That much.

"You want to go to the beach?" Anita asked walking behind me as I leaned against a post looking up at the sky. I turned and saw her, Ricky and A.M.

"We just have to go down the trail about half a mile," Anita said.

"Trail? I don't think so."

"No, Nicki. It's nothing like what those clowns put you through this after-noon. I promise."

"That's okay, it's too dark down there. Besides, my legs hurt."

"We have torches and I will be happy to carry you," A.M. said and then came and swept me in his arms.

"Put me down, Anthony Marcus," I protested but he was already walking with Anita and Ricky following.

True to her word, we were at the beach in less than ten minutes and the trail was nothing but a curved, downward path. A.M. put me down and I ran straight to the shore, taking off my sandals and putting my feet in the cool sand and cold water. It felt so good, that I couldn't help but smile.

I walked in the water for several minutes by myself and I couldn't stop myself from thinking about my parents. We came to the beach every summer. A cool breeze stopped the tear that was easing down my face. I turned back and from a distance A.M. was running to catch up with me. I stood still, wiped my face and waited. I didn't realize how far I had walked.

He caught up with me and we walked in step together.

"You still mad at me?"

"Hell yeah," I said, remembering my anger and increasing my stride.

"Ah, baby come on," he said taking me in his arms. "Let's kiss and make up," he said licking his lips and giving me my look.

"What you did was mean."

"I know. I'm sorry. But I wasn't going to let anything happen to you. You know you're my world."

"Well, I got news for you, you world almost went crumbling down."

"I'm sorry."

"I didn't appreciate what you did."

"I'm sorry."

"I was very scared."

"I'm sorry."

"I mean, I thought I was going to die out there."

"Nicki?"

"What?"

"Shut up and let me kiss you, please."

I placed my arms around his neck and pushed his mouth toward mine. His arms tightened around me just as our lips met. And, like always, I was in a dream state of mind as he kissed me with the tenderness I love to feel. I kissed him back loving the feel of every part of his mouth. He moaned under his breath and as his lips kissed the base of my neck, I swear my knees buckled under me.

I felt his arousal against me and dared myself to look at his face. His eyes were half closed, his lips half parted and I swear I never wanted him as bad as I did now to make love to me. I eased out of his embrace.

"What's wrong," he asked.

"Nothing."

"Nic, don't say nothing when it's something. What is it?"

"I'm scared of being out here alone. With you."

"What, why?"

"Because anything can happen, Morning."

"Not anything that you don't want to happen."

"I'm scared of what I want to happen," I said meeting his eyes.

In one move he pulled me inside his arms and began kissing me wildly, passionately as his hands moved up and down my back and I swear I didn't want him to stop.

He kissed my neck and my ears and then brought his lips back to mine as his hands squeezed me closer to him and I loved every minute, every second and every touch. And then, out of nowhere, Crystal's tear stained face appeared before my eyes. Traci's angry tone was in my ear and I could see Lisa throwing away her pills.

I gently pushed myself out of A.M.'s arms. His light brown eyes looked down into mine and I felt myself crying inside because I wanted to be with him so bad. His fingertips came across my lips. "You're so sweet, I could kiss you all day."

I looked away from A.M. I was trembling all over. I wanted to know what it would it would be like to have him kiss me all day and to make love but I was so scared. A.M. reached for my hand and pulled me back in his arms squeezed me tight and then looked back down at me. I could feel his hardness against me like I had so many times before when we were this close. He kissed me and I felt a tingling in the base of my stomach that traveled downward. I pulled him closer to me and returned each kiss.

His arms were totally wrapped around me and I felt so close to him but yet not close enough. His mouth left mine and once again traveled down my neck and my shoulder and I can't lie I wanted to scream cause it felt so good! My knees got weaker, my body was shaking all over and I didn't know what was happening to me. I just knew that I didn't want it to stop.

A.M. began whispering my name and telling me how beautiful I was and, in a matter of seconds, somehow the two of us were lying in the sand wrapped up in each other's arms kissing over and over again. A.M. held me as I lay atop him. He moved his hands slowly down my body as he continued to kiss my mouth and my neck and my whole body felt weak. He slid his hands under my shirt and gently rubbed my back and he looked at me with a look I have never seen before. "Nic, baby, I'm so in love with you," he whispered.

I couldn't stop myself from shaking, couldn't stop myself from trembling and couldn't stop the tears that I felt forming in my eyes. "I will love you for the rest of my life Morning," I said as a tear slid down my face and unto his.

"You promise," he asked, wiping my tears away.

"Always," I whispered and then touched his mouth with my own. Once again, his arms came around me and up my back. I began moving my body against his again and A.M. started to moan under me and I was surprised to hear myself let out a sound that came from somewhere deep inside me. Our kiss deepened and became more passionate. I wanted to feel his warmth against me and feel his heart racing against mine. I cannot explain the connection I felt with him.

I wanted him and he wanted me. I loved him and he loved me. I didn't question it. I knew it. Knew it like I knew the back of my hand. Knew it way down deep inside of me. Knew that as long as I live I would never feel like this with anyone else. He was the one, my one. I sat up and then pulled A.M. up with me. We sat close, eye-to-eye, hands to hands, heart to heart and soul-to-soul. "Show me A.M.," I whispered never being more serious in my life.

A.M. looked at me for a long moment without saying a word. His eyes never left mine and I could tell he was trying to figure out what I meant and to figure out if I was for real. I leaned my face closer to his and gave him a small kiss. "Show me how to love you for the rest of my life. Show me."

With gentle fingertips, he touched my face and held it in his hands as he kissed me over and over and then let his mouth travel down to the base of my neck and shoulders as his fingers unbuttoned my shirt and then slid it off. I nervously looked into his light brown eyes and then reached for his shirt. I pulled it off of him and let my hands move slowly down his muscular biceps. For moments, we sat quietly as our hands discovered each other in a way they had never before. His hands traced the outline of my collarbone and down to my breasts. I led my fingers across his Adam's apple and down his chest where I discovered a mole on his left side. He covered my hand with his, brought it to his lips, kissed it and then placed it back on his chest. Pulling me in his arms, his mouth found mine and he leaned backward with me falling on him. We rolled over and he lay atop me. His hands came up and pushed my bangs from my eyes.

"Nicki, I love you and I want you so much, but I'm...are you sure baby?" He asked then kissed me such gentleness I thought I had died and gone to heaven. I caressed his back, loving the feel of his warm skin against mine. I didn't want to let him go.

"Junior, where are you? It's getting late and we better head back," Anita's voice rang from a distance.

In an instant, A.M. jumped up and was reaching for both of our shirts. He gave me mine and I quickly put it on and hurriedly buttoned it up as he did the same. I had just buttoned the top button when I heard Anita behind me.

"What are you two up to?"

"Nothing, just checking out the place," A.M. said to his sister who was now standing only a few feet away from him. I checked my shirt once again and stood up and faced Anita and Ricky.

"This place is beautiful," I said to nobody in particular looking out at the ocean and feeling Anita's gaze on me. I was scared to face her. Scared for her to see what I was feeling for her brother.

"We better head back. It's getting late," Anita, said taking Ricky's hand in hers.

"You guys go ahead. We'll catch up," A.M. said.

"Don't be all night Junior."

"We're coming, Nita, alright?" A.M., said more sternly. Anita looked him over and then Ricky pulled her hand and they walked off down the shore. A.M. and I both watched as they walked off and after a moment turned and faced each other. I suddenly felt chilled and rubbed my hands up and down my arms. A.M. came and wrapped his arms around me and gave me a slight kiss.

"That was close."

I looked up into his eyes. "Tell me about it."

A.M. squeezed me and kissed the top of my head. "One day we will come back here alone and make this our special place," he whispered taking my hand in his.

"One day," I whispered back as he led me back up the beach.

"A.M. get up," I whispered.

"What is it?"

"Shh, just get up."

He slowly raised his head and looked at me with one eye opened. "What is it Nic."

"Let's go," I said pulling his arm and making him sit up.

"Where?"

"To see the sunrise."

In what seemed like five minutes, he finally got up and out the trailer. I tossed the keys of the Impala to him and ran to the car. He got in, started the car, and headed down toward the shore with him still trying to wake up.

"Come on, sleepy head, we're going to miss it. Step on it!"

"What is your hurry?"

"I always wanted to see the sunrise on the beach."

A.M. glanced at me, smiled and then shook his head. "What am I going to do with you, girl," he said yawning.

In minutes, he pulled up close to shore and we were there just as the sun began to come up. I grabbed his camera and took a picture just as seagulls were flying into the horizon as A.M. sat in the car with his head laid back. He was sleep again, I bet. I walked and took several more pictures and then turned the camera toward the car and got about two shots of A.M., with his mouth wide-open, snoring for the entire world to hear.

I eased back into the car, but on the driver's side, pushing A.M.'s dead weight over. It took some time but he finally moved over enough for me to get behind the wheel. I started the car and stretched my legs so that I could reach the pedals with my toes. I took the car out of park and started driving the coast, just as A.M. had. It was so exciting. I couldn't help but laugh aloud as I pushed the pedal with my feet until I was going fifty miles per hour. A.M. woke up and looked over at me.

"What the..."

"Look baby, I'm driving," I said smiling and looking over at him.

"Nicki, what are you doing," he said sitting straight up.

"It's okay. Look, I'm going straight and I ain't hit nobody."

"Baby, stop the car."

"A.M. look, I'm going straight. I'm okay, really."

"Okay, baby let's just turn around and go back. The tide is going to come in."

"Fine, alright," I said turning the car sharply to the left.

"Not that way! Turn to the right, the right!" A.M. screamed and made me all nervous, and the next thing I knew we were headed straight for the ocean. I screamed and let go of the steering wheel and sat in horror as the car hit the water.

"Shit, shit, shit!" A.M. screamed.

I looked over at him and then closed my eyes and started saying my prayers 'cause God knows I can't swim a lick.

It was ten o'clock when Ms. Emily and I entered the house tired as all get out. Ms. Emily turned on the light that lit up the small living room and I never been so glad to see this little tiny room in this little tiny house. We both fell on the couch at the same time and let out a deep breath. Spring break was fun, but I was glad tomorrow was Sunday and that I had school on Monday. I was ready to get things back to normal.

12

It rained twenty-six of the thirty days in April. Most say April showers bring May flowers, but here it was the sixth day of May, and there was nothing but more rain. Anthony looked out the window of his bedroom at the gloomy clouds and the rain hitting against the window and smiled. Nothing could make him sad.

He went over to his dresser and pulled out the top drawer where he reached way in the back behind his tee shirts and socks and pulled out a small black velvet box. He leaned against the drawer closing it with his body. He opened the box.

Inside it was his dream.

He looked at the small diamond solitaire nestled in the band of gold. A smile crept across his face. He couldn't wait to give it to her and see her face. And hear her answer to his question. Yes!

He closed the box and put it on the bed next to his coat and then went over to the mirror and checked out his clothes and hair. As he combed and patted his hair, he noticed that his hands were shaking. He wasn't nervous, just excited, anticipating. He pulled on his shirt, did a James Brown turn, laughed and grabbed his coat and the velvet box.

In his car, he placed the velvet box in the glove compartment and started the engine, which took a little time. Poor car hadn't run the same since Nicole decided to take it swimming. It was raining harder now and by the sound of the thunder and lightning it was going to get worse before it got better. He turned his wipers on high but it seemed the rain was getting harder and harder.

He reached Jackson Street and decided to pull over and wait the storm out. He popped the O'Jays, Survival in his cassette player and fast-forwarded to Let Me Make Love To You. He leaned back into his seat closed his eyes thinking about Nicole and how beautiful she was to him.

Twenty minutes later, his eyes sprang open as he realized he must have fallen asleep. He looked out the window, and saw that the rain had stopped. He sat up straight, started the car and pulled back onto the street. Then, just as soon as he got to 23rd he heard a loud popping sound and then his car began to vibrate forcing him to slow down. He cursed under his breath and stepped out the car. He had a blow out. He went back to the car grabbed his keys and went to the trunk. It made no sense to sit here and complain just needed to go ahead and fix it. He had told Nicole he would be over her house around eight and it was already ten 'til.

"Pass me the salt, Ms. Nicki," Emily said to Nicole who sat across from her at the small dinner table but seemed to be in another world. She was thinking about what A.M. had up his sleeve. All day at school, he kept acting mysterious and said that he wanted to go somewhere special tonight. She didn't have a clue to what he was up to and couldn't wait to find out.

"Nicole Williams, what's gotten into you? Will you pass me that salt, girl," Emily said more fiercely. Nicole looked at her as if she was strange and then passed Emily the salt.

"That Mr. A.M. really has you going don't he? Your head is all up in the sky. Come back down here to earth and finish your dinner. This fried chicken is delicious," Emily said, placing a spoonful of mashed potatoes in her mouth.

Nicole smiled at her across the table biting into her chicken. "You think I will ever learn how to cook like you, Ms. Emily."

Emily laughed, "If you ever stay in a kitchen long enough," she said taking a bite of her own chicken.

Suddenly Emily's eyes began to bulge out and her face began to turn gray. She tried to get up, but she was too close to the table.

"Ms. Emily!" Nicole screamed, fear suddenly taking a hold of her. She got up and went to the other side of the table and tried to pull her from the chair, but her heavy weight was too much for her small body to grab a hold.

Emily suddenly went limp and her face fell and hit the table. Nicole screamed.

"Ms. Emily! Ms. Emily!" She cried out as tears suddenly formed in her eyes and streamed down her face. She pushed the woman forcefully but she didn't move. She had to get help. She ran to the phone and picked it up and got nothing but silence. The storm knocked the power lines down again. She ran to the front door opened it, but before she could step out a tall figure was standing in front of her.

She looked up and into Glen Hall's eyes. His face was of stone as he stared down at her. "I heard screaming. What's the matter," he asked after a moment.

Nicole turned back around and went over to Emily's unmoving body.

"I don't know. One minute we were talking and then the next..." she stop unable to finish as tears continued to run down her face. Through a haze she saw Glen move toward Emily. He lifted her head and felt under her neck and then placed his head down to her heart.

"I don't hear anything. I think she's dead," Glen said turning to Nicole.

Nicole felt the floor come up from under her as she slid down against the wall her body shaking in pain. This couldn't be happening. Not again! Not ever again. She closed her eyes tightly not wanting to see the nightmare she was in.

"Did you call 9II?" Glen asked and Nicole only shook her head. Glen looked for the phone and saw it was off the hook on the floor. He went to it, listened to the dead silence and then placed it back on the hook.

He looked back at Nicole who was crumbled on the floor crying softly with her arms wrapped around her shaking body. He went to her and slowly picked her trembling body off the floor and pulled her into his arms.

He let out a deep breath as he held her. Held her like he always wanted to hold her. It didn't matter to him that she was crying or that there was a dead body lying only a few feet from them. He was holding her.

Anthony slowly pulled up to the curb and parked in front of the small house on 29th Street. As he turned off the lights he looked up and saw the front door was opened. He smiled as he remembered that Nicole likes the smell of the rain. He turned off the motor glanced over at his glove compartment and then glanced in the rearview mirror and saw somebody running trying to get out of the rain. He quickly got out the car, ran down the walkway and jumped on the front porch. He tapped lightly on the screen door and then walked in the dimly lit house and his heart stopped beating.

Emily was at the table her grayish face turned toward him, her blank eyes staring across the room. Anthony tried to speak, to call out for Nicole but his voice was trapped inside him. Suddenly the room lit up when a flash of lighting bolted across the sky causing him to jump. And that's when he saw her.

Curled up in the corner between the couch and the end table silently crying and shaking from head to toe. He quickly walked over to her, knowing she was probably scared to death and stopped dead in tracks when he saw her face. It was beaten bruised and blooded. Her lips and nose swollen and her right eye was almost closed.

"Nicki, baby, oh God, baby!" Anthony yelled as he knelt in front of her. He reached out to touch her face but she quickly moved away and then he noticed her clothes. Torn were her shirt, her bra, and skirt. Then he saw the blood oozing down her leg.

"Nicki!" He screamed in horror and then pulled her in his arms as tears started streaming down his face. "Who did this to you? Baby, who did this!"

Nicole looked straight ahead as Anthony held her. She felt his body tremble with loud cries that matched her own and the weight of his pain was too much for her to bear and she slipped away.

Anthony felt her body go limp and pulled away and saw her eyes were now closed. "Baby wake up. Please Nicki, please! I love you, I love you!" Anthony cried harder but Nicole just lay still in his arms.

Somehow he pulled them both off the floor and carried her over to the couch and laid her down as gently as he could. He ran to her bedroom and pulled the bedspread off the bed and came back and wrapped her in it and then lifted her in his arms as he continued to cry and curse everything around him. As he reached the door for the briefest second she opened her eyes and looked at him as a tear slowly rolled down her cheek. He didn't know then that he would never forget the look of pain in her eyes.

In a matter of minutes he made it to his house, rushed in and cried for help from his family. His mother and sisters came running when they heard him and shocked filled their faces as they looked at the bruised and beaten body that he carried barely recognizing it to be Nicole. Only his mother was able to speak. "Oh, my God, what happened?"

"She was...somebody..." Anthony cried out but stopped unable to explain the unexplainable as tears again began to stream down his face and seemed to pour from his very soul.

"Call 911!" Ann shouted.

"No!"

"Anthony Marcus call 911!"

"Mom, Ms. Emily is dead."

Ann looked at her son strangely not understanding what he was saying. "What happened?"

"I don't know. She was lying dead in the kitchen and Nicole was... if we call the police they're going to take her away. She has nowhere else to go. Please don't call the police. Please. Promise me."

Ann looked into her son's tearful eyes and nodded her head as her heart felt heavier for the fear and pain in his own eyes.

She instructed him to place Nicole on the sofa and then instructed her two youngest daughters to get towels a basin of water and blankets. She knelt in front of Nicole who at that moment tried to open her eyes.

"It's okay, Nicole I'm here. It's okay. Can you tell me what happened," she asked as she began to open the bedspread to look at the extent of Nicole's injury. Her heart sank as she saw her torn clothing and her bruised body. She glanced over at her son who stood only inches away and then back down at Nicole just as April and Ashley appeared with the towels and fresh water. She took a towel and gently stroked her face.

"Sweetheart, were you raped?" Ann asked as she wiped blood from around her lips. Nicole painfully looked into her eyes and slowly nodded her head. Behind her Anthony cursed and fell to his knees. She went to her son and shook him hard until he looked at her.

"Anthony Marcus, Nicole needs help. Go get Dr. Webster. Tell him we have an emergency. Hurry!"

He looked at his mother and then at Nicole and then quickly headed for the door.

"April, call your father. Tell him to come home. Ashley, come help me," Ann said and then turned back to Nicole. "Sweetheart we're going to help you okay?"

"Ms. Emily..." Nicole whispered.

"It's okay. I know. But we got to take care of you right now okay? Nicole you're bleeding and I'm going to have to take these clothes off of you so I can see where it's coming from, okay?"

"It hurts."

"I know, sweetheart. I know," Ann, said barely able to keep the tears from her own eyes as she looked down at the poor helpless child who was like another daughter to her.

"Ashley, I'm going to lift her up. I need you to get her shirt off first," Ann said looking at her youngest daughter and then with gentle hands she lifted Nicole up and piece by piece they removed all her of her clothing. Ann looked down at her right leg and noticed the blood. She took a towel and applied pressure to her thigh and was relieved to see the bleeding subside. It wasn't a deep cut. Then she saw one on her hip and then another at her waist. Her hand came up and covered her mouth. Dear God who would do such a thing?

She covered Nicole's body with a blanket and then placed a warm towel to her swollen eyelid. "Nicole, who did this to you?" Ann asked looking down at Nicole. "Do you know?"

Nicole closed her eyes and then slowly opened them back up and seemed to force herself to speak his name. "Glen."

"Glen. Glen Hall!" Anthony's voice came from behind them as he stood in the doorway with Dr. Webster from two doors down.

Nicole glanced up into his eyes and then closed her eyes and turned her face into the sofa and her body began to tremble as she cried. Anthony stormed out the door. His mother ran to the door just in time to see him speed off.

She turned back around and watched as Dr. Webster moved toward the sofa and opened his bag. She went to Ashley and held her shaking hands inside her own.

"Ash...who is this Glen Hall?"

"He's a boy from school. The one Junior had the fight with right before spring break."

Ann shook her head and pulled her daughter into her embrace closed her eyes and prayed knowing this nightmare was far from over.

Like a madman, he drove the streets of the Central District. Up Jackson Street across Empire Way down to 23rd and then down to 29th. He came toward her house and slowly slowed down and then stopped. Through tear filled eyes he looked up at the front of the house, at the porch where he had so many times saw her sitting talking to Emily. Where he had so many times saw her looking out the front window or sitting on the steps waiting for him to pick her up. Where they had laughed, discovered and shared secrets, dreams, and promises and stolen kisses way past curfew, under the light of the moon and a blanket of stars. His tears fell harder as rage filled his soul.

He drove down and over to 27th Ave, went to the third house on the left got out and knocked on the door of the dark house. Five times he pounded but nobody came. He looked around the street. It was so dark and quiet. It was if everybody had been swept away with the storm. Anthony ran around to the back of the house and looked inside the windows. Nothing. Nobody. He went back to his car got in and sped off just as more rain began to fall.

Block after block, he drove his eyes straining to see through the blinding rain and his blinding tears. He came to Swan's Pool Hall and stopped the car. He could barely hear the blues music coming out the door as a man drunkenly came out and stumbled to his own car. Anthony took a breath, cut the motor and went inside.

He looked around quickly, his eyes not seeing who he was looking for and was about to leave when somebody called his name.

"I said, what brings you here Mr. Washington?"

Anthony turned to face Robert Swan, owner and founder of the fine establishment that he was standing in, the king of First Ave, the stroll where his 'women' worked. 'The Man' that all the action in the CD had to come through, be it small time numbers, big time gambling or the drug of the month and prostitution.

"I was just looking for someone, Swan."

"Who might that be?"

"He's not here, so it don't matter," Anthony replied looking over the faces again.

"Well, from the look of things, it's a good thing he not. What's up, young blood, you look like you just lost your best friend," Swan said as he moved closer to Anthony and put a hand over his shoulder. "Maybe I can help you out."

Anthony stepped away from him. "That's okay Swan, I'm cool."

"And that's what I'm talking about Washington. I know you're down, brother. That's why I'm trying to rap to you. See, I need a little more assistance at the high school, you know where I'm coming from? What you play, varsity football and basketball? So I know you're pretty well known for a young blood. And I hear you got it going on with the ladies too. And that's what I need. You know someone who knows how to communicate with the people and someone that the people like. I mean, you know, Glen tries, but he ain't the friendliest bastard on earth you know what I mean?"

Anthony saw red at the mention of his name and had to calm himself down so he could speak. "Is he here?"

Swan looked Anthony over and didn't miss his reaction to his high school playmate's name. "Maybe he is and maybe he isn't."

"Don't bullshit me, Swan," Anthony said stepping closer to him. Swan laughed. The kid had balls. Big ones if he thought he could step to him like he just did. He peered down into Anthony's eyes.

"How bad you want to know, young blood?"

Anthony glared back at Swan. He knew what he was asking and any other time he wouldn't have gave Swan the time of day, much less step foot in this place or hold a piece of a conversation with the man. But he wasn't thinking about Swan. He was thinking of Nicole. She was at his house fighting for her life, lying on his couch stripped of her innocence, her dignity.

"Take me to him," Anthony said never taking his eyes off of Swan.

Ann went to the door at the sound of a car pulling up. Her husband ran up the walkway and into her arms and she practically collapsed.

"Baby, is she okay? How is she?" He asked going into the living room still holding her and looking over Dr. Webster's shoulder and the bruised up Nicole who once again had her eyes closed. He winced at the sight of her. "Great God, have mercy," he mumbled under his breath.

Dr. Webster stood up and looked at them both. "Damn fool cut her everywhere but at least they were superficial wounds and the bleeding has stopped. I didn't examine her internally. She's in too much pain. She needs to go to the hospital. There she could..."

"No," Ann cut him off and then turned to her husband. "Anthony, Emily is dead. If Nicole goes to the hospital, she's going to become a ward of the state and there's no telling where she will end up."

"Ann, the state's going to find out about Emily. So we might as well take her to the hospital where she can get help," Anthony said.

"No. I promised Anthony Marcus. He's scared," Ann said frantically.

"Where's Junior?" he asked looking around the house.

"I don't know. He knows who did this and I think he's gone after him."

"Oh God, no."

"You got to find him."

"I will. I promise I will."

Anthony Sr. drove his blue Cutlass as fast as he could up and down the wet streets by Nicole's house looking for his son's brown '68 Impala. He drove by the parks, the high school and down by the lake where he knew kids hung out but also knew no one would be out on a night like this. The rain was driving down against his windshield and didn't look like it would ever let up.

Finally, parked in front of a pool hall, he saw the car. He jumped out and ran inside the smoked filled parlor. His eyes quickly scanned the place and he didn't see his only son anywhere. This didn't make since. Junior wouldn't leave his car anywhere. He was about to turn around and go look down the street when he noticed a man come through a back door. He ran to the door and took a look outside through the driving rain. He heard the sounds of fist hitting flesh and the groans of pain. His heart almost leaped out of his body. He strained his eyes to follow the sounds his ears heard. In an alley, about a half block away, he saw somebody leaning over a body pounding his fist into it over and over again.

"Dear God, please don't let that be Junior. Don't let that be Junior."

He began to run up the alley just as his son stopped hitting Glen and began to stand up. Glen suddenly stood up and jumped him and down they both went again and then the sound of thunder ripped through the air. Only it wasn't thunder.

Anthony Sr. watched in slow motion as Glen's body crumbled in front of his son's feet. He quickly ran over and grabbed Junior by the back of his shirt and pulled him up. Tears were streaming down his son's eyes as he labored to breathe.

"Junior," was all he was able to say as he looked at him. His son looked into his eyes and then cried in his father's arms. "It's okay son."

Anthony Sr. walked his son down the dark alley and neither one of them ever looked back. Neither one of them noticed as the tall man standing in the shadows behind the trash dumpsters bent down and picked up the still smoking 38 caliber pistol, put it in his pocket and then go back inside the pool hall.

"Here, Junior take this," Anthony Sr. said handing him a small envelope. He glanced down at his father's hands and his own shook as he reached for the envelope.

"Here are your tickets. They are in the name of Carole and Steve Miller. Now listen to me. When you get to L.A., your grandmother Devon is going to be at the airport waiting on you. She's going to take Nicole to the hospital as soon as you land. Don't talk to anyone on the plane. If anybody asks what happened to her, just say you were in a car accident. If Nicole's wounds start bleeding, you're going to have the change the bandages. But, if she loses consciousness, you're going to have to get help. The flight is just a couple of hours so hopefully everything will be okay. Junior, son... I'll call you as soon as things die down here. But you might have to stay awhile. I don't know."

Anthony looked into his father's eyes and felt the weight of the world. He wished he could find the words to tell his father how sorry he was, how he wished he could turn back the hands of time. More than anything he wished he could climb in the Winnebago, head out to the shores, and go fishing or just hang out in the garage and clunk around on the Impala. Go do anything that could take him away from where he was now. Standing in the middle of Sea-Tac Airport saying goodbye to his family, his life.

"Dad, I wish..."

"Junior, save your wishes for the future, not the past. Remember that I'm proud of you and that I love you. And nothing will ever change that. Nothing."

Nicole stepped out of the bathroom with Mrs. Washington, Ashley and April. She wore one of Ashley's sweat suits and Anthony Marcus' baseball cap. She moved slowly through the airport with her head low to avoid the stares and the shame and pain she felt. Ahead, she saw Anthony Marcus embrace his father and she couldn't stop the tears from flowing from her eyes. Mrs. Washington squeezed her shoulders and pulled her in her arms.

"Nicole. You two are going to be okay. Don't worry. Don't look back. And remember we love you," she whispered.

"Mrs. Washington, I'm sorry."

"Sweet child. You have nothing to be sorry for. None of this is your fault. None of it! Now look at me. You take care of yourself. In time you will heal. You may not forget but you will heal, okay?"

"I don't want to go."

"Devon is going to take good care of you. She's the best. And you will have A.M. right by your side."

"They called their row. It's time for them to go," Anthony Sr. said to his wife. She let Nicole out of her arms. Her baby, her only son came to her and embraced her tightly.

"Take care, son," she said pulling away and looking up into his wet eyes with her own. "We love you."

Anthony Sr. came and stood beside her and took her hand inside hers. Ashley grabbed his other one and April hers. Each hand represented strength as each held the other up and said goodbye to their son, their brother, their daughter, their sister.

PART TWO:

That's The Way of the World

MARCUS

13

Damn, I was hungry. I looked at my watch. It was after eleven, so even the fast food places weren't serving breakfast now. I should have had breakfast at Jackie's this morning but there was no time. I had overslept and Jackie didn't even wake up. Hell, she was dead to the world this morning. Didn't budge an inch. She's been tripping lately. Sleeping like crazy and cranky as hell. I hope she wasn't using. No way. I didn't want to even think about that.

And I know she's not pregnant, well at least she shouldn't be. But something's wrong with her cause she sure as hell hasn't been taking care of things like she used to. All I know is she better straighten her shit up. I was cool with her as long as she was an asset, but lately she's been nothing but a liability. And one thing about me, I don't have any debts. Might have to drop her with the quickness.

I needed to get to the bank, but hell, I was hungry. I looked around and saw a Fatburger's up the block. Sure didn't want my day to start off with some greasy burger and fries but that was the only thing around. Hell, seems like there's a Fatburger's on every corner in Los Angeles.

I pulled my car in the drive-thru three cars deep. I glanced at my watch again, eleven o' seven. I picked up my cell phone and dialed Michael's. He answered on the third ring just as I was finally moving up.

"Talk to me."

"Say, Mike, it's me."

"Hey, cuz. It's been a minute."

"Yeah man, I know. Been busy lately."

"Well, I ain't mad as long as you been out there making money."

"That's all I do cuz, you know that."

"Well, since it's like that you need to be helping a starving artist like myself out. Being that we're family and all."

"Negro, you're living in the hills and sporting a Porche. Last time I saw you, you'd put on fifteen pounds so don't even play me."

"Ah, cuz, you know I'm packing mine. And hell, it grew over the summer."

I laughed in the phone. "Fool, you're crazy."

"Say, I learn from the best," Mike laughed back.

"And you know it. Listen, I heard on the radio that you were performing at Iguana's," I said, letting the top down on my ride.

"Sure am. You know I'm hyped."

"Yeah, I know. That's why I'm going to come down tonight and keep your ass on your toes. You know, make sure you taking care of business and not misusing the family name."

"Oh hell, I know I got to be on my p's and q's if the infamous Anthony Marcus Washington, Jr. is coming to the house. Cause if I don't, then you'll end up with all the ladies."

"Well, as my man Barry would say, sho you right."

"All right then. You want me to get a table for you and a couple of your 'friends.'"

"You can get the table, but I'm flying solo tonight."

"Not a problem. Nicki said she was coming too. You want to sit with her or would she cramp your style."

"Sitting with Nicki will only enhance my charm. You know how the ladies pay more attention when you with someone else."

"I hear you."

"How is she doing anyway? I haven't seen or heard from her in a couple of weeks."

"Hey, you're the one out there making all the money. Nicki's been around and doing okay far as I know."

"Good. Say you want to go shoot some hoops before tonight?"

"Nada. I got to go see my broker."

"Your broker, huh? You got a hot tip?"

"Yeah Latex. Cause I know your ass won't be going home alone tonight."

"Bye, Negro." I hung up the phone laughing at my crazy ass cousin. We were the same age. Actually, he was about two months behind me, so technically, I have had to school him all his life. Well ever since I've been in LA anyway. And believe me, seventeen years ago he was real wet behind the ears.

See, Mike's a singer waiting to happen. Hell, he's being trying to get discovered since he was a virgin. He could have made it a long time ago if his dad, my crazed uncle, would have stopped confusing him. Michael doesn't want to do anything but sing. That's all he wants. But his dad has had it in his mind that he should follow in his footsteps ever since Mike took his first step.

He's an only child. And Uncle Lewis' only dream is to have his only son wearing an overpriced suit, sitting in a oversized office, overlooking smog ass Los Angeles with the Law Offices of Washington, Washington and Associates on the door. But that's not how Mike rolls. And he finally told Unc this when he hit thirty. I guess it just takes some people longer. Anyway, like I said. Mike's cool. He knows who all 'the people' are and knows where all 'the parties' are. And now that him and his father haven't spoke in almost three years, we are all the family that each other have. Except for my girl Nicki.

The cars in front of me pulled up. I inched up and looked at the clear blue sky with thoughts of Nicole Chantel running through my mind. Nicki likes sky blue days, tall evergreen trees, snow-capped mountains, the smell of rain, ocean breezes, warm sand between her toes and me. I closed my eyes and felt the sun against my face. Damn, I hadn't thought about that in years.

In my lifetime on this earth there are some things I choose to forget and some things I can't forget. I don't remember painful things that I've seen in the past, 'cause in order to make a future, I choose not to. I don't remember the bad things I did yesterday, because in order to live today, I choose not to. But sometimes the smell of the ocean, the sight of a sunrise, or the words of a certain song will send memories through me that, even with time, won't die and go away.

Seventeen years has not erased the history, the chemistry and the arithmetic that Nicki and I shared. I mean we go back, way back. We have mixed and blended been tossed and stirred and when you add it all up we still can't be divided. Hell, I might as well go ahead and lay it out there and just say it like it really was; she was my first and only true love. Stole my heart right from under my damn nose. So why should I forget? That's just the way it is, the way it always will be and the way it will never be again.

But hey, that was then and now is now. And right about now if I let the ladies tell it, I'm just a dog, with a capital D-O-G.

I make no qualms about it. I am what I am. Get with it or get out of my way and hang your PhD's on the wall cause my BAD, is hanging well! And believe me, I'm not exaggerating. I only talk what I know, so don't be mad cause I got it like that. I'm the whole damn package.

I'm six-three and a half, two hundred twenty-five pounds of solid, smooth-dipped caramel colored skin that has never gone out of style. I still have my boyish grin that can't help but expose a pair of deep dimples even though I sometimes wear a full beard that covers my sturdy chin and goes up to what some have called, my bedroom light-brown colored eyes. No doubt, I am what I am.

So, see it's not my fault that the opposite sex has always practically thrown themselves at me. I have never had to ask for the draws. I mean, all I do is just be me and women just drop them. Now mind you, I don't get with just anything. I mean hey, I got standards. I have no kids and have never had any diseases cause I've been putting a coat of armor on my gold since the word go. And even though I have been down with my share of women, I have lived thirty-three years and still have yet to cross the color line. I loves my sisters.

But I like a quality sister. A sister with some class who has her stuff together, her own pot to piss in, and her ducks in a row. She doesn't have to be model-fine and model beautiful. Hell, models are too damn thin and these days are looking more and more scary than beautiful anyway. She just has to look good to me and have things going for her.

You know, have her own place, her own car, a job, and knows who her baby's daddy is. A sister that knows how to take care of herself and gets what she wants on her own. 'Cause I can't stand a sister that always has her hand out every time she sees me go in my pockets.

And yeah, I got pockets. The only thing fatter than Bad is my pockets. I got enough money to give every sister I have ever laid with, a crib, cars, furs, jewelry and some more. I just don't roll like that. Hell, I'm no pimp! Besides that kind of living don't do nothing but advertise and I'm not into people knowing my business. I'm private and low key. I got to keep everything on the low, low.

The only thing most people know is what I want to them to know. I can't let anybody know me like I know me except me. That's how I roll. That's the way I live. I keep everybody at a distance. I'm like M.C. Hammer used to say, 'you can't touch this'.

Now don't get me wrong, I'm not so untouchable that we can't do business. Hell, I couldn't make a living if I was. In my business, talk is all of the game. And a good talker is a good listener. Once I figure out what a person really wants, I got them buying even if they came just to window shop. That's how I am a success. I am Taylor Motors. My exclusive luxury dealership is the place that everyone including Donald Trump, has come to find the best luxury automobiles that their money can buy. My line of cars is Taylor Made to fit their wallets. That's the way I roll. That's my business.

So, I'm a dog, so what. I admit it. I am what I am. Besides, the ladies love it and deep down I believe I'm living the life that I am supposed to live. Shit! Just like Al Green says, love will make you do wrong. And sometimes when you do wrong, you just keep doing wrong. So hey, I figure why not just spread pieces of myself with all women. Hell, they're all lucky I share the best part of me. My BAD!

A car horn blowing from behind got me out of my stupid, egotistical, sad-ass state of mind. I had to laugh at my own damn self. Shit, if I didn't talk about myself, how else will all the lies get started? 'Cause if the truth could be told, I'd sure in the hell wouldn't tell it.

I glanced at my watch again and then looked around the area. It was eleven twenty and the streets were still pretty clear, just a couple cars at the grocery store across the street. Guess anyone that's anybody is at work. Where my ass needed to be.

Five more minutes passed by. Man, these people were slow. I could have gone to that Piggly Wiggly across the street bought my food and cooked it myself. This was crazy. The car in front of me moved on. It was about damn time. I told Ms. Thing in the window my order and then turned on the radio.

"Hey, that's my song," she said.

I looked at her, shook my head and turned it off. She looked at me like I had just stolen her purse or something and closed the little drive-thru window with force. Hell, I didn't care! She couldn't listen to her song now. I was hungry. She needed to go place my order so I can get out of here. I got things to do.

Again, I looked across the street. The lady that I saw a few minutes ago trying to start her car was still there, her car still not starting. I looked at her as she left her two kids in the car and went to use the pay phone. Her daughter in the front seat shrugged her shoulders in annoyance. The boy in the back was car dancing with a Walkman on. I guess that was his song too.

I looked at the woman on the phone again. From where I was sitting, I could tell she was angry and getting nowhere on the phone. Ms. Thing stuck her head out and thrust my food toward me just as the woman slammed down the pay phone, went to her car and let the hood up. I looked at my watch again.

"Say, give me three number two specials," I told my hostess with the most-est. I got that look again.

"Please," I added as nice as possible.

She answered by handing me my food and slamming the window in my face.

Eight more minutes passed as I waited for the rest of my order while munching on my chili cheese fries and pastrami sandwich. I hated to eat in my car. But today was an exception; I was a man on the move.

I looked back at the woman. She was looking under the hood of the car like she really knew what she was doing. She shook the battery cable, pulled her oil stick out, looked at it, put it back in, wiggled another cable, got back in the car, and tried to start it again. Nothing. Her daughter had a sour look on her face, her son kept bobbin' his head. Ms. Thing came to the window just as I about through with half of my sandwich.

"Here you go. That gon be sixteen fity-two," she said jacking up our English dialect, practically throwing the food at me. I reached in my wallet, pulled out a twenty, gave it to her, and drove off. I didn't even feel like waiting for my change. I just hoped the food was edible.

I glanced at the Piggly-Wiggly. The woman's brown hair was the only thing I could see of her as she leaned over her steering wheel with her head down. I eased my car next to her. I don't even think she heard me coming until I spoke.

"Hi."

She looked up at me, her eyes full of despair. I smiled at her as two other pair of brown eyes began to scope my car out. The boy in back let out a long whistle.

"Hush up, Jamal," the woman spoke to him looking at him through her rear view window and then back at me.

"You look like you can use some help."

She looked at me again as if trying to decide if she should give me the time of day. A little round man dressed in a Piggly-Wiggly shirt and blue Dockers stepped out of the store door, looked at us, and then stepped back inside the door where he continued to watch us.

"I don't know what's wrong with it. It just won't start," she finally said in a voice that was almost soft as a child.

"You want me to take a look at it?"

She looked at me as if she could tell if I knew anything about cars just by looking at me. I reached across the seat, grabbed the bag of food, and then opened my door. I went to her side of the car and leaned in the window.

"I don't mind, really."

She looked me over from the head to toe. Okay, I didn't look like Joe Mechanic, having just stepped out of a convertible Mercedes 500 and standing here wearing one of my many designer suits.

I pulled out one of my business cards and handed it to her hoping that would convince her that I might know a thing or two about cars and that I wasn't just some thug cruising the block trying to get my eat on. Okay, that is a little true. I was hungry.

She took the card and read the embossed print of Taylor Motors, with her fingers rubbing across the lettering. She looked into my eyes and after a moment smiled. I handed her the food.

"For you while you wait," I smiled back.

Both son and daughter perked up then. She took the bag, her pretty brown eyes smiling thank you. I took off my jacket, laid it on the passenger side of my car and rolled up the sleeves of my shirt, noticing the time.

I went around the front of the car and stuck my head under the hood. It didn't take me long to find her problem. It was her starter. I heard her open the door and come to my side.

"What's the matter?"

"It's your starter. It needs to be replaced."

She let out a long sigh, her hands on her small hips. I stood up and took a good look at her. She was tall and slender, dressed casually in khaki pants, a blue cotton shirt with a blue sweater tied loosely around her neck. Her hair hung loosely about her face. She had eyes like mine, flawless milk chocolate skin with no makeup. She looked more like a model instead of a mother of two.

The little round man at Piggly-Wiggly stepped outside again.

"Look, I could call a tow truck and have your car towed in."

She looked down at her feet without responding at first. "I don't want you to go out of your way. You've already done enough with the food and all."

"It won't be a problem. I was on my way to work anyway," I lied.

She looked back at me, with her hands up trying to block the sun out her eyes. "How much is this tow truck going to cost?" she asked and I could tell she felt defeated just thinking about it.

"Nothing. All I have to do is call Eddie and he'll come down and get your car and take it in."

She stood there quietly a moment.

"I'm only trying to be nice. I promise. Besides you've been out here so long you're about to give that poor store manager a heart attack."

She actually laughed, a beautiful laugh and then looked back at her kids who were both still busy with their burgers and chili-cheese fries.

"Look, I really appreciate the offer but I can't," she said facing me once again.

"Why?"

"I just can't."

"Why?"

"Look, I don't know you from Adam, okay. You could be a bank robber, or some murderer for all I know. People just don't go around helping people these days."

"And all I could be is just an exceptionally nice person," I gave her my most charming smile, but she wasn't buying as she stood there looking at me with her hands folded across her chest.

"Say, when I saw you from across the street, I could have ignored you, got my food and went on about my business. But I didn't. I'm just trying to help a sister out. Besides, I don't see anyone else coming to your rescue which means that I must be your appointed Black Knight."

"I don't know."

"Please, my mom made me promise years ago to do one good deed a day. And I'm off to a bad start since I practically told home girl off at Fatburger's across the street."

She laughed again, looking into my eyes and I could still tell she was hesitant.

"No strings," I said holding up my right hand like I had ever been a boy scout.

"Okay."

"Good," I said and then leaned into my car and got the cell phone.

"Good afternoon. It's a beautiful day here at Taylor Motors. I'm Gina Steel, how may I direct your call," my over zealous receptionist answered.

"Hi Gina, this is Marcus"

"Good afternoon, Mr. Washington. How are you today?"

"Fine, thank you. Listen can you patch me to Eddie please?" I asked hurriedly to get her off the phone.

"Eddie is at lunch sir, would you like to me to page him?"

"No, of course not. Let me speak to Steve then."

"One moment."

Steve came on the line and I gave him the details, the location, hung up the phone and opened the passenger side of my car.

"Your chariot awaits," I said holding out my arm.

"Where are we going?"

"Destination, Taylor Motors."

She looked at me about to object and I looked at her letting her know I wasn't taking no for an answer. She smiled. "Thank you, Mr. Washington."

"You're welcome, Ms.?"

"Kara. Kara Davis."

"Well Ms. Davis, let's get you and your kids out of this hot sun."

She turned to her kids who already had their car doors opened. The three of them got in and I went over to the driver's side of my car and joined them. I looked over at all three. I never pictured myself driving a car with a woman and two kids. All we needed was a dog to look like the perfect picture of the great American family.

We arrived at the dealership forty-five minutes later. In that time, I learned that Kara was divorced, and lived in Lynwood alone with her two kids who were out of school today because of some teacher's conference. She worked at a bank but took the day off to be with eight-year-old Jamal and eleven year old Kendra. They had stopped at the store to get some snacks and had planned to go on a picnic, but the old hoopty, her reward in the divorce settlement, had other plans.

I led them to the waiting area of the dealership where other significant others and children were waiting. I went to the garage and Eddie informed me that Steve had just called and was on his way in. I returned to the waiting area, told Kara the news and then excused myself to my office as I heard Jamal say "that car is the bomb," for the tenth time as his eyes looked across the showroom.

It was almost one o'clock and I was just starting my day and I never did make it to the bank. Damn! Oh well, that's life. I went to my office, sat down at my desk and reached for the phone as I placed my briefcase on the floor.

"Hello," Jackie's voice said sleepily on the line."

"You still in the bed?"

"Hi, why didn't you wake me when you left."

"I tried."

"What time is it?"

"Let's just say most people are at lunch."

"Damn, it's that late," she mumbled.

I took a long breath. "What's up with you, Jackie?"

Instead of an answer, I heard nothing but complete silence.

"Are you still there?" I asked after a moment.

"Yeah."

"What's up then?"

"Everything."

"What's that mean?"

"Everything. A lot of shit is happening."

"Like what, Jackie?"

I heard her breathe heavily on the phone.

"Like what?" I repeated.

"You wouldn't understand. I can't talk to you."

"Since when can't you talk to me?"

Another heavy sigh. I let a long sigh myself. This was like pulling teeth and I was nobody's dentist. I didn't have time for this. I had too much to do and was already behind schedule.

"I'll tell you what. Why don't you page me when you feel you can talk to me again, all right? It's been nice, baby."

I hung up the phone and, just as quickly, erased her face from my memory. I closed my eyes tightly, rubbing them with my hands, already feeling drained. She was using, no doubt. I've seen this before. I went through this with Monica. Monica was the sweetest person I had met in a long time and beautiful was a word that was not good enough to describe her. She was slender, had long, flow-ing hair that was all hers, and a smile that made the sun shine. But, within weeks, I found out that she was a straight up crack head. I tried to hang with her, tried to get her some help, but she didn't want it. And I swear, it did something to me when she died about a month after I quit seeing her. It really did.

And now Jackie, I don't know. I've known her for about two years. Took my time with her because at the time I wanted someone real instead of just my regular fly by night girls. Wanted someone to talk to or maybe see me beyond the obvious. Someone who could be down with me, and all the things I've got to do to be down myself.

And it seemed like she could be the one. She was a girl from the hood who understood the hood, yet knew there was something else out there and didn't mind working to get it. She worked for an insurance company and told me many times of her dreams to move up without lying down. She had class, style, ambi-tion, determination, and one problem I didn't know about until I hit it.

She was sex addict. A nymph. Had to have it. When we were together, she never wanted me to leave. Did things to me so I wouldn't want to leave. Pulled out all the stops. Had more toys than Toys R' Us. Begged me to stay the night with her and those nights would turn into days before I would retreat from her, feeling totally drained 'cause, I swear, we did nothing but go at it twenty four seven. She became more needy and greedier of my time. Practically blowing up my pager. It was like she was possessed by Bad.

But here lately she's calmed down. A lot. Too many things are different. Her motions are slow. Her speech sometimes is slurred and I know for a fact her eyes have been glazed over more often than not. And sex? It's almost like she's forgotten what it was. Something's not right. It just ain't, and hey, I got to cut her loose.

"Mr. Washington," A soft voice spoke on the other side of my door interrupting my thoughts. It was Kara.

"Come in," I said standing up and going to the other side of my desk.

"Hi."

I pointed toward a chair across from my desk. She sat down and I went back to my seat behind my desk.

"I don't mean to disturb you, again. It's just that I've changed my mind about getting my car fixed."

"Why is that?"

She didn't answer me but instead looked around the office. I noticed her eyes take in my big mahogany desk, my original oil paintings, and the floor-to-ceiling bookcase and cabinets behind me as her feet pressed down on the plush carpeting. Finally her eyes met mine.

"Quite honestly, Mr. Washington, I can't afford it," she said quietly and then added, "I should have never let you tow my car in. "

I leaned my body down into my chair and smiled as I met her eyes. "I thought you understood that the only reason I was helping you was because I wanted to. And who knows, maybe one day you could help me out."

Kara looked at me for a moment before answering me. "Oh, and let me guess what it is I have to do to help you. A blow job or maybe a quick tumble on your office desk."

I slowly sat back up in my seat. "Have I looked at you or said something that has made you uncomfortable or maybe offended you?"

Kara quickly averted her eyes and nervously began to wring her hands together. "No."

"Then why is it that you think all I want from you is something of a sexual nature? Look, I'm really am just wanting to help you. Not to belittle you, but I realize that you don't have a lot of money to spend for the upkeep of your car after just one look at your situation. And you told me that you were a single parent trying to raise two kids.

"My gesture toward you is because I understand that and I respect that. I have four sisters back home and I would hate to think that if a brother saw one of them down that they wouldn't help them out. I have not been there for them. But I'm here for you."

Kara leaned back into her chair before speaking. "I'm sorry, I misjudged you."

I met her eyes and smiled into them. "No sweat."

"But still, I don't know what to do to repay you for all the kindness you shown me."

I stood up and walked around to the front of my desk and leaned into her chair. "I tell you what. Why don't you go get one of the rentals and take your kids on that picnic you promised them while you car is being serviced? I'll make sure your car is delivered to your home before nightfall."

Kara stood up and awkwardly we touched slightly as her perfume danced through the air. She opened her lips to speak but I gently placed a finger on them before any words escaped out. I opened the door and led her to the rental office.

At seven o'clock, I stood at Kara's doorway and rang the doorbell. She answered the door wearing a short breezy dress that hung loosely and her face was all smiles as she moved aside so I could come in. I slowly stepped inside and quickly assessed my surroundings.

Candles were lit, soft jazz music was playing and a bottle of a not- too-expensive wine was sitting on a table with two wine glasses. She gestured for me to sit down on the couch. I did. She poured the wine in both glasses as I looked again throughout her apartment. It was small, quaint but very homey, very comfortable. Clean. Plants were everywhere and there was a large fish aquarium filled with goldfish.

She handed me a glass and looked into my eyes. I met her gaze and then we both sipped the wine not taking our eyes from one another. She smiled slightly at me and told me she was glad that it was I who had returned her car. I informed her that I wouldn't have had it any other way. She told me that she couldn't stop thinking about me. I told her the feeling was mutual. She leaned into my space and kissed me on the cheek, just barely touching my lips. I returned the gesture by stroking her lips with my fingers.

Again, our eyes met. She sipped more wine and I did the same. She then slowly let her fingers do the walking down my lower torso until she found what she wanted. A slow smiled crept across her face as she moved her hand in a circular motion. She then took both of my hands and laid them on her breast. I gently began to stroke her soft skin and then quickly buried my face into them and inhaled her scent. She smelled like crushed roses.

She buried her face into my neck, whispering wild and kinky things in my ears. And then, without shame, looked into my eyes and told me she never wanted anybody like she wanted me. She lifted her dress over her head and her hair slowly cascaded wildly against her face. She quickly began to unbutton my shirt and then, with shaky fingers, she undid my belt, unzipped my pants, and didn't stop until I found freedom. In a course of minutes, I was out of my clothes, wearing nothing but a condom and the woman with the two kids, who I found stranded at a Piggly-Wiggly, had straddled me and rode BAD until she screamed with delight and I moaned with pleasure.

Three hours later, I pulled into the parking lot of Iguana's and handed a brother my keys with a bill to let him know that I appreciated him taking extra care of my car. His young face widened into a smile about a mile long until he met my eyes and saw the seriousness in them. He calmed down, took my keys and then gently eased my 500 to safety as I headed toward the door where the smell of cigarettes and liquor immediately hit me in the face the moment I opened it.

A tall woman behind a booth grinning from ear to ear took my twenty dollars as a buff brother ran a metal wand up and down my person and then pointed me in the direction of the blaring music.

I swear there must be a video cam in the ladies room that scoped the parking lot, 'cause as soon as I cleared security, I was greeted by five different shades of beautiful black women. All of them wearing short skimpy skirts or tight fitting pants and all smelling good. I smiled, said hello and then had to squeeze through the narrow path they left.

I immediately looked toward the stage where my cousin was getting his groove on. I stood on the outside of the dance floor and, within seconds, three different women asked me to dance. I refused as politely as I could, trying not to offend any of them. I wasn't ready to dance yet. And if truth were told, I really don't like to dance. Not like I used to back in high school. I just like to hear good music. Since I didn't know which reserved table was for me, I decided to head toward the bar to get a drink.

"Excuse me," a female voice spoke as I tried to squeeze my way to the bar.

I looked down and noticed the woman and thought maybe I had bumped her and quickly excused myself if I had.

"Can a sister get your phone number?" she asked, looking me in the eyes. I looked down at her and studied her for a while. She seemed to be the same size all around, five feet high and five feet wide and had too much of other people's hair in her head. But, her smile was genuine. Real. So what the hell, it never hurts to converse.

"Now what do you know about me that makes you want to get my digits."

She looks at me slowly. Head to toe. The way I had looked at her. "Maybe I just like what I see."

"Well, hasn't anyone ever told you that what looks good isn't always good for you?"

"Who said I wanted anything good?"

I had to laugh at that. "So you're a woman who speaks her mind?"

"And, I'm a woman who's not afraid to go after what I want."

I smiled again. She had more rap than L. L. Cool J. Conversing with her might be all night thing. Not what I had in mind.

Luckily, a waitress looked my way. I had to seize the moment. When she asked me what I wanted to order, I spoke so low she couldn't hear me. When she leaned toward me and asked me to repeat myself, I whispered in her ear my order and then let my tongue tickle her ear. The woman beside me saw everything. Turned on her heels and left. I smiled at the waitress, apologized, promised to behave myself and to give her a nice tip.

The music stopped and Michael announced that the band was going to take a twenty. He came over to me all hyped up. We embraced, like cousins do. He did his Ray Leonard shuffle and I glared at him like Evander and held up a single, clinched fist. He dipped and dodged again before speaking. "How's it hanging cousin?"

"Long and hard," I informed him.

We both laughed.

Mike said. "That's why all the women in here are drooling."

"Don't hate me."

"Hell, I tried, but your ass is family. Come on let's sit. I need to rest my dogs."

I followed his GQ look to one of the reserved tables. Mike was dressed in all tan and in all silk. Had on a button down shirt, matching pants and jacket. A waitress quickly found her way to our table, asked us our poison and sashayed back to the bar with my cousin's eyes following her every move. When she was finally out of sight, he brought his attention back to me. I shook my head and laughed.

"Damn, cousin, if you got to look at it that long, then it's been too damn long."

"Tell me about it," he said taking another glance into the direction of the woman that stole his affection and probably gave him an erection.

"Mike, I can't believe you're not getting no play. I see these women drooling over you when you're up on that stage."

"I play when I want to play cousin."

"I hear you. So where's my girl."

"Nicki?"

"One and only."

"I guess a no show man. Haven't seen her. Haven't heard from her."

"Sure hate it. Would have liked to have seen her."

"Me too. She called me Tuesday, said she was coming on my opening night. This is my opening night. I don't know," Michael said. Hunched his shoulders.

Ms. Waitress brought over our drinks. I gave her a fifty and told her to keep them coming as my cousin drooled some more. She left. We raised shot glasses in a toast, downed them and continued our conversation where we left off.

I asked, "Is the great one in town?"

"Yeah, he just came off tour. Maybe that's what the deal is. You know a little qt."

I hunched my shoulders. "Whatever."

"I hear you. I still don't get that."

"I quit trying years ago."

We both said nothing for a moment. Then I changed the subject. "So, how long you're going to play here?"

"Couple days. Couple nights. Depends on if they like me."

"Hey, Mikey, they like you," I said trying to sound like that old Life Cereal commercial.

"Yeah, tonight they do, but tomorrow who knows."

I didn't say anything for a moment. Seemed to me like he was on a down trip all of a sudden. "What's up, Mike? Why the long face?"

"Man, you know, same old, same old. I've been playing clubs like this for years. Working my ass off and nothing has panned out. Sometimes I just get tired of this, man. I'm tired of singing everybody else's shit. I'm getting too old for this. I feel like if I don't hurry up and get my minute in the spotlight, I'm not going to get it at all."

"Mike, you're tripping. You got talent, son. You can give any other R & B artist out here a run for their money. And you know you can sing circles around the great James Fulton."

"So, why are brothers like Fulton who can't sing a note outside of a studio out touring and I am stuck up in some club singing his shit?"

"I know you don't sing his shit."

"Hell, no. But don't think I don't get asked."

"Straight? Man, that's like asking Patti to sing some of Diana's shit."

Mike shook his head. We both laughed.

"Exactly what I'm talking about. You don't know how many times I have stood on a stage and asked myself what does he have that I don't."

There was only one answer to that question and we both said it at the same time. "Nicole."

"Exactly! Marc, man, I have asked myself over and over why come that woman didn't fall in love with me."

"So you're still sweatin' my girl," I said laughing.

"Be serious Negro. How could I be with your ass blocking all the time? That's your bad. I'm sweatin' her man. I want what he got. Fame, fortune, women and more women."

I clicked my tongue against the roof of my mouth and leaned back deeper into me chair. Couldn't believe what I was hearing. "Mike, don't sweat him. That Negro's foul."

"Don't worry cousin, it ain't like that. I'm just talking. Everything is everything. Only thing I'm sweatin' are these fine ass women that are up in this club. Short ones, tall ones, oh la la ones."

I laughed and shook my head as Ms. Waitress returned with two more glasses in tow and my cousin's inquiring mind wanted to know her digits. She obliged him by writing them on a napkin and then wiggled off. We repeated our ritual, placed empty glasses on the table in front of us as Michael's eyes continued to roam the room. I reached over and pulled the light beige handkerchief out of his jacket and handed it to him.

"Here, Negro. You're drooling."

Michael took the handkerchief from me wiped his mouth and then bit down on it as a sister wearing a short-short skirt paraded in front of us for the fifth time. "Marc, how can you just sit there with all of these honeys parading around?"

"Easy. I had my bit of honey before I came here."

"Dog. Just straight up canine." Michael said standing up.

"Woof, woof!"

NICOLE

14

I checked my hair one more time in the mirror. It was in a funky mood. Doing it's own thing, going wild and every which of way no matter how hard I tried to straighten it out. Kind of like my man. I took a deep breath, grabbed a headband threw it on my head and turned off the bathroom light. In the bedroom, I threw off my robe and walked to my closet in my underwear and tried to figure what outfit I was going to try and squeeze in.

These extra fifteen pounds I was carrying around were sitting in all the wrong places and nothing I put on lately looked like a damn. But hey, it wasn't like I had anybody to impress. My man stopped looking a long time ago. I pulled down a red Donna Karan silk mini dress, slipped it on, looked in the mirror, pulled it off, and threw it on the bed. Next came my white Versace jumpsuit. Hell no! My ass looked like a beach whale. Then I tried my navy and green Gucci pantsuit and I looked like I was going to work. Scratch this. I just won't go.

I left the bedroom and headed toward the den to fix a drink and then went back toward the bedroom. I dropped down on the bed taking a long drink. I had to go. I promised Mike I'd be there and a promise is a promise. Besides, it would be good to see him, relax, laugh, and dance. Do shit I have not done since God knows when. I blinked my eyes. I didn't feel like crying. I didn't feel like feeling sorry for myself. I didn't feel like thinking about James and our so-called relationship. I downed the rest of my brandy, placed the empty glass on the nightstand, went back to my closet, and pulled out my black halter sundress and my black sandals. In ten minutes I was dressed, looking like a million pennies and ready to go.

It was hot. I let the top down on my convertible BMW and drove fast down through the streets to catch the wind in my hair. Marcus gave me this car for my thirty-second birthday. Michael gave me a diamond and sapphire pendant. James was out of town and didn't even call me. I turned on the radio. Mary J. Blige is singing, "I'm not gon' cry." Singing her face off. I changed the station. That was just hitting too close to home and right about now I was trying to run away. I popped in a CD and let Kenny G mellow me back out, calm my nerves, soothe my stirred up soul. I blasted it as I cruised toward downtown Los Angeles to Iguana's. I was suddenly glad I didn't stay at home. Alone.

Michael was on the stage when I came in looking very suave and very smooth singing his rendition of Peobo Bryson's 'I'm so into you'. He poured out note after note with such passion. You could see it with the way he moved. It was in his hands as he reached out to you. It was in the way he moved his lips when he wrapped his silky voice around each note and in his eyes. The brother made love to his music. He was so damn serious.

I spotted his playa, playa cousin sitting at a table eyeing a woman to his left who was trying to act like she wasn't paying him any attention. I smiled and snuck up on Marcus from behind. I lightly tapped him on the shoulder and went into my 'Q' mode. I place my hands on my hips and started waving my hand all in his face while swerving my neck in small circles.

"I know you not trying to get with her, Marcus," I said loud enough for Miss. Prissy to hear.

"Hey, Nicki," Marcus said standing up.

I stepped to him closer putting my finger on his chest. "Oh, so you just going to try and play me?"

"What's up with you, Nicki?"

"What's up with me? No, the question is what's up with you? Soon as I turn my back, you're always in some other woman's face. Have you forgotten about me, little man, Niquita and Chandrika? What's up with that? Don't make me have to call the child support people on your trifling behind cause you..."

"Okay, baby okay," Marcus, said smiling down at me. "I'm wrong, I'm wrong. But just tell me what I can do to make it better. What Marcus got to do to calm his baby down?"

"You want me to calm down?"

"Yeah, baby, I want you to be calm, you know, chill. I want you to be happy. What I got to do to make that happen?"

I looked around Marcus six plus frame to see if Miss. Prissy was still watching and she was with her mouth wide open. I looked back at Marcus and started batting my eyelashes real fast. "Well, if you would give me like twenty dollars so I could get my feets done I could be happy."

Marcus threw his head back laughing. "Come here girl."

I fell into his open arms laughing with him. He kissed my forehead and squeezed me tighter. "I've missed your crazy behind."

"I've missed you too Marcus," I said holding him just as tight and then pulled away just as fast. His embrace was too comforting and too much like home and I was too close to tears to stay there. I looked away from his knowing eyes and slid down into a chair and then looked at Michael on stage.

"Your cousin is on, Marcus."

"And you know that," he said sitting down and then waving at a waitress. I watched as she happily switched to our table smiling all the way. She leaned into his face so that he could get a zoom shot of her Wonder Bra and watched his eyes as he talked. Marcus gave her his infamous Mac Daddy smile showing those big dimples of his and I swear the girl was about to faint. She didn't care if I was his mama or the damn Queen of England, sitting across from him. Heifer just straight up ignored me! She was getting her drool on. He pulled her closer, whispered in her ear and she pranced on away.

"Marcus, Marcus, Marcus!"

"What," he said looking at me with his 'what did I do wrong look' looking like the little boy of thirteen I met twenty thousand years ago.

"So, how many women have you slept with?"

Marcus sat there with his dimpled smile struggling to keep a straight face and give me an honest answer. I glared into his eyes and decided to make it easy on him so I added, "Without a condom."

His smile broadened and he answered without hesitation, "Including you, none."

We both laughed and I then glanced back at the stage. Getting into Michael's groove. He looked our way, gave me a wink and I blew him a kiss just as our friendly waitress came back with our drinks, sliding Marcus a folded up piece of paper and mouthing call me with her lips. Marcus nodded his head like he was going to do just that first chance he got. Yeah right.

"Give it up Marcus. What's her name?"

"What?"

"Q or K"

Marcus unfolded the piece of paper and laughed. "Can we say Shaquanda-lisha?"

We both laughed and then Marcus slipped the paper in his jacket pocket.

"Oh, so you're going to keep it. What happened to your golden rule? You know no Q's and K's, no drama."

"I know Nicki, but did you see the legs on that girl?"

"My bad, your rule. Make it or break it."

"No, for real. I got to stick to my rule. I can't handle the drama. I just don't want to her to see me throw it away. She might get mad and slip a little something in one of our drinks."

"Um huh. So what's been going on with you?" I asked taking a sip of the brandy that he had ordered for me.

"Nothing much. Working hard and playing when I can."

"Brothers always got to play."

"Hey, this is a free country and I'm a free man."

"To freedom," I said lifting my glass. He lifted his and took a long drink as his eyes searched mine too damn long. I planted a weak smile on my face and looked at my hands as I tried to ignore his constant stare.

He asked, "So what's been up with you?"

"Work. You know show business is not all that damn glamorous. It's a lot of hard work."

"I hear the Great One is back in town."

"So I've heard," I said pulling my glass to my lips again. He has been in town three days. Three days! Think he would have called me? Say at least hi, I'm home. Had a great tour, thanks for setting it up, thanks for nothing, something anything. Not a word. Not one word. Hadn't even come to the house to get a change of clothes. Marcus reached across the table and touched my free hand looked all inside my eyes.

"Talk to me."

"There's nothing to talk about Marcus."

"Don't give me that Nicole. We have known each other all of our lives. You don't think I know when you're hurting or when you're sad?"

I looked into the eyes of my best friend wanting so much to tell him all my secrets and to share my pains.

"Nicki, I want you to be happy."

I blinked back the tear that was fighting to get out from behind my lids. Marcus was talking about something I long forgot how to want for myself.

"What's happiness, Marcus? I'm thirty-three years old and I swear I keep missing it. I thought I would be happy sharing my life with somebody that wanted to share his life with me. I thought it was the satisfaction of doing my job well and knowing that I made a difference in someone's life. But it's not, you know.

"I got life all wrong. I mean I should be doing whatever it is I want to do. Living the way I want to live. Being with whomever I want to be with. I mean I know I'm not the brightest crayon in the box but I finally get this. I should eat, drink, and be merry with anybody I choose. Right, Marcus. Right? I mean aren't you happy being with any and everybody? You do what the hell you feel with whomever you feel whenever you feel. In your game of life you make your own rules."

Marcus rubbed my hand inside his. "Why are you living like this, baby?" He asked looking at me waiting on an answer but I had nothing to say. I didn't come here tonight for this. I glanced back at Michael then back at Marcus who was still waiting.

"Forget I said anything okay?" I mumbled. "I came here to get away from my problems."

"Just answer me one thing. When was the last time that fool he made you smile?"

My shoulders began to shake and I kept trying to hear Mary J sing, but tears were slowly slipping down my cheeks anyway. Marcus lifted his hand to my face and wiped my tears as he held my eyes with his.

"Why do you do it, Marcus?"

"Do what?"

"Why do you guys have to have so many women?"

Marcus rose in hands in protest. "Hold up, first of all don't even put me and that Negro in the same boat. His ass is in a dingy and I'm riding in a luxury cruiser. I don't take things from women and I have never used a woman. I give a woman what she needs and what she wants. I make them happy for as long as I can. And when I see where I can't do that anymore, I step."

"And you don't see nothing wrong with that?" I asked my tears now gone.

"Honestly? No," he stated simply.

I looked at my friend for life and smiled. He is what he is and made no excuses for it. And hey, I admired him for being true to himself because it was a lot more than I could say about myself. "So you just going to leave a trail of broken hearts across the state of California."

"Don't hate, appreciate," Marcus said holding his hands out to put himself on display.

I laughed and looked into his smiling eyes. "I can't stand you, Anthony Marcus."

His eyes turned serious, as he once again seemed to look straight through me. "I know baby. I don't like you either."

"Yo people. What's up over here?" Michael asked coming to the table and pulling a chair from another one so he could sit. "I'm up there pouring my heart out and my two supposedly biggest fans and supporters are over here all huddled up and not giving me the time of day. What's up with that? Where is the love?"

"Oh, no Mike. I'm all in you. I felt you baby. See I was crying," I said smiling and rubbing my face searching for my dried up tears.

"Oh yeah, me too man. I was touched. Moved," Marcus added.

"Cuz, please. A Mac truck couldn't move you right now," Michael stated.

"Whatever," Marcus answered.

"So Nicki, when are you going to hook a brother up?"

"What do you want, Michael? You want my people to call your people."

"Hell, I want you to call me personally."

"Watch yourself son," Marcus said.

"Quit blocking," Michael said to Marcus and then turned back to me. "So, what about it?"

I looked at Mike, trying to read him. "What's up with you tonight. Why are you tripping?"

"I can't help it baby. I tripped when I fell in love with you?"

"Come on son, I taught you better, " Marcus laughed.

Michael ignored him, kept eyeing me strangely. "Come on Nicole, we've been friends a long ass time, you know. I think it's time we went on the next level. I've matured now, baby. I'm down for whatever you're down for."

"Michael, you're crazy." I said.

"About you baby. Marcus, tell her man. I'm saving all of my love for you. I'm not even getting any."

'That makes two of us,' I said to myself and then to Michael. "Let me sleep on it, okay?"

"Alright, and then you sleep with me."

"Say man, don't you need to go back on stage?" Marcus asked.

"Naw, I'm through for the night. I'm just need to get with the prettiest girl in the club tonight. You know what I'm saying?"

Marcus laughed. "Excuse my horny cousin Nic. But you know how we men are when we have been without for a couple of days, we lose our minds. He's delusional. Up in here thinking he's me and coming at you all foul and everything. But don't worry. I'll get him some help. A woman or a blow up doll or something."

I shook my head at them both. What would I do without them?

I can't scream. I can't even scream. All I can do is stand with my mouth gaped open, because my mind is unable to comprehend the meaning of words. I can't see. My eyes are suddenly blinded by a red vision of two people intertwined with each other in their own manner of lovemaking. One, a woman, I don't know, the other, my man. My James.

They are so engrossed in their passion that they didn't even notice me until a low groan finally escapes my lips. I know they are both looking at me, but still I can't see anything but that red vision.

I hear a scream, the woman. She begins to rustle about for her clothes and heads out the door in about twenty seconds flat. I sense James coming towards me. Unconsciously, I move back and bump into the dresser. Through the red, I could finally see him; his male, naked physique is unmasked before me. I look up and see his face. I could finally see his eyes.

"Why don't you make this easy and just go. I'll send you your things."

I look at him in horror. I know he didn't just say what I thought I heard.

"I want you to leave, Nicole," he spoke again more sternly.

I stood against the dresser dumbfounded, shaking my head from left to right. Something was definitely wrong with this picture. I'm the one that just came home and found him in the bed with some slut and he's acting like he's mad at me! Like I've done him wrong!

I finally found my voice and spoke. "What did you say?"

"Oh, you deaf now."

"Wait a minute. Don't you think you owe me some kind of explanation?"

"What else is there to say besides GO?"

"You, bastard!"

"Look. Why waste time playing games, Nicole? You and I have been finished for a long time. I don't need you. We're not married. We don't share the same bed and you haven't written a decent song in three years! Why are you still even here taking up precious space? You're useless to me!"

My body literally trembled with the anger of an earthquake and suddenly the red was darker and once again I could no longer see James. I stood still, shaking my head trying to focus my eyes and see him. My James, the man I had known, lived with and loved for almost ten years.

The sensitive loving man who, in a heartbeat, swept me off of my feet with his witty charm, great personality and sensuous voice. But he wasn't here. No, instead stood before me, was a twisted two-headed monster that I, no doubt, helped create.

Didn't I make him the star that he was? I can't believe this! All of a sudden I was dispensable! Didn't this man love me or care about me at all? How many times did he profess his love for me? Why was I being discarded like some used car? What was I, some late model Ford and now it was time for a newer and shiner version?

"Nicole! Didn't you hear me? I want you to get your shit and get out of my house. My money bought this house and paid for everything in it."

I felt my body tremble again. He was serious. Tears uncontrollable came to my eyes as my heart suddenly felt an unbearable pain. Like somehow, someone had literally stuck their hand inside my chest and began to squeeze the very life out of it.

I felt sick, like bile was coming from depths of my stomach and getting stuck at the base of my throat. I sob loudly and could still feel the hot tears that wouldn't stop falling, still unable to believe what was happening. How, in the course of one day, hours, no minutes, had my whole life, as I know it changed and turned upside down? Again!

James stared at me harder and curled his lips back before speaking. "How long did you think I was going to let you ride my coattail, basking in my lime-light, holding me back? Did you think I would carry you forever?"

"Carry me? Is that what you think you've been doing. I thought we had a relationship. A partnership. Hell, a damn commitment!"

"Woman, you don't mean shit to me," he said walking his naked torso away from me toward the bathroom.

My knees turned into jelly and my feet felt like two concrete bricks. This can't be happening. "What? James, how can you speak to me like this?"

He laughed as he turned toward me. "Nicole, you always have a hard time with the truth. Read my lips, I don't love you. Maybe I never did," he spit out like he had a bad taste in his mouth.

Those words were worst than any slap in the face and literally made me feel six inches tall. I was speechless, defenseless, and helpless against the evilness that seems to, no matter what, come back into my life and knock me down.

This can't be happening to me! I can't do this. I don't want to comprehend this pain or understand it. I don't want to live through it again. I am so tired of hurting and not being able to do anything about it. Rage overwhelmed me and I reached in the bureau top drawer and pulled out the revolver that was always kept there. I looked up at James who was now standing in front of the bathroom mirror. Before I knew it, I had my hand on the trigger, pulling it back. The sound of the chamber clicking made James turn around and looked back at me.

"What the hell do you think you are doing?" He yelled, walking back toward me.

I stared up into his eyes, not blinking. The cold barrel of the gun had some-how strengthened my bruised heart. "Take another step and find out!"

He stopped in his tracks. "You can't be serious," he said with a smirk on his face, but I smelled his fear. His eyes were looking at me as if he was searching for the woman who would do anything for him. I hope he saw what I felt. I wanted him to see the hardness and the coldness I felt. My fingers tightly gripped the gun.

"Try me. Give me one good reason why I shouldn't kill you."

"Nicole, be rational."

"Now you want me to be rational!" I screamed. I walked over to him, and brought the gun down toward his crotch, my eyes never leaving his as I slowly placed the gun on the tip of his penis with the coldness of the barrel. "Okay, I won't kill you."

"Nicole, what are saying? What are you doing?" James pleaded loudly as sweat poured from his head.

"What I should have done a long time ago. Put you out of your damn misery because you nothing but a selfish, conniving, low-life, black, mangy dog. How dare you! How dare you stand here and say that you didn't give a damn about me. That I mean nothing to you! Like you accomplished all that you are by your damn self. I made you! And I will break you if I have to! And that whore or anybody else won't even want you when I get through with you."

James fell to his knees and I placed the gun inches from his forehead. "Nicole, please. I'm sorry."

"Tell me something I don't know!"

"What do you want me to say? What do I have to do for you to get this damn gun out of my face?"

"How about that you owe your success to me. How about that without me you would still be singing in nightclubs and wouldn't have known what it was like to have a gold or a platinum record or what it feels like to win a Grammy. How about you're sorry for making me lose our child!" I cried out unable to hold in the tears of anger that were ripping through my body. For moments, I stood over him holding the gun through my blinding rage without a word between us.

"I want out Nicole. I just want out," he stated simply in a calm voice.

Hot tears once again formed in my eyes and burned my cheeks. Suddenly, I felt defeated, drained and unable to control the emotions that seemed to rip through my soul. I struggled within myself trying to hold in the pain that was fighting to get out.

"I'm tired of pretending," he said standing up and looking me dead in the eye.

"No!" I screamed inside as the pain in my heart got worse and then moved from my heart to my head; a slow, throbbing pain that seemed to engulf my whole body. I couldn't see his eyes anymore. I couldn't make out his face. But I knew he was still talking to me. I could still hear him.

"...I'm doing this for you Nicole..."

Was he smiling at me? What did he say? I tried harder to see him but everything was becoming so blurry.

"...I'm a star. I can't be with you and my music."

I looked harder for his eyes, but all I could see was his mouth as he stood there smiling, saying those awful wicked things to me.

"... I mean I tried to stay here as long as I could, but I can't anymore. It's over Nicole. I don't love you."

Suddenly, I felt an explosion. God, did I just have a heart attack? My body was shaking and my left hand became extremely hot and hurt something awful. I slowly opened my hand and tried to see it but everything was still blurry. Where was James? I could hear him, but I still couldn't see him. Why didn't he just shut up? Why was he saying those ugly words? He just kept saying them over and over again. "I don't love you. I don't love you."

I backed out of the bedroom, ran out the house, jumped in car and before I knew it I was on the Santa Monica freeway. I dodged in and out of traffic like a person possessed, my foot glued to the gas pedal. Tears were burning my face as I drove, blinding my vision. I knew I needed to pull over, but something in me wouldn't let my stop.

Finally, I exited off the freeway and went in a liquor store. When I walked in I saw how strange faces were gawking at my like I was from out of space or something. I went straight to the counter, asked for the first bottle I saw, paid the man and left.

I opened the bottle and took my first swallow before I reached the car door. The hot liquid burned my throat as it went down. I hopped back in my car, cranked it up and just started to drive. I didn't know where I was going but I knew I just had to get away. I drove. I drink. I cried. And then I drove and drink some more as tears continued to blind me.

I don't know how long I drove. It could have been minutes it could have been hours. But finally I got tired of driving. I spotted a clearing, a parking area, and a dock. I saw the ocean. I parked my car, got out, taking my bottle with me. I felt lightheaded as I looked at the bottle that was already half empty.

I removed my shoes, left them and proceeded to walk toward the ocean. There was a boat out and I could hear loud music coming from it. Stumbling I walked until I got to the shore, sat down and faced my life.

I've been here before, too many times. I swear my whole life has been nothing but a roller coaster. Just like the ride, I seem to always make it to the top and then somehow, I always end on the bottom. Rock bottom.

The first years were great. I had everything. It's funny that as a child, you take things for granted thinking everything is as it should be and will always be. You never think that the unthinkable can happen and take everything that you know and love away. But it can.

And somehow you pick yourself up and you get back on the ride of life. You start over, finding new hope, new people to share your life with and dare to dream again. Which is what it seems I've been doing my whole life since the death of my parents.

I took a long drink and felt it burn my insides but didn't care. I knew better than to drink on an empty stomach but I needed something to fill me up and take away this familiar pain.

I glanced out at the Pacific with the moon high above it. For moments, I watched the waves float in and rush out and upward only to float in again. It was peaceful, tranquil unlike my torrid and torn up soul.

At thirteen, I thought the death of my parents would be the most traumatic experience I would ever have to face. A part of me died with them in that fire and it seemed like years had passed before I was able to face a day without crying, feeling lonely or just missing their presence in my life. But I started over, accepting the hand I was dealt and their deaths.

My new friends and new home, first at the Haywood Home and then with Emily Nelson wasn't ideal, but it was comforting in knowing that I wasn't alone. Especially once I met Marcus, my Morning. He came into my life and gave me everything I needed. Friendship, laughter, family and a love I didn't know could exist. And no one could have been more surprised than I was.

From the beginning, he was everything I wasn't. Cool, confident, rough and tough, all-around school bully. He lied, cheated, stole, fought, pulled prank after prank and still everyone was either drawn to his charming smile or feared his dangerous attack. And he became my best friend. He listened like no one else ever did. He let me cry on his shoulder and then made me laugh in spite of it. And before I knew it I was in love.

Like magic, I was under his spell. I couldn't think straight when we were apart. I couldn't see straight when we were together. He became the first person I thought of when I woke up and my last dream at night. I was in hook, line and sinker. Sitting on top of the world, riding high on my roller coaster. Then I hit bottom. Rock bottom. Ms. Emily died. And I was raped.

Morning found me beaten, bleeding and bruised. Morning covered me, caressed me, consoled me, comforted me and carried me to help. Then Morning cried. Cried like rain. Cried like an angel in the sky. And I couldn't look at him and I didn't want him to see me. I heard him say he loved me. Over and over he said he loved me that he would take care of me. But Morning couldn't stop crying. Morning cried so hard that I felt his pain on top of my pain. I closed my eyes. I couldn't look at him and I didn't want him to see me.

I took another long drink, wiped the tears from my eyes and looked back out at the ocean. It took me fourteen years to say those words out loud or even think them in my mind. I was raped. It took me fourteen years to erase the guilt, the shame and the dirtiness that came with it.

It took me to hit rock bottom again.

I was thirty years old. I had just found out that I was six weeks pregnant. I was happy. I ran to James and told him the good news. He wasn't happy. He didn't want to be a daddy. He just wanted to be who he was. A star. He said some mean things. I said some. We argued. He pushed me. I fell. I lost our baby. Rock bottom. And things changed again.

He didn't leave me and I didn't leave him. He apologized but I didn't hear him. He didn't come to our bed and he didn't touch me. When he was home he stayed out for two and three nights at a time and I didn't ask. I couldn't care less. But I couldn't stop loving him. From day one, I loved the great James Fulton with an urgency that was out of this world.

He noticed me first. I had been in LA for six years, was a senior in college, living with Marcus, his cousin Michael, and their grandmother, Devon who was nothing but a saint living on earth. She took me in, took care of me, nursed me and became the mother I desperately needed. She made me finish high school and then sent me to college. She told me over and over that I could have whatever I wanted in life. I didn't have the heart to tell her what I wanted the most was lost to me forever.

In those six years, I pushed my friend away, day by day, year by year. No longer was he my Morning, but now he was my Night. My darkness. Because every time he looked at me I went to a place that I tried so hard to forget. He got the message. He stayed away. Sometimes for months at a time and I can't lie it hurt like hell when he was gone.

Michael and I bonded. He picked up where his cousin before had left off. I didn't know how much he knew about me. But if he knew the truth he never said. He treated me like his sister. I needed that. But a part of me needed more. And James seemed to know exactly what it was.

We met at a club downtown. I was with Michael, dancing and having a good time. Then there was a contest. Michael sang. Sang his heart out and blew the audience away. Then James came on. Singing only to me. He pulled me in the middle of the floor, got on bended knee and sang to my soul. Michael said it was a ploy. James won the contest. And James won me.

Weeks passed, turned into months and James did everything right. He sent me flowers, telegrams, and candy bouquets. He took me to all the exclusive res-taurants, nightclubs, and even movie premieres. He took me on weekend getaways to Vegas, Tahoe, and the Bahamas. He listened to my sad stories and loved my body the way it never been loved like it was a sweet, sweet song. In four months, I moved in with him. And then two months later, quit school with just a semester to go. I set into a plan that would launch his singing career to the top. I devoted myself my time and my energy to him and making him a household name.

I wrote song after song, hit after hit. I handled his promotional tours; got him interviews on radio shows, autograph sessions at record stores, and then later at his career skyrocketed, spots on various talk shows. I chose his record label and made sure that they gave him a good deal. I hired the best lawyer, best man-agers, dance instructors and voice teachers and never complained and understood that we couldn't get married just yet, because it could possibly damage his career as a sex symbol. Whatever James said he needed from me I gave, blindly, stupidly, and unquestionably.

I raised the bottle to my lips trying to wipe the taste of James from my heart. Why even now, did I even find myself loving him? I felt so disgusted. So alone. The motor of the boat started and it began to cruise further out into the water.

"Why the hell did you do this to me?" I asked aloud to the moon that I was sure laughing down at me.

I took another swallow of the liquid drowning my clothes as it poured down my chin and for some reason I thought it was funny so I began to laugh. To really laugh and then I started to cry again.

Suddenly, remembering where I was, I looked out at the ocean. The ocean which had so many times had been my peace, my tranquility every since I moved to this city. I rose up and walked to the edge of the water, letting the coldness caress my feet.

"To roller coasters." I lifted my bottle to the wind and took another drink. I closed my eyes and let the cool air brush against my face, freezing my hot tears. It felt so good, so cool. I wanted to feel it caress my entire body.

I dropped the bottle and proceeded to walk further into the water and before I knew it the water was up to my chin. I stood still and looked out as far as I could see. Water was all around me and it was pitch black. I needed to get to the other side where it was safer, brighter. Where there was a better world with no pain.

I looked out before me and suddenly I panicked. I turned around and faced the shore that seemed miles away. I didn't mean come out this far. I stepped forward and stepped into a hole and went down. My feet folding beneath me gave away to the current. I tried to find my way back up, but it seemed the harder I tried to come up, the further I went down.

My body grew tired and I no longer had the strength to try anymore. I saw my father telling me to be brave and then my mother kissed me softly on the cheek. Mrs. Haywood wiped my tears and then Ms. Emily squeezed me in her big arms.

Then I saw a mean, evil face sneer into mine as his hands held me down roughly and so tight that I grew tired and tired. I strained my eyes to see him but he let me go and suddenly I was floating. I felt my body drift away. I looked back behind me to see where the evil face had gone and then I saw him. Standing before me laughing, cursing me. It was James.

DEREK

15

Derek yelled into the wind, "Come on damn it! Come on!"

He massaged her chest harder and harder and then placed his mouth on hers, letting out short breaths into her, and praying to God that he was doing it right, having never once attempted this life saving technique in all the twelve years that he's known it. He pushed on her chest again and again, hoping that he was applying the right amount of pressure.

"Please God, don't let her die."

Finally she coughed and he watched as she opened deep brown eyes, blinking as she did and looking at him. He never felt so relieved in his life and let out a long sigh.

"Oh, thank God."

He bent over her and carefully looked at her praying she was all right. She looked at him strangely. He knew she was trying to recognize him, but there was nothing. He was just as much a stranger to her as she was to him. He looked into her eyes and right away saw fear. She tried to sit up and then almost instantly laid back down as her face told the pain she was in. He gently stroked her hair and removed a strand of it from her eyes. "Take it easy."

She looked at him and struggled to catch her breath.

"I thought I lost you."

"I'm not dead," she finally spoke hoarsely.

"No."

"I'm not dead," she said again.

"No."

She looked around as if she was looking for something or maybe someone. But there was nothing but blackness. Then she looked back at him with pain stricken eyes.

"My head," she barely whispered and then in seconds her eyes closed her and she slip back into unconsciousness.

He quickly picked her up and carried her limp like body toward his house, once again terrified that she wasn't it going to make it. She felt almost weightless. He laid her on his couch in the living room, knelt his ear to her chest just to make sure that she was still breathing and then quickly went and found the phone. He needed help. He spoke into the phone nervously noticing his hands were shaking.

"Say man, I need you to get over here."

"What's up," his younger brother asked excitedly.

"I don't know, I mean it's an emergency. I saw this woman drowning and I gave her CPR and everything and she came to for a minute but now she's out again."

"I'm three minutes away."

He hung up the phone and went back to the couch and once again listened for her breathing. She was still with him. He looked her over carefully in the dimly lit room and noticed her clothing was torn on the sleeve and badly soiled and there were scratches on the side of her face. He sat next to her afraid to take his eyes away from her as he could only imagine what happened to her out there.

Finally the doorbell chimed and he jumped to go answer it. Before he could say anything, Gerald rushed to the couch and began to look over the woman, his hands expertly checking her head and body. Never had he been more proud of him as he watched him examined her. It was like he was the older brother. He was in complete awe of him as he stood there feeling helpless.

Gerald removed her clothes and told Derek to go get a robe or something and some blankets. He rushed down the hall and into his bedroom and came out as quickly as possible.

"Did you see what happened?" Gerald asked when Derek returned taking the robe from him and gently put it on her, as she still lay perfectly motionless. Then he placed the two blankets on top of her.

"What did you see," he asked again.

"I'm not sure."

"What do you mean?" Gerald asked looking back at him.

Derek hesitated a moment before answering. "I don't know exactly. I was coming back from my run and at first, I saw her standing at the edge, I thought. But as I got closer, I noticed that she was actually in the water and she just started to sink. She never started to swim."

"Are you saying that she deliberately walked in?" Gerald asked applying an anesthetic on her face.

"Yeah, that's what it looked like."

Gerald said something under his breath as he placed a small bandage on her face. He let out a long sigh. "She's going to be all right. She doesn't appear to have a concussion and I don't feel any bumps or bruises."

"Then why is she unconscious?"

"She's not unconscious, technically. She's just passed out."

"What are you saying, man?"

"She's loaded. Smells like gin."

Derek let out a deep sigh. "I thought she was going to die," he mumbled honestly as his brother headed toward the kitchen and then stuck his head in the refrigerator. He followed him wondering what was in there that could help her.

"What are you looking for?"

"Something to eat."

"Oh."

Derek sighed again, relieved. He was just hungry. He remembered the meal he had began to prepare earlier, but now didn't appeal to him.

"Well hey, I made a steak earlier, you can have it."

"Nah, it's too late for something like that." Gerald said and then grabbed some deli meat, a tomato, lettuce and the jar of mayonnaise.

Derek took a seat at the counter and watched his brother make a sandwich, glancing once at the woman who still hadn't so much as turned over on his couch. Was he sure she was all right?

"She sure is pretty," Gerald stated taking a bite of his sandwich.

"Who?"

"The woman on your couch. What's wrong with you? Has it been so long that you have been with a woman that you've forgotten what they look like?"

"It hasn't been that long."

"I can't tell, big bro."

"What are you doing looking anyway? You're an old married man."

"Married, not blind and definitely not dead."

"Well, so is she," Derek stated remembering the huge diamond on her left hand.

"Maybe. But if she was so happy, I don't think she would have been out there trying to walk the Pacific, you know what I mean?"

Gerald took another bite of his sandwich as if the possibility of one contemplating suicide was a normal thing. "I mean if she was my wife, she sure in the hell wouldn't be laying on your couch."

"Your wife has slept on my couch before."

"Yeah, but now without me," Gerald said finishing his sandwich and then headed for the living room with Derek following behind. He looked down at the woman who still lay quietly.

Derek looked too and then bent down and whispered in his ear. "So are you saying you don't trust me or your wife?"

Gerald smiled and then stood up straight. "She's probably going to be here awhile. Maybe until morning."

"So, I shouldn't wake her."

"Oh, come on, you remember your college days, leave her alone, unless of course she's bothering you."

"No, of course not."

"Good. Just give her a couple of aspirin when she wakes up and she should be fine."

"All right."

"And relax."

Gerald then reached for his jacket and headed for the front door. "Page me if you need me, but I'm sure you won't, unless of course, you forgotten what to do with a beautiful, young woman."

"What are trying to say?"

"Nothing, old man, nothing at all. I got to go. I was on my way home and Sharon's probably worried sick by now."

Derek glanced back at the woman. "Say thanks, okay."

"No problem, Oh by the way. I trust my wife. Later man."

Derek stepped into the cold air with Gerald and just before he reached his car he yelled out to him. "Hey, give Sharon my love."

"That's quite all right, I'll give her mine."

He closed the door smiling, went into the kitchen, put on a pot of coffee. Next he went and took a quick shower, changed into some clean sweats and still the woman had not awaken, so he went back into the living room and sat down in a chair and turned on the television. But television was a bore and after playing remote control for a good forty-five seconds, he turned it off. Now what was he going to do? For some reason he felt uncomfortable and restless in his own house and couldn't seem to remember what it was that he would usually be doing.

He turned on the CD player and the sounds of Boney James flowed through the house. He sat there listening for a moment, his feet tapping to the beat. But after awhile, he still felt out of sync, almost as if he was in a strange land. Damn, this was weird. What was he doing before her?

He went over to the couch and looked down at her and wondered what was her story. Why had she tried to kill herself? To him, she looked as if she had everything going for her. Gerald was right. She was very beautiful. Her face was smooth milk chocolate brown with a medium sized nose, high cheekbones and full lips. Her black-brownish hair hung loosely about her shoulders. Derek found himself staring at her, guessing her to be around five-seven or eight and very shapely even in that bulky robe.

"You like what you see," her voice suddenly said catching him off guard, embarrassing the hell out of him.

"I'm sorry."

She tried to sit up and her hand went instantly to her head. "Where am I?"

"This is my home. I found you on the beach remember?"

"Yeah, yeah, I remember," she said looking about her and noticing the robe. "Where are my clothes?"

LOVE AND CONSEQUENCES

"My brother removed them. He checked you out. He's a doctor. And he said you'll be okay." Derek said hoping he sounded assuring.

She looked at him and nodded her head. "Can I get something to drink."

"I'll make you something, be back in a second."

He went into the kitchen and then once there, looked in his cabinets for some tomato juice.

"Where's your bathroom," she asked shakily and he turned around and saw that she was standing up. She looked drained all of a sudden, almost pale. He ran to her side.

"Down the hall to the right. Let me help you."

"No," she said pushing him away with one hand and holding her mouth with the other and then went into the bathroom while Derek stood there a moment not knowing what to do. Then remembering her drink, he went back into the kitchen, got the glass and then got the aspirin. Ten minutes later she came out the bathroom, looking a lot better.

"I hope you don't mind I used a towel and some mouthwash."

"No, that's fine. You feel better?"

"For the most part. My head is killing me though."

"Here, take these. It should help." He handed her two aspirin and the glass.

"What is this," she asked frowning at the glass.

"Just tomato juice."

She looked at him hesitantly and then placed the aspirin in her mouth and quickly swallowed from the glass.

"Now that wasn't that bad was it?" Derek asked after she gave him the glass. She shook her head and he then went into the kitchen and came back with some coffee and placed it on the table that sat in front of the couch. She sat down on the couch and he poured a cup of the steamy liquid for her and then sat down across from her in one of the chairs that faced her. Their eyes suddenly looked at each other nervously. She fidgeted with the robe and he began to pop his knuckles. She glanced at the coffee he poured for her and then looked back at him.

"You're not going to have any?"

"Yeah, I think I will," Derek said practically jumping up out of his chair and going into the kitchen to retrieve another cup. When he came back she was sipping her coffee and kind of gazing into the fireplace across the room. He poured some coffee in his cup, took a quick sip, burning his tongue in the process. The music went off and the house became unnerving. He felt uncomfortable again. Finally he spoke.

"I have some food if you're hungry."

"No, please, don't bother," she said politely and then continued to drink her coffee as he drank his trying hard not to stare at her.

She began to look around her and at the other rooms from her view. This house was fairly new and he was not one for decorations, so he was sure she didn't have much to amuse her. His sofa was black leather, his chairs white and there was a black marble coffee table and matching end tables by the chairs.

The dining room had the same type of table except it was white and there were two leather stools in front of the counter that separated the kitchen from the living room. There were no flowers anywhere, just a few art figures that he had picked up either at the swap meet or at the art gallery near Venice Beach.

There were a couple of paintings that a college friend of his did on the walls of the living room and a bearskin rug that sat in front of the fireplace. And of course he had a decent sound system and a too big television that sat in the corner of the living room.

He figured his house needed a little something extra, but what he didn't have a clue. He just likes to come home and look out his sliding glass door that faced the ocean. Her eyes met his again and he quickly thought of something to say.

"I really could get you something to eat, it's no problem really. I was about to come up to eat when I saw you..." he stopped in mid sentence realizing what he was about to say, not sure if he should and then curiosity got the best of him.

"Listen, I know it's none of my business, but maybe it would help if you talk about it. I'm a good listener."

"I've got nothing to talk about," she said tightly starring into the fire.

He looked at her in disbelief. "You obviously tried to drown your sorrows in some bottle of whatever and then tried to drown yourself in the Pacific Ocean and you say you got nothing to talk about?"

"Well, like you said it is none of your damn business," she said and then stood up and walked over to the fireplace, her back to him.

For a moment there was silence again and then Derek finally spoke. "Was it about your husband?"

"What makes you think I'm married?" she asked turning to face him.

"Isn't that a wedding ring you're wearing on your left hand?"

She looked at him strangely and then at the ring and before he knew what was happening she pulled off the ring and threw it into the fireplace.

"Just a ring."

"So that's why you walked into the ocean? That's why you wanted to kill yourself?"

"Damn it! I wasn't trying to kill myself," she said loudly, almost yelling.

"Well, from where I stood I think otherwise. And I just think that it would do you good if you would admit to..."

"I don't have to admit a thing to you and I don't care about what you think. You know all you men are alike. You think we're going to kill ourselves over you?"

Derek sat there trying to keep himself intact suddenly angered by her categorizing him. "You don't know anything about me and I would appreciate if you didn't judge me."

"No, look at the way you live. Look at this house. I know you probably think that you are God's gift to women just because you got a little money in your pocket and we ought to be grateful that you give us the time of day," she said sarcastically meeting his eyes.

Derek was out of his seat. "I'm not going to justify the way I live to you just because it bothers you. So let's just squash this whole conversation."

"No, let's not," she said looking around the house again. "From what I can tell you're living high aren't you my brother? Or maybe you're like the average African-American male and living high off your woman, because from the looks of this robe, it's a little too frilly for your taste?"

He walked over to her and stood as closed to her as he dared and looked at her between slanted eyes. "No woman has ever helped me do a thing. I am my own man and you don't have any idea what I came from to get where I am now. And I don't need somebody that I just pulled out of the Pacific Ocean who's life had to have been so desperately sad to come here and mock me!"

"Nobody asked you to!" she shouted.

Derek looked at her heatedly. "You know you're just like everybody else that I've tried to help. You're ungrateful and you're blaming me for the mistakes that you made because you expect me to fix them. Well, you need to wake up. I can't fix your problems and I shouldn't have even tried. I should have left your ass floating."

He walked away angrily, opened the sliding door and went out to the terrace. He needed some air. He suddenly felt trapped in his own house. He couldn't believe this. Every time he tried to help someone he got his accomplishments thrown up in his face.

He inhaled deeply taking in the ocean air and closed his eyes. He was not going to let this woman get under his skin in his own house. He knew who he was and what he was about. Sure, he had a nice home, but that doesn't make him shallow or superficial.

Growing up in rat infested projects in New York made him appreciate what he now had. Watching his mother work hours in a beauty shop just to make sure her three sons kept clothes on their backs and had food to eat made him strive to get where he was today.

And being the oldest, his mother often confided in him about her heartaches and the pressure she felt trying to raise the three of them alone. He vowed to make something out of his life just for her. He wanted her to have a nice home and to be able to buy clothes for herself instead of doing without for months because she had three growing boys and no husband to help her with them.

"I'm sorry. I had no right to say those things," her soft voice said behind him.

Derek stood there a moment longer and continued to watch the ocean hit against the beach and soon his anger subsided and he turned to face her. Her eyes were filled with tears that refused to fall, making him feel bad for blowing up at her.

"No, I'm sorry. I shouldn't have pried."

She nodded her head and then looked down at the floor. "Thank you for saving my..." she started as the tears that she had been trying to hold in suddenly fell.

Awkwardly, Derek placed an arm around her shoulders and led her back inside and placed her on the couch. He went to the bar and poured them both a brandy. She reached for the glass with shaking hands and swallowed it all in one drink before he even touched his. He sat on the other end of the couch, taking a sip from his glass as she sat perfectly still crying softly to herself.

Derek now felt totally helpless again as he watched her tears rolled down her face as some fell in the empty glass she still held in her hand. Quietly, he sipped his drink as he tried to make himself invisible, feeling guilty for witnessing what was no doubt, a painful situation for her.

"I found him with another woman," she said dismally staring at the floor, her voice barely audible.

Derek looked at the pain that was clearly in her eyes as she tried not to cry anymore.

"And I know it wasn't the first time, I mean let him tell it, it comes with the business. I just thought...that he would always love me."

She choked back tears, as if she was determined not to cry. "Our whole relationship was just a joke," she continued. "I've just been in his way, holding him back. I gave up my dreams for him, would have died for that bastard and now I'm in his way," she stopped and rubbed her eyes.

Derek slid closer to her on the couch. "You know, it's not good to give so much to someone that you lose yourself in the process."

She looked at him and half laughed. "Where were you ten years ago with this advice?" she asked.

He smiled before answering. "In my own bad relationship."

"Did she cheat on you?"

"Not that I know of."

"Then what happened?"

"Oh, let's just say that I didn't live up to her expectations. I didn't have all of this."

She looked up at him as if she had just noticed his presence. Her eyes met and held his for a long moment making him feel as though she could really see him. Like she had somehow connected to a part of him that he forgot existed.

"I feel so stupid," she said closing her eyes.

"You're hurt, you're not stupid."

"My man used me. And, I let him. Stupid."

"But you know, everybody does something stupid for love."

"That's 'cause we refuse to see what is right in front of us. We want it to be perfect, and we stupidly try to hold on when we know we should just let go. I can't do this love thing again. I can't give and give and give, over and over again only to have my heart trampled on. I don't need this shit!"

"I can't say the same. I want love again."

"Why? You just said you gave your all to someone only to have her throw your heart back in your face. You can't sit there and tell me that made you feel all warm and fuzzy inside," she said sarcastically.

Derek placed his drink down and stood up, walking over to the fireplace. He took the poker and shifted the logs feeling his body stiffen as he tried to erase the memory of his past. He didn't need this. He didn't need this woman coming into his house opening old wounds that had been long closed and long forgotten. And he certainly did need her reminding him of feelings of pain and loneliness that he had long ago suppressed.

"I did it again. I'm sorry. You know what, I know you're not the reason behind my anger. You're not the one that hurt me and I shouldn't... I shouldn't be here."

She stood up and Derek turned around and faced her looking at the sadness that was written all over her face and he swore he felt her pain, her anguish. Understanding her need to lash out.

"I need to go," she whispered as more tears came in her eyes.

"Wait. Please. Don't leave like this."

He moved closer to her and placed his arms around her suddenly scared she might head back to the sea.

She let the weight of her body press against him and cried in his arms unashamed and uncontrollably, reminding him too much of a familiar pain. He began stroking her hair as she cried and cried from deep within. He held her tighter wanting to comfort her and then whispered in her ear. "It's okay."

He held her tighter and tighter not wanting to let her go. She was so warm. He looked down at her and cupped her face raising it up to meet his.

"It's going to be okay," he whispered again holding her still until she became quieter, almost calm. He looked down at her noticing her puffy eyes, her swollen lips. She was beautiful. He looked deeper into her eyes and felt the desire to touch her lips with his own. And, just as quickly, he felt overwhelmed with guilt, for thinking the things he was.

He slowly pulled away and she looked up at him locking her eyes with his. Making him feel that connection again as they stood only inches apart. Derek quickly closed his eyes, hoping she couldn't see the desire that he was sure was on his face.

"Damn," he whispered under his breath opening his eyes again only to find her looking deep into them as if she could see his soul. They stood there for moments, without words between them. Derek slowly pulled away from her arms and went back to look out the terrace door and tried to regain some composure. He couldn't understand how she seemed to be able to get under his skin so quickly. He couldn't understand that as she cried on his shoulder about her jaded lover that all he could think about was kissing her.

He turned back around and faced her again. She looked so sad, fragile. And here he was being consumed with desire and wanting to make love to her.

He walked back toward her and stood as close to her as he dared. "Would you like something else to drink?"

Another tear slowly rolled down her cheek as she sank back down to the couch shaking her head. She cried out. "I just want to pain to stop."

He sat down next to her and took her hand in his and held it. "I know."

She leaned her head against his shoulder and slowly began to cry again. Slowly without realizing it, without hesitating he leaned over and kissed her on the cheek as he stroked her face. And this time when she met his eyes, he shamefully couldn't resist. He kissed her lips, fully and fiercely. And she kissed him back, eagerly and hungrily. His hands slowly moved about her body and she never once protested. Within seconds he slowly lifted the woman that he had carried from the ocean and carried her to his bed.

Her eyes opened. She blinked and then looked up at him. The whole night he had watched her. The whole night he had held her. Half of him afraid that she would try to leave if he fell asleep and the other half of him desiring her over and over like he desired no one in a long time.

"Hi," he said when she looked over at him.

She turned away from him. "I have to go."

"I know."

He was scared for her to leave. But what could he do to stop her. She didn't belong here with him. He sat up and cupped her face in his hands but she kept her eyes down avoiding his. He then quickly removed his hands from her. "I'll go get your clothes."

When he came back she was in the bathroom. He tapped on the door and handed her clothes to her through the half open door. He then went into the kitchen and began to make a fresh pot of coffee. After about twenty minutes, the door opened and soon she was in the living room fully clothed. He walked over to her searching her eyes but she still wouldn't look at him.

"Are you going to be okay?"

She nodded her head and then headed toward his front door. Not once did she look back as she exited his life as quickly as she had entered it.

ICE

16

I do what I do because I have to. Not because I want to or even like to but because I just have to. I sat quietly on the couch and waited for a woman I didn't like for what seemed like hours. I had already grown impatient with talk T.V. and the home shopping networks and had been channel hopping when I finally heard keys turn the lock.

Sheila came in and glanced my way. A slow smile formed on her lips before she spoke.

"Hey Ice. I thought I missed you."

I stood up slowly and stepped to her. "Why you so late? Where have you been?"

"To Anaheim to see about my father. He hasn't been doing too well."

I tried to listen to her, bend a little sympathetic ear, but like I said I didn't like her. I glanced at the briefcase she held in her hand. Reminded myself why I was even here. "Did you get with A.J.?"

"Yeah," she said heading toward the kitchen. She put the briefcase on the table and then headed for the cabinet where she reached in and got a glass. She went to sink, filled her glass with water and took long swallows before heading down the hall toward her bedroom.

I went into the kitchen and sat down at the table and opened the briefcase. Rows and rows of this country's founding fathers' faces stared me in the face. I didn't count them. Didn't have to anymore. At one glance and years of experience I knew what a quarter million looked liked.

I took the four folded bags out of my coat pocket and began to fill each one with the money until all of it but five thousand was in them and then carefully placed those four bags back in my pockets. With the weight of the cash and my nine-millimeter, my three quarter length leather coat now felt like it weighed a ton.

Sheila came back into the kitchen, wearing nothing but a short see through nightgown and a wicked smile. I looked up at her hoping her radar could detect my mood and detest of her. She stepped up to me putting one of her long legs up in a chair and giving me a full view of what I did not want to see. I closed the briefcase and stood up.

"Can't you stay awhile," she asked in her fake sweet tart voice.

"No."

"Come on Ice, I'm on fire, baby."

I didn't care if she was standing there with smoke coming out of her ears and if her fake hair was blazing. I wanted no part of what she was offering. I didn't like her. I didn't like being around her. And the only reason I was is because I had to.

I left her standing in the kitchen and went to the bathroom. No sooner after I had relieved myself, she was in the bathroom with me. Her hands were on me, unzipping the pants I had just zipped up, reaching for me. I pushed her hard making her fall hard on the toilet.

I looked down at in disgust. Her eyes were bugged out. Her lips looked dry and her make up couldn't cover up her natural ugliness.

She put her hands on me again. I grabbed her by both wrists and squeezed them as tight as I could with one hand as I tried to fix my clothes with the other, all the time feeling the weight of my coat. She freed herself from my hold and then pushed me back so hard I stumbled. Before I knew it, I'd slapped her. Slapped her three times.

Black tears began to roll down her brown face. She leaped toward me and I quickly moved and she fell to the floor by the door. I began to step over her, but she grabbed my pants leg and tripped me up. I stumbled on the floor next to her. She pulled on my coat, my pants leg, anything to keep me down on the floor with her. Both of our long limbs kept getting tangled up together. I was trying not to hurt her but damn I was getting tired of this shit and was about to go for my nine when she finally just let go.

She sat in the middle of the floor crying like a five year old. Big loud, choking sobs. Her nose was running. Her shoulders were shaking as tears spilled out of her eyes over and over and as her bottom lip was turned over like a sad clown face. I stood up. She reached for me and I stepped back. Her eyes looked up at me. Pleaded with me. She put something in my hand. I looked at the condom and cursed under my breath, closing my eyes tightly and wishing I could close my ears, cause now she was begging me for it.

I opened my eyes. Caught my own reflection in the mirror and froze. I didn't like what I saw. I didn't want to be here. And I didn't like Sheila. I moved away from her, and didn't stop walking until I made it to my car.

I started the car and pressed on the accelerator with a lead foot. I zigzagged out of the parking lot, barely missed hitting the parked cars of this condo's jacked-up residents. Soon, I was on the streets were I sped up even faster. I jumped on freeway after freeway, pressing my car to the limit.

I hit eighty, ninety, a hundred and twenty miles per hour. And still I wasn't going fast enough. I couldn't get away from what I was running from. Even with close to quarter million dollars in my pockets, I knew I couldn't get away from myself, and this hell called my life.

I slowed down when I reached the dirt road that led to my ranch located just south of Palm Springs. I eased my car into a covered garage and then entered the darkness of my 4,500 square foot home on the range without even gazing toward the rolling hills of my six acres. Straight away, I reached for a bottle of Jack Daniels and a shot glass, which I filled up and emptied four times before I felt myself even calm down a little.

I sat down in my deep brown leather recliner, closed my eyes, and listened to the quiet around me. No gunfire, no helicopters, no screaming, just quietness. Sheila's tear stained face appeared behind my closed lids. I poured another shot and downed it trying to erase her from my memory, but it was to no avail. She was a part of me, an ugly part. A part that reminded me of who and what I am.

A drug dealer, dope pusher, the man, gangsta, thug, whatever the hell you want to call it. I sold hash, marijuana, crack, cocaine, ice, heroin, uppers and downers. Whatever you desired. Over the years, I have made countless trips to Jamaica, Mexico, the Caribbean, Cuba and all across these fifty United States. Wherever and whenever, I boarded planes with enough drugs strapped to my body to send me to jail for at least three life times and have counted enough money to make me a billionaire twice over.

I've seen I don't know how many drive-bys. Seen kids as young as nine die at my feet because they wanted to run with the big dogs and thought they could be big ballers and shot callers. They see the big cars and the endless cash and think they can hang.

But that's not why I'm here. I wasn't looking for the life. I'm just living it because it was all I could do. Some people in life get choices. Some people get none. Where do you think I fit in? Beep, wrong damn answer, because right now, it really don't matter. I am what I have become, a menace to society. A man who's not fit to walk this earth on two legs because of some of the things I have done, a man trying to escape his own reality.

And so what if I am no longer on the streets and hanging out in alleys. I have paid my dues and moved my way up the so-called ladder. Now, I don't get my hands dirty by touching the product but instead I keep the money clean. I'm the laundry man. I know damn near a hundred ways to get rid of a quarter million and still have it come back to you when you need it without a trace.

But now I'm tired, damn tired. Tired of Sheila drooling at me every time I make a pick up. Even though I know that's my fault 'cause I never should have messed with her in the first place. But she caught me at a real low moment and I gave in to her constant come-ons and now she thinks she can have a piece of me every time she sees me. Always throwing in my face that it is her uncle who is really running things.

But what she doesn't know is that I don't give a damn. I let that monkey go a long time ago. Slaughter can only do to me what I let him do. His stupid idle threats have long expired. I'm at the end of my rope. I've been living this life a long ass time and it's time for me to make my move.

John Slaughter can kiss my black ass. He gets no respect from me. I'm just biding my time, sitting here waiting. Waiting on a new day. That's why, for now, I do what I do. Not because I want to or even like to but because, shit, right now I just have to.

NICOLE

17

I entered the house that I had spent the most important years of my life, the house that had healed me. It was early, quiet. I walked across the marble floored foyer and went into the living room and was still able to see my various memories still there. My many days spent in a welcome solitude and my many days filled with laughter. This house was my haven. My save place. Here, I was once again part of a family.

I looked into the fireplace and could see the embers of a fire that was probably from the night before. I could still feel its warmth. The winding staircase that led up to my old bedroom was on the left. It's beautiful brown arms glowing in the early morning sunlight that came in from the bay window.

In the kitchen, everything was still and still the same. The same appliances, the same table, the same small television on the counter that Anthony Marcus was always glued to and the same stools at the breakfast counter where Michael and I used to always sit. I looked at the stove. I could almost see Devon scrambling eggs and flipping pancakes. Just being here made me realize how much I missed her.

I came to her a scrappy teenager who had seen too much and had lived through too much pain. She took me in, nursed me, guided me, and no matter how much I tried to reject her love she kept on giving it. She gave me strength and told me over and over that I had a purpose in life. I needed her strength now, but now she was gone. All I have now is my memories. I don't even have the money she left me. Devon died seven years ago. Her best advice to me was that it is never too late to change your life.

For years, she worked for the rich, cleaning bathrooms she couldn't even use to feed her two growing sons and make sure they went to college. Her husband died of a heart attack when Marcus' father was twelve and she had to struggle to make ends meet. She liked to sew and for years she made clothes for friends and charged them a minimal price. Then, at age forty-five, a friend of hers talked her into designing clothes and before you know it, her designs could be found in Rodeo Drive's best stores. Six years later, she was a self-made millionaire. Her boys finished college and Lewis, Michael's father, even went to law school.

Her children grown and gone, she found this house and fell in love with it and moved in. For years, she lived alone and traveled abroad and then, when Michael's mother passed, he came to live with her. And then a year later, Marcus and I came. When she passed, she left the house to the three of us and left each one of her grandchildren, including me, two hundred and fifty thousand dollars.

Michael used most of his money to refurbish the house and invested in stocks. He lived in the house and lived off the interest so he wouldn't have to work and could concentrate on his singing career. Marcus bought Taylor Motors and now is making end over ends. Stupid me invested all of my funds into James' career and now have what--an ungrateful man who wants nothing to do with me?

I walked over and opened a familiar cupboard, found the coffee and began to make a fresh pot. I sat quietly at the breakfast table near the window and looked out at the morning sky, enjoying it's peacefulness and tranquility. Soon the coffee was ready and I got up to fix me a cup but then stop when I heard footsteps.

"Is that you, Nicki? "

I turned around and faced Michael as he stood on the last step of the back stairwell that led into the kitchen from upstairs. "I didn't mean to wake you."

He came across the floor and stood inches in front of me and his eyes began to search mine. He placed a finger on my soiled and torn clothing, his eyebrows raised.

"Are you all right," he asked with a concerned voice.

I looked at him briefly and managed to nod my head and then stared down at the floor and started counting the tiled squares on the floor.

"You made coffee," he stated looking about the kitchen.

I looked back at him as he reached into the cupboards and pulled out two cups and placed them on the counter. I sat down in my old seat at the counter as he poured coffee, added cream and sugar to mine and just sugar to his. He sat down beside me and sipped his coffee in silence. Every now and then he looked at me with an unasked question in his eyes and I yielded nothing but silence in return. Finally, when his cup was empty he turned and faced me.

"Talk to me," he said taking my hands into his.

I let out a heavy sigh. With Michael, I knew I never had to really say a word and I knew I could come to him with anything. He knew what hurt me and he was always there. He didn't understand or even like my relationship with James but he never judged me. He just listened to me. Sometimes he would give his advice, but most times not. He just listened.

But it was never easy talking to Michael. He had a way of looking at me that made me see myself no matter how much I tried to hide from myself.

I began to speak, slowly unfolding the scene I witnessed at my house the night before. His eyes became angered when I explained my rage and saddened when I spoke of my sorrow.

I couldn't tell him everything. I couldn't tell him how weak I felt and how, just maybe, I was trying to kill myself when I went into the ocean. I didn't want to see that part of myself in his eyes.

He comforted me. Holding me and stroking my arms, reassuring me that nothing else was going to happen. I was safe here. I was home.

Hearing those words I began to cry again. Just hearing those words made me realize how I had spent countless years looking for a place that I belonged. And every time I got comfortable with my surroundings, home was gone. Somehow, I had convinced myself that my life with James would last forever.

Michael continued to hold me until the tears stopped. We have been here before too many times; me crying and with Michael holding me. Finally I pulled away.

"You okay, Nicki?"

I nodded yes. I knew he knew I was lying. But I refused to keep crying and to keep hurting. I finally spoke holding in my tears. "Mike, tell me something."

"What?" he said as he wiped away dried tears from my face.

"How come I'm the last one to know that James was incapable of loving anyone but himself?"

"I don't know, Nicki."

"I mean, how is it that when it comes to James, I am totally blind, totally lost and totally in the dark."

"Nicki, don't do this to yourself. You did right by him. All you did was love him."

"But I needed him to love me. Why didn't he love me back?"

"Nicki, you have already said the answer to that question. He only loves himself. James doesn't have a clue on how to love anyone. He never could see or appreciate the kind of woman you are. You're a good woman, Nicki. You need to believe in yourself. You don't need him to make you, you. Hell, you know it's the other way around. And he's going to realize that when all of his shit hits the fan."

I sat there silently taking in his every word remembering how devoted I was to James and how I would have done anything in my power to make him a success. But that was before the baby. I hadn't felt like that in three years.

I gave up trying to light his path and let him go on his own. I quit caring what he did, if his songs were number one or how long his concert tours were going to last. So why was I so broken up inside? His words haunted me. I don't love you.

"And then there was the car accident," Michael was saying as he stood in the refrigerator taking out the milk, eggs, ham and cheese.

I looked up at him as he stuck his head out the refrigerator door.

"When were you in an accident?"

"Oh, so you are listening to me."

I sighed heavily, "I'm sorry, Mike. My head is not screwed on tight this morning."

He placed the items on the counter by the stove and closed the refrigerator.

"Look, Nicki, why don't you go upstairs, take a hot shower and find some fresh clothes. I'm sure the hot water will clear your head and make you feel better. By then, I'll have breakfast ready."

"I'm not hungry."

"Now how are you going to pass up my world famous ham and cheese omelet and my delicious buttermilk pancakes?"

"Well..."

"I didn't think you could. Now get on upstairs and get cleaned up."

Michael was right. The minute I stepped out of the shower, I felt a hundred times better even if I didn't look it. I looked into the mirror and stared into my eyes. I had placed a steamy hot towel on my face hoping some of the puffiness would go away, but it hadn't. There they were, like luggage, two big bags under my eyes carrying the weight of my tears and all my hours of crying. I wish I had some makeup.

I had washed my hair so I quickly blow-dried it and then pulled it into one ponytail in the back grateful that I had at least had a fresh perm. I found a new toothbrush, brushed my teeth and gargled. I went into my old room, looked in the closet, and was thankful that I still kept my old clothes here. I pulled out a pair of Levi's and found an old UCLA sweatshirt. In the dresser, I found underwear and socks and quickly got dressed as the smell of food began to linger in the air and my stomach began to growl.

I started down the hall but stopped when I heard Michael talking to somebody. I ducked into Michael's room and looked out the window. Marcus' car was in the driveway. I sat on the bed. Damn, facing Michael was bad enough but facing Marcus was going to be even tougher. He knew me inside out. I can't lie to him or hide from him. I can't fool him. He's going to ask every detail of what happened last night until the moment I walked into this door. I took a deep breath and headed down the stairs. They both turned and faced me when I reached the kitchen.

"Breakfast is ready, Nicki. So dig in where you fit in," Michael said smiling at me.

I crossed the kitchen and pretended to look at the food on the table. "Yeah, everything smells ready."

"Hey, Nicki, " Marcus said in a somewhat quiet tone and I could tell that

Michael had already told him about my situation. I looked at the floor and then at him as I nervously played with my hands before speaking.

"Hi."

"How you doing?"

I met his eyes and saw just the hint of disgust and anger in them for my relationship with James. I couldn't take his 'I told you so and James' is nothing but a flea bitten mutt' routine. Right now, I hurt. And when I hurt, no bad mouthing words were going to make me feel better. I held my head up high and looked him straight in the eyes as I spoke.

"Look, I know Mike's probably told you why I'm here and believe me the last thing I want to do now is to relive that whole scenario over again. So please, if you don't mind, spare me the pain of repeating the details. And please don't start in on bad mouthing James. I've heard it all. I know what you're going to say. I just can't deal with all that right now. I just can't."

The last words out of my mouth just couldn't come out without a whimper. I quickly brushed new tears from my eyes while my friend stepped closer to me. His eyes softened and his arms opened before he spoke.

"Come here."

I fell in and the damn broke. He squeezed me tighter, and the river overflowed and I couldn't stop it. Tears just came out of nowhere and out of everywhere. Tears from yesterday, yesteryears and maybe even tears of tomorrow poured from my soul. I just couldn't stop.

And he held me. He rocked me and squeezed me until no more tears fell. I finally pulled away and stared at a place on his polo shirt that was wet with my tears. His hand came under my chin and pulled my face to his. Gently, he kissed my forehead and then smiled into my eyes. I felt so totally safe and so totally ashamed of my behavior. How many times had I been here?

"I'm sorry. I shouldn't be giving you a hard time one minute and then crying on your shoulder the next."

"Hey, I can take it. Besides, this is your shoulder, whenever you need it. It's always here. And so am I Nic. Whatever you need, I'm here."

I looked up into my best friend's eyes and knew he meant every word. Knew I could count on him at any time. Knew I wasn't alone.

"I know."

"So you want me to go over there and jack that fool up, thrash his car, burn his bed? Hey, just say the word and it's done."

I couldn't help but smile at what he said as it reminded me of the Anthony Marcus I knew so long ago. Always looking to take someone out. Nothing at all like the serious businessman, Marcus Washington, that he was today.

"That's okay. I just need that shoulder."

He squeezed me in his arms again. "Anytime baby. Now come on let's eat some of this good food my cousin fixed up here. A brother like me is starving like Marvin."

He pulled out a chair. I sat down and then him and Michael joined me. Just as Michael was about to pass the platter of pancakes my way, the doorbell rang.

"Damn, a brother can't even get his eat on," Michael said going to the door as Marcus stood up and went to turn on the television. I poured myself some orange juice and sipped it slowly as I heard Michael raise his voice in the living room.

"What's the hell is this all about?" Michael was shouting.

"I have a warrant," A male voice spoke from the living room.

Marcus and I looked at each other and two of us hurriedly headed out of the kitchen. Michael was standing in the foyer talking to a short white man wearing a pale blue powdered suit waving a badge and a folded piece of paper. He looked up when he saw us come into the room.

"Nicole Williams?" he asked.

I looked at him in horror. "Yes."

"I'm Detective Johnson and I have a warrant for your arrest. You are being charged for the murder of James Fulton."

My knees buckled under me, as a slow scream seemed to come from the pit of my stomach. "No! No!" I yelled, not feeling the hot tears that eased out of eyes once again. This can't be happening. It can't be.

"What the hell are you talking about," Marcus shouted out taking the warrant from the man's hand.

I watched as his eyes quickly read the piece of paper and then crumbled it up and threw it on the floor. I didn't kill him. I couldn't have. God what have I done? What have I done?

"This is bullshit," Marcus spit out at the officer.

The man ignored him and approached me grabbing my hands and placing them behind my back.

"Step back man, get your hands off of her," Marcus said pushing him.

"Look I'm just trying to do my job."

"Well, right about now I think you need to find another job. You're not taking her anywhere," Marcus shouted standing inches in front of him.

They stood there glaring at each other as Michael and I looked on in total disillusion.

"Say, Collins, get in here. We got a situation," the officer turned and yelled out the door.

The door soon opened and another man walked in. I looked at him and shook my head with disbelief. This can't be happening.

MARCUS

18

My father once told me about change. Told me there are some things in life that you never know are going to happen. No matter how hard you try to plan, map out or follow a certain direction, your life will change in an instant, over and over again. And no matter what you do, you can't stop change. If it's in your deck of cards, it's coming. Change is what controls your life and it's what you have to accept. The only thing certain about change is that you never know when it's going to happen until it happens. It's secret is it's element of surprise. And it was here.

I never knew that I would watch the police drag her away with her hands handcuffed behind her. I never dreamed I would feel such sorrow as I stood motionless unable to stop it from happening. Unable to do anything but stare out at the street until the car was out of sight and there was nothing left to see.

I ran to the car and retrieved my address book. Quickly my fingers went through the pages until I found the number I was looking for. I pulled out my phone and dial the numbers. I spoke hurriedly, urgently and couldn't remember my exact words but I just knew that I had to say something, do something, anything to help her. I looked back at the house as if she would still be in the kitchen. I turned on the ignition, stepped on the gas and sped down the street. I didn't realize Michael was beside me until I got half way down the block.

At the police station we were told what I already knew. We couldn't see her. But we had to be here. We sat on cold benches in the middle of a cold hallway. Strangers walked by. Some in uniform, more in handcuffs. And we sat and sat and watched time slip by on the huge clock that faced us.

Out of the corner of my eye, I saw Michael looking just as confused and angry as myself. Neither one of us cared for James, neither one of us wanted Nicole with him, but neither one of us could ever come between them. And now I'm wondering if either one of us even tried.

Michael turned to me and told me again what Nicole had told him just hours before. She spoke of James' betrayal, she talked about being angry and hurt but she never let on that something like this had happened. Never did. We were clueless. I stood up and pulled out my cell phone and called Jackson again.

"Jack, this is Marcus. How far away are you?"

"I ran into some traffic on 10. Could be here a while."

I listened to dead air not wanting to know the answer to my next question but had to ask it anyway. "Give me worst case, Jackson."

"She could be denied bail."

I squeezed the phone so tight my hands began to throb. "But this is her first offense."

"Doesn't matter if they're talking capital."

My insides started doing some serious flips. I couldn't believe this was happening. I hung up the phone. Michael's eyes met mine. They looked like mine.

I sat back down on the bench and felt my body slowly go numb. I couldn't feel my own breath. And I couldn't stop thinking about and cursing James Fulton's very existence. I should have done something! But I did nothing. I stayed clear of their relationship. I silently sat by and did nothing even if I knew something between them wasn't right. It was her life, her choice. The most I did was listen to her whenever she was so fed up she had to vent out. But I did nothing.

Three hours later, they led me into a small room after I had been searched like I was a permanent resident. After I lied to one and told him I was her attorney and slipped five bills to another to see her. I took a seat at a wide table that had two chairs.

Seconds later another door opened and Nicole came in accompanied by a officer who led her to the other seat and then stood only inches away from her not once acknowledging my presence. I instinctively reached across the table to touch her but the officer quickly stepped up. I looked at him and then looked into her eyes.

I suddenly recognized the look that had haunted me for years. The look of despair, anguish, fear, pain, confusion, anger and emptiness all rolled up into one. The look that said she needed me, but couldn't tell me how. I felt like I was six inches tall and like I was sixteen years old again. Finding her hurt beyond repair.

I sat there. Quietly. But in my mind I cursed everything under the sun for what she was going through. My father's words echoed in my ears. I hated change. Always had a hard time accepting it. Change has never been good to me. But it was here. I could feel it all up in my bones. Felt its presence the moment they put those handcuffs on her wrists. Saw it now in her tear-stained face and her haunting eyes.

I sat there. Promising myself to get her out of here. Promising myself to take her away from this pain. And this time I was going to do it right and not let her push me away when I knew she needed me the most. I was here to catch her when she fell.

Suddenly Nicole met my eyes as if she just realized I was sitting across from her. Her lips began to tremble and I couldn't fight my urge to hold her. I stood up, pushed the officer out the way. I knelt down in front of her and embraced all of her that I could. Felt her body shake and give in to the aching sobs that were now rumbling out. I squeezed her tighter. Let her pain absorb me. Whispered in her ear that I would do everything possible to get her out of here. She kept crying. It was if the tears couldn't stop. I stroked her hair and arms that were handcuffed behind her. And her tears kept on falling.

"Come on man you got to go," the officer said tapping me on my shoulder. "Time's up."

I let her go. Stood up and watched him take her away.

An hour later, after I had talked to everybody that was anybody, I was faced with the fact that I had to leave her. There was nothing that I could do. I couldn't stay with her. I had money and could get my hands on thousands more but I couldn't get her out. I couldn't do anything. The wheels of justice surely didn't turn on the weekend and the way Jackson was talking they might not turn at all in her favor.

Michael and I drove back to the house in complete silence. Neither one of us still couldn't believe what was happening. Just this morning the three of us were about to sit down to have breakfast together.

Now Michael and I walked into the house and found cold pancakes and hot orange juice sitting out on the table. I watched as Michael picked up the food and threw it in the trashcan, plate and all and then poured the orange juice down the sink.

He finally turned to face me and I could see the brother's question in his eyes. But this time I couldn't answer him. I left Michael in the quietness of his home with his own thoughts. I had too many thoughts of my own to deal with.

DEREK

19

Assistant District Attorney Derek Alexander walked into the Los Angeles County Courthouse. He had just heard about the biggest crime this courthouse has seen since the O.J. Simpson case- the murder of famed singer James Fulton. He felt his blood pumping rapidly throughout his body.

He knew for a fact that his name was on the list for this case. His boss had just last week told him that he was impressed with his work and that the next big case would be his. And this was it. And he couldn't believe his luck because it should be an open and shut case. He already talked to the detectives and he already knew that they found the murder weapon at the scene with the prints. Case closed.

Derek walked into the conference room and sat down among his peers and soon after the two detectives assigned to the case came in. They briefly told everyone that they have the accused in custody but however she did not make any statement. Derek felt relieved. It was best this way. They didn't need her to say anything and then say the police coerced her. Get her attorney present.

"Who is representing her?" Derek asked.

"That is unknown at this time," Detective Johnson stated. Derek nodded his head with thoughts of the best way to get her convicted of first-degree murder. He looked through the file that was on the table. Saw the pictures of the crime scene; the victim, the gun and then their prime suspect mug shot.

Derek's heart stopped beating. He couldn't believe it. It was her! The woman he pulled out of the Pacific. The woman he took to his house. The one he made love to!

He shook his head in disbelief and clumsily knocked over a pitcher of water that was in front of him. Everyone in the room turned and looked at him as he jumped up when the water began to run off the table and wet his pants just as someone joked and asked him if he was having a little trouble holding his water as the others laughed.

Derek looked around him and quickly excused himself, practically running out of the room and down to his office. He paced the floor, his mind racing. What was he going to do? How was he going to explain this? How in the hell could he have slept with a cold-blooded murderer?

He quickly removed his wet trousers pulled out some sweats from his gym bag, put them on and then plunged down in his chair as question after question ran through his mind.

Had she set him up? Did she see him jogging on the beach and decided to fake a suicide attempt by plunging into the ocean just so he would save her and boom she had an alibi?

And how she seduced him with those big brown sad eyes and those big crocodile tears? She planned the whole thing! The way she cried in his arms, pressing her body into his. Yes, she knew all too well what she was doing to him was driving him crazy with desire. And the way she looked at him, the way she practically held him with her eyes.

Damn! How could he have been so stupid? Had it been so long that he slept with a woman that he didn't even recognize a set up? Was he so desperate for a woman's touch that he didn't mind sleeping with the first one that came his way? A murderer!

Derek suddenly felt sick to his stomach as little beads of sweat formed on his forehead. He felt his hands become sweaty and his stomach began to tie up in a big knot. He began to stand but instantly was forced back down when a pain from his stomach shot through him. What was he going to do? How can he explain that he slept with the accused right after she killed her husband?

There was a knock on his door and before he could respond his brother Gerald rushed in with a surprised look on his face and threw the front page of the Times on his desk.

"Tell me you are surprised as I am," Gerald spoke before taking a seat across from Derek. Derek let out a heavy sigh and barely glanced at the paper. He didn't want to see it. Instead he looked over at Gerald, and even found that difficult.

Another knock was at the door. His colleague, Sarah McAdams stuck her head in the door.

"You decent?"

"What?" Derek answered still trying not to look at the picture on the front page that stared in him the face.

"You have on pants or are you in your BVD's."

"Oh, I'm cool."

Sarah pushed the door ajar and strolled in the office letting out a long whistle. "Damn, Alexander you are one lucky dog! Oh, Hi Gerald."

"Hi, Sarah," Gerald uttered even though it seem like Sarah didn't care he if spoke or not. She was obviously excited about something.

"What are you talking about?" Derek asked.

"You know who got the Fulton case don't you?"

"Who?"

"Who do you think?"

"You?"

"You, knucklehead. Looks like you in there. Get with me later. I want to hear your strategy," Sarah voiced happily and then headed for the door. "Nice to see you again, Gerald," she threw over her shoulder and then closed the door behind her.

As soon as the door closed the two brothers eyes met.

Gerald asked. "You got time for lunch."

"Definitely."

They sat across from each other at a sandwich shop that was across the street from the courthouse. On the brief walk over they remained completely silent. Both were wrapped up in their own thoughts. Drawing out their own conclusions as they tried to answer the million-dollar question that was on everybody's mind.

A waitress came and took their order. Gerald ordered a BLT and Derek a turkey sandwich, even though he couldn't even phantom the thought of eating right now. He stared out the window, looking toward the courthouse steps. His steps. His throne.

Gerald stared at his older brother noting the tension in his eyes. "The paper didn't mention her drowning. So I take it they don't know you found her at the beach."

"They don't know the half of it," Derek admitted letting out a long sigh.

Hesitantly Gerald asked, "What happened after I left?"

Before he answered Derek met his brother's eyes and then let out another long sigh. "I slept with her."

"Tell me you're joking, man."

"Gerald, I made love to a cold-blooded murderer! I wouldn't joke about a thing like that."

"Do you really think she did him?"

"I don't know," Derek, acknowledged staring out the window and then looking back as his brother again. "I don't know what to think. I mean when we were together, it was so right. I didn't want her to leave."

"Did she even mention Fulton?"

"She didn't say his name, but she did tell me how she found him with another woman in their bed. She gave me this long account on how he somehow turned everything around and then totally rejected her. Telling her that he didn't want or need her anymore.

"But she never ever said anything about a gun. She never said he attacked her or that she had to defend herself against him. Which leaves me no choice but to think that she planned our whole encounter. She saw me, and she swooped down and seized the opportunity to have an alibi. I'm a witness that can put her far away from the crime scene. A witness she could easily seduce and then have tangled up in her web of lies."

"But you yourself said you saw her first, walking into the Pacific."

"I was out running. The lights were on at the house. She knew someone had to be around."

"I don't know, D. It sounds like just a coincidence to me."

"No. It sounds like my job just went down the drain to me."

* * * * *

"Say, Alexander, I hear you're the HNIC," the young officer guarding the interrogation room door said as soon as Derek walked up.

"Let me in," Derek said formally ignoring his remark.

The officer pulled out his keys, opened the door and began to lead the way but Derek quickly grabbed his arm pulling him back.

"Alone."

"All right now, you're the man," the officer stated backing up and then closing the door behind Derek.

He entered the room without once looking at the woman that he had met only once and had without haste taken to his bed. He quickly walked over to the double glass mirror, pulled the blinds down and then walked over to the table and reached under and turned off the small microphone. She slowly turned around and faced him as he began to walk toward her clapping his hands in a slow motion.

"For best performance as an outstanding lead actress, the Oscar goes to Ms. Nicole Williams."

She looked up at him her face full of wonder.

"Oh, now wait a minute. I think you deserve two Oscars. You actually look surprised to see me."

He took the one of the chairs across from her and put it right next to hers and sat down with his face inches from hers. "I feel like we need to reintroduce ourselves to one another," he began with his breath hitting her face as he spoke in a low voice. "I guess when you so willingly fell into my arms and into my bed you failed to mention that you are cold blooded killer. I guess you thought that part wouldn't turn me on."

Tears quickly formed in her eyes and she ashamedly lowered her eyes from his.

Derek raised his hand and wiped the tears from her eyes as she flinched at his touch and as more tears began to slide down her face.

"You are good you know," Derek said getting closer to her face. "I mean I can't tell you how terrified I was when I plunged into water after you. I had to dive in over and over again before I found you. Then when you were unconscious I thought you were dying or maybe already dead. And then you awoke just for a second. Just long enough for me to see the pain in those big brown eyes of yours.

"In my home, I watched you as you laid on my couch looking so beautiful and innocent as you slept. And I couldn't stop thinking about how tragic that this beautiful woman tried to end her life. I kept asking myself why didn't she want to live, what was missing from her life? And then I thought, maybe you were like me. You know, alone and lonely for the companionship and comfort of someone special.

"God, I felt so guilty when I realized that even as you slept I wanted to hold you, soothe you and yes make love to you. But little did I know that what I desired to happen was all part of your master plan."

"No," she cried out in a raspy voice.

"Oh come on now!" Derek practically yelled at her. "I admit I'm a little slow but I have finally figured out my role in this motion picture of yours. I played the part of the sucker. The dumb smuck who finds the beautiful woman that fakes an attempted suicide and then pleads her way into my bed just hours after she killed her husband!"

Suddenly he stood up and begins pacing the floor, his body seething with anger as she watched him.

"Please you've got to help me. I'm so scared," she cried out again.

"Help you. You want me to help you? You have just screwed up my life and you're asking me for help? Everything that I have worked so hard for is finished because of you!" Derek roared at her. "And why? Why me? Did our paths cross somewhere in the past and I just can't for the life of me remember when? Did I do something to someone in your family or run over your damn dog? Why have you destroyed my life?"

"Why are talking to me like this, what about me? I'm the one facing murder charges," she screamed back at him.

Derek walked back to her and leaned over his face directly in front of hers. "And guess what? The very man that pulled you out of the great Pacific is the same man that is supposed to make those murder charges stick. You're looking at the lead prosecutor who has been assigned to your case," he stated.

"No, this is not happening."

"You're right. It's not. But isn't that exactly what you planned," Derek began as he once again started pacing the length of the small room. "Forget that I have worked my ass off for this office for over six years! Forget that I have had to dot every 'I', cross every 'T' and win every case I have ever been assigned. I have had to keep my private life private and in public make sure I was on my best behavior, because I tell you, you never know when they're watching you.

"For six years I have lived like this, basically having no life outside of my career. And guess what, it paid off. Thanks to all my hard work, I have made a name for myself and have become a respected prosecutor. But now, thanks to you, I find myself right smack in the middle of a scandal. Can't you see the headlines? 'Murderess Nicole Williams beds Assistant District Attorney, Derek K Alexander hours after she knocked off her old man!' All my dreams, my whole career is all over, all over, because of one very sweet piece of ass!" Derek concluded standing as close to her as he dared, his body fuming with anger.

"I haven't told anyone about you. I won't mention that you found me and that...that you saved my life."

"You expect me to believe anything you say to me now?"

"Yes! You saved my life. I owe you..."

"I don't want you to owe me anything. I don't even want to know you," Derek said with disgust.

"And you don't have to. Look, just take my confession and there won't even have to be a trial. I killed my husband."

Derek looked at her as more tears began to stream down her face as she continued. "Everything that I told you before is true. I just didn't tell you everything. I didn't tell you about the gun. I was so angry and hurt when James said that he didn't love me. That hurt more than finding him with that woman. I felt sick and my heart ached so bad I thought I was dying.

"I just didn't understand how he could be so cruel. How could he just treat me like some washed up dishrag or something? I loved him. And God help me, I still do. You don't spend ten years with somebody and cut off your feelings in a second's notice. At least I can't. But he could. He had no problem standing there just moments after he slept with that woman in our bed and then telling me to get lost and to get out of his life. He had no problem hurting me!

"After everything we've been through together he deliberately hurt me by telling me that he didn't love me, that he didn't want me! I just wanted him to shut up and take back all the things he was saying to me. So I pulled out the gun. I didn't shoot it at first. I just held it on him. But he wouldn't shut up.

"He just kept telling me over and over that he didn't love me. And I don't even know how or why but I fired the gun. And I didn't even stick around to see where I hit him. I turned and left. I didn't know I killed him until this morning when the police picked me up."

Derek stared at her hard as she spoke. She was either one hell of an actress or she was telling him truth. And God forgive him he believed her. He walked over closer to her.

"How many times did you fire the gun," he asked calmly.

"Once."

"Are you sure?"

"I'm positive. What difference does it make if I killed him?"

"Because your husband was shot six times," Derek stated brutally and watched as her face twist in horror.

"No, that's not true! I couldn't have shot him that many times and not know it. It was just once. I shot the gun once and left."

"After you fired the gun what did you do with it?"

"I dropped it on the floor."

"What room where you in?"

"We were still in the bedroom."

"He was murdered in the living room, as he came in through the front door."

"What are you saying?"

"What I'm saying is that from what you just told me and if it is the truth..."

"It is the truth. I have no reason to lie to you."

"If it is the truth," Derek repeated and then continued. "And once I know the time of his death, then I will know for sure that you were not the one that kill him. After all you were with me most of the night. That I'm sure of."

"Oh God. I didn't do it. I didn't kill him."

"But you tried. Maybe you had someone else finish the job."

"Go to hell," she shouted at him angrily.

"No, that's where you will go if you don't cooperate with me. My ass is on the line here. I can keep my mouth closed and never tell anyone that I ever laid eyes on you before today. Or, I can, once again, save you. And in order for me to even think about doing that, I want to hear every damn detail of that day including what you had for breakfast that morning. No lies, no games and I better damn well be able to find proof to everything you tell me.

"I want to know if you made one phone call after you left that house or made any stops before you reached that beach where I found you. And believe me, I will check out everything you tell me with a fine toothed comb. I want a list of all your friends and your family, what they do for a living, if you talk to any of them at any time that day, and if anyone of them would have gladly finished the job you started. Do I make myself clear?"

"Yes."

Derek pulled out the small tape recorder from his jacket pocket. "Start talking."

ICE

20

Everything was foul and has been every since that damn Fulton got his. Seemed like this whole city has just turned upside down. Stupid Sheila was blowing up my pager. Every three minutes the damn thing was beeping like crazy. She even put in a 911 thinking that would make me hurry up and call her back. But I don't work like that. She didn't own me and no matter what she thought she didn't control me.

Hell wasn't it enough that I housed her ass in that $400,000 condo and bought and paid for damn near everything she had. Wasn't she rolling her ass down Rodeo Drive in a shiny new Corvette that I bought and buying up everything at the drop of a hat?

Uncle Johnny wasn't putting her down like that. I was. She needed to be happy with what she had instead of wasting my time talking about what she thinks she wants. Hell I had more important things to do. Like come with a plan to get my ass out of her and her Uncle's life.

My cell phone rang. I looked at the caller ID. It was Slaughter. I picked up on about the sixth ring just to mess with him.

"Yeah."

"What's up, Ice Man?" Slaughter's voice said all too clear and for once I hated the clarity of wireless remote.

"'Sup, Slaughter."

"I need to see you."

"About?"

"I'll tell you when you get here. I'm waiting," the bastard said and then hung up. Damn. Didn't even ask me if I was in the middle of something. I hung up his line and then dial Sheila's digits. I don't even think the phone ring before she picked it up.

"Ice. I need to see you."

"So does your uncle."

"I need to see you before he does. It's important."

"Whatever it is you better speak your piece now 'cause right about now I'm rolling to see him."

"It's about Fulton."

"The singer."

"Yeah. I was with him the night he got it."

I sat up in my seat. Paid her trifling behind a little more attention. "Didn't know you knew him."

I heard her let a long breath and could picture her rolling her eyes in her head. "Like I'm the only woman you lay down with."

More like the only woman I didn't want to lay with is what I wanted to tell her but I just gave her a cool whatever.

"Look Ice, if the police come asking me anything, I'm gonna say I was with you."

I was about to blow her off but my curiosity got the better of me. "Why?"

"Cause I just don't want no static."

"Why should LA's finest come messing with you? Did you pop him?"

"Hell no. You know that his so called wife was arrested for that."

"Just because she was arrested doesn't mean she did it."

"I'm sorry about it, 'cause I'm putting my money on her."

"Then why are blowing me up 911?"

"Damn, Ice can't you just cover for me?"

I thought about it. Thought about it for about two damn seconds.

"No." I hung up the phone.

Slaughter was drinking a glass of red wine when I walked into the Jake's Bar and Grille. A half empty plate sat in front of his fat ass on the table with the remnants of steak and fried potatoes left on it. His favorite guard dogs, Tre Dog and John Jr. a/k/a Assault and Battery were trying to look inconspicuous at another table across from him.

I looked around and saw some peeps in the back playing pool. I nodded to them just to let them know I see them. A few nodded back and some didn't. Which was cool. I wasn't in the front line anymore and I like it that way. I figure the less people that knew me the better.

I slid in Slaughter's booth just as he was trying to pick steak out of his teeth with a damn knife. He had his head half cocked to one side, mouth wide open and was trying to stick that knife between tooth number sixteen and seventeen. Guess he never heard of a toothpick or dental floss.

I rubbed my hands across my tired eyes. "'Sup, Slaugher."

He brought his eyes to mine and folded one of his hands around his glass. "Got a job for you."

"What else is new," I said nonchalantly. I didn't mean to sound like I didn't give a damn but unfortunately I'm one of those people that can't fake the funk. I say everything as I see it and feel it. Which I know pisses Slaughter off but hey, if he don't know me by now, then the hell with him.

He gave me his glare that was suppose to intimidate me but only made my ass laugh which didn't make things any better. Then he started loud talking me and asking me if I was dissin' him. Which made A & B looked over at our table like they were going to do something.

I threw my hands up let the shit go. They just didn't get it. I was just ready for this man to state his business and let me rise up out of here. There was no need for polite conversation. Hell, we weren't friends. I didn't like his ass.

Slaughter growled at me. "There's a run Thursday that I need you to handle."

I shook my head. "No can do, J.S."

He glared at me. "What you mean you can't do it? You do whatever the hell I tell you to do!"

I looked at him and wondered if Sesame Street came on back in his day cause I swear he didn't know what the word NO meant. I stayed calm. Maybe his ass was suffering from that Alzheimer disease and he didn't know what he was supposed to know.

"Look, Slaughter, my job duties have been redefined. I don't touch the stuff."

Slaughter eased back in his seat and I could tell he was trying to think of a new approach. "Ice I don't have no one else, you understand? A.J. ran into a little situation and business still got to go on. I'm asking you this one time. You're the only other person I trust, son."

Got to hand to Slaughter, he wasn't too proud to beg when it came to moving the product. But he was damn unfortunate. I knew if I did it this one time there would be another time. I had to stand my ground. "Sorry, Slaughter, I'm not the one. Get your boy Tre Dog over there. He needs to learn the ropes."

I stood up. It was time for me to go. Slaughter grabbed my shirt and growled at me.

"I'm not asking anymore, boy."

I peeled his greasy hands off me and glared down at him with all of the anger and hatred I had built up inside of me over the years. "I'm too old to be your damn boy. Too old."

I bounced.

NICOLE

21

I slowly got of the cab. I don't know why, but I had to come here. Marcus and Michael had picked me up but I told them that I would meet them at Michael's later. Michael hesitantly called a cab for me while Marcus stormed to his car. I knew they wouldn't understand, but I need to do this. I had to come here. Maybe if for no other reason than to just the make it all real.

My body still felt shell-shocked, my mind in total disillusion and my heart heavier than it has been in a very long time. Death was all around me and I really didn't know how to go on living and why it was important for me to exist. I have nothing. I was on the bottom of that roller coaster again and I swear this time I had no intention of getting back on. I didn't see the point.

Slowly, I walked holding a single red rose in my left hand trying to focus on the pretty blue sky and the sun shining against it. My eyes burn with a familiar wetness. I didn't want to cry. I didn't want to be sad. I had to have happy thoughts. I wanted to have happy thoughts. I kept walking. Making myself feel the breezy wind and the sun's warmth against my skin, but tears came anyway. I could hear birds in the distance, singing harmoniously in the trees. I tuned in and tried to hum along. But the tears still fell. Then I saw him.

There he was. His name carved in stone, his body lying in the ground. I knelt down and traced the letters and they felt hot to my touch. It was real now. I could no longer lie to myself. There it was in big bold letters. Here was the spot that held my James. I placed the rose down and tried to ignore my hallow insides.

"Today is so pretty," I heard my own weak voice say aloud. "It reminds of the times we used to go on picnics in the park. When you used to sing to me."

My voice was shaky as I spoke and more teardrops hung heavily against my eyelids. I wiped my tears with the back of my hand and then placed my hand on the headstone that spelled out his name. Touched the dirt that held his body. Blinked back my blinding tears. Tried to fight back my memories of that night but they just kept coming.

I could see him with her. In the house we built. In the bed we shared. Her body being caressed by the same hands that used to touch mine. Her mouth being touched by the same mouth that had moments later curled in ugliness and said hurtful and unkind words.

So, why was I here crying my heart out? Why did I feel like I was living via remote control and didn't know how I was supposed to make it without him? Telling me what to do, how to feel, where to go and how to think. All the things that I despised about him I missed the most and instead of feeling any sense of freedom I felt hollow inside. Empty, vacant, void of life and love.

Why?

How many ways did James try to show me that he didn't love me and make me see the writing on the walls? Flaunting woman after woman for me and the whole wide world to see. Nobody knew about me. Nobody knew there was someone at home waiting on him or his call, needing his love, understanding, compassion and gratitude. I was a non-entity to him. And he was my life.

The moment I stepped into Michael's home I let out a long sigh. For the most part I was glad I was here considering the fact that I could be confined to a jail cell for the rest of my life. Literally living a nightmare.

Every second I spent there I felt literally drained of air. Each night I fought to sleep and couldn't stomach the meager food that was brought to me. For hours, all I could do was stare at the ceiling trying to figure out how my life had once again become so messed up.

Nobody could have ever told me that after meeting the great James Fulton I would be accused of his murder. I went into the den and poured a shot of Vodka and closed my eyes and swallowed it in one drink. Tears burned behind my lids. Tears of pain, disgust, agony, gratefulness, God, I almost spent my life behind bars. The mere thought of it sent chills down my spine and my hands shook as I poured another drink. Swallowed it and held back more tears.

For days I stayed behind bars as others decided the outcome of my life and as I contemplated the end of it over and over and over. Everything about my life was nothing but confusion. I wasn't sure about anything. Didn't know what to believe about myself. I couldn't even convince myself that I didn't kill James. In my heart of hearts I didn't know.

I didn't know what I wanted to do when I picked up that gun. Didn't know if I wanted him dead. 'Cause no matter how many times I asked myself that question, I couldn't come with a clear answer. I didn't know.

I headed up the stairs and made my way into the bathroom. My own reflection scared me. My hair uncombed, my face almost unrecognizable to myself.

Deep circles enclosed my eyes. My usual brown skin was blotchy, dry looking. I got a hot towel and began to scrub my face. Tried to wash away the ugliness that faced me in the mirror. But the same face stared back at me.

I went to the shower. Turned the water on as hot as I could stand. Scrubbed every inch of my body with soap over and over again. Washed my hair at least four times before the musty smell of that cell went away.

I stepped out of the shower, dried off and then wiped the steam from the mirror. In the reflection I still saw her. I got a comb and began to comb my damp hair. Gobs of my mane came out in the comb.

I placed the comb down and went into the bedroom. Michael had brought my clothes over and I headed toward the closet to get my robe. As I slipped it on I looked at myself in the full-length mirror and again I didn't recognize myself. I walked over to the mirror looked closely, but couldn't find the woman I used to be.

Gone was the extra fifteen pounds I had carried around for months. I had lost that plus some. My ribs were under a thin layer of skin. My stomach was beyond flat. It looked hollow. Even my breast seemed smaller. I looked closer at my face. Those were not circles under my eyes. My eyes were sunk in. My whole face was sunk in. My high cheekbones sat above empty layers of skin. Tears slowly made their way to my eyes. I became a blurred vision. I didn't know who I was anymore. And maybe James didn't either. That's why he no longer wanted me.

I lay across the bed. I was so tired. I closed my eyes and prayed for sleep. I just wanted to sleep and never wake up and face this nightmare called my life. I wanted peace. Quiet. Stillness. But my mind wouldn't rest and my heavy burdened heart was tearing into two.

I needed another drink. I went downstairs and headed for the den. Once again I hit the bar and poured this time a tumbler full of the liquid pacifier and pain quencher. With shaky hands, I held the glass to my lips then closed my eyes as I felt the warm liquor fill my insides.

I left the den and headed into the music room as I wondered where Michael and Marcus were. It was so quiet. In a corner near the stereo, I noticed a box from Bon-a-fide Records. I went to it and opened it up. In it I found various CD's from different artists. My hands picked up each CD as I looked through it. Then suddenly James' face was staring up at me from the cover of his latest CD.

I took it out and held it in my trembling hand as I read the back of the cover. I walked over to Michael's stereo system and placed it in the changer. Immediately, James' voice vibrated through the room. I literally felt a chill run up my spine. His voice was raw, scratchy, and almost unrecognizable or maybe I've forgotten it already. I don't know. It's been a long time since I heard him sing. This was in fact the first time I ever listened to his last CD.

I wrote four of the songs, including the title track, Love Doesn't Know My Name. I wrote the songs, but I didn't go to the studio to hear him record it. I didn't produce it; I didn't go with him to the radio station to promote it once it was released. I did nothing. I had nothing to do with the making of James' last accomplishment except writing the four cuts.

And now those songs were a mirror reflection of what I was feeling. Lost in Loneliness, My Broken Heart, and I Can't Remember When I Hurt This Bad. It was like those four songs were some kind of premonition. They were all about me, what I've been feeling, what I've been going through and what I couldn't get away from. They were my words, his voice, my pain, and his death.

I sat on the couch and continued to listen to James as he for once spoke to and understood me. I eased back on the couch, took another drink and waited for the pain to stop.

DEREK

22

Derek slowly brought his jog to a walk, panting hard and taking deep breaths. He looked across the sky and then at the ocean ahead, marveling at its beauty. The sun was just about to set and the ocean had an orange glow. He squinted his eyes at a figure ahead. A woman was sitting at the shore drawing with a stick in the sand as her hair blew carelessly in the wind. As he came closer he recognized her. Derek picked up his pace and stopped at her side. He looked down at her as she continued to draw nothing in the particular in the sand, never once acknowledging his presence.

He knelt down beside her and looked at her profile. It had been weeks since he has seen her, stood next to her or sat next to her. And even though every thing inside of him told him she was like poison for him, he couldn't stop thinking about her. All the weeks that have passed, every one left them thinking about her eyes and the feel of her inside his arms. He closed his eyes at the memory and then quickly opened them back up.

She turned his way and looked directly into his eyes, as a small smile tried to cross her lips but didn't reach her eyes.

"Hi," Nicole said, her voice huskier than he remembered.

"Ms. Williams," Derek said.

She let out a small laugh. "It's a little late for that don't you think."

"Late?"

"Formalities," she said turning her face toward the ocean again leaving Derek with more memories of that night.

"How are you," Derek asked after a moment.

"Can I get back to you on that?" she answered simply.

Derek looked out into the ocean and then at her again. "Look, I need to apologize for my behavior when you were brought in. It was just I was so...surprised and caught off guard."

Her eyes looked directly at him as she again let go of a small smile. "Counselor, don't feel like you know me. We slept together, that's all but you don't know me. So there's no need for an apology, you were doing your job."

Derek sat still looking at her realizing that she was calling what they shared that night exactly what it was; two strangers meeting one night having sex. So, why couldn't he? Why was he remembering every fine detailed moment that he spent with her?

"Doing your job and looking for the truth," Nicole spoke suddenly but this time not looking at him. "And the truth is, I don't why I slept with you. I know you didn't force yourself on me, but I don't know if I seduced you. I saw you wanting me and I needed that. I needed to feel everything that I saw in your eyes, but I couldn't. Not even as I lay in your arms," her voice trailed off.

Derek sat there stunned at her words. She told him she used him and he had to admit he admired her for her honesty.

"You still have that brandy up there in that big old lonely house of yours," she asked him suddenly taking him out of his thoughts.

"You think my house is lonely?"

"No, just you," she answered as she slowly stood up.

Derek stared at her a moment without comment wondering how it is she thinks she know him. "I choose to be alone."

"I hate being alone," she sadly said looking out at the ocean and then back at him. She started walking toward his house. And he followed.

Inside, she went into the living room. He went into the kitchen. She fixed herself a brandy. He made fresh coffee. He then sat in his favorite chair. She went to the terrace door and looked outside. She looked almost peaceful. He felt too uncomfortable. She suddenly turned to face him. He thought of the feel of her lips, her soft skin, her warm body, and his bed downstairs. He shook his head as if that would erase the scene flashing behind his eyes. It was too quiet in here.

"You mind if I put on some music?" Derek asked.

"Your house."

Derek rose out of his chair and retrieved the remote from a top of his television. He pushed buttons and soon the sounds of Anita Baker's 'I Apologize' filled the room.

She took a seat on the sofa. "Umm, that's nice."

Derek went to the bar and poured himself a glass of brandy. He walked back to his favorite chair, sat down and took another sip of his drink.

"You write music, right? Do you play any instruments as well?" Derek asked trying to find a safe conversation.

"Say, let's not talk about me. Tell me about you. Where are you from, where is your family? Why do you choose to be alone? What skeletons are hiding in your closet?"

Derek looked at Nicole as she sat there obviously waiting on him to answer. "Okay. I'm from New York. Born in Harlem, raised by the greatest mother in the world. I have two half brothers. I'm the oldest. Gerald, the typical middle child complete with delusions, illusions and many, many issues, is a medical doctor about to start his own practice. He's married to a wonderful woman, has three beautiful girls and two badass dogs. My younger brother, Darius, is a sophomore at UCLA, plays for the Bruins. And then my mother, Rose is currently in Europe, traveling with my Aunt Paulette. And that's me in a nut shell."

"Sounds like you all are close."

"We're all we got as my mom used to say."

"That's nice. Now tell me about you."

"I just did."

"You gave me the reference off of your job application. You have a mom, an aunt and two brothers. Tell me about you. I want to know what makes you, you."

"What, the silver lining version is not good enough? You'd rather hear about what it was like to grow up poor in the projects of an inner city that was full of gangs, junkies, dope pusher, pimps, prostitutes and I must not leave out the rats and the roaches? You want to hear that by the time I was five there was hardly anything I hadn't seen?.

"Women getting beat up in the middle of the street, junkies dying on the curbs, prostitutes working in alleys and behind abandoned buildings. You want to hear how I gave my mom a hard time always getting in one thing or another, but she didn't understand I had to be tough cause there was no one but my mom and me? Or, how about I tell you about how I used to go to the neighborhood store and steal chicken so we could have meat for dinner. But hey, don't feel sorry for me because things did get better.

"My mom got married when I was six and soon after, my brother Gerald was born. That's when I found out that I was supposed to have a father. So, I asked her where was my father and she said that he just couldn't be with us, that it was too hard for him. I never asked her another thing about him, not even his sorry ass name. As far as I am concerned he was just a sperm donor. A real father doesn't walk away.

"Anyway, when Gerald was about four, his father had a stroke and died. So there we were again struggling. My mom worked as a beautician and Gerald and I practically lived in that beauty shop. We came home from school, went straight to the beauty shop, and waited on her so we could all go home and eat dinner. Sometimes that wouldn't be until after ten o'clock at night. I remember my teachers thinking I had a sleep disorder because I fell asleep in school everyday. It's a wonder I learned anything."

"And look at you now, Mr. Assistant District Attorney."

"That's only because my mother was determined to get us out of there. She hated living in those projects. She would cry so hard sometimes she had Gerald and me crying and we didn't even understand. We knew no different. Everybody we knew lived in the projects. But when I was fourteen that's when things changed for good.

"She was dating this sharp dresser named Avery. That brother was always clean. He wore those big-brimmed hats; platform shoes and sported one of those long leather coats. Gerald and I knew he was going to be our ticket out of the ghetto, because he was smart and anybody that dressed that damn good had to have money. Then one day my mother caught him stealing money out of her purse and she burnt him on the face with a pressing comb and threatened to kill him if he ever showed his face again. Last I heard, that brother was still carrying that pressing comb on his face." Derek laughed as he remembered Avery running from their small apartment.

"Soon after the burning, my mother found out she was pregnant. But she didn't cry about it, or worry about it or wonder how she was going to be able to feed one more mouth and keep her vow not to get on welfare. It seemed like when she was pregnant with Darius she got stronger. And the stronger she got, the harder she drove my brother and I. She buckled down on us and made us do nothing but homework. She said we had to get good grades so that we could get scholarships and go to college. And on days I didn't have homework she made me go to the library and read the encyclopedias and bring her a report on what I read. I can't tell you how much I hated it. And I can't tell you how grateful I am now. When my friends were going to parties and hanging out, I was at home or stuck in some library studying. My friends were still hanging out when I got accepted at NYU. And they were still hanging out when I graduated from law school." Derek took a deep breath and looked at the woman that he had just met only weeks ago. "How did you do that?"

"What?"

"Are you a Psych major or something? I mean I haven't talked that much about myself in years."

"I just wanted to know what makes you tick, you know what drives you. Now I do. Although, I still don't think you shared any of those bones rattling in your closet."

"Maybe I don't have any," Derek said standing up and taking their glasses to the bar where he refreshed their drinks. He walked back and handed hers to her and then sat on the table in front of her feeling her eyes on him the whole time.

"You mean to tell me that you don't have one secret that nobody else knows about," she asked looking directly at him.

Derek smiled as he thought about what she asked him. There was one secret blaring in his mind right now over the many he's sure if he took the time to think about were there. The night he found her. Derek sat his glass down on the table next to him.

"What about you, Nicole. What are your secrets? What makes you, you?"

"Now looks who's the Psych major. Trying the old reverse psychology trick.

Only I'm not falling for it tonight. See, the more I talk about me, the more pain I feel. And the more pain I feel the more I drink. And you don't have enough alcohol over there to erase my pain. And, besides, the more I drink the more I'm afraid that we would do something that we would regret later."

"Who said anything about regrets," Derek asked meeting her eyes.

"Some things don't have to be said."

"Well, maybe some things need to be. Look I'm not going to lie to you. I hate the circumstances that we met under. I have sat in this room and closed my eyes and wished it hadn't happened but it did. But if I were to sit here and do my job and search for the truth as you say, I would tell you that I liked being with you under any circumstances. And for the record, the biggest secret that I have in my life right now is that I'm having a hard time sitting here and not kissing you."

Derek took one of her hands in his as his words floated through the space between them.

Nicole looked into his eyes before speaking. "Derek, I am just enough on this side of sober to know what you're saying and to know not to react to it. And, for the record, I'm more than flattered. But this is not six weeks ago and I'm no longer at the bottom of the pit. I'm scraping my way up to the top, but I don't want to step on you in the process. You're really a nice man. You saved my life, literally but I..."

"Don't want to have any regrets," Derek said flatly taking a deep breath and letting go of her hand.

She looked into his eyes momentarily and then averted them to a spot on the floor. "So I guess this is part where I leave."

Derek stood up in front of her and held out his hand. "Let me make sure you get home safely."

Once in the car, they were completely silent as Derek concentrated on the road and Nicole sat and listened to the music that came from the radio. Before long, he was by her side of the car holding the door open for her. He helped her out and stepped back afraid of what he might do if they were too close. Everything that needed to be said was already said. Now he just needed to get her in this house and walk away without looking back and never see her again. As they reached the door, she pulled out her key and turned to put it in the lock.

"Here, let me get that for you," Derek said taking the key from her. Then the inevitable happen. Their fingers touched and he found himself looking deep in her eyes. They stood there silently for moments. He had no idea what she was thinking, had no idea what she was feeling, but he knew what he was feeling and what he had to do.

He placed his lips on hers and kissed her softly, yet passionately, as he pulled her inside his arms letting out a low moan as desire swept over him like a small tidal wave. He couldn't believe how much he wanted her. He was breathless with desire. Why was this happening? Finally, he pulled away from her and just looked in her eyes and it was as if the world had stopped spinning on its axis and the wind had stopped blowing.

"Goodnight," he finally whispered.

"Goodbye, Derek."

MARCUS

23

The papers in front of me made no sense. The words and numbers of the financial statements seemed all jumbled together. I couldn't concentrate. I closed my eyes and rubbed my temples and forehead trying to refocus. I was tired. I hadn't slept soundly in weeks. I couldn't. I was worried about her. Constantly.

Every time I go over to Mike's, I find her the same way. Sitting in the dark, either drunk or already passed out. But it's not the drinking that bothers me. It's her eyes. They look so damn empty. There's no light in them. No hope. No life. They just look void, like she has had enough and wants to give up. That's what bothers me.

If I could I would stay with her for twenty-four hours a day. But, besides my business needing my attention, she has told me more times than once to leave her alone. To give her some space, some breathing room, some time to get over her loss. I try to do this. Everyday I have gone in to work, only to get little accomplished. Everyday I have given her some space to go through what she's going through. But I swear I want to invade her space. I want to take her and shake her until she becomes herself again. I hate seeing her like this. Hate it. There were too many memories, too many.

"Good morning Mr. Washington," Gina spoke as she came into my office. I glanced at my watch. Was it already eight thirty? I've been sitting behind this desk since six.

"Good morning Gina," I said looking up at her. She gave me her brightest smile and then poked out her lips, as she no doubt noticed the paperwork scattered about my desk.

"It already looks like you've been here awhile. All work and no play isn't good, Mr. Washington."

I stacked the papers in a pile. "It's not as bad as it looks. "

"Would you like me to order some breakfast for you or get you some fresh coffee?"

Gina eyes glanced at my empty cup. I had already had three and didn't need a fourth. "I'm okay. But get what you want and please close the door behind you."

Gina stepped away from my desk and headed for the door and then stopped when she reached it. "Mr. Washington, is everything okay?"

"Of course. Why do you ask?"

"I don't know. Something's different. You just seem sad."

I looked at Gina with raised eyebrows then smiled to reassure her. "I just have a lot on my mind Gina. Nothing to worry about," I said hoping that would pacify her. I wasn't in the mood for conversation.

"Okay then," Gina said as she walked out of my office and closed the door.

I took a deep breath and leaned back in my chair. Sad. I looked sad. Gina didn't know the half of it. Six weeks ago, I watched my best friend get dragged off to jail, charged with the murder of her live in boyfriend, and I haven't been the same since. Mike once said that Nicole is my other half. That whatever she goes through, I go through. Said we're like some weird kindred spirits. Mike doesn't have a clue either. Once upon a time Nicole was my world and my world got turned upside down and so did I. And now it was once again upside down.

When most people look at me they see the money, the job, the women, the games. Hell, I'm a master of disguise. I don't like the real me to be seen. But sometimes the man I am inside sneaks out and takes a look at what I'm really doing, watching me go through the motions of trying to act like everything is everything.

But when my world is turned upside down, the real me takes over. I start wondering about everything and find myself not able to pretend anymore. That's probably what Gina saw, the real me. The real me, that doesn't shake and bake, or put on a front of living life as I damn well please; the real me that has experienced pain and loss in ways that I never thought possible.

Sure, I'm able to take care of business by day and play hard by night. I'm my own boss, have more money than I know what to do with and so many women I have to fight them off. What more can a successful businessman want? I shook my head. Do I really want to go there?

"Mr. Washington, Michael's on line one," Gina's voice interrupted my thoughts. I quickly picked up the phone.

"What's going on cuz?"

"Hey, Marc. Say, have you to talk to Nicki?"

"No, what's up?" I said while trying to figure out Mike's tone. It seemed a little, I don't know maybe... sad.

"I'm worried about Nicki, Marc," Michael said and then let out a long breath. I leaned back into my chair and took a deep breath also. I was more than worried.

"Where is she?" I asked suddenly filled with anxiety.

"I don't know."

I sat back up in my chair. "What do you mean you don't know Mike?"

"She's not here."

"I'll be there in twenty minutes." I hung up the phone, grabbed my keys and headed for the door.

"Mr. Washington, there's another call for you," Gina said as I passed her desk.

"I'm out, Gina."

"It sounds important. She says she calling about your friend Nicole."

I grabbed the phone. "This is Marcus Washington."

"Mr. Washington, hi. My name is Vivian Jasper. You don't know me but I'm a neighbor, well I was a neighbor of James Fulton."

My hands tightly griped the phone at the mere sound of that name. I took a deep breath before speaking. "What can I help you with Ms. Jasper?"

"Normally I wouldn't be all up in nobody's business, but since the murder took place I've been keeping an eye out on the house."

"How did you get my number?"

"Well, a long time ago, Ms. Williams gave me your number in case of an emergency. She said I was to call you or a Michael Washington if ever there was trouble."

Alarm bells were going off in my head as she rambled on. My body tensed up. "Ms. Jasper, please tell me. What's the emergency?"

"Well, it's really no emergency. I mean it could be but really not one where we need to call the police or anything. At least I hope not."

"Ms. Jasper, please. What is it?"

Instead of answering me she took a long breath and held the phone without saying a word for what seemed like hours. "About an hour ago, Ms. Williams pulled into the driveway of the house and went in. At first everything was quiet but now I'm hearing noises. I mean it sounds like there is some kind of disturbance, maybe even violence. I just hope nothing has happened to her."

I slammed down the phone.

In twenty minutes I was in Nicole's driveway. I jumped out of my car, ran up the walkway and entered the open front door. Immediately I felt cold. I scanned the living room noticing turned over furniture and broken glass everywhere. Dried blood stained carpet, a taped outline. I crossed the room. A 16x20 picture of Nicole and James obviously during happier times was staring up at me.

Through the cracked glass, I could still see him smiling down at her as she looked dreamily up into his eyes. I went into another room, stepped over broken lamps, trophies, awards, framed gold albums, more turned over and broken furniture. I headed down the hall toward the back of the house. The smell of liquor lingered in the air.

In the bedroom I found more havoc. Clothes, jewelry, shoes and cologne bottles were thrown about everywhere. The bed, stripped naked, showed a shredded mattress. The dresser sat empty of drawers, their contents again on the floor.

The room had been totally ransacked. Totally destroyed. And still there was no sign of her.

I ran into the den. Found nothing but turned over liquor bottles and more broken glass. There were more broken pictures and more discarded awards and plaques thrown about the room. And yet still she was nowhere to be found.

I looked in the five guest bedrooms, the kitchen, the dining room, the exercise room, the private theater, the study, her office. Found nothing but total chaos. My breath quickened as I began to retrace my steps. I knew she was here.

I looked in the same rooms a second time this time more thorough. Checked under beds, in closets, behind furniture. I hit the bathrooms. Remembered there were six of them throughout the house. Check all six. Still found no Nicole.

I returned to the living room, stood amongst the wreckage, and tried to remember this house. I had only been here maybe three or four times over the six years that they lived here. I couldn't remember if there was a special place that Nicole had. At my grandmother's house, I knew her favorite room was the kitchen. Here, I didn't know about her. Didn't know her dislikes or favorites. Didn't know if she was happy or unhappy. Didn't let myself think about it.

I held my head down in shame. I had let her down. I wasn't there for her. Despite the years of friendship we had shared and all of the tough times we faced together, I let James come between us.

I went outside. Looked at her parked car in the driveway. She was here. I knew she was. I headed toward the back of the house. Opened the gate of the twelve-foot brick wall that secluded the area. Big shade trees blocked the April sun from the patio and offered a cool breeze. The twenty-foot pool looked void of any visitors. Beyond it's concrete walkway, a plush manicured yard lay around it with a single garden to the left. On the right there was a barbecue pit, iron chairs, tables and a swing for two. It was so peaceful and quiet out here. Nothing was disturbed. Nothing looked out of place.

I noticed the roof of a smaller house. I walked down stairs and found another plush yard that was immaculately kept. This area was more shaded. More trees. Just as I put my hand on the door of the house, something told me to turn around. I turned and faced the trees then hurried toward them. There she was in a hammock asleep. I finally let myself breathe and said a short prayer.

I picked her up and carried her toward the smaller house. I opened the door and found it to be clean and not destroyed like the main house. Gently, I laid her on the couch. In the bathroom I found clean towels, wet one and then came back to her sleeping body.

I looked down at her and at that moment she looked like she was sixteen again as she lay there sleeping. My hands trembled at the memory. I placed the towel gently on her face, washing away dried tears. In a matter of moments she opened her eyes.

"Marcus," she whispered softly with the scent of the gin hitting me strongly in the face. I ignored it. Kept right on wiping her face.

She sat up slowly. Looked about the room and then back at me. Her eyes were full of sadness. Despair. Pain. She leaned her body toward mine. I saw it trembled and held it before the first teardrop fell.

On the drive home, she stared emptily out the window. Her eyes focused on nothing in particular. Every now and then she would let out a heavy sigh, maybe her way of letting me know she was still breathing because I swear I couldn't hardly watch the road for looking over at her.

When we arrived at the house she headed straight upstairs. Before I could say a word, she turned and asked to be alone. I stood there for a moment and watched her go up. And I swear it was hard as hell not to follow her.

Michael came in from the kitchen. I had called him from my cell on the way over here to let him know she was with me. We both went into the music room. Michael sat down at the piano bench and looked out the window and onto basketball court.

"Is she alright?" Michael asked after a moment.

I took a deep breath and went to sit on the couch. I glanced at my watch. It was only ten fifteen. It seemed like the whole day had already gone by.

"Yeah, I think so. She went to the house, trashed it like you wouldn't believe."

"How did you know to go there?"

"Would you believe a nosy neighbor called me just as I was about to come over here? Said Nic had been over there for a couple of hours."

"She must have left just after I drifted off. She was here when I got in about four. I didn't hear her leave."

I took a long look at Michael. His eyes were swollen from lack of sleep. "Why don't you go on up man? You look dead on your feet. I'll stay here."

"Marc, we can't keep watch over her like this. She doesn't want us to."

"Mike, I know, but I have to do something."

"But what man? I mean I have never seen her like this."

I said nothing and looked away. Hell, I've seen worse. "She's going to be alright, man."

"If she doesn't drink herself to death first," Mike said and then started playing with the keys on the piano. He was right about that. I tried not to let her drinking bother me but it did. Kept telling myself that it was her sadness and grief for that no good dog man of hers that made me worry but it was more. It was all of it. Nicki was on a downhill fall to nowhere and she didn't want anybody to stop her. She wanted to crash.

Michael looked over at me. "What if Nicole never comes out of this?"

"She will Mike."

LaTANYA WHITMORE

"How can you be sure, man? I mean look at her."

"I'm sure because I know her. I know her better than I know myself. She's been through worse and has survived. She's going to survive this too," I said to my cousin as if my life depended on it. It did.

NICOLE

24

The fresh smell of coffee woke me up. My eyes opened and the brightness of the sun seemed to burn into my skull. I closed them again and slowly sat up and faced the wall. My whole body felt weak, empty, and hollow. I slowly opened my eyes and looked around the room. The clock on the nightstand said one thirty. On the dresser in front of me was a tray that held a single cup of coffee. I slowly got up and went to it, inhaled the aroma and then quickly sipped the brew, feeling some life creep back into me as memories of this morning flashed before me.

I had walked into the house and immediately felt the emptiness of it. I went through the whole house. Through every room, hurriedly and then came back to the living room. This time I looked about the room more carefully. Noticed the turned over pillows on the couch and the residue of a white powder on my cherry wood tables. Saw my many pictures lying on the floor that had once hung on my walls and sat on my furniture. Pictures I had bought at art auctions, pictures of James and I. I picked up the 16x20 picture and looked at a smiling James as he stood there with his arms around me and as I gazed into his eyes. I read the words at the bottom of the picture that were printed in the foreground.

I can't exactly remember
what it was that made it seem impossible
for me to live without you.
There was a loneliness that you filled
an emptiness that lasted a lifetime but went away
the moment you possessed me.

I stopped reading. A huge lump formed in my throat but couldn't hold in the anger inside of me. I felt my body shake. Trembled like an earthquake. Tears were in my eyes before I realized it but I could still see smiling James. Hot, angry tears burned as they slid down my cheeks as I continued to look at the picture. I heard a voice sob and cry out loud and I swear it wasn't mine.

My clinched left hand opened up and I dropped my purse and keys at my feet. The picture became blurry. The faces distorted, unrecognizable. I flung it across the room and watched it hit the wall as glass shattered about. It was a lie, nothing but a damn lie. Everything in this house was a lie!

I picked up one object after another and threw it. Nothing here was real. Nothing here was mine. It was all him and his stupid lie. James had filled this house with old lamps and antique chairs and furniture and pictures, saying they represented what he had accomplished. Like I had nothing to do with his success.

"You stinking, selfish bastard!" I screamed out loud and sent lamps sailing in the air and crashing to the ground. I knocked over all four of those ugly antique chairs that had sat so formidably in this room. I had hated those chairs. I pushed over tables, statues, plastic plants in golden pots. I was totally out of control. And I wasn't through.

I went into the music room. Walked over to his wall of fame. I knocked off all of his precious awards and trophies. His three Grammies, his American Music Award and his Soul Train award, I threw them all across the room. His framed gold and platinum records. Threw all eight of them to the floor. Even though I wrote each and every one of them, they meant nothing to me. He never said thank you. Never once said thank you to me in those acceptance speeches. Never. It was all about him. Such a lie!

I stormed into our bedroom. The last place I saw him. I immediately went to his closet and pulled out all of his clothes and hurled them on the floor as tears continued to stream down my face and as I cursed his very existence.

I went to his bureau and knocked over his favorite bottles of cologne, his diamond Rolex watch that I had given him after his third album went platinum and the gold nugget ring that he wore on his right pinky finger. Like a woman possessed, I pulled out the drawers that held all his socks and tee shirts that were all so neatly folded and dumped them unto the floor. In the mirror, I caught a glimpse of the bed.

I turned around and went over to it and pulled all the cover from it as the memory of James and his woman's body entwined in my sheets went through my mind. I went into the bathroom, found the scissors came back into the bedroom and began to slice the mattress into shreds. I left the room still crazed with anger.

I went back through the rest of the house. In each room I found a different lie. In each room I destroyed it. Destroyed everything about the great James Fulton. I headed back down the hall into the living room. My eyes were finally free of tears. My anger subsided. I was finished here. All the lies had been destroyed. All the fake happiness diminished.

I reached the living room and bent down to look for my purse. I stepped over the pictures and statues that I had thrown about the room. Then that's when I saw it, the outline on the carpet. I moved the chair that I pushed over earlier and unveiled the spot where James must have laid as he died. I now noticed the blood stained carpet. I looked about me, horrified. Dried blood was everywhere. The walls, the curtains, the furniture, everything was covered in blood.

A low scream escaped my lips. I began to feel sick to my stomach. Once again I found tears in my eyes. And I couldn't stop myself from crying. I cried so hard that I literally felt like my insides were going to come out. I came here to take back my home. I came here to destroy him and his memory, to destroy his lies and the deceitfulness. But I swear I never wanted him dead. Never.

I went into the den, grabbed a bottle of gin, and took a long strong drink; swallowing hard trying to drown out the scene my mind wouldn't let me forget. I headed out the back door. Out of that house. For the longest time I just stood still, gasping for air. The next thing I remember is Marcus holding me.

I looked around the room and then placed my now empty coffee mug down. Oftentimes I came to this house, this room just to feel safe, loved. But right now, the only I thing I feel is alone. I pulled on my robe and headed down the hall. I needed something stronger than coffee.

I passed by Michael's room, saw him asleep, and kept on going until I reached the den. Before I reached the bar, I saw Marcus out of the corner of my eye. I let out a deep breath and sat down on the couch instead. Marcus looked my way, got up out of his chair, and knelt down in front of me. "You feel like getting something to eat?"

"No," I answered. I wanted a drink.

"Are you okay?"

"I will be if everybody stop asking me if I'm okay," I said glaring at him. His eyes changed from concerned to hurt and I wanted to take back the words, but it was too late.

"Marcus, you can't fix this. You don't even understand this. Why don't you just go back to work or go get with one of your women or whatever?"

"Maybe I'm already where I want to be."

"Maybe I don't want you here Marcus. There's nothing you can do."

"I'm not going to let you push me away. Not this time."

"What gives you the right, Marcus? Who appointed you my damn guardian angel," I yelled, going over to the bar.

"Our friendship, Nicki!" Marcus yelled back at me.

I turned and looked at him. Saw a piece of the man I used to know years ago. The one that used to hold me, touch me and made me feel safe, loved. I poured brandy into a glass and drank it all in one swallow. Damn I give anything for that feeling right now. As if reading my mind, Marcus moved closer to me. Took the glass out of my hands and then pulled me into his arms and then his hands began to stroke my hair as he held me. I rested my head on his shoulder as I held him back. And the tears didn't come.

For the briefest moment I felt safe and that everything was all right and as it should be. I was not in pain; I was okay. I was not alone; I was loved. I was not empty. Marcus pulled inches away from me and looked down in my face. His eyes went all inside me.

"Don't push me away Nic," he whispered. "My life is nothing without you in it. I need you."

I watched as his face came closer to mine. As his lips came closer to mine. His eyes left mine and then for seconds stared down at my mouth and I watched his. He kissed my forehead, my eyes and then suddenly slipped away.

I watched him as he walked over to the bar, poured himself a shot of brandy and then stood with his back to me. I stood still not knowing what to do or how to react. Hell, I wasn't even sure what just happened. I went to the window and looked outside. I soon heard Marcus come up behind me stopping only inches away. I wanted to turn around and face him to look in his eyes. But I couldn't. His hand touched my shoulder.

"Call me Nic. Whenever you need me," he said and then walked away. I turned and watched him walk away and leave the room. As soon as he was gone I went to the bar and poured myself another drink. Tears formed in my eyes but didn't fall. I wanted to scream. I needed him now.

"So, what shall we have?" Michael asked as we looked over our menus. We were at a steakhouse downtown LA and I can't lie I didn't want to be here. But he kept insisting until I gave in. Insisted that I get dressed up, do something with my hair and go out on the town with him. I looked over the menu again. I didn't really have an appetite but I guess I had to pick out something since we were here.

"Steak and lobster sounds good to me, what about you Nicki?" Michael said looking over his menu at me and then placing it on the table. "Hey, look at me, what's up?"

I met his eyes with mine and forced a smile on my lips. He was trying so hard to keep my spirits up. And I wanted to also. I wanted to find joy in listening to birds sing or watching the sun set against the Pacific. I just didn't know how. I couldn't believe how much joy I lost when James died. I used to love to go for long drives and just marvel at the colors of the world.

I loved the beautiful shade of blue the sky was and my favorite season was the fall when all the beautiful trees were in full bloom and yards were full of autumn leaves that made me want to jump in. All the simple things that used to make me smile were now gone. But why was that? James didn't hang the sun. But he hung the moon in my life. That's why my joy was gone. But I was not going to think of James tonight. For Michael's sake I wasn't going to let thoughts of James ruin our evening.

"Taxes," I said after awhile smiling at him.

Michael looked at me with a silly grin back. "Crazy girl, what do you want to eat?"

"You got a couple of dollars on you, don't you?"

"Yeah," Michael answered hesitantly.

"Okay," I said letting my eyes roam the menu again. "I want a nice big juicy steak, no, no, no. I want lobster, and oh crab legs and hordes of shrimp! And a big, big baked potato oozing with butter and a huge salad."

"Is that it?"

"And we got to have champagne, the best champagne that your money can buy?"

Michael looked at me a long moment and I could read the hesitation and concern in his eyes. "It is just wine, Mike."

"Sure, why not. Anything else?"

"Yeah, I think I do want that steak."

Michael shook his head and called for the waiter and gave him our order, requesting that the champagne come first. "You sure got a hell of an appetite tonight. Brother could go bankrupt just trying to feed you."

"Oh, I know you can handle it," I said sliding deeper into my chair and taking a look around the restaurant. It was small and charming and where we were seated was private and could even be romantic. I looked over at Michael with thoughts of Marcus. It has been a whole week since I've seen him. 'Call me whenever you need me.' Those were his last words to me. And I hadn't called, cause I can't lie I didn't even know what to say. "He almost kissed me."

"Who almost kissed you?" Michael asked.

I looked at him strangely.

"You said he almost kissed you. Who?"

I looked away from Michael. Couldn't believe I had said that aloud. I looked back at Michael who sat waiting on an answer. Just then the waiter came to our table with the champagne, opened it, then filled both of our glasses and left. Michael raised his glass to me and I raised mine back.

"To good friends," he said and I touched his glass with mine before taking a long sip.

"Have you talked to Marcus?" I asked after a moment.

"He's at the house every morning when I come in. He doesn't say much, makes small talk and then leaves. Why, what's up?"

I looked at Michael in amazement. That was impossible. I've been there all week and haven't seen him at all. Marcus has all but disappeared every since that day he found me at my old house.

I stared at Michael. "What's going on Michael, you two babysitting me now? What, Marcus comes in while I'm asleep and stays there until you come home? What are you guys trying to pull!" I said angrily. I didn't appreciate being watched like some damn baby. I'm a grown woman and can take care of myself.

"Nicole, calm down. First of all we're not babysitting you. We're just worried about you. Both of us are. We are just trying to be here for you."

"I don't need this shit, Michael," I said looking around the table to make sure people weren't staring at us. I was angry but I wasn't trying to cause a scene.

I didn't need someone recognizing me as the woman who was accused of killing James Fulton. I took a deep breath, picked up the bottle and refilled my glass.

"Nicki, take it easy, baby?"

"Don't tell me to take it easy Michael."

I tilted my glass and emptied it and then glared back at Michael who sat looking at me as though he hadn't done anything wrong.

"Nicole you can't get mad at us for caring about you. We're family Nicki. If I were in your shoes, I would want you by my side. And so would Marc. He would want you by his side. So don't ask us to step aside and pretend like nothing is happening to you. It's happening to all of us. Stop acting like you going through things alone, because you're not. And you know deep down you don't want to. We're all family Nicki. We stick... " Michael stopped in mid sentence but his eyes didn't leave mine. "Marcus almost kissed you. Well, I'll be damn."

I turned my eyes away from his. I wanted another drink, but my glass was empty. I reached for the bottle and refilled my glass. Once again I turned my glass up, emptying it before I placed it back on the table. Michael sat across from me waiting on me to say something, but I had no words. Our food came out and we ate in mostly silence, only commenting on how good the food was. He ordered more champagne and we both refilled our glasses, me more often than him. I pushed my food away when I couldn't hold anymore and watched Michael finish. He smiled at me and laughed and reached over and wiped butter from my nose. I heard myself giggle and for a minute didn't know where that sound came from. And before long I was laughing harder because it felt so good.

"That looks good on you."

I looked up at the figure that came with the voice that stood at the center of our table. "Hi Derek."

"Hi yourself," Derek spoke staring down at me and I quickly looked away from his burning eyes.

"Hey, Alexander, right, the Assistant DA," Michael said extending his hand to Derek.

"How are you doing?" Derek asked Michael even though I still felt his glare on me.

"Nicole, are you going to introduce us?" Michael asked.

"I'm sorry, Derek Alexander, Michael Washington."

"Nice to meet you," Derek said.

"Say would you like to join us?" Michael asked and I kicked him under the table. He made a face and then reached down to rub his leg.

"Sure why not," Derek said and then Michael signaled for the waiter again to bring another chair, which he placed between the two of us.

"I would offer you something to eat but as usual Nicki ate up all the food. But we do have champagne, would you like you a drink? I'll get the waiter to bring another glass."

"No, don't bother. I can't handle too many things inhibiting my mind when I need to concentrate on something else," Derek assured him never taking his eyes off of me. "It's good to see you. Out."

"Well, you know, a girl's got to get out every now and then and have a little fun," I said cheerfully, a little too cheerfully. Damn that champagne.

"So the two of you are just having a grand old time, uh?" Derek asked.

"A blast, we've been sitting here talking about...what were talking about Michael?" I asked turning to Michael.

"Um, I don't know, sex," Michael blurted with a smile and I kicked again under the table but this time kicked Derek.

"Ouch!"

"I'm so sorry," I said covering my mouth trying not to laugh. But the look on his face was funny. "Maybe I'm the one that's too inhibited tonight."

"The only thing you are is radiant. You have a beautiful smile," Derek said now smiling in my eyes.

I looked away from him and looked at Michael who sat staring at us both. "Excuse me, I need to go to the ladies room."

The three of us rose from the table. I lost my balance and bumped slightly into Derek. I said excuse me again without looking into his eyes and hurried to the bathroom.

Inside, I washed my hands and splashed cold water on my face as I looked in the mirror. What the hell was wrong with me? Why did Derek unnerve me? Make me feel uncomfortable and relaxed all at the same time. And Michael. What the hell was that comment about? We had not been talking about sex. Was it possible that he knew that Derek and I slept together? He couldn't have. I looked around the bathroom to see if anyone was in there with me. I didn't have to use it but for some reason I didn't want to come out. Then again, there's no telling what Derek and Michael were talking about. I bolted out of the door.

When I got to table Michael was sitting alone and the extra chair was taken away. I let out a deep breath and sat down. "So you ran him off uh?" I asked.

"Yeah, he had to go," Michael answered strangely.

Something wasn't right. His mood has changed. "Is something wrong Michael?"

"No, of course not. I've ordered coffee."

"Michael you're lying to me. What did Derek say?"

"Who said he said anything?"

"You know I hate it when you answer my question with a question?"

"And I hate fake ass people," Michael said frankly.

I looked directly into Michael's eyes. "He told you we slept together."

Michael shrugged his shoulders and sat up in his chair. "Well it definitely wasn't hard to figure out from the way he talks of you. I can't believe the brother was that foul Nicki after you shared with him what happened with James. I mean for him to come at you when you were the most vulnerable is just pretty damn low if you ask me."

"It wasn't like that Mike. I wanted him to take me to his bed." I said and then shamefully looked away. "Michael, I know you got his great self image of me, and in your eyes I live on a pedestal but right now I can't live up to it. I just can't."

Michael reached across the table and grabbed my hands and I looked back into his eyes. "Hey, you know what I'm sorry. It's not even my business. And for the record, no matter what you do, to me you're still live on that pedestal. I love you."

"And I love you back Michael."

ICE

25

I looked out of the rearview mirror. There was no mistake. That was the third time I had noticed the car behind me. It was a dark blue Mustang that had been following me since I hit Slauson Blvd. I pulled into a parking lot of a bank and eased myself into the line of drive-thru tellers. In the mirror, I watched as the Mustang sat idle in a parking spot behind me. I laughed as I recognized Slaughter's boys in the car. A & B were trying to keep tabs on me. What was up with that?

The car ahead of me pulled off and I was at the window not ready to make a deposit or a withdrawal. I didn't even bank here. I looked back at A & B and then eased my car out of line and made my way around to the front of the building where they were still parked. I eased my Lexus facing them and let my window down when I was just inches from Tre Dog's face.

"'Sup boys," I said leaning out of my car window looking into their car to make sure they weren't holding a piece or something. Hell I sure was.

A look of surprise came over John Jr.'s face. "Oh, hey Ice, what up man?"

"You tell me. You've been tailing me for twenty minutes. What gives?"

"Nothing man. We're just up in here about to do a little banking."

"Is that right?" I asked looking back at Tre Dog. I was so close I could smell the cheap wine he probably had with breakfast.

"Yeah, Ice. You know everything is cool. We didn't know you bank here too," John Jr. answered.

"And I didn't know you boys knew how to drive," I said glancing around our surroundings. Had to see what was around me just in case our friendly conversation became unfriendly. I then turned my attention back to Tre'Dog and looked at him with the disgust I couldn't disguise.

"You two are trifling. How long are you going to do what that old man tells you? I bet you two don't piss unless he gives you permission."

Tre's' eyes glared back into mine. Brother acted like he was a little perturbed, like he wanted to jump in my shit. I patted my breast pocket with my right hand and let a slow smile form on my lips. "Down boy, you don't want to hurt yourself."

"Man, why you always talking to me like I'm some kid, Ice. You ain't better than me!"

I laughed at his pathetic self. "You don't see me asking how high every time Slaughter says jump."

"And that's on you, Ice. You know Slaughter gone mess your ass up, cause your ass didn't do that job like he asked," Tre answered. Acting like he finally discovered he had some balls.

"So, that's what this tail is all about? You boys on a mission for Slaughter?"

Tre'Dog turned away and I looked over at John Jr. who was looking away from me as well.

I took my car out of park. "You tell his fat ass to remember he started this, and I'm going to be the one to finish it."

I eased my car from the parking lot and headed back down Slauson without looking back 'cause I knew without looking that those two dummies were still parked trying to put their one brain together and figure out what to do next. They might not know what to do, but I do.

I had access to all of Slaughter's money. I knew where all of his shit was warehoused and when each and every shipment moved and left this city. It would be only a matter of time before I totally took everything he has worked me so hard to get away from his sorry ass. Yeah, it was definitely time for me to make my move.

I drove another five miles down Slauson and then pulled over at a hamburger joint. Might as well get me a greasy burger to go with my foul ass mood. I parked my ride and got out. The drive-thru was so long that I might as well go inside. I went in and stood behind some kid who didn't know what he wanted.

I looked down at him. He looked no more than sixteen and was dressed in head to toe street gear. He had on matching shirt, pants, hat, socks and even shoes. He was a walking billboard. I let out a slight laugh and he turned around and looked at me. I looked down at him, stared at his wannabe-self, and shook my head. His baldhead was too big for his skinny little body that was draped in gold chains around his neck, a gold watch and a ring that went across his whole hand that read 'Hard'. He glared up at me showing me his gold grill in his mouth.

Young blood was smelling himself and thinking he could just step to me. Here I was minding my own damn business and this kid wants to step to me. I know what it is. All that damn rap music has got their ass confused. They sit around all day listening to Ice Cube, Doctor Dre, Scarface, Master P, Snoopdogg and every other Dogg and think those brothers understand what goes on for real. They need to recognize those people are nothing but entertainers and they get paid to mess with their little egos.

I continued to look down at pint size and finally decided to speak. " 'We got a problem?"

"I ain't got no problem, you got a problem," he answered in a voice that couldn't make up it's mind what octave in wanted to be in while his eyes continued to glare at me.

"Yeah, I'm hungry. Are you through with your order?"

"Naw, I ain't through yet and I don't appreciate you rushin' a nigga."

"Don't mean to rush you, but you been here awhile. Do you need some help? Can you read?" I asked suddenly. Hell, patience left me when I got out the car. I didn't have time for this. If little man didn't hurry up and get out of my way I wasn't going to be responsible. It was only so much little shit I could take in one day, first A & B, now this. I had business to take care of.

"You trying to be funny?" half-pint asked getting in my space as his street gear touches my designer suit.

I looked him dead in the eye. "If you don't step back the joke's going to be on you."

"Yo, what up Ice." Another youthful voice said coming through the door. Young blood stopped looking at me and went over to his partner. I turned myself and thought I was seeing double. Homeboy was laid in the same gear, just a larger size for his beefed up size.

"Hey dogg, what up!"

"Can I help you?" The girl behind the counter said to me giving me her attention. I glanced at the board above her, ordered a number four, paid her and then sat down at a table where I could wait for my food and check out my environment.

"Say Ice, you see that Lexus out there? I gots to have me one of those, you know what I'm saying." Dogg said to Ice. Ice went to the window, looked out the window and let out a long whistle as he looked at my car.

"Yeah, that's hard. I'm a have to knock one of those off myself."

"Say you know who car that is?" Dogg asked.

"Naw man. I didn't see. I was up in here trying to get me some food before old dog up there started trippin'." Ice said.

"Who that?"

"Hell if I know. He just trying to be all in mine, you know."

His eyes met mine as he spoke and I let him know I wasn't in the mood for his bullshit.

"Sir, your order's ready," the young girl at the counter, said to me.

I stood up went to the counter and got my food. I went over to another counter got a couple of extra napkins and then headed for the door. I slowly walked to my car. My left hand held my food, and my right hand was itching. I looked back at the boys who had now stepped outside and then got in my car. I began to back out and then looked in my rearview mirror. Ice was staring at me. With my own damn eyes.

Sheila didn't have her ass at home and a part of me was relieved cause I swear I was in no mood for her bullshit. A & B, who were back on my tail, were parked right outside Sheila's complex. For eight days, they've been tailing me for as long as I let them, which was never too long. I let them follow me to places they already know, to the bank, to Sheila's and Frank's Place. Hell, I even let them tail me to the damn store and the car wash. Then I lose their ass in Compton or South Central so I can make my real stops and head home. I hadn't seen their trifling father and was in no hurry, cause it was no telling what I was going to do when I do.

I looked out the window of Sheila's condo. Junior was standing outside the car talking to a kid. I looked a little closer and noticed that was the same kid from burger joint. The one I penned Dogg. I snapped open the window and listened. Dogg was looking for a buy and was standing holding out cash to Junior. His boy Ice suddenly showed up and the three of them began to laugh. Tre'Dog stepped out of the car and they began to smoke a joint. I closed the window. They were trippin'.

I heard the key in the lock and Sheila came in all smiles when she saw me. "Hey, Ice man. How's it goin' baby."

I glanced at her and noticed her glazed eyes. Here lately, Sheila stayed high. I looked at her empty hands. She didn't even have the briefcase. "Where's the money?"

"Oh, I didn't go today," she said slowly.

"You didn't go," I said staring at her.

"Naw, man."

"Why not?"

"I ain't got to go everyday. That money and shit ain't going no where."

"Except up your damn nose. Does your uncle know you're using?"

Sheila started to laugh and stumbled near me. "You think I tell my uncle everything? Shiiiit!"

I headed for the door.

"Where you going?" Sheila slurred at my back.

"Away from you," I said and then headed out the condo and into the garage. I drove to the east exit. In my rearview mirror I saw Tre'Dog and Junior still smoking a joint with Dogg and Ice. I eased on away. Still seeing Ice's eyes looking like mine.

DEREK

26

Derek stood quietly at the AmericanEagle terminal watching the incoming planes at LAX. He quickly checked his watch and sighed heavily as he noted he still had another ten minutes before the flight from New York was due in. He looked around the area and decided to take a seat facing the window. He hadn't been there more than two minutes before a familiar voice spoke behind him.

"What are you doing here?"

"I should be asking you. Aren't you supposed to be at work?" Derek asked standing up looking at his brother.

"Mother called me last night and asked me to meet her," Gerald said.

"Why, she asked me over three weeks ago to meet her flight?"

"Well, she hasn't been able to get in touch with you lately and so she called me."

Gerald glanced at a plane that was coming down the runway. "She's not the only one who hasn't been able to reach you man. What's been up?"

"Just work," Derek said evasively and then walked over to the window.

"You're still working on that Fulton murder case aren't you."

Derek nodded. "Yeah, it's been over two months now and there are still no leads as to who killed him."

"But we know for sure it wasn't his girlfriend?" Gerald asked walking over to the window. "The girl you found at the beach that night. It wasn't her even though we know what she walked in on."

"It wasn't her, Gerald."

"You sure about that, D."

Derek turned and faced Gerald. "What's with the questions, man? You, of all people, know she was with me that night."

"I know D, it's just something about all of this doesn't smell right. I mean why haven't the police been able to come with a single suspect."

"Because they are wasting time. There were fibers all over that living room that have yet to be identified. It's like the police have already decided it was Nicole and they are not going to even bother looking at any other evidence. Even though they have released her, I know for a fact they are still watching her and pointing fingers at her and only her."

"Maybe that should tell you something," Gerald said halfway under his breath.

"Maybe that should tell me what?"

"Be realistic, D. Some things are just obvious."

"Leave it alone, man," Derek said sternly looking at his brother with threatening eyes.

"No I won't leave it alone. Damn, Derek! Have you even thought about what this would do to your career?" Gerald asked becoming angered.

"Let me worry about my career and you just go save some more damn lives!" Derek yelled in his face. The two stood silently staring back at each other.

"You've fallen for her, haven't you?" Gerald asked suddenly.

"What!" Derek exclaimed.

"She's got you dangling on a string like a damn puppet. And now you're going to just throw away everything for this murderess."

"She didn't kill him! You don't know her. You didn't spend but two minutes with her!"

"Oh, but you spent the night with her so you know her better." Gerald said sarcastically. "D, I know I'm out of line, man but..."

"You're damn right you're out of line." Derek interrupted his anger seething. "I am so sick of hearing this bullshit and I can't believe I'm hearing it from you. You were there! You know she was with me."

"But I don't know if she's not a murderer, D. And neither do you."

Derek stepped closer to his brother. His eyes enraged with anger, his voice tight. "Gerald for the last time..."

"Derek," a woman's voice called from behind him. He turned suddenly and looked into the eyes of his mother who unbeknownst to them had already stepped off the plane. "Is everything alright son?"

"Yes," Derek said quickly and then placed his arms around her in a tight embrace. "Hey, you look fabulous. I've missed you."

"I've missed you too," she said softly and then let him go and looked over at his brother. "Gerald are you going to give your mother a hug or are you just going to stand there and marvel at my beauty."

Gerald smiled and came over and embraced his mother. "Well you are beautiful, mother," he said standing back looking at her.

"I always said you were my favorite son."

"Hey, I thought I was," Derek said.

"Well actually Darrius is," Rose smiled.

Derek reached for her hand and the three of them headed through the terminal.

Gerald began to question his mother about her trip to Europe and she excitedly told him her favorite things and all the shopping she had done while Derek only partially listened. They went to the baggage claim area, picked up her luggage and then Gerald said his good byes, promising to meet with them later and would bring his wife and kids with him. Derek nodded. He looked down at his mother who seemed to be studying his face a long moment. He briefly wondered if maybe she had asked him something and felt guilty for not giving her his undivided attention. His mind was on other things.

Derek watched as Linda Avery filed her nails intently, as she sat at the table in the interrogation room, popping her gum and swinging her right leg. She was a secretary at Bona Fide Records and Derek had asked her to come in for questioning after reading a report that one of Fulton's neighbor's saw Ms. Avery at the house the day of Fulton's death and on several other occasions. The report made mention that the police had questioned her the day after the murder but found no reason to question her any further. Derek disagreed. It could be possible that Ms. Avery was the last to see Fulton alive. He walked into the interrogation room. She stopped filing her nails and looked up into Derek's eyes as he gave her brief smile.

"Thank you for coming, Ms. Avery. I'm Derek Alexander." Derek said as he retrieved a chair, pulled it to the table, and sat next to her.

Linda nodded and tried to discretely take her gum out of her mouth. Derek, watching out of the corner of her eye as she put it under the table, placed a file on the desk and opened it up. He looked over at her, gave her another brief smile and she smiled her own toothy grin.

"What can I do for you sugar?" she asked not able to hide her Georgian accent.

Derek glanced at her silently. Noticing her hair, her makeup and her dress. Everything about her was overdone. Her blond hair stood at least three inches high at the top, her makeup thick and her dress was tight, short and loud. He glanced down at her swinging leg that hiked up her skirt to reveal her thick thighs. Derek looked back in her eyes. He guessed her to be about forty, but the file in front of him said she was twenty-eight.

"Ms. Avery, I know you have already spoken to the police, but I would just like to clarify a few matters in your statement," Derek said glancing down at the typed paper in front of him then back at her. She was going through her purse and finally her hands came out with a cigarette and lighter and she quickly put the cigarette in her mouth.

"I'm sorry Ms. Avery, this is a non-smoking facility," Derek said just before she lit the cigarette. Linda glanced at him, smiled her crooked smile and then put the cigarette and lighter back in her purse.

"What do you want to know Mr. Alexander?"

Derek pulled out a small recorder and turned it on. "I hope you don't mind. It's the way I take notes."

"Whatever floats your boat, sugar," Linda said still swinging her leg.

Derek began. "How long did you know Mr. Fulton?"

"Three years."

"And how well did you know him?"

Linda looked at Derek a long time. He was sure she was assessing what he might already know and trying to decide how much information she wanted to repeat or disclose.

"We was lovers, honey," Linda said candidly as she looked down at her nails, picked up her file and began filing them again.

"How long were you lovers?" Derek asked.

"Does it matter?"

Derek was taken aback. "Well one might think it's irrelevant, but just for the record, how long?"

"Three years, honey."

"I see. And what about Ms. Williams, how long have you known her? Three years as well?"

"No, I really didn't know her until about a year ago. She really stayed behind the scenes a lot. She would come into the studio with him but James never made it seem that their relationship was anything but professional. And she didn't either for that matter. It wasn't until I started seeing him at the house that I even knew they lived together. Yeah, they sure had me fooled."

Linda reached in her purse and pulled out another stick of gum. She put the gum in her mouth with shaking hands. Derek knew she probably wanted a cigarette instead.

"So, you would go see him at his house. Did you see Mr. Fulton the day he was killed?"

"I saw him."

"You were the woman Ms. Williams found James with, am I correct to say?"

Linda looked away from Derek without answering.

Derek looked down at her statement that the detective had taken the day after the murder. "Based on your statement to the police, you had called in sick that day so it's safe to say that you didn't run into him at work."

Linda sat up straight for the first time, stopped swinging her legs, and faced Derek head on. "Look, James and I spent the whole day together. We went shopping, hung out in Malibu, and then went to his place. Everything was going fine until she showed up."

Derek watched Linda closely. "So you believed she killed him?"

"Believe! Sweetie she was not happy to see me, let me tell you. And if looks could kill I would be dead right along with my James."

Derek watched Linda a few more minutes as she batted her eyes and tried to act like she was the victim in all of this. "Ms. Avery, where did you go after you left Mr. Fulton?"

"Where did I go? Why?"

"Just for the record." Derek stated.

"I went home. I...I was so distraught, I just went home."

"Did anyone see you?"

"Are you accusing me or something, Mr. Alexander?" Linda asked excitedly.

"Just for the record," Derek said pointing at the tape recorder.

"No. I live alone."

Linda sat back against the chair, pulled out a cigarette and lit it before Derek could object.

"Thank you for coming in Ms. Avery."

Derek stood up, turned off the recorder and showed Linda out. She was a basket case. And she was definitely a suspect.

Three days later Derek pulled into his garage just as the sun was setting. He thought about going running but then changed his mind. He got out of his car and then closed the garage. He went into the house and was instantly welcomed by the smell of good home cooking. He entered the kitchen and smiled as he saw his mother standing over the stove. Boy he was glad she was here.

"How's my favorite girl?" Derek asked going over to hug his mother from behind.

"Boy, you scared the living daylights out of me. You better quit that sneaking," Rose said turning and hugging him back.

They embraced a moment and then Derek went to peak inside the pots and pans on the stove and looked in the oven where he found smothered pork chops, mashed potatoes, cabbage, hot water cornbread, corn on the cob and even a peach cobbler?

"Now, you know you wrong coming over here spoiling me for a day."

"You could eat like this everyday, if you found you a woman and settled down," Rose winked at him and then turned back to the greens.

Derek went to the counter and sat down on one of the barstools. "Alright now, don't start that again."

"Don't start? You're the one that better start something. You already done let Gerald get married before you and he has three girls. Before you know it, Darrius will be out of college and married with kids."

"Don't let him hear you say that."

"I'm talking to you, son. What are you waiting on?" Rose asked turning to face Derek again.

Derek looked away from his mother's eyes, and went to retrieve a bottle of juice from the refrigerator. He took a long swallow and then returned to his seat still not answering her question. He had no answer.

Not one she wanted to hear anyway. He had resolved in his mind that marriage was not for him. His career was too demanding and there were many, many things he wanted to accomplish before he even thought about being responsible for somebody else's life. Sure, he enjoyed the company of a woman. What red-blooded male didn't? And sure he would love to have somebody to talk to and share his ambitions with, but marriage? He just couldn't see it. He went out on that limb once only to get struck down. There was no way he was going to set himself up again.

"You hungry?"

Derek looked at his mother who was smiling over at him and smiled back. "Shoot, yeah!"

"What's up my people?"

They both turned around to see his younger brother standing in the doorway with a pretty brown-skinned girl that came to his waist. His mother turned and rushed to her youngest son, hugging him tightly.

"Look at you, you're losing weight. Come in here and get something to eat."

"Hey, you don't have to ask me twice. I smelled that food two miles down the road." Darrius said, smiling from ear to ear. "Oh, I'm sorry, this here is Monica. Monica, these are my peoples. My mom Rose, my egg head brother, Derek."

"Nice to meet you," Monica said politely.

"Nice to meet you too, honey," Rose said.

Derek stood up and shook her hand and then scooped his younger brother on the head. "What's up, bubba?"

"Hey D. You going around looking like you lost your best friend. You look tired, brother. Stop letting that j-o-b get to ya. Get you a girl and handle ya business."

"Don't worry about me young man. You just handle your business."

"Oh, I'm taking care of mine. Ain't that right baby?" Darrius said turning to Monica who stood blushing.

"Alright, you two go wash up. Everything is about ready," Rose said and Derek was thankful she changed the subject for Monica's sake.

After dinner, Derek and Darrius washed the dishes and cleaned the kitchen and then soon after Darrius and Monica left. His mother had eaten and sat down on the couch to watch the television but had fallen asleep. Derek went to the television, turned it off and turned on the radio. He found his favorite jazz station, poured himself a brandy and went out to the terrace. The ocean breeze felt cool against his face as he sipped his drink.

He sat down in one of his loungers and forced himself to look to the right. He knew exactly where he'd found her; right over there, near the coral reef. Right over where he always ended his jog. He closed his eyes and remembered seeing her go under not once but three times before he could reach her. He had pulled her out of the water and placed his lips on hers. They were cold, yet soft. So damn soft. Just like the rest of her. Derek opened his eyes and took another sip of his drink and placed it on the glass table next to him.

No matter how hard he tried to forget, he just couldn't. No matter how many times he tried to forget what she felt like in arms, he couldn't. He couldn't forget her lips, her neck, and her eyes. He just couldn't get her out of his mind.

He wanted her. It was so clear to him. He wanted her then and even more so now.

"Feel like some company?" his mother asked behind him.

"Sure," Derek said turning to face her.

"It's so beautiful out here," Rose said taking a seat next to Derek. "I never imagined this in New York. Everything there was so crowded. Here, it's just open space. Breathing room."

"Yeah, you're definitely right about that," Derek said looking out at the ocean. They both sat in silence awhile enjoying the ocean breeze and listening to the waves crash against the shore.

"So, Gerald tells me you're working on a big case," Rose asked after a moment.

"Yeah, pretty high profile. Pretty complicated."

"Tell me about it anyway. I'm no college graduate, but I think I can catch on."

Derek looked at his mother and realized that he wasn't going to get around this conversation. She was set on hearing about it and once she was set on something there was no way around it.

"It's a murder case and there is a lot of publicity because he was a singer."

"Oh you're working on that Rick James case?"

"No mama, not Rick James," Derek answered smiling. "James Fulton."

"Oh, okay, I heard of him. Well who killed him?"

"Right now we don't know."

"Well, I read in the paper, they arrested his girlfriend."

Derek took a deep breath before speaking. "They did but they let her go. There wasn't enough evidence against her."

"So now the police are looking for another suspect. Um huh. So what do you think? Do you believe she killed him?"

"No," Derek stated flatly.

"How can you be so sure?"

Derek looked at his mother and smiled briefly. "You know, you're the one that should have been an attorney."

"Don't evade the question," Rose said smiling back at him.

Derek shook his head. She will never change. She always had a way him to make him tell her whatever she wanted to know.

"She was with me on the night of the murder, mother. I'm really her alibi."

"Her alibi? How on earth...you know her personally?" Rose asked sitting straight up in her chair.

"I met her the night of the murder, right out there," Derek said pointing to the ocean. "She was drowning so I pulled her out."

"You saved her life?" Rose asked excitedly.

"Yeah. I brought her here, called Gerald, he checked her out and said she was alright."

"That doesn't mean anything. She could have done it before she came out here."

"The coroner's report says his time of death was well after midnight."

"And you don't think she killed him after she left here?"

Derek looked away from his mother's eyes, picked up his brandy and swallowed the rest of it. He felt his mother's eyes on him and only hoped she didn't see what he was trying to hide.

MARCUS

27

I made it to Mike's at around midnight and found Nicole asleep on the couch. I went over to her and gently touched her arm. "Nicki."

Slowly she opened her eyes and looked into my mine. Moved her mouth like she was looking for words. "Morning?"

I froze. She hadn't called me that in years. Memories began to flood me. Took me back to a time where everything was so different. Where everything in my world was the way I wanted and needed it to be. I looked back at her and her eyes were closed again.

I lifted her up. She rested her head on my shoulders, her lips brushed against my neck. I shifted her in my arms as I moved through the house. In her room I laid her in the bed. She didn't stir. For moments I stared down at her wondering if everything was ever going to be right again. I reached down and touched her face, leaned over and kissed her forehead and suddenly her fingertips touched my fingertips and then slowly wrapped themselves around my hand. Her eyes flickered. Looked into mine. She spoke softly. "Stay with me."

It was around five thirty when I got out of bed. And I swear I didn't remember sleeping at all. Seemed like all night long I kept one eye opened and the other one maybe half shut. I just lay there holding a woman that I hadn't held like this in a long ass time. Dismissed the fact that she smelled mostly of stale liquor, sweat and her unique womanly musk. I just held her.

In the wee hours she cried in her sleep, a soft cry that was followed by reaching hands. I embraced her in the fold of my arms. Stroked her hair and face until she quieted. Placed small kisses on the back of her head and ears. Pushed her hair aside and kissed the back of her neck. Just held her and closed my eyes and let myself remember a time when holding her like this was as natural to me as breathing. Let myself dream of first: our first dance, first kiss our first fight. The first time I got lost in her brown eyes.

My eyes popped opened like a springboard. I began to exhale deeply, do a little reality check, did whatever it took to regain my composure. I shouldn't have lay down with her. I shouldn't have let her pull me in her bed. I already came too close to kissing her. I didn't need to be aching for what used to be.

I stumbled down the back stairs and went into the kitchen. I looked in the refrigerator and found it bare except for a half carton of eggs, a half-gallon of outdated milk and some covered dishes that I didn't want to uncover.

I realize that my cousin is more out then in but this is ridiculous. And it's not like the brother can't burn. He can cook his face off. Damn, it's no wonder Nicki's on a liquid diet. There is nothing here to eat. One thing is for sure, there's going to have to be some groceries up in this camp if I'm going to stay over one more night.

I reached for the phone, called my favorite breakfast spot that was about a block from Taylor Motors that delivered. I ordered croissants, blueberry muffins, assorted fruit and hazelnut coffee. I then ran back upstairs, hit the shower, shaved, and dressed just seconds before the food arrived and my no food having cousin came creeping into the kitchen.

"Damn, it smells good up in here."

I turned my back with my food in my hands blocking his path to my grub. "I don't think so cuz. This is real food and I am real hungry."

Michael looked at me with one of his I'm doing him wrong looks. "Come on Marc, why you treating your favorite cousin like that?"

"Say Negro you know that don't count when it comes to some food. Every man for himself," I said placing my bags on the counter and then fanned the air with my hands to fan the scented food his way. "Um, the aroma of fresh bread."

Michael sat down at the table across the room. "It's okay. I'll remember you next time I fix my grilled salmon."

I went to the cabinet grabbed a couple of coffee mugs then picked up my bags of food and sat them down on the table. "Alright, you can get you lame self a muffin or two but don't drink all of my coffee."

Michael quickly jumped up and retrieved two plates from the cabinet and then reached in for the contents of my bag. "Um, croissants, blueberry muffins and hazelnut coffee. Hazelnut?"

"What?"

"Hazelnut?"

"Why you all frowned up and saying hazelnut like it's bad medicine?" I asked reaching for a croissant and letting it melt in my mouth. Um Heaven.

"It's sounds like weak medicine. I mean how strong can it be. Where's the perk in hazelnut?"

"It's not supposed to be strong. It's soothing, relaxing."

Michael's eyes met mine before he spoke. "Let me guess. You once got with a girl named Hazel."

I smiled. "Very soothing, very relaxing."

"You're sick."

"Hey, don't knock it 'til you try it. Go on, broaden your horizons."

"That's okay. Me and my Mr. Coffee over there like it very black and very strong."

"And don't forget very hot," I said biting into my second croissant.

"Are we still talking about coffee?"

"My bad," I smiled, taking another bite and washing it down with my hazelnut coffee. Michael leaned back into his chair and began to tear into a blueberry muffin.

"Speaking of hot," he said as he finished off his muffin and then gave me direct eye contact letting me know he was about to go fishing all up in my business.

"When I got in last night, you know around three-thirty or so, I decided to check in on my house guest. Little did I know she would be keeping company that time of night or morning as the case was."

I finished off my coffee and then leaned back in my own seat. "What's your point, Negro?"

"My point is that I'm a little po'd. I mean this here is my crib, my bachelor crib. And if there's going to be some freakin' going on then I should be the one doing the freakin' or at least getting freaked, you know what I'm saying."

I had to laugh at my cuz, cause he was seriously tripping. His new vow of celibacy was a good three months old and he was seriously weak from lack thereof.

"Mike, man why don't you get you a woman so you can get your mind out of the gutter about me and Nicki. You know me better than that."

"Oh, I know you all right. I know you like that. I know you want to get with that, you know?"

I stood up out of my seat. I didn't want to hear half of what he thought he knew about Nicki and me. "Look Mike, you need to check yourself," I said with more anger than I wanted to.

"Marcus, why you getting all riled up? Could it be that what I just said just might be a little bit true? I mean damn man I hardly ever see you. But every since Nicole's been staying here you have been here everyday, on her like white on rice. So when I see you up in her bed quite naturally I thought hey, you know."

"No, what you saw last night was me being true to my friend, my best friend for over twenty years. Twenty years! I have never walked away from her when she has needed me and I never will."

"That's my point Negro. You care about her so much that nothing can make you make stop caring. Nothing."

"And what's wrong with that?"

"Nothing, man. Hell, I commend you and your friendship with Nicki. I admire it. I mean it's so rare to see a friendship between a man and woman that has survived for so many years despite James and the numerous women in your life."

"If you admire it and commend it then why are you jumping to all these conclusions?"

"Because you're not jumping through shit," Michael said standing up. "I mean come on man, the summer you and your family came down here she was all you could talk about so I know damn well she was more to you than just some 'friend'.

"And I was here when you guys first moved here. Nicole was going through something horrible. Now I didn't know all the details, but I know she was in pain. And so were you. But that didn't stop you from being devoted to her. When she hurt, you hurt. When she cried, you cried with her. You wouldn't breathe unless you knew she was breathing. Whatever she needed man you made sure she had it, no matter what it cost you. No matter if it meant you letting her go. That's more than friendship cuz. A hell of a lot more."

I sat back down in my chair as the weight of my cousin's words fell on my shoulders and the memories of long forgotten years haunted me as they had in the wee hours of the morning; memories of another me, another her, at another time. Kissing memories, touching memories. Laughing happy memories. Memories I couldn't forget no matter how hard I tried.

"Look, Marc all I'm saying is that you and Nicki are like a story that has a beginning but no ending. She's like this incomplete sentence, this dangling participle in your life out there just hanging. How long are you going to leave her out there? How many times are you willing to lose her? She's right at your fingertips and you won't reach for her."

"Mike, you need to..."

"What's up fellas?" Nicole's spoke as she came down the back stairs.

I instantly met her eyes wondering how much she heard but her eyes told me nothing. "Good morning. I ordered breakfast."

She walked over to the table and took a seat. "Is this hazelnut coffee?" she asked reaching toward the small canister.

"Yeah," I answered feeling Michael's glower on me. I poured some coffee in the mug that Michael didn't use and then had to reach around Michael to get to the sugar who didn't miss the opportunity to bump my arm as I did. I briefly looked into his "I told you so" eyes and then gave Nicole the sugar.

"Sorry, there's no milk, but there's some creamer in the bag."

"Thanks."

"Aren't you going to eat?"

"No, this is fine for right now okay."

"Okay," I said looking her over. Unlike last night she looked more restful. It was as if a good night sleep and a fresh shower had lifted the weight of the world from her shoulders. Her damp hair hung loosely about her face that shone naturally. And I could tell she was trying to make an attempt to sound, if not feel, good. She pulled her robe tighter to her and sipped her coffee silently. Michael, who had been busy with his Mr. Coffee, came and sat down with us at the table with his cup of instant pick me up and grabbed a muffin off the plate.

"So, did you sleep okay?" he asked her in between bites.

"Yeah. Although I vaguely remember getting into bed."

"Well when I came in last night you were snug as a bug in a rug." Mike said looking at me.

"So you came in pretty late last night?"

"Yeah, the crowd kept asking for encores. Man it was wild."

"Why you up so early now? Aren't you tired?" Nicole asked in between more sips of coffee.

"Dog tired. But I can't sleep. See, I'm supposed to be meeting with this agent tonight and I am so hyped up. My stomach is tied in knots."

"Michael how many times have I told you, you got it? Talent, looks and you know the ladies love you. Any agent that signs you will see nothing but dollar signs. Take your butt on upstairs and catch some z's before you fall all over the man."

"It's a woman. Zora Winston. You know of her?"

"Everybody knows about Z. She's the best in the business. You sign with her and you are in there. She'll hook you up."

"Yeah?"

"Yeah. Now go to bed."

"Alright then. Thanks Nic."

Michael stood and then kissed Nicole on the cheek and then faced me. "Thanks for breakfast cuz."

"Anytime. But look, you mind going to store and getting some food up in here? We can't live like this, right Nic?"

"Sure can't," Nicole said grabbing a croissant and biting into it.

"Yeah, alright. Later."

Nicole and I both watched him head up the stairs and then turned toward each other at the same time. The slightest smile was on her face. Looked good. She finished the croissant and coffee and then stood to put her cup in the sink.

"So why haven't you left for work yet?" she asked.

"Are you trying to get rid of me too?"

"No. But you don't have to baby sit me."

"Well what are your plans for today?"

"Nothing much. I mean I'll probably just hang out here for most of the day. It's not like I have a job to rush off to."

I stood up and put the remainder of the food in fridge. "You know what I want to do today?"

"What?"

"Jump in the Benz and load the CD player up with some serious music. I'm talking Rick James, Parliament, Cameo and Barkays and then just head out to the coast. Maybe to the beach house."

"Yeah?"

"Hell yeah. That is if you come with me."

"What about work?"

"Have you've forgotten that I'm the owner slash president slash CEO of the company. I go when I want to go. So come on, let's do this."

"I don't know Marcus. I don't know how good of company I would be. I don't want to be a wet blanket."

"The only way you can do that is by saying no. Come on. We can let the top back, you can kick off you shoes, lay back, and let your feet hang out the window."

Nicole walked over by the window and looked outside. And I could tell from her body language that she was itching to get out from these four walls that she has secluded herself into.

"You throw in some Lakeside and Prince and you got a deal," she said turning toward me.

I was going about eighty, the top was down while Parliament was making our funk the P-funk and Nicole was laid back with a pair of dark shades on her toes tapping out the window and her hair blowing wildly in the wind. We both were singing loud and off key while trying to remember all the words to the psychedelic groove and dance in our seats all at the same time. And she was smiling. Laughing.

"Say Marcus, you remember that time I went fishing with you and your family up to Whidby Island?"

"Yeah. And you wanted to see the sunrise over the ocean. So you talked me into getting up early the next morning and we drove on the beach."

"Boy that was a blast. You were flying down the beach in the Impala. You had to be going about ninety."

"Actually it was only about fifty. And if I remember every thing was cool until you decided you wanted to drive and drove us right into the ocean."

Nicole busted out laughing. "The look on your face when we hit the water."

"First, I thought we was going to float out into the ocean. Then after I realized we weren't, all I could think about was my dad."

"Boy, he was pissed."

"Pissed? The man put me on lock down. I couldn't drive my own car for two weeks. Couldn't talk on the phone or go anywhere but school. Shoot, man those were the hardest two weeks of my life."

"Yeah, that's when your dad started calling me Eve, saying I would get you kicked out of Eden. I don't think your dad liked me much after that."

"Nah, he liked you. He just didn't think you needed to behind the wheels."

"Can't say that I blame him," she said leaning deeper into her seat.

I glanced over at her, caught her smiling, looking happy as she talked out the side of her neck with Cameo. I sank down deeper in my seat, got into my gangsta lean as I cruised down the highway with my best friend by my side. Life felt right.

An hour later Rick James had us Busting out of L 7 square by the time I was pulling up to the beach house. Nicole had her eyes closed and was singing loud and popping her fingers so hard that at first she didn't even realize that we had stopped. When I cut off the engine she opened her eyes and looked around.

"I can't believe it," she said stepping out of the car.

"What?" I asked grabbing my CD case to take in the house just in case we were still in our funk mode.

"It looks the same."

"It is for the most part," I said heading for the door. I opened it and let her in first. She walked passed the entrance that led past the kitchen and straight to the living room and then unto the terrace. She stood at the sliding doors looking out at the beach and pacific below us.

"I haven't been here in years."

I placed the CD's on the coffee table and walked up behind her.

Nicole let out a long sigh. "I've forgotten how beautiful it is."

"Kind of takes your breath away uh," I said looking over her shoulders.

"Mind if I open the door, Marcus?"

"Get on out there," I answered pulling the door open for her. She stepped outside and closed her eyes. I watched as the wind blew across her face and through her hair as her white dress blew across her legs. She looked so peaceful.

I left the doorway and began to load the CD player up with a different beat. Jazz. A little Kenny, Najee, Alex and Kurt. Nicole hadn't been here in years but I have often made this my weekend getaway. Kept a well-stocked wine rack downstairs, steaks in the freezer, old and new movies and lots of music. But phones and pagers were not allowed. When I came here I got away.

Just like Nicole had that first summer we spent here. This is where my grandmother had brought her countless of times. And I swear, each time Nicole came home she looked more at ease, more at peace with herself. Like she did today. Maybe it could last. Which is what I was hoping for.

I reached into the freezer and took out a couple of steaks. It was barely eleven. By five or so those babies will be ready for the grill. I went downstairs and grabbed two bottles of wine came back up and placed both in the fridge. Then I went outside and got the small cooler I had packed from the trunk of the car. Inside, were some cheeses, cold cuts, sodas, and potato salad that I had stopped to get on the way down along with some bread and crackers. Had to get this girl to eat.

I went back inside the house, put everything where it needed to go, pumped up the sounds on the stereo and then went out of the opened terrace door. Nicole was stretched out on a lounge chair barefoot with her shades on.

"You look relaxed," I said before sitting in a chair next to her. I touched her arm with a cold soda and she jumped and then pushed me lightly with her hand before taking the soda.

"I was."

"Am I disturbing you?" I asked playfully.

"No. You're giving me exactly what I need as always and you know it."

"I try to oblige."

"Marcus?"

"Yeah?"

"Thank you."

"You know you're always welcome."

I pulled on my shades and leaned back into my seat letting the warm sun hit against me being thankful that I changed into a wind suit. Glancing over at Nicole, I could see that her eyes were closed. I closed mine and drifted back to the scene in the kitchen with Michael earlier this morning. Kept hearing him ask me about a dangling participle. Dreamed. Slept.

A bird squawking above my head woke me up. I jumped, tasted old soda in my mouth, and then rubbed my sleepy eyes. I glanced at my watch. It was just twelve-thirty, but I swear I had been asleep for about three hours. I looked over at Nicole. Her mouth was wide open and soft snoring noises were coming out of it. And women say they don't snore. Where is a video camera when you need one?

I went into the house where Kenny G was tearing up his soprano sax. In the kitchen, I took the bottles of wine out the freezer and placed them in the refrigerator. Next, I took out the cold cuts and cheese and made some sandwiches as I danced in tune with Kenny and played my air sax.

The terrace door opened and I looked up just as Nicole came walking in looking like a summer breeze. Warm. Inviting. I stopped dancing. Hell I stopped breathing. I watched her move across the living room like I was watching a movie in slow motion. Noticed her every graceful and feminine movement. The sway of her hips, the way her breast shifted softly in her dress, the way her arms swung freely as she moved, the way her eyes lit up when she smiled.

"One of those for me?"

"Uh?" I asked finding myself speechless.

"Are you okay?"

"Yeah."

"You sure? You looked like you spaced out on me."

"I'm fine. I just was thinking about something."

"Well, chill Bill. I'm going to wash my hands. Those sandwiches look good."

She left the room and I finally exhaled. Damn my cousin. He just had to go messing with my mind. Had to go digging in my business uncovering old bones and old feelings.

Nicole came back grabbed a sandwich, a soda and then went and plopped back down on her chair. I came out with my food and joined her. She ate. Ate like she hadn't had a decent meal in months, which I knew was true based on what she's been through and the fact that my cousin didn't seem to think that food was an essential part of the daily health plan. She took her last bite and then pushed her empty plate aside. Took one long drink of soda and then belched like any man I know.

"Oh, excuse me," she said laughing lightly.

I laughed with her. "It's okay, just means good food."

"I feel like walking what about you?"

"Cool," I answered, finishing the last of my sandwich and removing my shoes and socks.

We raced down the stairs and practically ran out to the shoreline where the sand was soft and the ocean water was cool as it brushed our feet. We walked side by side for long moments without saying much. Every now and then our arms or hands would touch just enough to feel each other's presence. Guess there wasn't much to be said. We were just enjoying the moment. Maybe even wrapped up in our own solitude, our own thoughts. At least I was. Kept thinking about the past, the present, but couldn't see the future. Nicole's voice finally interrupted my thoughts.

"You know the last time I came out to the beach I almost died."

"What are you talking about?" I asked turning toward her.

"That night I found James with that woman. I just walked out into that ocean and waited for it to swallow me up."

She looked into my eyes with all seriousness. I was speechless. She continued. "For the briefest second I didn't care if I lived or died."

I stopped dead in my tracks. A part of me went stone cold. She noticed I wasn't walking with her and walked back toward me. She reached up and touched my face with her hand.

"Marcus, I'm not always as strong as you want me to be, okay? Sometimes it's too hard when I find myself in a place I never thought I would be."

I looked down into her eyes. Heard what she was saying. But couldn't help the feeling that I was having. She wanted to die because of that low class mutt and I wanted to kill him all over again. I wanted to dig his ass up so I could kill him, plain and simple. I started walking. Fast. Pacing. Trying to think of way I could kill that foul ass mutt again.

"Marcus, please, calm down. Please."

"I'm calm Nic. Okay. I am really," I said turning to face her again. "It's just that I hate that he hurt you so much."

"I know. Which is why I didn't always tell you everything that went down between James and I. But that's neither here nor there. I'm talking to you about one night. I need to tell you everything that happened that night because I don't want anything to come to you that you hadn't already heard from me. Now, are you going to listen to me?"

I looked at her wondering what it was I didn't know. "Of course."

"Okay, like I said, I was drowning. But Derek, you know the prosecutor that was assigned to James' murder case? He saw me out there and he basically saved my life. From what he told me, I was unconscious. He did CPR, called his brother, who is a doctor, had him check me out and he assured Derek that I was fine, which is why I didn't end up in a hospital."

She paused and began to increase her stride as I absorbed all this as preliminary information to what she was really trying to tell me and tried to shake the eerie feeling that was suddenly creeping up on me.

"At his house," Nicole suddenly continued. "We talked a lot. I told him about James and what I walked in on. I didn't tell him about the gun though. It just never came up. I don't think at that time I even remember getting the gun and shooting at James. Maybe I had already blocked that part out. I don't know. I just remember talking to Derek and him making me really comfortable. It was like as he listened to what I said, he really heard me. You know what I mean? Didn't criticize me or judge me. Just listened. Like it really mattered what I had to say. Then one thing led to another and..."

"He didn't..."

"The question is did I? And the answer is yes."

We both stopped walking and I literally felt my blood boil. Evil thoughts were creeping into my mind about a man that I knew no matter what Nicole said had probably taken advantage of her situation.

"Marcus, I knew Derek was attracted to me and that made me feel special. Wanted. And I needed to feel that way. I'd just found James with another woman. He had just told me that he didn't want me, didn't love me. And here was this man, a complete stranger making me feel special. Desired. Like a woman is supposed to feel.

"And when he kissed me, I didn't resist. In fact I invited him, welcomed him to every part of me. But in the end the joke was on me. I woke up feeling cheap and degrading. I had finally sunk down to James' level."

I stepped closer to her and touched her face with the tips of my fingers. Nicole just told me she slept with a complete stranger and still it didn't change how I felt. Nothing could. My cousin's words echoed. I kissed the top of her head and then embraced her in my arms and squeezed her close to me.

LOVE AND CONSEQUENCES

We sat on the beach for the rest of the afternoon. Watched the sky change and waited on the sun to set. Reminisced on days when we were kids. Only talked about the happy silly days. Never talked about the sad days or about the days that changed both of our lives. And that's okay. I was just happy for today and happy to be with her and laugh with her.

After the sunset we walked quietly back to the beach house. We grilled the steaks, ate and sipped on two bottles of wine while watching Cooley High. I stretched out on the couch while Nicole sat on the floor. I don't know how many times I dozed off. Kept waking up seeing only bits and pieces of a movie that we had sneaked in to see when were kids. I awoke at the end were Preach was running from the graveyard. Nicole was silently crying.

"Marcus, promise me that that will never happen to us."

"What's that Nic?" I asked sitting up.

"We'll never have some stupid misunderstanding or lie tear us apart."

I kissed the top of her forehead and prayed.

NICOLE

28

When Marcus and I returned from the beach house two weeks ago, I promised myself that I was not going to allow myself to wallow in self-pity. I was going to keep my head up and try to focus on getting on with my life. I have been burying my head in the sand long enough.

Two days later, I contacted my attorney and James' accountant and decided to get my finances in order. I needed to quit ignoring the bills that were being forwarded to this house and take care of things. But to my surprise, I had nothing to take care of things with.

James' accountant returned my phone call only to inform me that I'm going to lose the house. It turns out that besides not paying the IRS for the last two years and owing the record company close to eight hundred thousand dollars he also went behind my back and got a second mortgage on the house that was in arrears over eight months. Not to mention that two days before he died he had cleaned out all of our joint accounts so I was virtually penniless.

But even though I don't have a dime to my name, I woke up this morning telling myself that today is not going to be like yesterday and every other day before it since James' death. Today, I'm not going to feel lonely or depressed or unloved. Today, I'm going to get through it with my head held high because my life depends on it.

No longer am I going to feel inadequate or feel that I can't make it without James. So what if everything I have done since I was twenty-three years old revolved around James. It doesn't mean that I can't survive and go on living and find a new purpose in my life.

But then the mail came and I received a letter from my attorney. A woman name Debra Codell has a child by James. James has a two-year-old child. A daughter, James has a little girl. I feel more than anger or hatred. I feel down right betrayed.

I didn't care about the house. I didn't want it and planned on selling it anyway. I don't care about the money. I don't give a damn because if push comes, to shove I know I can go to Michael and Marcus and all of my money problems would disappear. But for James to have a child after he repeatedly fought with me and told me vehemently that he never wanted a child is so unbelievable and unforgivable. Throughout our relationship he wore condoms because he wanted no children! The bastard pushed me down the stairs making me lose our child because he never wanted children!

I sat back in my chair taking another sip of the vodka I held in my hand hoping that it would ease the pain that seem to engulf my very being as hot tears rolled down my face. Even in his grave, James still has the power to hurt me and prove with a definite finality that he didn't love me.

I swallowed the rest of my drink, stood up, and went to the bar in the dimly-lit room to refill it. The lights flickered on and off for a second. A storm was near. I walked over to the window. I listened as thunder continued to rumble across the sky and saw the lightening from a distance. I pushed the window open just slightly and let the cool breeze sweep across my face. As I inhaled, a memory from my own childhood came to mind. I loved to be play outside when it rained. Another tear fell from my eyes as I wondered if my unborn child would have like the smell of rain.

I took another sip and moved back to my seat. It was so quiet here. I loved this house. I closed my eyes and remembered when I first came here how safe I felt. But now I felt nothing but scared and alone. Just like I did when I first lost my parents. I tried to picture my mother's face. It was so hard now. It's been so long.

Sometimes it amazes me how much I still miss my parents. It's been twenty years yet it seems like yesterday I was screaming for my father as I watched our house go up in flames. That night, that birthday was the beginning of my end. Ever since then, I have known nothing but pain. Sure, I've tasted some happiness here and there but every time I think I'm where I'm supposed to be, my little happiness is slowly taken away.

And I'm tired. I'm so tired of this shit. All I want is my freedom, my sanity and to be pain free. I hate feeling like this. I didn't want to feel this. I didn't want to be like this. I was supposed to be over my grieving period and on with my life. I was supposed to be laughing on the beach with Marcus and remembering old times and having dinner with Michael and toasting a happier life. I wasn't supposed to be drinking myself into oblivion night after night because that was the only way I could fall asleep. And Lord knows I just want to sleep. I just want to sleep and wake up and find the pain gone. But it never goes away. It haunts me. Just like before. And just like before, I had no one to share the pain with.

As close I was to Michael, I couldn't share my pain with him. There were things about me that Michael didn't know. I had secrets from him. And Marcus. God Marcus, knew everything about me and Marcus felt my pain. But Marcus blamed himself. And I hated that. My pain was not his fault and it never was. So I only had myself. I was once again on my own.

MARCUS

29

The house was dark and I swear my heart sunk to my feet, knowing what I was going to find. Silently I entered the music room and found Nicole sitting in her favorite spot with her back to me. I walked closer to her before speaking.

"You all right?"

She turned and faced me suddenly and brought her hand up to wipe her tear stained face. "Yeah," she whispered to me in the darkness without meeting my eyes.

I looked at her closely as she kept her eyes from mine and as her body language spoke to me telling me otherwise. One minute she was rubbing her hands up and down her arms, the next she was wringing her hands together. I watched her for a moment. A long moment, knowing damn well I was getting on her nerves. But I didn't care. This had to stop.

I knelt down in front of her and lifted her chin so that her eyes would meet mine. They were red, puffy and too damn sad. Anger crept inside of me at the speed of lighting.

I hated everything that was happening to her. I hated James for existing and even more so for getting his sorry ass killed. I hated the fact that Nicole wanted to be nothing but this sorrowful woman that sat in this chair and held onto a tumbler glass like it was her life support.

She didn't have any hope in her eyes. She was gloomy and wanted to wallow in her doom. It was like she had given up and was just waiting to die. It was like...like before. When she was raped.

Nicole and I never talked about the rape. We never spoke about the one night that changed out lives forever and ripped everything that we had, we knew and believed apart. We couldn't. She couldn't tell me of the shame, guilt and pain that she went through any more than I could tell her of the horrifying anger, guilt and hatred I felt.

All we could do was withdraw from each other and deal with it in our own way apart from each other. I wanted to go to her. So many times I wished I could have told her some kind of words of comfort and let her know that I did not blame her or think bad of her because of what happened.

But I couldn't. My guilty conscience wouldn't let me. I couldn't face her.

And before I knew it we drifted apart. And now I'll be damned if I let that happen again. It took us years to rebuild our lives. I wasn't going to lose her again. I couldn't lose her again. I wanted, no, I needed the young girl I met years ago to look back at me. I wanted her happy, smiling, joyful, kicking my ass, cussing me out. Anything! Anything to let me know she was alive.

"You can't keep doing this," I said pushing a strand of her hair from her face.

Nicole let out a heavy sigh and blinked back tears. "And you can't tell me what to do."

"Nicki, I'm not trying to tell you what to do. I'm only trying to tell you that this is not good for you."

She stood up and walked away leaving me on my knees to stare at an empty chair. "Then why don't you tell me what has been good for me, okay? Was it good for me when my parents died and left me an orphan? Was it good for me when I was placed in a home for homeless girls and then in a foster home? Was it good for me when Emily died and all the other rotten things that happened in my life? Why don't you tell me Marcus, cause in all of my years of living I seemed to have missed the good shit!"

For moments I knelt there unable to tell her what she needed to hear. Everything I could think of didn't seem to justify the pain she was going through now anymore than it did her previous pains. But how could I not say anything.

The sound of glass made me look up. She was at the bar now, glass tumbler in one hand and canister in the other. I went to her. Place both of my hands over hers.

My eyes pleaded. "Please don't do this."

Hers glared back. "What would you rather I do, hide behind a brick wall and pretend that shit don't bother me like some people do!"

I caught the criticism she threw with impeding anger. "This bothers me!" I yelled.

"I don't give a damn about what bothers you!" She yelled back in my face and pulling her hands away from me. "I'm tired of worrying about what bothers everybody else. From now on I'm taking care of me. I'm doing whatever makes me happy!"

"I want you happy too. But this is not happiness. And you know it isn't."

"Go to hell!"

"Damn it Nicole don't you know how much I care about you? I cannot watch you destroy yourself!"

"Then turn your back!" she spit at me and then picked up the glass canister again daring me with her eyes to say or do anything.

I stood still all of ten seconds. I watched her pour Vodka in her glass until it was filled to the rim. Watched her place the half empty canister back on the bar.

Then, before I realized it, I took the glass from her and threw across the room. Then I picked up the canister of Vodka, the gin, the scotch, the brandy and all six of those pretty crystal tumbler glasses and threw every one of them against the fireplace. By the time I was finished, the whole room reeked of liquor and scattered glass was everywhere.

I looked at her long and hard and I swear I couldn't feel myself breathing. "I can't turn my back!"

She met my gaze with a hard glare and I could literally see her anger building up inside of her. Her eyes became small slits and her mouth curled up and said the most hurtful words she has ever spoken to me.

"I HATE YOU!" she yelled as she ran up on me and started hitting me with balled up fist. I stood there unable to do anything, my whole body went numb.

"I hate you, you low life bastard. I hate you, James Ful..." She stopped in mid swing. Her eyes looked directly into mine.

I watched her body shake, tremble and I didn't know what to do. Part of me wanted to go to her, hold her, comfort her. But I couldn't. I was still hearing those three words.

So I stood there watching her body tremble. Watched the tears fill her eyes and fall slowly from heavy eyelids. Watched her lips quiver as she tried to make sense of everything that was happening.

"I didn't mean that. I didn't mean you," she whispered.

I felt myself breathe and then pulled her in my arms. "I know," I said squeezing her body into mine. Holding her until she pulled away.

"I'm sorry," she said looking up at me.

"It's okay."

"No, it's not Marcus. Nothing is okay," she said as she walked across the room. She went straight to the bar and pulled out the half a gallon of Vodka that was kept under it, found another glass, filled it up and took a long swallow before looking at me.

"Nothing is okay. But you don't understand that, do you? You don't understand my pain, my loss! This is my life and I have to handle it the best way I can."

"By drinking yourself to death? You call that handling things?"

"I call it surviving!" Nicole shouted as she stood in front of me letting out deep sighs that seemed to heavy for her to hold anymore. I watched as she swallowed the rest of her drink and placed the empty glass on the table.

"Marcus, I would give you my right hand but right now I can't tell you what you want to hear? I'm just too tired. I'm tired of everything! I'm tired of feeling this pain. I'm tired of knowing this loneliness. I'm tired of everybody wanting me to get over what I feel!"

"I'm not asking you to get over what you feel. I just don't want you to give up. I want you to get on with your life. And if that means letting him go then do it. Hanging onto him is not going to make him come back just like it didn't make him love you."

The swing of her left hand left the right side of my face burning and my mind in total shock. "How dare you! How dare you speak to me about love when you have done nothing but spend your life rejecting it? All you have ever done is hide behind your brick wall, your invisible line where no one dare cross without a personalized engraved invitation!

"You, Mr. Unreachable, Mr. Untouchable, Mr. Selfish and I don't give a damn about nobody but myself! You have done nothing but spend countless hours with countless women and you're even proud of that fact! You don't know shit about love. You don't have a clue about what I'm going through!"

I looked into her angry eyes and I swear I didn't know what to say. Didn't know how to respond. The only thing I knew was that those words seemed to cut me to my very core. And I couldn't speak. So I just crept my selfish ass back behind my damn brick wall.

A sound woke me from a deep and frightful sleep. All night I tossed and turned. Kept seeing angry eyes. Kept hearing hurtful words. I glanced at the clock. It was 4:15 and the sun was nowhere near the sky. I silently crept down the hall.

Her room was empty. Her bed untouched. I hurriedly went down the back stairs, passed the kitchen and then into the music room. The foul stale smell of the mixed liquor lingered in the air. The front door open and I ran to it. It was Michael coming in from the club. We both looked at each other silently then he followed me back into the music room.

"What happened?"

I didn't respond. I was trying to remember how long I had slept and where was she! I stepped on a piece of glass. Saw blood oozing out of my foot and hopped over to the couch sat down and began to search my now throbbing foot.

"Where's Nicki?"

"What?"

"Nicki. Is she asleep?"

I looked into my cousin eyes. "I don't know where she is, Mike."

Michael looked around the room again and then walked over to the coffee table where he found a piece of paper with Nicole's handwriting and began to read it aloud.

Dear Marcus and Michael. I needed some space and
some time to myself. Please don't worry about me.
I'll be okay. I just need to be alone. I will call you. Nicole.

LOVE AND CONSEQUENCES

I rose from the couch. Forgot about the broken glass and my bleeding foot and took the note from Michael. I read the note myself. Then read again as if the words would change.

ICE

30

I stepped out of the shower, walked over to the mirror and wiped it with a towel so I could shave. The mirror fogged back up as quickly as I wiped it and I could only see my eyes staring back at me. I lathered up my face, grabbed my razor and began to shave even though I could not see my whole face. It wasn't like I needed to anyway. I could do most things without thinking. I finished shaving, put down the razor and then stared deep into my eyes looking for what others see when they look at me. I quickly closed them feeling myself shudder. I had no idea of who I was or who I used to be. I couldn't see my eyes anymore. They were the kid's. The young punk I ran up on in the burger joint that day, the young punk whose eyes has haunted me every since.

I believed in messages. And his eyes had a message. The game has changed and it's time for me to get out. Now! If I want any resemblance of a real life, I got to get out. I have wasted so many years, giving up so much and have nothing but an empty life to show for it. I have to take care of Slaughter, Sheila and this whole life I'm living. I'm tired of lurking, hiding, sneaking and pretending I am down when I don't give a damn about none of this shit. I got to make a clean break, get away from my life so I can live my life. And there is no way I can do that unless I reinvent myself. I want to look in this mirror and know that there is a real man staring back at me.

I left the bathroom, went into my bedroom, and quickly got dressed. I went to the dresser, picked up my piece, my keys and headed downstairs and out the door where I jumped in my car and sped off. I made the trip to the land of la la in record time blindly led by rage and with only one thought. Slaughter has got to go.

I went straight to Jake's Bar and Grill. Sure enough, Slaughter's car was parked out back. I pulled up right beside it and went in through the back door. The sound of an old Ashford and Simpson song was coming from the jukebox. I answered their question with a resounding no. Nothing was good to me right now.

In one glance I check the small joint out. A man and a woman were playing pool. She was leaning her body all into his as he showed her how to guide the stick and then kissed her on the neck. I watched her smile and then turn and kiss him deeply on the mouth.

Behind them in the mirror I could see Slaughter. He was getting up from his favorite table in the corner. I watched him in the mirror go toward the bathroom. I looked around again. Noticed two other men sitting at the bar in front with a plates of half eaten food in front of them. That was it. No one else was here except I knew Pam or Jake himself had to be in the kitchen. Slaughter's boys were nowhere to be found.

I looked at my watch. It was a quarter to nine. I had been standing here in plain view all of three minutes and no one even looked my way.

The woman at the pool table laughed and I looked to my right again. The man was rubbing his hands up and down her backside, down her thighs and back up under her dress. She wrapped one leg around him, then as if remembering where she was put it back down.

At that moment, Slaughter came out of the bathroom and went back over to his table for one and sat with his back toward me. I reached into my pocket and my hands felt for steel. I could feel sweat beading across my head. It's been a long time.

I wrapped my hand around my piece with one finger itching at the trigger. I took several steps forward until I was so close to him that I could see the hairs on the back of his neck. I watched him chew his food and then slowly eased my hand out of my pocket holding my piece and brought it up toward his head.

The woman let out a slight moan. Slaughter picked up his coffee took a sip and then continued to eat. In the mirror beside me I could see now that the woman was sitting on the pool table her head thrown back as the man rested his head in her lap. He kissed her thighs, her breast and then pulled her face to him and kissed her long and hard.

I looked away. Back at Slaughter who was now sucking a bare pork chop bone. I brought my hand up again. The kitchen door opened. Pam came out, gave the two at the bar more coffee and then went to the other end of the bar and picked up empty plates.

"I love you, Carolyn."

The man's voice made me turn back toward them. I looked at the woman; saw tears in her eyes as she looked at him. She kissed him and then whispered to him. I read her lips. My body went cold.

I looked back at Slaughter. Gripped my piece tighter and held it with both hands as sweat poured in my eyes. There were five people in this damn hole in the wall. Five! And I had to take them all just to get the one. I had to do them all just to get my freedom. I had to pop Jake's daughter, Pam, who just had her twenty-eight birthday last month. I had to make the meal of the men at the bar their last meal. I had to drop the man that had rubbed his woman's thighs on top of a pool table early in the day in the middle of this dingy bar and grill. I had to make sure Carolyn never told him she loved him again. I had to, just to get my freedom!

I squeezed the trigger. Slaughter slowly put down his fork and sat perfectly still. Pam looked toward the men at the bar. The men at the bar looked toward the couple at the pool table. The couple at the pool table looked at each other. Their eyes locked on each other. No one looked my way. But they felt me. They all felt my presence at the same time and dared to move or even look at me. I was death staring them straight in the face and they all chose not to look.

I stepped forward until I was directly behind Slaughter and placed my nine at the base of his head. John Slaughter tensed up and stared straight ahead.

"'Sup, Slaughter."

"Ice, you're as good as dead," he said darting his eyes to the mirror and making eye contact with my reflection.

"I got the gun. You're in here alone and you're not even strapped. So tell me again whose dead."

Slaughter placed his hands flat on table. "I guess you don't mind going to prison for the rest of your life."

"I have already spent my life in prison. Today I'm breaking out."

"You got the balls to pop me in front of all these people."

I looked around the place. Pam was frozen solid at the counter with the same puppy dog eyes she used to give me before I laid her down last year. The old men at the other end both stared ahead with food in their mouths that they couldn't swallow. Behind me, Carolyn's man stood in front of her as another tear fell from her eyes. I turned to Slaughter. "What people?"

Slaughter laughed.

I pushed the gun against his head and his laughter stopped. I stepped in front of him, keeping the gun on his head and knelt down in front of him looking at the center of his pupils. "You got two choices. One, I blow your brains out of your head before you process your next thought. Two, you watch me walk out of that door and out of your life. You forget the day we met and that you even ever knew me. You forget the kind of car I drive, the color of my eyes, the color of my damn skin. You forget I even exist. And if you got to think about it John, you're a dead man. I know everything about you, even your damn breathing pattern. I made you John. I know your operation inside out. I will start a war and make your family love your enemies. This is our last conversation. You understand old man?"

Slaughter nodded his head and then diverted his eyes to the bar like I wasn't even standing over him with a gun to his head. "Pam, can you get me another cup of coffee?"

I stood up and watched as Pam came to his table with the hot coffee her eyes staying on Slaughter the whole time. She poured his coffee and then went back to the counter and began to wipe it again. I looked at the two men. They both went back to eating. At the pool table, Carolyn's man lifted her off the table and pulled her in his arms. They shared a kiss. He rubbed her backside. She whispered to him and again my body went cold. I headed back out the way I came and jumped in my car. I started the engine glancing in the rear view mirror to make sure Slaughter wasn't crazy. Instead I only saw my eyes staring at me. I know who I am and who I used to be. I used to be the young punk at Fatburger's but now as of this moment, I'm a man. I pressed my foot harder on the gas pedal and drove faster. Carolyn's whispered words echoed in my ears. She didn't know it but she saved Slaughter's life. I looked ahead at the road in front of me with only one thought. Love is a powerful thing.

PART THREE:

All About Love

NICOLE

31

"Hello."

"Hi Mike, it's me."

"Nicki? How are you?" His voice was warm, genuine, and sincere.

"I'm good."

"It's been too long."

"I know."

"Why don't you just come home then?"

"Where's home Mike?"

"Hey, mi casa es su casa."

I briefly smiled into the phone. "I love you."

"Back at you."

"How's Marcus?"

"Truth? I don't know. He's slipped back into his old habits. Don't see him much."

"I miss you guys."

"Then come home. There's no reason for you not to be here."

"I have my reasons."

"Whatever they are they're not good enough. Tell me where you are so I can drag you home where you belong."

"Quit trying to be a bully. It's not your style."

"Oh so you don't think I will uh? Girl, I will drag you here by your weave, kicking and screaming all the way."

"Yeah, right."

"Oh, you think you know me so well?"

"Like the back of my hand."

"Well, I know you too. I know you need me."

I hate it when he's right. I let silence creep between us.

"Come see me Nicki."

I didn't speak. This is not what I wanted. I just wanted to hear his voice. I wasn't ready to see him yet.

"Come on, girl. You know I'm not too proud to beg."

"How's your singing coming?" I asked hoping to change the subject.

"Come see for yourself. I'm still at the club for a couple more weeks."

"I'll think about it. See you later, friend."

"Nicki?"

"Yeah?"

"You're taking care of yourself, right?"

"I am. Bye, Michael." I slowly hung up the phone and let out a deep breath.

That was hard, real hard. But I'm glad I called him. I needed to call him. It was bad enough that I left in the middle of the night the way I did. Sure, I left a note, but Michael and Marcus deserved more than that. Especially Marcus. I shouldn't have let over two months pass before even calling them. I don't even know where that time went.

The night I left, I felt like the world was caving in on me. Like I was back in the Pacific drowning. And I was going down kicking and screaming all the way. Didn't care who went with me. Didn't care who I hurt in the process. No one could save me this time. Didn't want them to. I was my own destruction.

So I left. Left in the middle of the night and without saying goodbye to the two most important people in my life. But I had to leave that way because I knew they would have tried to stop me. And I had to leave before I totally destroyed everything between us.

But that was yesterday and today is today and I have finally left my past in the past. Now I had to fix the present. And I knew I had to do that by getting on with my life. And by un-hurting the people I hurt the most. I had to see Marcus.

I still can't believe the things I said to him and the things I did. I hit him twice. Told him I hated him, twice. Said mean, ugly, hateful untrue things. And then saw the hurt in his eyes. How could I be so cold? Why did I have to lash out at the one person who has never let me down? I had to see him. Had to make things right. I just don't know how. But I know I will find a way. Had to.

Friday night, I found myself downtown in the midst of thick smoke and sweaty bodies. Wall to wall people were dancing, singing and seriously partying. I found the stage and watched him. His voice was clear as crystal over the microphone. He was the ringleader. Everybody was following him. He sang, the crowed echoed. He danced, the crowd grooved. He was in his element and loving every minute of it.

His eyes found me in the middle of the crowd. His face widened into his beautiful grin and I couldn't help but to reciprocate. Quickly he brought the song to an end, told the band to take twenty and rushed his sweaty body to mine. He squeezed me so tight I came off the floor. I had to scream for air. He let go. Looked down at me and then kissed me fully on the lips.

"Damn, I missed you," he said once our lips parted and as I struggled to regain my breath.

"Michael, you took my breath away!"

"That's what you did to me the moment I saw you," he laughed and then looked me over from head to toe checking to see if I was all in one piece. "You look good."

"And you lie terribly as always. You see all the extra pounds on me."

"That's what I'm talking about. Brothers like a little meat on their ham hocks." Michael said rubbing his hands together and licking his lips.

I punched him lightly in the chest. "You were fantastic up there. You had the crowd rocking."

"Yeah?"

"Most definitely."

"Come sit with me."

I followed him to a reserved table at the back of the club.

"So, can I get you something? Coke, Pepsi, Seven-Up?" Michael asked as we sat down.

I laughed and shook my head. "It's okay, Michael. I can handle a drink or two without getting zooted. But no, thank you. I'm cool right now."

"Well, what about something to eat? There's a fantastic buffet table set up near the stage. Got plenty of food. Hot wings, little cute sandwiches, potato salad, vegetable trays, fruit trays, skrimps"."

"No, that's okay, I don't have much of an appetite."

"No appetite or just no appetite for food?"

I looked at him suspiciously knowing all to well where this conversation was heading and played along. "What's that supposed to mean?"

"I mean everybody's hungry for something. Why don't you tell me what you're hungry for and I'll see what I can do to hook you up?"

"Oh no, Mike, don't start none and it won't be none. I know you don't want me getting all into the details of your love life."

"What you want to know?"

"Everything. What lucky lady is getting all that love?"

Michael let out a small laugh, his eyes dancing and for a brief second he reminded me too much of Marcus.

"What's love got to do with it?"

"Umph, typical brother uh."

"I'm not typical. Maybe I don't have time for love?"

"You make time for sex."

Michael fidgeted in his seat and pulled at his ear. I knew his tale tell signs and decided to probe some more.

"Am I embarrassing you, Mike?"

"Maybe."

"Oh uh, uh. You're not getting off that easy. No fair, give me all the juicy details," I said propping my hands under my chin, ready to listen to all. He evaded my glare. Played with the candle that was on the table.

Finally he spoke, "There's nothing to tell."

"What do you mean nothing?"

"Just what I said."

"Michael, please. I just saw you on that stage singing and dancing your head off and practically driving every female in this club crazy. You can't tell me a good looking brother like you is not getting yours."

Michael look down and shook his head.

My mouth fell open. "You're joking right?"

He held his head up and stared me dead in the eye. "Hell no."

"Michael you do still like women don't you?"

"Nicki!" Michael exclaimed, almost knocking over the candle he had played with earlier.

"Hell, people change. I mean married women are waking up to their gay ass husbands all over the world."

"Well, not me. I loves me a beautiful chocolate brown skin woman and the way she smells and feels next to my skin when are bodies are umm..."

"Alright, now! So I hear you talk that talk, but you're not walking that walk. What gives?"

"You really want to know?" Michael asked his tone more serious than before. I looked in his eyes. Remembered why this brother and me were so close. Missed him.

"Talk to me."

"Emptiness."

"I feel you."

"Do you? Cause it seems everybody wants to think that a man has sex just to be having sex, but it's not like that with all of us. I hate being with a woman and then getting up to leave because I realize that I have no reason to stay. I want emotional intimacy, Nicki. The physical is played out. I want my woman feeling me when I look at her. I want to know what kind of day she had just by looking at her."

"Damn, Mike, I never knew this about you."

"What you're surprised to know that I really want to find someone special in my life?"

"No, I'm surprised you're not having sex."

"Oh, because I'm a black man I can't choose to be celibate? Surely you didn't think I was like my cousin going around messing around with half the female population of America."

"No, I didn't think that. Speaking of your cousin, how is he?"

"So, now we get to the real reason why you are here."

For the second time my mouth fell open. "That's not true. I came to see you."

His eyes glared at mine telling me he knew better.

"I did come to see you Michael."

"Okay, so you see me. Now tell me what's up with you and Marcus."

"Nothing I'm just worried about him."

"Worried about him or worried about seeing him?"

"Why would you say that?"

"Come on now, I know something went down between the two of you."

"What, did he say something?"

"No, but neither are you."

I took another deep breath and looked around the club again. Michael reached across the table and took both of my hands in his. "Look you don't have to talk about it if you don't want to. Just know I'm here okay?"

I looked into his eyes and saw all the familiarity that I loved about him. "I know."

He rubbed my hands with his.

"So, Mike tell me about this single I hear you're working on."

"Been keeping tabs on me?"

"Well, I can't help it. Everybody that's anybody is talking about you. Are you excited?"

"I'm scared out of my mind."

"Yeah?"

"Nicki, you ever have a dream come true?"

"Scary as hell."

"But I wouldn't be so scared if I had a songwriter like you in my camp."

"Okay."

"Okay? Just like that?"

"Yes, just like that."

"Do you have any idea how much I love you," he said and then kissed me on the cheek.

"Save the charm for the ladies Michael. I'm not buying."

"You sure know how to cut a brother. Couldn't you have let me down easy?"

"Not my style. So when do you go into the studio?"

"Z's working on locking me down hopefully in the next couple of weeks. Are you going to come with me?"

"Try to stop me. Now get your fine self back on that stage. You're public is calling."

Michael rose out of his seat slowly letting go of my hands. "And you called me fine. Baby, you have made my night." He kissed me again on the cheek.

"Get on out of here."

He laughed and took a step backwards. "Are you going to stay?"

"Maybe."

"Please. Just for one song. I've been working on something I would like you to hear."

I looked around the club as Michael disappeared into the crowd and then finally joined his band on stage. His happy disposition seemed to spread. The audience seemed to sense his return to the stage. I sat back in my chair with my chest stuck out. Michael had a serious following. I was so proud of him and so happy for him. A waitress came up to me and asked me what I wanted to drink. I shooed her away just as Michael began to speak.

"Hello everybody. I'm glad you all stuck around for my second set." Applause came loudly. The women were whistling and the guys were definitely barking.

"Thank you. You are too kind. Thank you. Right now I want to do a little something that I've been working on for quite awhile. It's an old song that when I grew up listening to it I didn't realize it said so much, I just liked the melody. But now, now I realize that this song pretty much expresses my outlook on some things that as a man I have been guilty of overlooking. Now I know the fellas are not going to want to hear this but say men, I think we've been dogging our women."

Every female in the club applauded. Myself included.

Michael waited for the cheering to calm down and then continued. "What I'm trying to say is they know more than we do about life, love and the whole scenario and we dog them out because they get it and we either don't get it, don't want to get it, choose to ignore it or play by our own damn rules."

"Talk to them Michael." A female voice ringed out among more applause.

Michael looked out onto the audience a moment and then went to take a seat at his piano. "But you know what? There isn't but one set of rules. And why, oh why, do some many of us, including myself, spend countless hours, days, years trying to change the rules I do not know. But I know better now. I want better now. This is where I am. This is what I know. Let me lay this on you."

Like magic his fingers glided across the black and white keys at first playing a simple tune, one that I slowly began to recognize from my youth. I stood up from my seat, moved through the crowd of screaming women to try and see him better. One lady was acting faint. Most were just waving their hands; smiles on their faces eyes closed as they too recognized the melody. Michael's voice sounded like pure silk as it wrapped around each note.

Paint a pretty smile each day.
Loving is a blessing yeah
Never let it fade away
It's all about love yeah

I couldn't believe it. I hadn't heard that song in years. Back in the day, Earth Wind & Fire was my group! And his rendition sounded just like the original. His background singers were on it, his sax and trumpet players were blowing it and Mike was on the keyboards ripping it up. Before I realized it, I was swaying back and forth with the crowd, feeling this serious vibe and getting caught up in Michael's voice and my many memories. His words soothed me, moved me and grooved me back in time.

"How many of you out there know what I'm talking about?" Michael asked the crowded club. A thunderous roar of applause, screams and more rang out as Michael continued.

Mmm, mmm!
Talking to yourself is fine
Makes you feel much better
Know just where to draw the line
My dear, my dear.
Bound to fall in love one day
surely and you need it.
pretty smile will always say
my dear, yeah.
Ooh ooh ooh ooh
Ooh ooh ooh ooh
Ooh oh ooh ooh
Ooh ooh ahh.

"Come on ya'll sing that part with me." Mike said as his eyes found me and smiled into my eyes. I gave him a big smile and blew him a kiss after kiss. The crowd immediately joined in on the next line.

Feel it, feel it, feel it yeah.
yeah, yeah, yeah,
yeah, yeah, yeah
yeah, yeah, yeah.

"Sing Michael," a woman behind me yelled in my ear.

"Go head, man," a man joined in.

"Handle your business, son."

I stopped swaying. I knew that voice. I slowly turned around. Standing right behind me with the biggest smile was Marcus. He lowered his eyes to mine. Looked all inside me. Said two words.

"Hey baby."

Tears were fighting their way into my eyes and I didn't know what to do. I wanted to hug him but I knew I had no right. I wanted to just feel the warmth of his arms around me and feel that kiss on my forehead but I had no right. Not after the way I spoke to him last. Not after the harsh words I said. Guilt quickly took residence all inside my bones and it brought his roommate fear.

I felt my insides shaking. Then my outside and I didn't know how much longer I could stand up. Somewhere far away I could still hear Michael singing, still here the music playing, and the crowd grooving. But I felt totally alone in the spot I stood in except for the man before me.

I looked at him and in my mind apologies were rolling off of my tongue. Over and over again all I could think about was how sorry I was. But the words weren't coming out. They were stuck in my throat. Choking me. I looked down at the lit dance floor. Watched it flicker on and off at the speed of my beating heart. I couldn't breathe.

"Are you going to stand there all night or are you going to give me a hug?"

I raised my eyes toward him. Saw his outstretched arms and then felt their warmth around me. I let out a deep breath. I couldn't remember the last time something felt this good. He squeezed me tighter, harder, strong. Held me for a long ass time. Rubbed my back, kissed my forehead and then held my hands in his as he looked down at me with the smile that I knew so well.

"Marcus, I am so sor…"

"Hey, I don't even want to hear it. That's water under the bridge."

"But the things I said, Marcus. I was so wrong. I didn't mean any of it. I was just so full of pain and I lashed out…"

"Damn woman you are the most stubborn person I know. What does a brother have to do make you be quiet?"

For the third time tonight I was left with my mouth wide open. Marcus' eyes were smiling and he let out a laugh and soon I was laughing and smiling with him.

"Now that's better. Let's dance."

"Uh?"

"Baby, we are at a club, in the middle of the dance floor and my cousin is up there getting his groove on. Get the lead out and move your butt," he said bobbing his head to Michael's rendition of Lakeside's Fantastic Voyage.

He let go of my arm and started moving to the beat, straight old-school style. Broke out into the muscle. I had to move on that. Jumped right in with him for a moment then started the doing the gigaloo. He smiled as he joined my move then switched up to the snake. I snaked him back and then started prepping on him. Then next we both started to smurf. We were partying seriously until he broke out and started to pop lock and I had to quit because I couldn't stop laughing. He grabbed my hand and led me off the dance floor.

"I knew you couldn't hang. Just old," Marcus said as soon as we reached the door. I caught my breath and inhaled some smoke free air as soon as we were outside.

"How is somebody that is doing the pop lock going to call me old? I don't think so."

Marcus handed the valet attendant his ticket and then turned to face me." At least I can still do it. Your butt's so old you forgot how."

"Marcus, please. I can do anything you can do. I just didn't want to embarrass myself like that."

"Oh, alright. Whatever you say, baby."

His car pulled up in front of us and Marcus grabbed my hand again. "Come on."

"Where are we going?"

"I haven't seen you in two months. I'm kidnapping you. Jump in."

I looked at him a moment trying to access what he was up to, gave up and then got in the car. Right about now a ride in a convertible Benz under a starlit sky seemed to be the right thing to do. I eased back into my seat and took my shoes off just as a Parliament CD began to play. I looked over at Marcus. He started snaking with the steering wheel and then put the car in drive. We car danced all across town.

Why we were at Taylor Motors, I didn't know. He took a remote control, pushed a button and a garage door that I never noticed before opened. He drove inside, turned off the car, let the door back down and then finally looked over at me. I was about to ask why we came but he placed a finger on my lips to shush me.

He got out of the car and then came and opened my door. I stepped out into the semi-lit garage and followed him to a door where he took my hand, still not saying a word.

He led me down a dimly-lit narrow corridor. Then we came up on the big, glass window that faced the showroom. Rows and rows of beautiful cars sparkled brightly about the room, everything from shiny new Mercedes Benz's to his collection of classic convertibles.

His office was just ahead. We went inside and I waited for him to turn on a light, but he didn't. He led me around his desk and as we headed toward his private bathroom I stopped walking.

He turned around to face me with a finger on his lips and pulled me forward. We headed to what I thought was a glass shower but before I could think to say anything he took the remote out of his pocket and pushed more buttons and the floor began to drop down. I grabbed his arm with my other hand at the sudden movement. He pushed buttons on his remote again. I looked about but couldn't tell what that function did until I looked at the remote in his hand that was flashing 'Alarm Set' in red letters.

We stopped moving and the door slid open. Marcus stepped out first. Reached and turned on the lights that gave a blue glow. I stood there in total awe.

"Oh my God. This is beautiful. This is unbelievable," I whispered as I looked around the large loft apartment that had to be close to at least twenty five hundred square-feet.

To the left of us, was a huge U-shaped kitchen that had an island and a long counter with bar stools in front of it, filled with built-in stainless steel appliances. The counter tops were dark blue marble with specks of gray. And there was a beautiful solid dark blue marble floor throughout the entire area.

"This is beautiful. When did you do this?"

"Awhile back."

I turned around and looked around the rest. There was a big comfortable navy leather sectional couch that had an old-fashioned cushioned bar behind it and faced a smoked blue glass table with a blue marble base. And then there was an entertainment unit that housed a huge stereo system and the biggest television I had ever seen.

"How long ago?"

"Um, about four years ago."

"I can't believe you never brought me here."

Just ahead of the living area there was a marble, navy, jacuzzi tub with beautiful chrome handles. And in front of that, behind a blue acrylic half-wall, was the biggest bed I had ever seen with a dark blue velvet comforter, sky blue sheets, about ten pillows and a mirrored glass on the ceiling.

I couldn't help but smile as I turned around and faced him. "Oh, I see. This is the babe cave right?"

Marcus face went into a huge smile. "Now why does it have to be all that?"

"Player, player. You're talking to Nicki, okay. Don't lie and try to deny. I'm feeling you all up in here."

"It's not what you think, Nic."

"Uh, uh."

"For real. This is my haven, not my harem."

"Marcus, please. Just how many women have you slept with?"

His smile left and his eyes became serious. "Why you always throw that up in my face?"

"Throw what?"

"The number. It really ain't all that."

I gave him the evil eye. "Marcus come on now, the Badman has been out there playing hard since the seventh grade."

"I was young."

"And?"

"I've slowed down."

"Slowed down?"

"Yes, you know matured."

"Matured yes, but it's not like you're out of the game, player."

"Well, just for the record, I'm not the one out there chasing. Women see the way I'm rolling and they do what they do. And hey as a man, I do what I do, get my satisfaction any way I can."

I stared up into his eyes. "You say that like you're missing something."

"And you say that like you haven't known me since I was thirteen. Like you don't know me. If you want to figure out this player's game, ask yourself why he is playing."

I looked at the seriousness of Marcus' eyes. For seconds I let my mind travel back in time when he and I were *he and I,* and then just as quickly fast-forwarded to reality. "Hey, this is getting a little deep for me, maybe I just need to get out the player's mix altogether."

He switched gears on me, winked and threw out that dimpled smile. "That's fine too. Have a seat, " he said gesturing for me to sit down on the couch as he headed for the kitchen.

"No, wait, back up. What do you mean ask myself? You're saying that I'm to blame for your womanizing ways?"

Marcus stopped in his tracks and turned toward me, his eyes once again so intense. "My ways, as you say, are just my way of dealing with losing you."

I was taken aback. I stared into eyes. I couldn't believe he went there; to our past like it was only yesterday that we stole kisses in his parent's kitchen. For moments I was speechless, caught up in my own memories. Remembered the way he used to hold me, smile at me and make me feel.

"You want anything?"

"What?"

"I'm thirsty. You want something to drink? " he asked as he backed slowly into the kitchen once again switching gears.

I nodded and then sat down nervously looking around this beautiful blue haven a little more. It felt so secretive. "Say, Marcus, there are no doors or windows in here. This is totally private. "

He came back with two glasses of iced tea and sat down on the couch next to me. "Exactly the way I intended it to be. I told you nobody knows about this place, nobody. This is my private haven. Everybody thinks I'm always closing myself up in my office when, actually, I've slipped down here to fix me a little something to eat, maybe watch a flick, take a hot shower, listen to some music and nobody knows otherwise. The only entrance is the one we came in and these four walls are sound proof."

"But when you come down here aren't you worried about what's going on up there?" I asked taking a sip of my drink and then placing my glass on the coffee table next to his.

"No. I have cameras all over the showroom, my office, my garage and the main garage. And I can watch everything up there from down here on those monitors," he said pointing up above our heads. "And my computer over there is tied into the others upstairs so I can keep an eye on every transaction. So, see I'm covered. I can literally run my business from my home."

"This is your home?"

"Yeah, one of them."

"Why you living like this?"

"Like what?"

"Secluded."

"Damn, I guess I can't hide anything from you. Not even my loneliness," Marcus said while his eyes looked even deeper into mine. I took a long swallow from my glass, trying to assess his mood. Everything he was saying, every move he made was somehow out of place. I couldn't remember the last time I saw him like this. He seemed so...so vulnerable.

"I did this place 'cause I felt like I was being swallowed alive in my old house in Santa Ana. I mean, what was I doing with a house that had eight bedrooms, four baths, a pool and a guesthouse and I'm by myself? So I sold it and renovated this place."

"And lived here in secret?"

"Well, it just happened that way."

"So why did you bring me here?"

"Why, what do you mean, why? I haven't seen you in two months, you know. The club was cool but I wanted us to go some place where we could chill converse, catch up. It's really not that hard Nic, I just wanted to be with you. I missed you."

I looked into his eyes for seconds feeling my heart swell up in my body and then leaned my body so that it pushed his "That's got to be the sweetest thing you have said to me in a while."

"Well, you know I have my moments," he said with all sincerity.

"Yeah you do," I said as tears tried to form in my eyes and so I decided it was time to change the subject. "And so does your cousin. He was on tonight."

"He definitely was that. The boy finally listened to me and did some quality music."

I popped Marcus on the back of the head. "You didn't have anything to do with it and you know it. And anyway, anything Michael does is quality. The man is talented," I said with peacock pride and then reached for my glass and lifted it up. "To Michael's success."

Marcus picked up his glass and clinked mine. "To my cousin."

We both took a respected drink. Marcus licked his lips and made them make a popping noise before speaking. "I still can't believe he belted out Earth Wind & Fire."

"Earth was my group!"

"Earth was my group. You didn't even know who they were until I turned you on to them."

"That's bull, Marcus."

"Who had all their albums?"

"That's only because I didn't have a stereo."

"Who got the tickets to their concerts?"

"You stole money from the cash register at your dad's restaurant to get the tickets. And if I remember correctly, we wouldn't have even gone if it hadn't been for me when your father caught your thieving behind and put you on lock down." I popped the back of his head again.

"Okay, okay, now. Why is this trip down memory lane getting me in trouble?" He said standing up and then walked over to his stereo system.

"Well, you started it Anthony Marcus. You always think you know everything."

"Anthony Marcus. Wow, it's been a minute since you called me out like that."

"I always call your whole name when I have to get my point across to your thick head."

"Oh, is that right? So, what's your point?"

"That I knew EWF first."

"Whatever. I knew them better."

"Oh, so you think so?"

"I know so."

"What album was All About Love on?"

"That's the Way of the World," I answered proudly. No matter what Marcus thought I knew I knew my group.

"Some people say that was the best one."

"You get no argument out of me," I said standing up and going over to another stack of CD's just next to him. He had a nice collection of old school and new jams. I watched as he took a CD out of the case placed on his system and then picked up a remote.

"Yeah, all the nice cuts were on there. Especially this one," he said and then pushed the remote.

A familiar beat filled the room followed by the sensuous slow moan of Phillip Bailey. I looked up at Marcus.

I said, "Reasons."

He whispered, "Yeah."

"That was the song."

"Correction, that was our song," Marcus said, placing the CD's and the remote down. He moved closer to me and before I realized it he had me in his arms.

I looked in his eyes, smiled and then placed my arms around his neck. Slowly, he guided me, and without thinking, I followed his lead. He held me close, strong but not tight. Placed his face next to mine then rubbed it against my neck. After a moment, I rested my head on his shoulder. Got lost in the song, in the movement of our dance. Couldn't remember the last time I felt so relaxed and so damn good. I sang softly.

Marcus arms held me tighter. His hands lightly caressed my back and lingered at the base of spine. His breath was warm against my neck, tickling my ear. I snuggled in closer to him as he began to sing too. Not loud, just barely enough for me to hear him and to let me know he was feeling the same grove that I was.

Phillip Bailey hit notes higher than the sky as I closed my eyes and floated in Marcus' arms. Floated and drifted. Drifted and floated. Grabbed onto some serious memories. Reminisced about happy times that made me wish for things unchanged. I held onto my Morning. Like Cinderella, I didn't want the clock to strike midnight.

I looked up at Marcus as memories once again started flooding my mind. I thought of a basement birthday party, park picnics, his 1968 Impala. In every memory there was this song, slow dancing and Marcus. And I was so happy, so damn happy.

Marcus touched the side of my face with his hand as he stared down into my eyes the same way he had the last time we were this close. That time at Michael's when we were in the den. When I felt like he was going to kiss me.

My heart began to race and I felt my knees weaken. I averted my eyes from his. Took a deep breath. Tried to get my heartbeat back to normal. Tried to tell myself that this was crazy. We were just dancing, nothing more, just a dance.

I slipped my hands from around his neck and let them rest on his shoulders. He took my left hand in his right, held it just above my heart. His face moved closer to mine.

"Every time I hear this song I think of you and our sixteenth birthday. What about you? Do you ever think about that night?" He asked in a voice that was sensually deep. I was so enthralled by his eyes and his voice that I couldn't find my own so I just nodded. Seconds ticked off complete silence that spoke volumes as he stared down into my eyes and as I looked deeply into his seeing our past starring right back at me. I saw our first kiss, whispered words, warm embraces.

He placed the side of his face against mine, his lips lightly brushing my ear as he began to speak. "I remember how we danced song after song and how you laughed. I had never seen you laugh so much or look more beautiful. You were so beautiful. And I was a nervous wreck."

"Nervous, why?"

"Because I knew how you felt about celebrating your birthday and I wanted everything to be perfect."

LOVE AND CONSEQUENCES

"It was," I said honestly.

"Yeah, it was a perfect night. One minute we were dancing, laughing, and acting crazy and then this song came on and ...and all I could think about was kissing you." He moved his mouth from my ear and looked into my eyes with such intensity and spoke with such blatant honesty that I trembled from head to toe.

"I want that night again, Nic. I want our song back."

We stopped dancing. Our breath became one and my body literally felt weak in his strong arms. I couldn't move and I wasn't even sure if my limps could hold me.

He was standing so close to me. All in my space and I couldn't tear my eyes away from his. They held me. They were like a smoldering fire that had me glued to the very spot I stood in. I couldn't move. I couldn't move even if someone was chasing me.

I watched as his face came closer to me, his lips only a breath away from mine. And even though a tiny voice in my head was telling me to step back I started anticipating their touch against mine. I wanted to know this. I wanted to feel this feeling. And I was scared out of my mind.

MARCUS

32

I looked at her and hoped she knew just how serious I was. Prayed she did, cause I swear I never been more serious in my life. I knew I was way out on a limb. Way out in left field. But damn, I just couldn't help myself. I've been waiting for this moment for seventeen years!

I stroked her hair and then nervously touched her face as I lost myself inside of those brown eyes that caught my attention at a locker so many years ago. I stared down at her shapely lips. Hungered to touch them with mine. I wanted to feel them so bad. I tried to hold back but I couldn't wait any longer. I was so damn anxious.

I placed my lips against hers. Felt her softness and tasted her pure cane sugar sweetness. She kissed me back.

And I let go.

Let go of everything that ever kept me from this moment. I closed my eyes just as my mouth covered hers and my tongue ravenously savored her sweetness in a long, lingering kiss. It had been years since we've touched like this. Years! And it was still the same. Power. Magic.

I embraced her tighter. Felt her body melt inside my arms and continued to kiss her deeply and passionately, as she matched my urgency with her own. She tugged gently on my bottom lip. Darted her tongue softly against mine. Drove me out of my damn mind! I caressed her face her hair and my lips never left hers. With each breath I kissed her and God as my witness, I never wanted to stop. I picked her up in my arms, held her suspended in the air. Held her until I felt her inside of me. A moan escaped from deep within me. I felt like a drunken man, like that brother who once said he was drowning in the sea of love as I kissed her over and over and over. Somebody needed to help me because I couldn't help myself. I just couldn't.

Slowly I eased her body back to floor still holding her and still touching her lips with mine in small kisses. I couldn't breathe. I didn't want to. My body shuddered and my heart felt like all my African ancestors were pounding wildly on Congo drums. Our lips parted. I touched her lips now swollen from my touch with my fingertips, feeling their softness and already missing their touch against my own. My eyes looked deeply into her eyes. And I know I was like an open book and that I was revealing all that I had tried to hide for so many years. But it was too late. It was too late for me to change what just happened. Too late for me to deny it, cover it up, make excuses or even apologize for it. Her lips began to move slightly but no words came out. She placed her hands inside mine. I intertwined my fingers with hers. I leaned my head on top of hers, felt her breath mix with mine, and felt her heart beat my beat. For moments we stood in the very place I've always wanted to be, together. And I swear in all of my dreams I have never felt anything like this in my life. Like time had stood still and it was on our side. Finally.

And tears were in her eyes.

I didn't understand. My heart was pounding so hard that I thought it was going to burst. I wanted to kiss her again but I dared to breathe much less move afraid to wake up from my dream of dreams. She slid her fingers from mine moved them toward my face with a look I never seen before, captivating me as a single tear slid down the side of her face. I wanted to say things I hadn't said in a long time. The words were on the tip of my tongue. But her tear filled eyes stopped me. Kept me silent. Wishing, hoping, dreaming, anticipating, aching.

She moved her lips closer to mine brushed them softly against me in a sweet kiss, never taking her eyes from me. I covered her hand with mine, kissed the inside of her palm and then stared down into her eyes. My heart was about to split open. I have dreamed of this for so long. I couldn't let go. I just couldn't.

I kissed her face, tasted her tears and her body crushed me against the couch. I closed my eyes tightly, then looked back into hers, feeling my defenses break down even more. I couldn't mask my desire and want for her. I couldn't hide what I was feeling. I felt naked down to the bone. Exposed. I never wanted anyone in my life the way that I wanted her. I wanted her forever in my arms. Our bodies as one, twisted, tangled, entwined, wrapped totally around each other. I wanted to lose my heart and my soul, taste her from head to toe, make love to her until the stars fell from the sky. I ached for her.

Her body trembled in my arms. Her eyes were bearing into mine, drawing me in like a magnet making me realize that after all of these years, all of this time, and all of the women, she was still able to mesmerize me like no other. I embraced her face as my heart put words in my mouth. "Nicole these past months you have been away, I have been going crazy thinking about how important you are to me and how much you mean to me. Nic, you're what's missing in my life. Baby, I want you so."

She brought her lips to mine, stopping my words as she slid her tongue in and out of my mouth, making me weak as she pleasured me with her sweetness. I felt her body against mine, her softness against my hardness. Our kiss heated and intensified, as her hands moved up and down my back, and as mine wrapped around her totally, unable to let go.

LOVE AND CONSEQUENCES

I reached behind her for the zipper of her dress, slid it slowly down her back as I began to kiss and nibble on her neck and shoulders. She took a step back from me just as her dress quietly hit the floor at her feet. For seconds I just looked at her. Took all of her in and stood in awe of her beauty. Her hourglass figure was breathtaking as she stood in all her splendor wrapped only in black lace and the three-inch black heels that she slowly stepped out of. I walked around her, stood behind her. Admired, adored and appreciated everything that she was. Just the sight of her aroused me. She was simply beautiful, *so incredibly beautiful.*

I caressed her shoulders, then wrapped my arms around her pulling her back against my front as I kissed her neck, her ears, her shoulders and her back continuously. She let out a soft moan every time I kissed the base of her neck on the left side. I unhooked her bra, slid it off of her shoulders and then began to gently massage her breasts with both hands. She turned her face to me. I kissed her mouth fully, deeply. Let my tongue explore every part of it as she turned her body in my arms and then moved her hands to my waist and began to pull at my belt.

I watched as she undid the buckle and then slowly pulled my shirt out of my pants. I couldn't believe what was happening. My dream was coming true. My fantasy was now reality. My body involuntarily flinched as she began to undo the buttons on my shirt and then slid it off my shoulders. She traced her fingertips across my chest and then followed her feather like touch with butterfly kisses. *The words were on the tip of my tongue.*

Once again, I pulled her back to my front and eased my right hand down until it was inside those sexy black lace panties. I felt her heat, her softness. With gentle fingers I slowly began to massage her intimately, as I still kissed her lips and squeezed her harden nipples with my left hand. She leaned her body into mine, her body slowly moving to a rhythm up against me. I found her groove.

I moved my lips from hers and began to kiss her ears and down the left side of her neck stopping at that spot that once again made her whimper as my right hand massaged her and then slid inside her. I stroked her, caressed her, and moved to her rhythm as it changed its beat. She called out my name, told me to wait. Called me A.M., begged me not to stop. I continued to kiss her neck, caress her nipples and stroke her center all at the same time. Her body gyrated against me. She turns to face me, her mouth opens, her breath short pants. I watched her eyes, felt her body tighten, and then like a butterfly she fluttered in my arms. I held her for seconds, kissing her lightly on the lips and then moved my tongue down her neck to her breasts. She held my head crushed to her bosom, calling out my name over and over as I caressed them with my tongue.

I slid those sexy black lace panties down and rubbed and caressed her curvaceous body loving the feel of her skin. I knelt down in front of her and carefully helped her step out of her underwear. She stood in front of me totally naked and once again I couldn't take my eyes off of her. She was so beautiful. And then I saw them. The light, discolored thin scars on her left thigh and hip. My body tensed up as I painfully remembered that night that I had found her beaten and raped, the night that I lost her. I pulled her to me and held her tightly as the tightness in my chest grew and burst wide open. I traced my fingers up and down the scars and kissed them over and over wanting to erase away all of the pain they had caused her.

I stood slowly, and in one motion I picked her up, with one hand around her shoulders and the other under her legs I carried her to my bed. She sat in front of me and began to remove my clothes, completely undressing me and then pulled me toward her. We kissed. Softly. My own body was shaking, as I leaned forward until we were both laying in the bed in each other arms. Her eyes told me all I needed to know, as I still couldn't believe that she was here, in my bed, in my arms. Finally.

I pulled her on top of me. She straddled me, placed her sex against mine. I pressed her body toward me so that I could kiss her breast as she began to grind against me. I caressed her body, rubbed it, and teased it. I slid my tongue back up her neck, around her ears and back down her neck again. I couldn't get enough of her. I rubbed her backside with gentleness and then held her as she moved it up and down and in small circles, driving me crazy with desire. I was aching to be inside her.

As if reading my mind she eased me inside of her. She felt so good as she moved her body up and down, riding me, squeezing me, taking me in inch by inch. I looked into her beautiful face. Our eyes locked onto each other as our bodies moved in tune with each other, found our rhythm, our tempo, slow, easy, smooth, serious, and so sensuous.

She brought her mouth to mine.

I kissed her.

Fervently.

I looked deeply into her eyes.

The words were there on the tip of my tongue.

I grabbed her hips.

Got lost inside her.

Moved deeper.

She closed her eyes.

Grabbed the headboard.

Began to ride me.

Bumped and grind me.

Her eyes opened, looked all through me.

I went deeper.

Her mouth opened.

She begged me not to stop.

I didn't.

Made me promise I wouldn't stop.

I promised.

She let go of the headboard.

Slid me in and out of her.

Had me moaning.

Feeling intoxicated.

Totally disoriented.

I pulled her body to me.

Kissed her.

Deeply.

Caressed her.

Closely.

Stroked her.

Gently.

Rolled us over.

Got back into her groove.

The words were on the tip of my tongue.

My body was sweating fire.

Her legs wrapped around me.

I grabbed the headboard.

She looked all inside me.

I got deeper.

She kissed me.

I started writing my name.

She moaned so loud.

I started writing her name.

She let out another deep moan and made me believe she saw God himself.

I let go of the headboard.

Lifted her body off the bed.

Held it close to me.

Cradle it.

Rocked it.

She told me to keep it right there.

I kept it.

Told me not to stop.

I couldn't.

She bit my shoulder.

She called me her sweet Morning.

Called me by my full name.

Gave me that sweet tongue again.
The words were. . ..
I shifted.
Changed my position.
Increased my stride.
Squeezed her backside.
She felt so good that I was loosing my mind!
She pulled me closer.
She pushed me in deeper.
She squeezed her muscle tighter.
I saw God, his son and a couple of disciples.
I moved my hips against hers.
I was the up to her down.
She was the back to my forth.
On the tip...
I moved sideways.
She moved in circles.
I slid in and out of her.
She pulled me in deeper every time.
She grabbed the headboard.
I pushed the footboard.
The bed didn't know which way to run.
A fire grew inside me.
I was a volcano.
I was about to erupt.
I pushed harder inside her.
I didn't want to let go.
I pushed deeper.
I didn't want it to end.
I pushed deeper.
But I couldn't hold back.
I couldn't contain the fire.
The words were on the tip...
I looked down at her.
She was watching in the mirror.
I gave her a show.
Did a dance for her.
Gave her slow hard daddy long strokes.
Her eyes locked in on mine.
She was holding onto the edge.
I told her to let go.

She breathed heavy short breaths.

I couldn't breathe.

The fire was building

I moved faster.

Got deeper.

She moaned out my name.

I told her to let go.

Her hands reached for me.

She grabbed me.

Pushed me.

Held me.

I pushed deeper inside of her.

Gave her all of me.

She looked at me.

Looked all inside me.

I watched her orgasm.

Felt it.

Saw her eyes fill with tears and slide down her face.

That moved me.

And before I could understand it, my body erupted and exploded into spasms.

I held her.

Tightly.

Looked down into her beautiful face.

Said her name about a dozen times

Gave her tender kisses and pieces of my heart.

The words were on the tip of my tongue.

NICOLE

33

I awoke suddenly. Sat straight up and looked about my unfamiliar sur-roundings and the sleeping body next to me. My hand instantly went up to my mouth. What have I done! This couldn't be true. Surely we didn't. I looked under the sheet that covered us. Saw our two naked bodies. Covered them up quickly. Surely we did. I closed my eyes and behind them saw us dancing one minute and then the next... he kissed me.

And like a flower I blossomed. Opened up and welcomed his passion.

His lips were sweet, soft, tender, loving. His strong arms held me close to him, tightly, swept me off my feet. I was in his embrace feeling his heart pound and his deep moans were driving me wild. I never felt so wanted. I never wanted someone so bad. Never had I felt such gentleness, tenderness, sweetness and bliss-fulness in a man's arms. Never had I experienced such passion. His loving was so good that I know I would walk a hundred miles just to experience it again. And his words, the things he said to me, moved me and had me reaching for him. And then the next thing I knew I was undoing his shirt, caressing his beautiful eat me up caramel brown skin that was like fire to my touch. I ran my hands up and down his person loving the feel of his muscled chest just before his mouth tenderly found mine again. He kissed me, held me, caressed me, picked me up, laid me down and made love to me totally and completely.

I opened my eyes and looked down at Marcus as he slept looking like the young boy I knew so long ago. I couldn't believe that the man that had made love to me last night was the same as the kid that taunted everyone in school. The bully who had everyone scared of his size, the sound of his voice and the wild glare he would get in his eyes, the boy that won my heart and became my best friend. He was such an incredible friend. Always looking out for me. Always hav-ing my back. Always down for me no matter what. And now I don't know. I don't know what do think, what to feel, what to do. I don't know. My body began to tremble and I wiped the tears from my eyes before they fell. How could I have let this happen?

I looked around for my clothes but couldn't find them on my side of the bed. I eased up out the bed holding the top sheet against me. Marcus' bare body was suddenly exposed and I put my hand to my mouth to stifle my own sound as I let my eyes roam over his nakedness. He was lying on his stomach. Looking so good with his sexy bowed legs, and his strong muscular back and shoulders that put the Greek god Adonis to shame. He shifted in his sleep. An arm reached for the empty space I just vacated. I went to the end of the bed, pulled up the comforter and gently covered him up and began the search again for my clothes. It was like they had disappeared. I looked all around the floor then I finally spotted my bra on the nightstand next to him. I walked quietly over to his side, again checking to make sure he was still asleep. I don't know why but I was shaking all over.

I moved like a mummy wrapped in the sheet trying to get to my bra and tripped over something, got tangled up in the sheet and hit the floor hard. I lay there a moment. Holding my breath, closing my eyes and hoping against hope that the sound of my thud didn't wake him. After a few seconds of him being totally motionless, I finally opened my eyes and began to rise up.

I looked to see what I had tripped over, Marcus' pants. I untangled my feet and grabbed my bra and continued my search knowing all to well that I couldn't leave here in a bra and a sheet. I have seen some strange things in this town but not that damn strange. I found my panties by the bathtub. Looked across the room near the couch and saw my shoes. Now if I could just find that damn dress I could be on my way. I needed to get out of here. I needed to think to breathe.

I heard Marcus stir in the bed and stopped dead in my tracks, afraid to turn around. "Nic," his voice ranged out in a sexy deep, morning gruffness that both startled and excited me.

I slowly turned and faced him as he sat upright in the bed with the blue comforter covering only half of his lean bronzed body. His eyes gazed into mine through half opened slits that held me to the spot I stood in. He licked his lips and I had to hold my breath to keep the moan deep within me from escaping out. I was so turned on it was ashamed. It took some time but my voice finally remembered how to speak.

"Morning."

He smiled, yawned and covered his mouth all at the same time and then ran his hand across his low cut hair and then back down to his side. I averted my eyes and spotted a piece of my dress sticking out from under a pillow by the couch. I looked back at Marcus and got trapped under that same gaze that seemed to see all through me. Again, he licked his lips. His slit eyes looked hungry. I felt like a fawn suddenly found under the scrutiny of the king of the jungle.

"Come here."

He held outstretched arms toward me. I wanted to move but my feet were like led. I wanted to run and jump in his arms, feel his warmth, get wrapped up in his caramel sensation but I couldn't move. I stood glued to my spot, watched as Marcus rose out of the bed intimidating me with his mere presence as I remembered the way every part of his muscled body felt and the way it had loved every inch of me up down sideways inside out tenderly and deeply. Giving me nothing but pure pleasure that brought tears to my eyes.

He reached for his pants that were on the floor, slipped them on and walked toward me. He stopped inches in front of me. Stroked my face with gentle fingertips. Spoke to me in a sexy whisper, "Last night was so incredible, so beautiful."

"Like a dream," I heard my inner voice say out loud.

Marcus kissed me like a butterfly, murmured softly in my ear, "A dream come true. After all of this time I never thought we would be like this. I never thought I would feel this way again Nic."

I looked into his eyes as tear number one began sliding down my face. He brushed it away and then kissed my eyelids. His arms came around me and surrounded me in his warmth. The sheet that I was struggling to hold onto was beginning to slide down. His lips found that spot at the base of my neck that made my knees go weak and a moan escaped from my mouth as my hands reached for his broad shoulders and held on.

Marcus was whispering my name and kissing me with some serious tenderness. My lips thirst for his. My breasts ached for his caress. My womanly parts wanted to feel his manly parts in the worst way. I was crazy, crazy, crazy, crazy with desire and want for him to touch me everywhere and to never stop. And I was so scared. I was so damn scared.

My whole body trembled from head to toe as tear number two fought its way from my lids. I was so confused. I knew this man. I've known him almost all of my life. But I had never, never known him like this.

Through trembling lips I called his name. With shaking hands I pushed him away and backed out of his reach, away from his touch, his lips. I pulled the sheet back up around me, held onto it like a safety net. He looked at me with confusion in his eyes.

"What's wrong?"

"Nothing. I just want to go."

"You want to go?"

"Yeah."

"Why?"

I lied, "I'm hungry."

"You know I'll fix you anything you want."

"No, please that's okay."

"But it won't take but a second."

I let out a long breath, felt myself getting agitated and practically yelled at him, "No Marcus. That's okay. I just need to go."

He stared at me a long minute and then stepped closer to me his eyes never leaving mine. "Why?"

I trembled. Closed my eyes shut and tried to squeeze tear number three back but couldn't stop what was already flowing.

"What is it Nic?"

Tears number four five six and seven were flowing freely from my eyes like someone had struck oil. "I don't know."

"You don't know what?"

"What to do."

"About?"

"What I'm feeling."

He tilted my head back so that I had to look into his beautiful light eyes. "What are you feeling?"

I took a deep breath, blinked back more tears. "That last night was a mistake."

His eyes changed from confusion to hurt in a matter of seconds. "A mistake? What... what are you saying? What was a mistake?"

My eyes once again filled with water as I looked into his. "Us, everything. Last night shouldn't have happened."

He dropped his hand from my face, took two steps away from me but didn't take his eyes away from mine. "How can you say that?"

"Because I don't know how else to say it, Marcus."

For seconds he stood looking at me like he never seen me before and then walked toward the bed and snatched his shirt from the floor and angrily put it on. I stood still as he began to pace the floor trying to sort through my mind for the right words to say.

"Marcus, you and I have been so close for so long and now I feel everything is so confusing. It's just that now that we have slept together..."

"We did a little more than just sleep in that bed last night," Marcus interjected.

"I know!" I said with more emphasizes than I wanted to and then looked away, afraid for him to look in my eyes. A creepy silence stood between us. I looked back at him, could see him grasping at my words, my tone, sizing up my body language, and drawing conclusions.

He finally spoke. "Last night didn't mean anything to you, did it?"

"No, I mean yes. "

"Well which is it?"

"I don't know what it meant. That's my point. Everything feels so complicated."

"Complicated?"

"Damn it Marcus I'm not a fool! I know your game, Mr. love em and leave em! I know I was probably the only woman you have ever known in your whole life that you haven't slept with," I blurted out without thinking and from the look on his face I wished I could take it back. "I didn't mean that the way it sounded. I just..."

"Want to walk away from me like you did with Derek. Isn't that just like the pot to call the kettle black," he said in a tone that was so harsh and cold that if he hadn't been standing there I would have sworn he was someone else.

I looked down at floor for a hole that I could crawl into, a hole to hide from my own transgressions. "I can't believe you said that. That is so unfair," I said looking back into his eyes.

He looked at me with eyes of steel his nostrils flaring as his breath came out in hard pants. "You want fair Nic? How fair it is for me to open up to you and tell what I've been keeping inside for almost two decades only to have you throw it back in my face? How fair is for you to lay in my arms last night and give me an idea of what could have been and hope for what could be and then this morning tell me it was a mistake!

"But hey no matter, right. This is just Marcus, your best friend. The good old lap dog that has always been there to catch any bone you throw his way. This is not going to affect him or change our relationship. We can go back to the way we were. All is fair in friendship, right. Well bam! That's where you run into my infamous brick wall. That's where I draw the line. There's no going back!"

For moments I was shocked beyond words. I couldn't remember the last time I saw him this angry and I sure as hell couldn't believe what he was saying. "What are you saying Marcus. You just want to throw away our whole entire friendship, our entire relationship because we had sex!"

"Why not? You expect me to pretend that last night didn't happen because it's complicated."

"I don't expect you do anything!"

"And that's my point, Nic. I'm not expected to do anything except what I've been doing for years and that is nothing," he stated dryly. "I should have done nothing when I saw you at the club last night, but I brought you here. If I had done nothing we wouldn't have talked we wouldn't have danced. I wouldn't have kissed you and I damn sure wouldn't be standing here looking like a fool because I made the mistake of looking in your eyes and telling myself that you wanted what I wanted!" he finished angrily.

"Marcus I did want..."

"To have sex with me, yeah I got that!" he yelled and began to pace the floor. "And you call *me* a player! You tell me about *my* game! You should have been telling about yours, cause I didn't even see you coming. And that's the shit that bothers me, Nic. I mean hell, I thought we were best friends you know share everything. Why didn't you come to me correct? We could have work something out, you know. I could hook you up on the regular. Tuesdays and Fridays sound good to you?"

I stared at him with disbelief. He was straight up tripping. "Okay you know what, I'm going to let that go because I can see the bricks stacking."

"I'm not putting up a wall, I'm just calling it as I see it," he threw in my face.

"Oh, so you're conscious of what you're saying and are intentionally hurting me?" I yelled back at him as tears streamed down my face. "I don't believe this. You of all people know that I have been to hell and back these last couple of months and have finally pulled myself together and you're going to stand there and call me a whore and make me out to be some desperate woman."

"Those words never left my mouth."

"Well what do you call that little remark about Derek and your little blasé comment about hooking me up on the regular!" I shouted my body trembling with anger.

Silence stood in the empty space between us. I felt my body shake all the way down to my fingertips as I stared into Marcus' fiery eyes with my own, as neither one of us backed down, neither one of us gave in. I wanted to scream. I wanted to shout. I wanted to take him and shake him. I wanted to go back to yesterday. Damn, how did we get here in the middle of all this pain? I blinked my eyes breaking our stare and then stepped closer to him. He looked at me with eyes full of the pain that I caused.

"Marcus, I'm sorry. Don't you know you're the last person in the world that I want to hurt? I need you."

"Nicole don't..."

"No, you don't understand. You mean the world to me. You're my best friend. I need you, Marcus. "

"What about me Nic? What about what I need?" The pain in his words hung in the air like a thick cloud of smoke that was choking him and tears instantly filled my eyes. "Last night meant something to me, Nic. Hell, it meant, everything! It wasn't about the sex. I gave you all of me. Last night I let go of everything. My pride, my ego, my heart ... and now you want me to what? Step back over some stupid invisible line. Do you have any idea how hard... how much... "Once again his words faded into the space between us.

His eyes pierced into mine as he place his right hand over his heart. "You're here Nic. You always have been. From the moment I first met you, I was yours for whatever you needed me to be. When you needed me to be your friend, I was there every day because I honestly cared about you. When you needed love, I gave you all that I had and wished ten times over that I could give you more. And then when you asked me to give you space, I backed off. But I never let go. I couldn't."

I stood stunned beyond words as his eyes looked into mine as he stepped back. "But now I know I have to."

I watched as he took the remote out of his pocket along with his keys. Through watery eyes I saw him punch in codes and then placed the keys in my hand. "The door's open, you can take the Benz."

I looked up at him but his eyes didn't meet mine. "You're asking me to leave?"

"It was a mistake for you to be here in the first place, remember?"

Fear took over me. I looked away from him and found myself once again shaking, feeling almost tormented and wondering if I walked out that door would I ever see him again. Tears were once again in my eyes. I had finally pushed him away and I didn't know what to say or what to do or how to fix this. "Marcus. Don't do this, please. We've been through so much."

His light brown eyes finally looked agonizingly into mine as a tear slid down his face. "We've been through too much, Nic. I can't do this anymore."

I stared into his tear filled eyes as the impact of his words hit me so hard I thought I was going to die. I stood there for moments, unable to move, unable to speak. My body shook uncontrollably. I had hurt him. I hurt him so deep. I reached for him, but he turned his back. I called out his name, he didn't answer. I hurt in places that had no name.

His phone rang and he immediately went to answer it. I listened as he mumbled words into the receiver only because I was still to dumbfound by his last words to move. He hung up turned toward me but it was like he didn't even see me. His eyes shifted about the room. Something was wrong. I don't know what but something wasn't right. I could feel it all over.

"What is it? Marcus, look at me."

He looked up at me as if he just remembered I was still in the room. "Nic, please, you just need to go," he said turning away from me.

I slowly went about the room, grabbed my clothes and got dressed as I shamefully hung my head.

Thirty minutes later, I walked into the back door of the Michael's and found it all too quiet. "Mike?" I called out. His car was in the driveway so I knew he was here. I don't know why I came here. I knew I wasn't going to tell him what just happened with Marcus. I just didn't trust myself to be alone.

"Mike, where are you?"

"I'm upstairs."

I headed up the back stairs toward the bedrooms. Then slowed down my stride. "Are you alone."

"What?"

"I said are you alone?"

I entered his bedroom and saw a suitcase on the bed and found Michael going through his closet for clothes. "Where you going?"

"Hey," he said walking to me and giving me a kiss on the cheek and then as quickly went back to packing before I had a good chance to look at him.

"Mike, what's up?"

"Marcus didn't tell you?"

"Tell me what?"

"I'm sorry Nicki, I just thought you two were, I mean I saw you guys leave together last night."

"What happened?"

"It's his dad. He's in the hospital."

I ran down the hall showered changed clothes and threw clothes in a suitcase. I don't know what I packed as I hurriedly moved about the room. Twenty minutes passed and I heard a car horn outside. I looked out and saw a yellow cab. I dragged my suitcase down the stairs just as Michael was at the front door. He grabbed it and we both headed out.

An hour and a half later I was seated between Marcus and Michael in first class seats of an American Airlines 747 jet headed for Seattle. I hadn't been home in seventeen years. I never wanted to go back. But as I stared at Marcus, as he looked solemnly ahead, I knew I had to go.

MARCUS

34

Angela was the first person I saw when I stepped off the plane. She hurriedly ran to my arms and I held my oldest sister as tightly as I could. I closed my eyes and felt her tears against my shirt. Bodies were pushing by and bumping into us but we still just held onto each other. God, I missed her so much and it felt so good just to see her.

"Junior! Oh, it's so good to see you. I'm so glad you're here," Angela said.

I released her and then looked down at her more thoroughly. She had finally picked up some weight, had salt and pepper hair that was cut in a stylish fashion and now wore glasses, but I would know her anywhere no matter how many years had passed. I hugged her again. "I'm sorry I wasn't here."

"You are now and that's all that counts," Angela said pulling away from me and wiping my dampened eyes. I looked away from her and behind her were my other three sisters. I couldn't help but smile as each one came into my arms and hugged me like I had never left. I looked at all four of them noticing the changes that seventeen years had made and had not made. Ashley looked just like my mom. Anita favored dad more and April resembled me so much it was unbelievable.

The five of us stood in a semi circle talking and laughing and for a few moments it was like I was home for a family reunion. I turned to Angela. "How's mom?"

"Strong as ever," Angela said smiling. "And can't wait to see her son."

I smiled a moment as I thought about my mother. "What about dad, how is he?"

"He's holding on."

"What do the doctors say?"

"Doctors, smoctors what do they know? Seeing your knucklehead is going to be his best medicine if you ask me. Oh my God is that Nicole?" Angela asked suddenly.

I had forgotten that Nicole and Michael were standing behind me witnessing our reunion. Nicole walked up to my sisters and they each hugged and embraced her like they had done me.

"I can't believe it. You're still hanging out with this bum?" Angela asked.

"Well yeah, he kind of grew on me," Nicole said. Her eyes met mine silently asking me what to say. I looked away.

"I have to say I'm shocked too after all these years," Anita said.

"I'm not surprised. They were hopelessly in love," Ashley spoke and April laughed behind her.

Michael coughed behind me.

"Say, you guys, cousin Mike's here," I said stepping aside.

"Little Mike. God, look at you. I know you're given the ladies hell in LA," April said.

"How's it going," Michael said extending his hand. April ignored it and pulled him into her arms and then soon each of my sisters hugged him. Soon after we all started walking through the airport picked up our luggage and headed out to the parking lot, playing catch up along the way.

We reached Anita's van, she and Ricky had three boys, with little Ricky being a little terror since he was the oldest and the angriest since his parents divorced when he was only seven. April just got married last year. Ashley has her own law practice downtown and was making more money then most of the men in her profession and was not wasting her time trying to be with no one special person 'cause in her words she was having too much fun. And Angela, who was about to turn forty next month, was the mother of ten-year-old Tasha, a girl that she adopted two years ago and had a special 'friend' in life but didn't want marriage either. They all stayed pretty close to my parents and still spent most holidays, especially Thanksgiving at the house on 43rd.

The seven of us piled in the van and Anita drove as I looked around the city I had called home for the first sixteen years of my life as my sister questioned Nicole and Michael endlessly about life in L.A. I sat quietly listening to all of them talk almost at the same time and I had to smile. I had forgotten what it was like. It felt damn good to be home.

Within no time, we reached the hospital and I fell in step behind Angela as she led the way inside and into an elevator. We reached the sixth floor and I stepped out first and held the door for everyone else to get out.

"He's in room six twenty," Angela said.

I looked at my surroundings and noticed the doctors and nurses hurrying by barely meeting any of our eyes. The whole atmosphere was serious, sad and solemn. The laughter and noise that the seven of us had shared in the van was nowhere to be found as we each walked through the halls. My chest suddenly felt tight.

Angela turned down a corridor and I followed. I then caught my breath. Up ahead of us my mother was coming toward us holding a pitcher. She glanced up at me and her hand went up to her mouth and tears were instantly in her eyes. I moved past Angela like I had once done on the basketball court and ran and pulled my mother in my arms. Her body shook in my arms as I squeezed her tighter. Tears were pouring out of me like crazy and I didn't care who saw. I held her and held her until she pulled away and looked up at me smiling through her tears.

"Anthony Marcus, oh my baby. Look at you! You are your father all over."

She brought her hand to my face and touched each corner of it. I took her hand kissed her cheek and pulled her back in my arms. She looked the same, smelled the same and I never knew I missed her so much until now. She hugged me tightly and then pulled away again. "I'm so happy to see you. You're all grown up now. Look at you. And Nicole, oh my, girl come here."

Nicole moved forward and my mother and her hugged and more tears poured from the three of us.

"It's good to see you Mrs. Washington," Nicole said through her tears.

"Oh, it's good to see you. You look wonderful. And Anthony's going to be so happy to see the two of you are still together."

Nicole looked at me nervously again with the same question that I still didn't have an answer for.

"Oh, mom, there's Michael," I said.

My mom turned and found Michael and embraced him as well and then grabbed my hand. "Come on, you're dad's waiting to see you."

I followed her lead and entered the room on shaky legs. My father was lying in the bed with the remote to the television in his hand and with black glasses perched on his nose. He glanced our way once and then again when he noticed me. I can't describe how I felt when his whole face seemed to light up when he looked at me. I hurried to his bed before he stepped out of it and we hugged like we had done at the airport so long ago. Again I felt my chest tighten inside and let the tears fall. I have never been so happy to see anybody.

His hands patted me on the back several times and I heard him sniff a couple of times before he pulled away and looked up at me at me. "What are you doing getting old on me, old man," I said looking into my same light brown eyes and smiling his smile.

"You look good, son. You look damn good," he chuckled and then lay back against the bed. My mom came over and fixed the pillows behind him, her face smiling from ear to ear. I sat down on the bed.

"Dad, you look good too. How are you feeling?" I choked out blocking out the machines that were hooked up to him.

"Right now I couldn't be better now that I've laid eyes on my only son."

He pulled me in closer and whispered in my ear. "You know all these females have been fussing about me night and day. It's good to have some back up."

"Yeah, that's what I'm here for dad," I told him.

"Anthony, guess who else is here?" My mom said.

My dad looked around the room and spotted Nicole in the crowd and then looked back at me and hit me lightly in the chest. "I didn't raise any fool did I? You know to keep a good woman by your side."

"Well, Nic and I are, we're just friends."

"Hey, hey Ms. Nicki, " he said as he held his arms up. I watched as Nicole hugged my father and he whispered something to her that made her laugh like I hadn't seen her in a long time. Then Michael stepped forward and received his hug as my dad asked about his brother. Michael told him Uncle Lewis was fine and was unable to make the trip but sends his apologies. And I wasn't even mad at him for lying.

For the next forty or so minutes we all sat talking and laughing and reminiscing about old times. Every now and then a nurse would come in and stick her head in the door and remind my dad that he needed rest and he would shoo her out telling her he knew what he needed and it was all right here in this room. She would let us be for about ten minutes and return again. The last time in she came in talking about the doctor was on his way with a specialist and wouldn't be happy to see a room full of people. My dad shooed her again. I smiled and continued to sit on the bed wishing I could spend the night.

The door opened again and this time an elderly man came in with another female in a lab coat.

"Mr. Washington, I've told you to limit your visitors to two at a time," the elderly man spoke.

My dad looked from his bed at the graying man. "I know doc, but my son just got here from out of town and everybody had to see him. Now where is this specialist you wanted me to meet?"

"Hi, Mr. Washington. I'm Dr. Ashton, and Dr. Lexington asked me to...oh my God, Mr. Washington. It's me Crystal."

"Crystal?" Nicole and I said at the same time.

She turned and looked at me and then at Nicole. And then the sounds of laughter came as the two of them embraced and as I reminded my family who Crystal was. They all vaguely remembered the girls Nicole stayed with at the home but hadn't seen since we left.

"Dr. Ashton?" Dr. Lexington spoke, wanting to know what all the commotion was about. Crystal looked his way and walked over to him, whispered something in his ear and he quietly left. She closed the door behind them and then turned back toward us smiling ear to ear. And our reunion was on again. We hugged and Nicole and Crystal cried and then Crystal got down to business.

She was a Nephrologist and she quickly explained my father's condition. His kidneys had failed and he was going to have to start receiving dialysis three times a week. And he could have a long life living with dialysis but a kidney transplant would be better. However, a wait for a kidney could be a long process and he would still have to be on dialysis until one became available. And that's where we fit in.

As his children any one of us could be a match. My sister's and I all didn't hesitate to say we wanted to be tested. And even Michael said he wanted to be too, cause he was family too. I looked at my cousin and felt nothing but love. His dad might not come through, but he does. Every time.

Crystal spoke a little while longer explaining the testing procedure, the transplant and recovery period for my father and the one who would give the kidney. I don't know why but for some reason, hearing everything from her made it easier. Even though we haven't seen each other in years, I felt I knew her and could trust her to be honest about my father's condition.

"Well, I've got to go but I will be back soon to talk to all of you and you guys can page me at anytime if you have any questions and concerns. We will need to get started with testing as soon as possible." Crystal said and headed out the door and then turned around again. "It's good to see you Badman, and Nicole, call me girl." She smiled waved and left.

We spent the next few minutes talking about who we thought was going to the best candidate for the transplant and we all now had our own expert opinions. My mother quickly reminded us that none of us could be sure of anything until after the test and that Crystal is the specialist. Nicole grinned from ear to ear and I could tell she was happy to see Crystal doing well for herself and I can't deny so was I. I even wondered about my other musketeer, Lisa and how she was doing.

Before long, my dad was yawing and I looked out the window and it had gotten dark outside. Still sitting on the bed, I arose, stretched out my aching legs and turned to my dad who was trying not to look like he was tired.

"I guess we better get going, old man. It's getting pretty late and you need your rest."

"What do you think I do here all day, run the marathon? I've been in this hospital for days while they poke and prod me trying to find out what's the matter with me while I'm sitting here in this bed bored to death. They don't even have cable, no ESPN, nothing. Shoot, I wish I could just go out and crank up the Winnebago and go fishing."

"You still have that old thing," I laughed.

"Not the same one, a new, bigger and better one," he said and smiled back.

"I don't know why," my mom spoke. "We don't need that big old thing. Don't nobody like to go fishing any more but him. Anita's boys don't go for that camping and fishing. And we can't even talk Tasha into riding in it."

"Well dad, as soon as you get out of here, we're going fishing." I said. "And we'll even take Mike with us and show him a thing or two."

"I'm going to hold you to it," Dad smiled.

My mother began to push us all out the door and one by one we all kissed dad goodbye. I reached the door and then turned around one last time. "See you tomorrow, old man."

"See you tomorrow son."

We had to squeeze tighter in the van to make room for my mother who sat in the front seat. Michael and I sat on the end of the second row with Anita and Nicole between us. We drove through the city toward my old home passing through downtown. I pointed out the space needle to Michael and the Center that Nicole and I use to hang out at. Anita informed us that there was a mall in the middle of downtown now and that the public market was still the best place in town to shop.

We all agreed to give Michael the grand tour of the city being this was his first time here. I couldn't wait to see things myself. Just looking out the window at the skyline of downtown I had forgotten how beautiful Seattle was. And then we passed by the floating bridge and I just couldn't help but remember all the nights I had spent looking out at that bridge, with Nicole. I glanced over at her and she was looking dead at me and then quickly looked away. I guess memories were creeping up on her too.

We reached the house and Michael, Ashley, Nicole, my mom and I got out. Anita had to go pick up her boys but before that she was going to take Angela to get Tasha from her friend's house and drop April at home. We all agreed to get together for dinner tomorrow with my sisters promising to bring their families to meet me.

I turned and faced the house. Except for the color, (it used to be gold, but now it was painted white) it still looked the same as the day I left. I walked up behind my mother and opened the door of the sun porch so she could go in remembering all of the rainy days I had spent out here. Inside things were different but things were the same. I was glad to see my parents had some new furniture.

The living room was completely new, but the dining room was exactly the same except for the new drapes. And it was still filled with my mom's plants. I headed straight to the kitchen, found the same kitchen tables and then headed out the back door and looked out at the porch I used to sit on when I skipped school. Old Ms. Jenkins' house was gone and it was just a vacant lot, which made the view even better. I could see clear to Rainer Ave.

I looked around the first floor longer, going into my parents room and then into Ashley's. She has been staying with my mom since my dad went in the hospital and took over Angela's old room.

"Say Mike, follow me," I said and practically ran up the stairs. I went straight to the front of the house and walked into my old bedroom and turned on the light. I stood in awe. It was like I never left. There was the same bed, same dressers, same couch, table and desk. It was unbelievable. I didn't know what to think. A part of me was happy but a part of me felt sad that my parents were somehow just waiting on me to come back. And I didn't.

I opened the closet almost expecting to see my old clothes hanging in there but they weren't. Except for my old letter jacket from high school. I pulled it out and put one arm through the sleeve and it came practically to my elbow. I took it off and hung it back up and then noticed the boxes on the floor of the closet.

I opened one up and saw all my trophies, metals and awards from high school. Michael picked up another box and carried it to the couch. It was full of all of my old albums, eight tracks and cassettes.

"Man, you had quite a collection in here," Michael said. I turned to face him just as Nicole and Ashley came in the room.

"What are you two up to?" Ashley asked sitting on my old bed. I didn't answer because I was too busy watching Nicole's reaction and I could tell she felt like she had walked into a time capsule too.

"Commodores, EWF, Rick James, Emotions, Parliament, Prince, man, you got all the seventies stuff. This is serious," Michael said looking further into the box.

Nicole moved slowly and sat next to him. I noticed her smile as she went through album after album. We were all in that box me and her, us, together. Damn just being in this room reminded me of how close we were and how crazy I was for her. Our eyes met and for seconds I got stuck in the past.

"Say Marcus, where is your stereo, I've got to hear some of this," Michael said to me making me tear my eyes away from Nicole.

I looked around and sure enough my old stereo/cassette player was still on the built in shelf by the window.

"If you really want to hear it come to the basement. There's a real system down there," Ashley said.

They both stood up with Michael taking the box with him.

Then Ashley turned to Nicole. "Oh, Nicole, there's another box in the closet with some things that my mom got from your old house."

Nicole looked at me and I went to the closet and came out with a box that had her name on it and put in on the table in front of her.

She opened it and the first thing she pulled out was my old leather coat that I had given her. She picked it up and held it close to her and I swear I wanted to tell her she didn't have to hold that coat cause I was right here. I was right here. I sat down next to her as she looked over at me.

"I remember the day you gave me this," she said softly.

"So do I," I admitted and then asked what else was in there before I found myself acting on a feeling. I cursed under my breath, hating myself, for thinking the things I was thinking. I was supposed to mad at her!

Nicole reached in and pulled out her journal and then her notebook that when she opened I could see was full of papers that said 'Dear A.M.'

"Let me see those," I said sitting closer so I could read. Nicole pulled the notebook close to her chest so I couldn't see it.

"No way," she said through a teary smile.

"Why, you scared I'll know how crazy you were about me? You know the feeling was mutual," I said with all honesty. *I hated myself! I was supposed to be mad at her!*

We held eyes for seconds and then Nicole pulled the notebook down and began to read aloud.

Dear A.M., I'm sitting here waiting on you
to pick me up and I can't lie, it's hard to just wait.
I want to be with you always. I know it sounds crazy, but it's true.
You make me the happiest person in the world and I want to feel the happiness
you give me every second of my life. I hope I give you happiness. Peace out,
my ride's here."

I looked down at the words on the paper and I was sixteen again, and she was my girl again, sitting on the porch, waiting for me. My heart was playing tricks on my mind. She turned the page and then read another one to herself as more tears formed in her eyes. I looked over and silently read with her:

Dear A.M., I can't explain all that is in my heart.
Sometimes I feel so overwhelmed that my emotions
burst right open and turn me inside out.
Baby, I love you. I love holding you, kissing you,
touching you. I love your name because it reminds me
that everyday is a new day that I get to spend with you.
I love you because you're my best friend and
because I feel your love. Thank you for loving me baby.
Until Morning.

She closed the book and we both sat there in silence. Memories of us years ago went crazy inside me. Back then I knew she loved me. I knew it every time I saw her eyes smile when she looked at me. But just seeing it on paper seemed to validate it all over again. The memory of last night went through my head. I could still feel her soft body under mine and could still her whisper my name over and over. I reached over and touched her face and she looked at me with sad eyes. Then I remembered how she had said that last night was a mistake. I slowly stood up and went to the door mumbling to her that I was going to check on Michael.

NICOLE

35

I couldn't stop the tears. I read the whole notebook and my journals and the tears just fell constantly. The feelings that I had for Marcus and had pushed deep inside me were resurfacing with each page I read. I had loved him so much. And I know he loved me. I know he did.

I stood up and looked around the room, his old bedroom. I walked over to his desk and could almost picture him sitting there and me sneaking up on him as he did his homework. I sat down in the chair and pulled opened the top drawer. Inside were some papers that were barely legible because the writing had faded. I couldn't make out a complete sentence.

I don't know how...Nicki, believe me when... Baby I love you with...

Each one said practically the same thing. I tried to remember a time when he had a hard time telling me something but I couldn't remember. I placed the papers down and then went through another drawer and found some pictures.

There we were at the Center laughing and posing in front of the Space Needle. There was another one of us taken in front of Franklin High. Another one of us with Crystal and Lisa on our sixteenth birthday in the living room downstairs, and then one of me on Christmas Day that same year. Then there were two pictures of both us on New Year's Eve. In one we were kissing in front of the Pike Place Market with fireworks in the background. The other picture caught us just looking at each other with our future in our eyes.

"Say Nicole you want something to eat?" Ashley said from behind me.

I turned around and faced her. "No, I'm fine. Where's your mom?"

"She went onto bed. She's been stressed out with dad being sick and all and now I think with Junior here she can finally let herself get some sleep, you know what I mean."

"Yeah, I'm glad. I'm glad we came."

"I see you found some of Junior's pictures," Ashley said coming toward me.

I looked down at me hands and then took the pictures with me to the couch and sat down. I looked at them again and smiled. "I can't believe so many years have passed by. It seems like these pictures were just yesterday."

"Yeah, I know what you mean," Ashley said and then came and sat down next to me.

"God, we were so young."

"And so in love. And it's good to see you two together."

I stood up and walked over to window and took a deep breath. "Ashley we're not together, together. We haven't been since we left here. We just couldn't find our way back. There were a lot of times that I wished we could but it just didn't happen."

"So what we read in the papers about you and the singer James Fulton was true. You two were a couple?"

I looked at Ashley a long moment as her words penetrated my mind. James and I was a couple. Is that all the papers called us? Was that all I was to James, if even that?

"Look Ashley, the biggest mistake I made in my life was letting James Fulton in it. But that's in the past now and I want to leave it there. And I've been struggling for months to do just that so please don't ask me about him or our so-called relationship. I will tell you this. I didn't kill him. I did try to hurt him for hurting me, but I didn't kill him and I don't know who did. And I'm not going to spend the rest of my life trying to figure out who did. I got to do like your brother told me and just let go."

"And what about Junior?"

"What about him?"

"Did he have anything to do with the murder?"

"What? Why would you even think that?"

"Because I know how much he loved you and I know he would do anything for you."

I turned and faced the window and tried to stop the tears from forming in my eyes. Marcus left his home because of me. He left his family and never came back because of me. "I'm sorry for taking your brother away," I said through trembling lips.

"Look Nicole, I'm sorry. That's not what I was implying. You know even though a lot of years have passed, none of us has forgotten what happened to you, none of us blame you and all of us, all of us still think of you as family. No matter what is between you and my brother now, you're still my sister. And I'm awfully glad that you came here to see about my dad, because we need you both."

I turned and faced Ashley again and saw tears in her eyes and then walked back over near her. She reached out and hugged me and I can't lie I felt like an enormous weight had been lifted off of my shoulders. "I'm glad to be home."

We finally let go of each other smiled and then laughed as we both wiped our own tears away.

"I'm going to go ahead and turn in," Ashley said and headed for the door and then turned around. "Oh I brought your bags up you want me to put them in here?"

"No," I answered maybe a little too quickly.

"Okay, okay. I'll put them in my old room right next door? I've been sleeping downstairs."

"Sure, if it's okay, with you."

"Okay, Well, I guess I'll see you in the morning."

I looked around Marcus room one more time and then headed out before I got trapped in more memories.

When I got downstairs, I could hear the light pulse of the bass coming from the basement and Michael and Marcus sharing a laugh. I walked past the living room and the dining room and went into the kitchen.

The green appliances had now been replaced with black modern ones. I looked to the left where the stove was and remembered a stolen look, precious words and tender kisses. I backed out of the kitchen. In the dining room again I remembered a Thanksgiving, lots of hugs, and even more tears. I had to face it. Memories were everywhere. I was here in the present without a clue about my future and nowhere to hide from my past.

I headed downstairs. Eased down the stairs slowly. I didn't want the guys to hear me or see me. The pulse of the music was louder. I walked toward the den noticed the pool table to the right and stood still for a moment. Remembered the countless times Marcus and I had played a game of pool. The bet was always the same. The winner got to kiss the loser for as long as he wanted. I always won.

To the left of the pool table was the card table. There, Marcus thought me how to play poker. And I beat him every time. Then he showed me how to play strip poker. I always lost.

I looked at the door in front of me that was partially closed. The music had stopped and I could see Marcus going through stacks of albums as Michael leaned against the bar. I suddenly remembered the bar in Marcus' loft apartment below his dealership. It was just like this one.

Suddenly Marcus looked up and right at me. His eyes held me.

"Say man, check this out," Marcus said and then the sounds of the Ohio Player's came on singing 'Let's Love.'

I entered the room, just as Michael began singing with the record, my eyes focused on Marcus. I moved toward him asking him to dance with my eyes. Without a word he moved closer to me. His arms came around me and I let out a deep breath so thankful that he didn't push me away. I needed a truce. I couldn't fight with him. I couldn't stay away from him. I had to be with him, especially here. Surrounded by our memories. I let my head lay on his shoulders, closed my eyes. Imagined myself being sixteen and dancing with the guy of my dreams.

He squeezed me tighter.

I did the same.

We danced.

I opened my eyes. He looked all inside them. Our eyes talked and talked and talked.

The song ended but our eyes still held onto their same conversation. Another song came on. It wasn't in my memory bank and only lasted about a minute and half. And then there was the sound of the needle moving and then complete silence.

We stopped dancing.

Marcus spoke in a whisper. "I'm glad you're here."

"I wouldn't be any place else."

He let go of my hand and then walked to the stereo and turned it off. I looked around for Michael but he was nowhere to be found.

MARCUS

36

"So what is it about this city," Michael said as he came into the kitchen and leaned against the dishwasher. I had been up for over an hour, showered and came down here to fix breakfast. I was on my last batch of pancakes.

"What are you talking about cuz? I told you I was going to take you on a tour and show you the sights. Hold your draws on and sit tight," I said checking to see how hot the griddle was.

"I should ask you did you hold onto yours last night," Michael said.

I stopped stirring pancake batter and gave him a look.

He smiled and then moved to a chair at the table. "Come on Marcus. Damn, I'm just saying it must be something about this city that has turned you and Nicole into two different people. I didn't even recognize you last night cousin. Or was last night just a carry over from what started the other night when you two left the club together."

I peeped over at Michael and began to stir my batter again. "So, you just going to sit over there and just straight up be nosy?"

"Well, you know me and my inquiring mind."

I poured batter on the griddle in a perfect circle and watched as it began to make bubbles. I poured some more until I had six perfect circles as Michael stared at me waiting on me to answer him.

"So, you're just going to ig me, cuz?"

I glanced at him without saying a word.

"Okay, well I guess that silence means that the other night when you two left together you handled your business."

"A true gentleman never kiss and tells." I said and turned over my golden brown and perfect pancakes.

"And while you were lip locking her did you tell her where your head and heart is?"

I went to cabinet and got a plate down and put it on the counter.

"Something like that."

"And?"

"And what?" I asked taking my perfect pancakes off the griddle and putting them on the plate.

"And what? Do I detect a little attitude? What the hell did you do to her?"

"Why are you assuming I did something to her?"

"Cause, I know you, man. You got game but when it comes to matters of the heart you are little lax."

"For your information cuz, I laid it all out on the line, alright. I left no room for doubt. I told her exactly what she means to me."

"So what happened?"

"Exactly what I wanted to happen. I mean she was in my arms and I was holding her and everything was everything."

"But..."

"Nah, man, you're not hearing me. There were no ands, buts, ifs or maybes. Everything was correct, right, hell even beautiful. Had me thinking we were getting back what we once lost. But the joke was on me. She put it on me and then didn't want anything to do with me. "

"What, back up, she played the player?" Mike asked amused. "Damn I love that girl's style," he laughed.

I stared at him in disbelief. "You know everybody is always saying I'm throwing up brick walls, but the minute I put down my defenses not only do I get my heart stomped on, my own cousin laughs at my expense in my damn face."

"I'm sorry Marc, I don't mean any harm but you got to laugh at the irony of this, man. "

"Yeah, well I'm just cracking up on the inside. Ha."

"Marc are you sure that's the way it went down?"

"I woke up and found her frantically looking for her clothes and trying to hurry up and get out there. She didn't even want me to touch her. Hell, I'm straight canine. I know how a dog hunts; you get your bone and you go home. That's what she did what did with that prosecutor. I just didn't think she would do the same with me."

"But come on cousin. That don't even sound like her, man. I know she cares about you."

"Yeah, in that brotherly, sisterly, best friend kind of way. That night didn't...it didn't change anything."

"But still man you two were together and you yourself said it was a beautiful thing. Hell that's got to count for something."

"Well in her words, it was a mistake."

"She said that?"

"Yeah."

"Damn, that's messed up. So what about now? Hell last night you were dancing with her, what was that about?"

"I never said that I didn't care about her, or want or need her in my life!"

"Alright man, chill."

"No why don't you chill? I wouldn't even be in this predicament if you hadn't been your normal nosy ass self digging up old feelings and talking about dangling participles and incomplete sentences making me believe that I could complete this damn chapter in my life."

Mike laughed. "Negro, don't be mad at me because you can't get over that woman. Hell I wish you would so I could step to her."

"You step and that will be your last step."

"Hey, I'm just saying, you need to shit or get off the pot. Nicole is too beautiful of a woman for you to be feeling sorry for yourself and half stepping. Now if I were in your predicament, I'd let her play me like a baby grand piano, 'cause ain't no way in hell, I'd sit around and do nothing and lose the chance I had to be with the one woman that I loved. But hey that's just way I play, player." Michael said heading out the kitchen.

Within twenty minutes, my mom, my sister and Nicole came in at looked about the kitchen at the spread I had prepared. On the table I had pancakes, sausage, bacon, eggs, hash browns, fresh squeezed orange juice and fresh hot coffee. Ashley walked over to me smelling like strawberries kissed my cheek and I kissed her back. My mom greeted me with a hug that I didn't want to let go of. Nicole and I made eye contact, smiled at each other and then she took her seat at the table next to my mom.

"Anthony Marcus, everything looks wonderful," My mother said cheerfully.

"I still haven't forgotten what you taught me," I said sitting across from her just as Michael came strolling in the kitchen to join us. "Oh, oh my cousin is trying to show out. You did good Poppi," he said cheerfully like he hadn't pissed me off earlier.

I ignored him and stole another glance at Nicole realizing I was wishing I could see her first thing every morning.

"Come on cousin, bless the table so I can get my grub on." Mike said sitting down.

We touched and agreed and I led us into prayer more thankful than I had been in a long time. After our Amens, plates were passed forks were busy and glasses were turned up. In between bites we shared conversation laughter and memories. The phone rang three times first Anita, then Angela and then April.

All of them wanted to know what time we were going to the hospital. My mom told them each of them that she had already spoken to my dad this morning. He was doing fine and wouldn't mind if we came later this afternoon after church. I looked at my mother as she said this. Couldn't remember the last time I went to church.

The five of us walked into New Hope Fellowship Missionary Baptist

LaTANYA WHITMORE

Church for the nine thirty service and sat on the second row. I was in between my mom and Ashley with Nicole and Michael on the end. We got there during devotion period just in time to sit down and stand up as we sang 'Guide Me Over Thy Great Jehovah'.

"Remember Brother Cooper?" Ashley whispered in my ear pointing toward the front of the church to the man leading the hymn. I smiled and shook my head. I couldn't believe that man was still alive and kicking. I took a closer look around the church and found things pretty much to be the same. The piano and organ looked the same. The same banner and covenants hung on the left wall. Usher Board number five came in still wearing blue suits and white gloves looking all prim and proper.

I glanced over at my mom. She turned and sang loudly in my face. I smiled. My mom could cook her face off, raised five kids, put me in my place when I stepped out of line, ran two restaurants with my dad but couldn't carry a tune across the street with directions. Her hand came up between my arm and she leaned her head toward me a second smiling a smile I could look at all day.

"Anthony Marcus, you remember Pastor Jones?" she asked.

I glanced at Ashley and asked with my eyes if it that was the same pastor that used to put us to sleep on those rare occasions that mom and dad dragged all five of us to church and Ashley only smiled. I turned back to mom and smiled as I held a deep sigh under my breath. This was going to be a long service.

One of the deacons then informed us that it was time to collect the offering and soon baskets were being passed around. The sound of rustling paper and coins clanging echoed in the half-crowded building.

When all the money was collected, all of the deacons took the baskets and exited the sanctuary. Then, an elderly minister in the pulpit stood and I wondered if that was Jones but then decided not when he asked us to come forth for alter prayer. My mom who was still holding onto my arm pulled me up front and I, in turn dragged Ashley out with me while most of the crowd just joined hands at their seats.

For about five to six minutes the minister prayed stretching his words out in his sermon like voice while the congregation did back up uh uh's, yes Lord's and have mercy Jesus'. When the prayer ended, my mom let go of my hand, dabbed at her eyes with her handkerchief and led the way back to our pew. Nicole and Michael both gave me a mischievous smile as I sat down.

No sooner had we sat down, a group of people came in and stood in front of the congregation and asked us all to stand. I glanced at Ashley as I remembered a cheer she used to do a long time ago. 'Stand up, sit down, fight, fight, fight.'

Suddenly a key was hit on the organ that I hadn't even notice, anyone had sat down at. The congregation started clapping and saying a bunch of amen's. The organist fired up again this time accompanied by the piano, guitar and drums. Where did all of that come from?

Then the choir started marching in from the back looking like they just stepped out of a Kirk Franklin video and the whole congregation joined in singing a hip hop version of 'We Come to Praise His Name' complete with a funky bass line from Parliament's 'Flashlight'. My mouth was slightly open as I again looked at Ashley. Surely I was not in New Hope Fellowship Missionary Baptist Church on the corner of third and Jackson.

The choir made it to the choir stand and blessed us with another song and then the congregation was allowed to take our seats. Then a brother about my age came waltzing in and headed straight to the pulpit opened his bible and adjusted the microphone.

"That's Pastor Jones' son. He's good," my mom leaned in and told me. I took a closer look. That couldn't be. There was no way. That couldn't be Leroy Jones, Jr. up there in that pulpit in a robe holding a bible just as good as he used to hold dice when we played craps behind Franklin High.

"He's real good and know the word, yes he do," my mom informed me. I took another look at Ashley who smiled and nodded and then looked back at Leroy who seemed to be making direct eye contact with my mom and then asked the congregation to stand. Once again we stood up and gave young Jones our undivided attention.

"Let's us go to the Lord in prayer," Leroy began and everyone once again joined hands, bowed their heads and closed their eyes. "Lord we come lifting our brother, Deacon Anthony Washington up to you this morning." A chill went through me when I heard my father's name. I closed my eyes tighter and as both my mom and Ashley squeezed my hands harder I found myself concentrating on the words coming from Leroy's mouth wishing they were mine because I suddenly became aware that I didn't know how to pray for my father.

I felt ashamed that I had to let somebody else pray for me. I listened intently as he asked God to heal my father's body and to have mercy on him and guide the doctor's hands as they touch my father. I felt my body tremble and held onto my sister and mother's hand even tighter.

Then he asked God to clean us up and make us strong where we are weak and to forgive us of our sins. Tears began to roll down my face as Leroy asked God for forgiveness of my sins because I never thought to ask for myself. The only time I went to God's house was when I was told to go by someone else. I hadn't stepped foot in a church since my grandmother was alive. I never went on my own to seek Him. And now I needed Him and didn't know how to ask.

My body shook as guilt and shame took over. I didn't want to be in His house and not be in His presence. Three words seemed to form in the pit of my stomach and move up and through me until they were resounding in my head and in my heart. I tuned out Leroy, my mom, Ashley and everyone else in the church. I knew they were still around me praying. I wanted to pray with them but I knew

I had to talk to my Father. I let the three words resound inside me until they were upon my lips. Over and over I repeated, Lord forgive me.

Ashley pulled my arm gently and I opened my eyes and noticed everyone taking their seats. I sat down, wiped my face, and looked up at young Jones who was opening his bible to a scripture. I leaned over and read with my mother. Soon the congregation was clapping and stomping, shouting and dancing as Leroy preached and taught us the word. There was one more song, one more prayer and one more offering and then we were dismissed. I looked at my watch. It was eleven thirty. I couldn't believe two hours had passed.

In less than an hour we were at the hospital and found Crystal in the room with my father. Then before we could all greet him and have a seat April, Angela and Anita came in as well and the small room was crowded. Crystal nodded at my dad and then he asked to have a moment alone with his children. My mom looked at him and asked without words what was going on and he assured her everything was fine and she, Nicole, Michael and Crystal left the room.

My father looked at me as I sat on his bed and then reached for my hand and then looked at my sisters.

"What's up, daddy?" Angela asked.

"Girls, come here. Come sit next to me."

The four of them crowded around him and the five of us looked at our father with concern but he just lay there first with a stiff expression and then with his easy smile. "I love you all with all of my heart and I hoped I have showed you that over the years."

"We know that dad," April spoke. "And we love you too."

"I know you do baby girl. I know you do. And I know all five of you are willing to give me a part of you just to keep me going a few more extra years and I love you more than words can say for just wanting to."

Tears suddenly formed in his eyes and he let go of my hand and wiped them away.

"We love you old man," I said reaching for his hand again. He looked up at me and smiled my smile.

"Junior, girls, there's still a chance that none of you will match me, a big chance. And if that's the case then I want you to know it's okay. I don't want any of you to feel bad or inadequate. It will just mean that it wasn't in God's plan you understand. Everything under the sun is in His hands and will work out according to His plan. If none of you match me it's okay I have options. I can do the dialysis thing and still live my life pretty much like I am now. Sure, I'll be limited to some things but I can still travel a little and run my business and be there for all of you.

"I may even get to L.A. to see what my boy's been up to all of these years and go do some fishing on the Colorado River one day. I'm not giving up my life and I'm not going to be a bitter old man about things I can't change. I got too much living to do and a pretty woman by my side. There's not too much more I want. Now, that's all I wanted to say. Anita, give Junior that Kleenex box."

Laughter broke out in the room as Anita passed the Kleenex box among the six of us, and soon my mom and Nicole came in. Our eyes met and I smiled and then looked at the door waiting on it to open again but it didn't. "Where's Mikey?"

"Talking to Crystal."

We spent hours with dad and then Crystal came in and said she wanted to get the testing done on all of us tomorrow so we could quickly put my old man out of his misery and get him out of this hospital as soon as possible. "Okay, everybody out now. Mr. Washington needs his rest and so do you. I want you all here bright and early at seven sharp."

I looked at my watch it was six thirty and according to my stomach way past time to eat. Everybody started saying goodbye to my dad and when I reached his bed he asked me to wait so he could talk to me alone. I turned to my mom, she smiled, kissed my dad goodnight and then left the room.

"What's up old man?" I said taking a seat at the foot of his bed as I smiled down at him.

"Junior, I know it's been a while but I thought I could talk to you man to man."

"Okay."

"Son I love you and I only want what's best for you. You may feel that I don't have the right to tell you how to live your life because you have spent so much of your life on your own, but that still doesn't change that you're my son, Junior."

I looked into his eyes and immediately felt tears form in my own. "I've missed having you in my life dad. I'm sorry that... that I didn't come back. I just couldn't... "

"Junior, I know you had your reasons and I'm not questioning your decision. I'm just saying that from the looks of things you have made a good life for yourself. And I'm proud of you son."

My body began to tremble from deep within as more tears formed in my eyes. It seems like I have waited so long to hear those words but I know I have done nothing in my life to deserve them. "Dad, you don't..."

"Junior, I look at you and I see a good and decent man. And I like to think I had something to do with that, huh?" he said smiling and scooping my head with his hand.

"Yeah, more than you know." I said wiping at my face.

"But, son, you got a issue."

"An issue?"

LaTANYA WHITMORE

"Yeah, isn't that what you young people say."

I laughed, "Yeah all right. So what's my issue?"

"You're a proud man. And ain't nothing wrong with having pride but sometimes pride can get in the way of what you really need in life. You understand, Junior?"

"I hear you."

"Do you, Junior? Nobody is promised tomorrow. We all have to make the best of things now. One day you're going to wake up and see that your whole life has passed by. I would hate for it to pass and you not get what you deserve, what you want because of pride."

"Dad   what..."

"Look, when you and Nicole left I knew there was a fifty/fifty chance that you might not make it. I even expected you not to. As much as you two loved each other back then, you were just too young to deal with that much hurt and that much pain."

His words surprised me, caught me off guard. I found myself looking down at the floor. "I tried every way possible to be there for her."

"Junior, I'm sure you did. I know you did. But did you let her be there for you? Did you tell her how you felt, what you lost?"

I stood up from his bed and went and looked out the window. "What I lost. God. She cried every single night for six months. Two months after we left she started going through the motions of a life she didn't recognize. She wanted everybody to believe that she was okay. But I knew better. Her eyes were so empty. But she would get up in the morning get dressed, have breakfast. We started school. She went everyday, did her homework, eat dinner. Sometimes she went to the movies, to a basketball game. She loved to go to the beach. But at night when the house was quiet, when we all went to our separate rooms, I would hear her. For six months, she cried every single night. And so did I. I would go to her bedroom and lean against her closed door. Wishing like hell I could just go in to hold her. I just wanted to hold her."

"But you never opened the door did you?"

"No."

"And you never told her how you sat out there every night."

"No."

"Why?"

"Maybe deep down I knew that we didn't have a chance. That I would never get her back."

"Tell her now."

I turned around and faced my father with disbelief. "What?"

"Open the door to your past son. It is the only way to get to your future. "

"You want me to bring up the past, the painful past to her when I know it will do nothing but hurt her? I can't do that. "

"Why not?"

I couldn't believe he actually wanted me to consider this notion of his. "Why not? Why should I?"

"Because time doesn't heal all wounds. It just covers them up. You have to deal with and face your past no matter how painful in order for you to move on. That is the only way you two are going to be able to work things out."

"There's nothing to work out Dad. Nicole and I are cool."

"Oh, so you're satisfied with the way things are between you two, being just friends? You're content? Or are you just going through the motions wanting everybody to believe that everything is okay? Son, your feelings for her haven't changed. You still look at her the same way you did when you were sixteen, Junior."

I looked in my father's eyes, hearing the truth in his every word.

"Hey, what's up?" Nicole said coming into the room.

I looked at her with my dad's words still ringing in my ears as she smiled in my direction causing my heart to literally leap inside of my chest.

Her eyes went from me to my dad. "Is everything okay?"

"Yeah, we were just catching up, you know talking about old times when you guys were kids," my dad said behind me.

I tore my eyes from Nicole and looked in his direction afraid of what he was going to say next. "Say we better get going," I said to Nicole while keeping my eyes on him. I moved toward his bed and gave him a hug.

"Put pride aside, Junior," he whispered in my ear.

I looked down into his eyes one last time and then walked to the doorway where Nicole was waiting. "I'll see you tomorrow old man."

When we reached the hallway everyone was waiting.

"Nicole, we're going to have to get together and catch up," Crystal said walking over to Nicole.

"I know. There's so much we got to talk about. When are you off duty?"

"Technically right now until tomorrow morning."

"Say why don't you come and have dinner with us?" Michael asked jumping in their conversation.

"That's a great idea Chris," Nicole said excitedly.

"I don't know," Crystal said hesitantly.

"You got to eat just like the rest of us don't you?" Michael added making serious eye contact with her.

"That's a splendid idea," My mom said turning to Crystal.

"Okay, if I come, please no hospital talk, no questions about the procedures tomorrow or anything. I got to unwind from this you know what I mean. I leave my office here."

"Well, in that case, please allow me to escort you and help you unwind,"

Michael said offering Crystal his arm. She looked at Nicole and then me and then Nicole looked my way and I let a small smile reach my face before leading the way out.

At the house, dinner was waiting. My mom had called Diane, the head chef at our restaurant, and told her to send the works. We walked into the house to the aroma of hot, fresh soul food. And right on time, April's husband, Gary came in with Angela's daughter, Tasha, and Anita's boy's R.J., Quinton and Jordan. It looked like Thanksgiving in the first week of August.

We all piled in the dining room blessed the food and began our feast on collard greens, potato salad, black-eyed peas, corn on the cob, ribs and hot water cornbread. Mike said he and died and gone to soul heaven. And I am not even lying when I say I was feeling the brother.

After dinner most of the guys retired in the living room and half watched the Mariners play the Oakland A's while the women stayed in the kitchen talking and cleaning and putting away food. After awhile, I eased in the kitchen in search of a something for my sweet tooth.

"So what's the story on you two. Did you guys elope?" Crystal was asking Nicole as the two of them washed dishes. Nicole turned around when she saw me head toward the stove in route to the last slice of apple pie. I tried to act like I couldn't find the silverware so I could hear her answer. Her eyes briefly met mine and I reached around her to get a fork out the drawer and began to eat my pie as I looked back at the two of them.

"Hey Badman," Crystal said.

Nicole laughed at the mentioned of my old nickname.

"I mean Marcus," Crystal corrected coming and giving me a brief hug.

"Say Crystal, where's Lisa?" I asked to get subject off of Nicole and I, which seemed to be the topic on everyone's mind.

"Would you believe her and Tim are still together, have five boys and live in Mercer Island."

"Five boys," Nicole and I both said at the same time.

"Five. Kept trying for that girl but after the fifth boy, Lisa said that's it. And to make sure everyone understood she named the last one Omega and got her tubes tied."

"Get out," Nicole laughed.

"I kid you not. You know Lisa," Crystal smiled.

"Whose Lisa?" Michael asked coming into the kitchen.

"Another one of my girls," I informed him and winked and then took another bite of my pie.

"Excuse me?" Mike asked confused.

"Lisa, Crystal and I were 'his girls' in school. He thought he was the bad man on campus and bullied anyone who messed with us," Nicole told Mike.

"So that's why his head is so damn big, you guys created this."

"Pretty much," Crystal said looking at Michael. He met her eyes and it was pretty clear that the two of them were more interested in just friendly conversation. A shot of jealousy shot through my bones.

"Say, let's go for a drive," I suggested.

"Cool, I've been waiting on my tour," Mike said still not taking his eyes off of Crystal.

"We can take my car," Crystal said and before long the four of us followed her out to her convertible Mercedes. Girl was after my own heart.

We cruised around downtown, passed the Center with Crystal showing us the mall and what store had closed and what new store had opened. We then hit the piers showing Mike the Totem poles and Ivar's Restaurant, the place that had the best clam chowder in the West. Then we went by the public market and Crystal promised to bring him back during daylight so he could get all the shrimp he wanted.

After that we hit Chinatown and, I know I just ate but the smell of the food had my stomach rumbling. Next, we headed toward the bridge and we pointed out to Mike that Mercer Island was the city on the other side. I thought Crystal was going to turn around but she jumped on the bridge and headed out. Nicole, Crystal and I screamed out like we used to when we went through the tunnel. Mike thought we were insane.

"Pass me my phone, Nicole," Crystal said. They were both in the front seat and Mike and I were in back, top town, cool breeze blowing as we flew about 50 mph to the sounds of an old Najee cut on the radio.

"Say, old woman wake up," Crystal said when she got on the phone. "If you're not sleep then what are you doing? You need to tell that man to get off you. You have enough kids. Yeah right, whatever. Guess what? I'm ten minutes away from your house so get up and put some clothes on and open the door. I'm bringing company. Never mind who it is. Yeah, it's a man. Matter of fact it's two. 'Cause I got it like that, bye." She hung up the phone, laughing and sped on across the bridge. Then after a few turns on a quiet residential street she was blowing her horn in front of a lavish two-story house.

The four of us piled out and the door slowly opened up. Tim was standing in the doorway trying to figure out who we were. Crystal led the way, kissed him on the cheek and went in the house.

Tim turned to me and looked me up and down and then smiled. "Say man, what's up? When you get back?" he asked tapping my fist with his.

"We just got in yesterday and Crystal thought it only appropriate that we come over and disturb the peace in your neck of the woods."

"We?" Tim said looking at Mike and then at Nicole. "Oh my God, Nicole," he went to her and pulled her in an embrace.

"Hey, Tim," Nicole spoke softly.

"I don't believe this. Wait until Lisa sees you. Come in, come in," Tim said stepping aside.

"Say, man, this is my cousin Michael from L.A."

"Nice to meet you man."

"Crystal, what is wrong with you coming over to my house after nine on a Sunday night," Lisa said coming down the stairs not noticing the rest of us yet. "You know how long it takes me to get my brats to sleep? They're hard heads don't never...Oh my God! Oh my God!"

And after that I don't know what she said cause her Filipino lingo took over as she grabbed Nicole in a hug and the two of them looked at each other smiling away. "I don't believe it. After all of these years, girl you look good. Oh my God! Timothy you see Nicole."

"Yeah baby, I let her in," Tim answered.

"I don't believe it."

"Look baby. Whose that?" Tim asked pointing in Michael and my direction. She looked at Mike first and tried to figure out who he was and then her eyes met mine and her mouth flew open. I stepped up and gave her hug that lifted her five foot two frame off the floor. She squeezed me tight and then I eased her to the floor. She looked at Nicole and I over and over again shaking her head.

"I can't believe this. I thought I would never see you two again."

"Well, here we are in the flesh," Nicole said.

"When you get in?"

"Yesterday."

"And you just now came to see me."

"We had a little business to take care of Lisa," I informed her.

She led us to the den as I introduced her to Michael and as Tim went to get us all something to drink.

"So tell me, how long have you two been married and how many kids do you have," Lisa asked no sooner after we sat down on the couch. Nicole looked at me and I hunched my shoulders.

"No marriage," I answered.

"No kids," Nicole added.

"Oh, so you two just living it up and shacking."

"No shacking," Nicole said under her breath. Tim brought us all a glass of lemonade and we sipped quietly as Lisa digested Nicole's and I situation or lack there of.

"So, you two decided to sneak back in town just like you left." Lisa asked.

"Actually my father is in the hospital and we came down to see about him and found Crystal as his doctor."

"No kidding. She's a great doctor. I'm glad she listened to me and went on to med school. Cause you remember she had a hard head and thought she knew everything but I told her she should make something of her life."

"Okay, Lisa we don't have time for you to jump on your soap box. I just wanted to bring them out here so they can say hi and for you to go through the initial shock because I know you were going to go ballistic. But we better be going, guys. We have a long day tomorrow," Crystal said standing up.

The rest of us stood up too and said a brief good bye to Lisa and Tim and promised we would all get together like old times. When we got to the car Crystal asked me to drive and hoped in the back seat. Mike hoped in right beside her like I knew he would.

NICOLE

37

The soft sound of music lightly drifted through the walls. It took me a minute but I finally recognized the soulful sound of Marvin Gaye voice as he sung 'What's going on.' I looked at the clock. It was three minutes after midnight and even after a quick relaxing shower I still couldn't find sleep. I eased out of the bed ran my fingers across my hair and began to pace the floor and before I realized I was on the other side of Marcus' door.

I leaned my ear to it and listened intently. Marcus was singing along and his voice was just as soothing as Marvin's. I tapped on the door and entered the room before he answered. The small lamp by the bed gave the room a kind of a purple glow. Marcus was stretched out on the bed wearing nothing but shorts and I can't lie I had to catch my breath at the sight of his muscular chest. He rose up to a sitting position when he noticed me.

"I'm sorry did I wake you?"

"No," I whispered. "I couldn't sleep anyway. You either I see."

"Not a wink. You come to keep me company?"

"Sure."

"Have a seat," Marcus said patting the bed with his hand. He eased up to the top of the bed and rested his head on the headboard. I went to the other side sat and leaned next to him.

"So what are you listening too," I asked then felt dumb, like duh.

"I found my old Marvin Gaye greatest hits cassette."

"I'm surprised you're not playing an eight track," I joked.

Marcus laughed lightly. "I'm sure I can find you one," he said and then pushed me slightly on the arm.

"You and you're music. I've forgotten how much you love it."

"My dad's influence."

"Is that right."

"Yeah, he used to say if you can't say it sing it."

"Wise man."

"Yeah, that he is."

Silence fell in the room and then the song 'Mercy, Mercy, Me' came on. I looked over at Marcus. His eyes were sad.

"You worried about your dad?"

"Yeah."

"He's okay Marcus."

"Yeah, everybody keeps telling me that. He's told me, my mom, Crystal, everybody's told me. But I don't know that. I can't see it, Nic."

I pulled his face toward mine and looked directly in his eyes. "He's going to be alright."

He nodded his head and then shifted his body toward me. "What if he's not Nic? What if none of us match and he has to get on some machine every other day for the rest of his life? What kind of life is that?"

"One that he can live Marcus. Your father is not dying. This is not a life or death situation, just a life-changing one. He is a strong man and your mom is a strong woman and they are going to get through this together. Be grateful for that."

"How can I? I've been gone for seventeen years and in my mind every time I pictured coming home I imagined finding my father messing with some car in the garage not lying up in some hospital bed or being hooked up to some machine!"

"Marcus, no. You're looking at this the wrong way. All you see is the negative. Baby, close your eyes and flip this. On Monday your dad goes on the machine, on Tuesday he goes fishing. Wednesday he goes back on the machine and Thursday he tinkers out in the garage all day. Friday he goes back on the machine and then leaves for the weekend with his wife to go see his son in L.A. On Monday morning before he leaves L.A. he goes back on the machine and by that night he's at home having dinner with his wife. Tuesday morning he's up cooking her breakfast. Wednesday he goes back to the machine, by that night he's kicking it with his daughters. Thursday he spends the day at the restaurant. Friday he's on the machine and then spends the weekend with his grandchildren taking them camping and fishing up at Whidby Island. Flip this Marcus. He's living. Baby, he's living."

Marcus looked at me a second and then brought his arms around me and in seconds I felt his body trembling in my arms. I held him closer and rubbed my hands across his back. He squeezed me tighter and I felt the moistness of his tears against my shoulders and felt his silent cries. I kissed the side of his face, stoked his back and held him like he's held me so many times.

His body finally quieted and he pushed away from me slowly. I looked at him but he didn't meet my eyes.

"I can't believe I did that," he whispered.

"It's okay. I understand."

"But I don't. I can't remember the last time I cried and this whole weekend I just been a crying fool."

"This weekend you've been overwhelmed. You've seen you family for the first time in seventeen years. If that didn't move you I'd think something was wrong with you," I said making him look at me.

"What about at church?"

"That was something between you and God."

"I couldn't pray for my father, Nic. I felt guilty for not going to church. I felt guilty for not asking God to forgive me for the things I've done in my life and I couldn't pray for my dad. I have messed up so much, Nic. So much. I feel like He won't heal my father because of the kind of life I've been living. I feel like He won't forgive me because I only came to Him when I needed Him."

"He doesn't work like that Marcus. Your life has nothing to do with your father's illness and God's miracles. And I know there is nothing that you have done in your life that He won't forgive you for."

Marcus looked at me a moment shaking his head. "How did you get to be one profound woman, Ms. Nicole Williams?"

"I have good friends," I said hugging him again.

He squeezed me back and kissed my forehead. I leaned back into his arms as we listened to end of 'After the dance' I closed my eyes a second and could imagine us dancing at Faces a long, long time ago. A smile crept across my face. "Marcus you remember Faces."

"I remember dancing to this song and you stepping on my toes," Marcus chuckled.

"Lie. I was very light on my feet," I said lightly elbowing him in the side.

"That's 'cause you were always on mine."

"I can't stand you," I said smiling.

"I don't like you either."

We both laughed and then Marcus yawned and closed his eyes as he pressed his body closer to me.

"Are you sleepy now?" I asked.

"I'm restful."

"Restful uh."

"Yeah, I got this little peace thing going on right now."

I raised my head. "Okay, well I guess I can go on to bed now."

"Nic, don't leave," he whispered opening his eyes and looking directly into mine and just like that I was stuck like glue to my spot like I was the other night when we made love.

How does he do that? How does he make me not want to move when I know I need to run as fast as can? But he looks at me and I get trapped by those eyes that make me think of things I long ago pushed aside and dream dreams I used to dream.

A part of me was screaming for me to get out of his bed but I refuse to listen. Practically all of my life, Marcus has been by my side through hell and back and there was no way I was going to not be by his when he needed me to be.

"I'm right here," I whispered and then eased back down into his arms.

Instantly I felt his warmth around me and I can't lie, sleep was the last thing on my mind. Marvin's soulful voice started singing 'I want you' and I felt every nerve on my body wake up and my body temperature rose at least thirty degrees higher as Marcus breath brushed across the back of my neck.

"Marcus?"

"Yeah," his sleep thick voice answered sexy deep.

For seconds I lost my train of thought, got caught up in the lyrics of the song and the feel of Marcus against me warm, covering me like my favorite blanket. I finally remember that I had called his name for a reason.

"Marcus, can you um, turn off the music?"

"The music?"

"Yeah, it's keeping me up."

"Sure."

In one motion he rolled over clicked off the cassette player and placed his arm back around me. "That better?"

"Yeah," I lied.

Now it was too quiet. All I could here was his breathing and was that my heart pounding? And that lamp of his that gave the room a purple glow was messing with me. On the wall I could see the shadow of us lying together as one.

"Marcus?"

"Yeah."

"Can you turn off the light?"

"You don't like the light either?"

"No. I like complete darkness."

"Not a problem."

He rolled over again turned the light off and then was back spooning my body. His breath again was warm against my neck.

"Um, you alright now?"

"No," I answered truthfully.

"No," Marcus said rising up looking down at me. "What else can I do for you?"

I stared up into his eyes and then down at his sexy lips and could almost feel them on mine. Two nights ago he looked at me the way he was now and kissed me all over and loved my body so good I screamed his name over and over.

"What? I uh…. Nothing. It's okay. Go to sleep. I'm sorry, go to sleep."

"You sure?"

"Yeah, go to sleep."

"Okay, goodnight Nic." he said and eased back down and pulled me back in his arms.

Okay, I can't do this. I tapped him on the arm, the bare muscular one. The one that was attached to his broad shoulders, wide chest and six-pack abs that led down to...

"Marcus, I'm sorry I don't want to bother you."

"I knew you wanted something," he whispered in my ear and I could tell he was smiling.

"Yeah I do."

"What do you want?" Marcus asked squeezing me in his arms.

"Could...could you put a shirt on?"

"A shirt. Do I smell? I took a shower," Marcus said raising up and smelling under his arms.

"No, crazy. You don't smell. Your body is just a little...warm."

"Too hot?"

"Something like that."

He leaned back and pulled a t-shirt off the floor, slipped it on and then snuggled back against me. "Now we sleep, right."

"Yeah," I said letting out a deep breath. "Well good night, Marcus."

"Good night Nic," he said and then leaned in and gave me the sweetest briefest kiss on my mouth. Not a deep kiss, or a long kiss. But just enough kiss with a taste of his tongue to make me want some more. I licked my lips tasted him then closed my eyes and searched for sleep.

"Say Nic."

"Yeah."

"This is nice."

I opened my eyes glanced at the moon shining through the window. "What's that?"

"Falling asleep like this."

"Yeah it is," I said knowing if I got any sleep it would be a major miracle.

Silence crept in the room and all I could hear was his breathing. Once more I closed my eyes and let myself relax in his arms. After a moment, Marcus body started moving, shaking the bed and then he let out a laugh.

I asked, "What's so funny?"

"It's a trip how everybody thinks we got married."

"Yeah."

Marcus yawned. "And think we have kids too," he said sluggishly.

I shifted in his arms closed my eyes remembered dreams of years ago.

"Thank you, Nic."

"For what?"

"Being here."

Silence.

Snoring.

MARCUS

38

"Marcus, Marcus, wake up."

I opened my eyes and turned and looked at Ashley standing over me. "Okay, okay. What time is it?"

"It's five o'clock."

I peeped toward the window and saw the dark sky looking back.

"We have to be at the hospital by seven, remember."

"Yeah, okay. I'm up," I said stretching and then looked down at the sleeping body in the cuff of my arms. A smile came across my face.

"You going to get up?" Ashley asked.

"Yeah," I said reaching over and turning on my lamp and then turned back to her and watched her ease out the door.

Nicole moved slightly in my arms. Slid one of her legs in between mine. Got comfortable like she wanted to catch the second half of her sleep. I pushed her hair from her face and then placed a light kiss on her forehead and then one on her eyelids and then lightly brushed her lips with mine as her eyes flickered open.

"Good morning," I whispered stroking the face that was only inches away from mine with my fingertips. Her brown eyes looked into mine, and that part of me that makes me male decided to join the party. I shifted my body to the left only to find her most feminine spot. Her eyes closed and her lips fell slightly open and I dove in, kissing her soft lips.

Her arms came up around me and I slid my hands down the length of her body. She was so warm, so soft. Memories of the night we shared stirred me. I wanted her so bad. Her arms slid down my back and she squeezed me closer and I was at that the point of no return. I let my tongue move down the base of her neck and onto the swell of her breasts as she started calling my name over and over.

"Marcus! Marcus!"

"Yeah," I whispered.

"Marcus wake up. Wake up!"

I shook my head, opened my eyes and in the darkened room I looked over into Nicole's face. Her eyes were wide open as we lay face to face. I stole a quick look at the clock. It was four forty five. I lay startled a moment.

"Did Ashley come in here?"

"No."

"Damn," I said rising off of the bed. I made it out of my room and into the bathroom. I was dreaming big time.

We made it to the hospital at six thirty. Crystal met us in the waiting room bright and cheerful like she had gotten about twenty-four hours of sleep to brief us about the procedure. I glanced at my mom and could see the weight of everything in her eyes. I went to her and kissed her cheek. "It's going to be okay," I told her.

"I know baby. God's got this," she whispered and then patted my face.

I looked up at Crystal just as she spoke. "Okay, everybody. Let's get started,"

My mom gave each of us a brief hug and said she was going to go sit with my father. Crystal then left the room with Angela following right behind. I fell in step behind April.

"Marcus," Nicole called out.

I turned around and waited as she walked over to me.

"No worries, okay," she said looking up at me.

I nodded and then she reached and gave me a short kiss. I looked down into her eyes, squeezed her hand and then followed my sisters.

After the procedure, I came back to the waiting room and found Nicole asleep in a makeshift bed of two chairs. I knelt down in front of her just as Michael's spoke from behind me.

"Hey Marc."

I stood up and faced him. "Hey."

""So now what?"

"We wait." I said glancing back at Nicole.

"It's hard to let go, uh man?"

I looked at Mike from over my shoulder. "Mind yours."

"I'm just stating the obvious cousin."

"No what's obvious is the way you've been pushing up on Crystal."

"I'm not pushing no harder than you."

"What's that supposed to mean?"

"Hey, whatever you want it to mean, cousin."

"Yeah, okay, whatever," I said glancing back at Nicole as she slept. I liked looking at her face.

"Although I will say this," Michael said interrupting my thoughts, ideas, hopes and dreams. He wanted to converse so I took the bait he put on the line.

"You'll say what?"

"Even though we're related we have two different styles, you know two different approaches."

"Oh, so you know my style."

"Yeah, you laid back with yours. You sit back, throw out subtle hints and before you know it the woman's coming to you."

"Is that so," I said laughing and shaking my head.

"Yeah, I heard your call last night, soft music playing. Marvin Gaye at that. Door opens, footsteps move across the floor another door opens no more footsteps. A little quiet conversation, a little laughter, and then more soft music. Smooth."

"Damn man, you don't miss a thing."

"I'm right across the hall man, I got ears."

"Well close your big ears, Dumbo and get out of mine."

"Come on cousin, I'm just glad you're stepping up to the plate. It's a different angle but it seems to be working for you, making her do what you want her to do. Come to you. You're on top of your game and I'm happy for you. Now see if it was me..."

"Uh, uh Mike. I have heard enough of your loveology 101."

"Hold up, is that my cousin with the player, player degree hanging high on the wall using the 'L' word."

"Enough Mike, it's too early in the morning."

"So, is that what you told Nicole when you bolted down the hallway to the bathroom this morning."

I glanced at him. "Okay man, that's it. I'm going to make sure you hook up with Crystal cause you definitely need a life."

"That's all I wanted to hear. Matter of fact, I'm going to go see if I can help her in anyway. Peace."

He left the room. I shook my head. Mike's smooth too. He always knows how to divert my attention.

I turned back toward sleeping beauty wanting to be her Prince and kiss and wake her up. Like she kissed me earlier. She suddenly moved and almost fell out the chairs.

"Ouch."

"You okay."

"No. These chairs are way uncomfortable."

"Here, take this," I said handing her a Kleenex from the box on the table.

"What for?"

"Catch that slob action off the side of your face."

"What," she said her hands going instantly to her dry face. "You play too much, Marcus."

She eased up and rolled out of the chairs slowly and then walked around moving her neck from side to side.

"Come here," I said grabbing her hand and then pulling her toward a straight back chair at the table where some cards were set up. She sat down and I began to massage her neck, shoulders and back. I looked down into her face. Her eyes were closed, her mouth slightly parted and little purring sounds were coming out of her. "How's that."

"Wonderful. You're good at this."

"I'm good at a lot of things," I told her.

"Yeah, I know. How did the testing go?"

"Okay."

"Where's everybody else?"

"I don't know. I've only seen Mike so far."

"Are you worried?"

"No. A good friend of mine told me not to."

"Good. If it will help I want to get tested too."

I stopped rubbing her shoulders because this feeling that I can't explain came over me. She reached up and touched my hand. I held it a moment and then she stood up.

"Let's go see your dad."

We entered my father's room and he was lying in bed staring up at the ceiling, as my mother lay asleep on a cot beside him. Nicole went to him and kissed him on the cheek.

"Good morning, Mr. Washington."

"Hey, Nicole. You look rather rested this morning."

"Well, I don't know how considering I just slept in two chairs in the waiting room. How are you doing today?"

"Oh I can't complain as long as I get to look at his ugly face."

I moved in and grabbed a hug from my dad. He patted me on the back. "Don't hate old man. This face as a way with the ladies."

"I'm not so old and you need to slow your roll."

"Alright dad. I hear you."

I took my seat on the foot of his bed and Nicole sat in a chair just as the door opened. All of my sisters entered the room.

"Hey, Junior we were looking for you," Angela said and then gave my dad a hug.

The door opened again and Michael came in spoke to everybody and then a few minutes later Crystal came in. Angela gently nudged my mom. She looked around the room and then stood up and moved by my dad's side placing her hand in his.

"Hey everybody. You all here?" Crystal asked. No one answered with the obvious. She walked over and stood facing my dad. "Mr. Washington, we ran test on all of your children and even though some of them were possible matches, none were..."

I tuned her out as I felt the bottom of my stomach come up to my throat. Ashley was standing beside me and I felt her body tense up and I reached out and took her hand as I tried to remember everything Nicole had told me in the wee hours of the day.

Still I couldn't believe this. I looked over at my dad's face and it hadn't changed since Crystal first came into the room and my mom was staring straight ahead at nothing.

Crystal voice cut through my thoughts. "….but your nephew Michael is a perfect match."

All eyes went on her.

"What did you say?" Anita asked.

"Michael's a perfect match."

"I am?" Michael said from the corner of the room. Nine pairs of eyes moved to Michael.

Crystal walked toward him. "Yes, you are. Now, like I explained before, it's a simple operation for Mr. Washington but your recovery will take longer and you will have to stay in the hospital longer so we can monitor your progress. We can do the surgery tomorrow but I really want you to think about this and be really sure."

"There's nothing to think about. I'll do it."

"Hallelujah, praise God!" My mom shouted and then hugged my dad and then went and hugged Michael.

I looked up at my dad who had tears flowing from his eyes. I went to the head of the bed and hugged him and we both shed tears of joy. A hand came over and pushed me out the way.

"Move Junior. Oh daddy, I am so happy," Ashley said hugging my father.

The rest of my sisters came and hugged my father one by one and I walked over to my cousin who still stood in the corner. "I wish I knew what to say, Mike."

"Come on cuz, don't sweat it man. It's no biggy."

"No Mike. This is a real…a real biggy. Thank you, man. Thank you." I said pulling him to my arms just before more tears fell from my eyes. "You are truly my brother. I will never forget this."

"Hey you know, blood is blood and thicker than mud," Mike said.

"Blood is blood, Mike."

"Hey can I get some of this," Nicole said and we pushed apart and held her in our circle. Soon my sisters all came over and so did my mom.

"Say now you can't overwhelm him. He has a big operation tomorrow," Crystal said.

"Oh, no. I'm an only child. I loved this. Bring it on. Bring it on," Michael said and we all bum rushed him again.

"Say man, you scared?"

It was five-fifteen about an hour before the surgery. I eased into a chair next to Michael's bed. I had just left my dad's room where my mom and sister's were going to stay until it was time for the surgery. Nicole was in search of some coffee.

"Scared? What do I have to be scared of? Man, I have the best-looking doctor in the hospital operating on me. The way I see it I'm in good hands," Michael smiled at me.

"Mike, you got a one track mind."

"I can't help it man. She's the one."

"Is that right?"

"I'm trying to tell you, man."

"Alright," I said and then moved closer to the bed. "Look Mike, I can't tell you how thankful I..."

"Marc, come on. You can't spend your life thanking me alright."

I looked at Michael like he was crazy. "Mike, what you're doing is saving my father's life."

"I'm only repaying him for saving mine."

"What are you talking about?"

"I'm talking about the month before you and Nicole moved to California when my mom died. When your family came up for her funeral. Your dad was there for me. I had watched my mom dwindle away to nothing in six months while my dad had affair after affair. He barely came to the hospital. He barely gave her a decent funeral. And before my mother's body was cold in her grave, I walked in and found some woman in her bed.

"It took your father to pull me off of that cheating bastard. I had my hands wrapped around his throat. I was going to kill him. I swear I was. But he talked me out of it. He made me realize that my mom would hate it if I spent one second in jail for killing his trifling ass. He wasn't worth it."

I stared at Mike in disbelief. I never knew. Never.

"And another reason I'm doing this is for me," Michael continued. "I want to prove to myself that I'm not like him. When someone needs me I can be there. I won't run. I won't hide. I'm not a coward. When Anita called and told me about your dad, I called him before I called you. And where is he now. He hasn't even as so much picked up a phone to see about his one and only brother. But hey that's my dad."

He reached across his face and quickly wiped the tear from his eye that was threatening to fall. "Say cuz, why don't you go see what's taking my cutie pie so long. I'm in need of some TLC."

I looked down at Mike for a second as he tried to down play what he was about to do and I couldn't explain the admiration I had for him. All of this time he had led me to believe that the riff between him and his old man was because of his singing career. He didn't want me to know how ignorant his father really was. I said a silent prayer of thanks for the father I had and the cousin I had and then went in search of a pretty mocha chocolate doctor and her brown skinned friend.

NICOLE

39

I looked at Marcus' profile as he drove admiring the growth of his two-week-old beard. He glanced over my way and I immediately diverted my eyes to the windshield in front of me. Out of the corner of my eye I could see him looking at me, smiling and then looking back at the road. I smiled and then looked out of my side window. We were on the way to the hospital like we have been every day for the past week and a half. His parents and sisters were at home preparing a feast fit for a king in celebration of Michael. He was coming home.

The surgery had been a success and Mr. Washington was released five days later. Ever since he has been home him and Marcus have been thick as thieves. They stay up all night talking into the wee hours of the morning, the sound of their laughing voices drifting up into the bedroom I sleep in. Every night Marcus' whole family was there for dinner and I never saw Marcus look happier as he laughed with his family. Then one by one bodies would go home or off to bed until it was no one left but Marcus and his dad. I tried to hang with them on a few occasions. But sleep would catch my butt and I would stumble on up the stairs fall into bed and drift on some memories of long ago and not so long ago.

Coming back here as brought back so many memories, especially at Marcus' house and especially in the den. Every time I walk down those stairs I see myself at fifteen, sixteen years old looking for A.M. to go see what we are going to get into next. We were so close. And then there was the party, the party that changed everything. He kissed me, asked me to be his girl and made all my dreams come true. Back then the only thing I knew how to do was to love A.M. That was all I wanted. We were the couple that everybody knew was going to make it. We loved each other so hard and so strong and nothing and no one was ever supposed to tear us apart. We were supposed to be Lisa and Tim, married with a house full of kids.

"Oh, oh. I think I made a wrong turn. This doesn't look right," Marcus said bringing me out of my thoughts.

There was a lot of construction on some of the streets so Marcus had thought he could find another way to the hospital. I looked out of my window and didn't have a clue as to how we had gotten where we were. "Things sure have changed," I said looking out the window as I recognized some of the street names but didn't recognize the area. Everything looked different. Where I thought I would see something it was gone. "Say there's Jackson Street up there. It's a major street. Turn right."

Marcus turned and we both searched for something familiar but didn't recognize the new stores and new office buildings in new shopping centers. He drove a little further and crossed 23rd Street. Now I knew where we were. At least I thought I did until I saw a new park off to the right.

"What happened to all the houses on this block," Marcus said.

I looked out the window on his side. "I know. Everything is gone."

We drove a little further and then finally started seeing some houses. Only they were not the houses I remembered. I remembered big freshly painted house with nice lawns, fenced in back yards, flowerbeds. Now the few that were still standing, and it wasn't many 'cause I swear it was like every other lot was empty, were barely standing and in need of a paint job and some serious lawn care. Cars were parked in yards, windows were boarded up and graffiti spelled out obscene words on vacant houses that I knew were once filled with loving families. Marcus turned right and we found ourselves on 29th Street.

"Slow down," I said as I looked on the right side of the street. We drove slowly and then when we got to the middle of the block, Marcus stopped the car. It was gone. There was nothing there just a vacant empty lot. I sat staring straight ahead at the nothing that was in front of me. I heard the car motor turn off and then felt Marcus' hand cover mine. I turned and looked into his eyes and then back at the vacant lot as my own eyes began to fill with tears.

"I remember the first time I came over," Marcus began to speak. "I rode my bike all the way as fast as I could after you called me. I couldn't wait to see you. And remember we both rode our bikes all the way to Seward Park and back. Then when we came back and we sat on the porch, and I remembering rubbing your legs. We spent a lot of times on that porch. I liked that old porch."

I smiled through my tears. "Yeah I did too although I didn't when I first saw it. I swear the first time I saw this place I wanted to run. It was old and small and I think it leaned to the right. And those big green country chairs were a sight. But I have to admit I ending up spending a lot of days rocking in those chairs watching the rain or waiting on you to come by."

"And I would get here and find you and Ms. Emily snapping beans or shucking corn."

"We went to the market almost every weekend and got fresh vegetables. She loved vegetables and fried fish."

"And don't forget barbecue goat," Marcus laughed.

"Oh, God, how can I."

"The look on your face when you saw those boys pulling that goat," Marcus laughed again. "Girl you jumped on my back so fast."

"Like you been around dead goats all your life," I said facing him.

Marcus let out a small laugh and then looked past me into the direction of the vacant lot. "Guess Ms. Emily showed us both some things. I like the talks we had. She was cool you know. I guess that's why she was such a good teacher. She had a way of relating to people."

"She liked you too. The first time you came over she said 'I like that Mr. A.M. and I think he's stuck on you.' I liked to have died." I said laughing at the memory and looking back at the vacant lot almost able to see us in the kitchen talking as I lost the struggle to keep more tears from falling from my eyes.

Marcus' hand came across my face and wiped away my tears. "Yeah, I guess she had me figured out from the start. She knew I was crazy about my brown-eyed friend."

I turned and looked into his eyes again and this time I didn't care about my tears. "How can it be gone? How can there be nothing here when everything here changed my life forever. One night, one person took away my happiness, and now I look out here and it's like I never existed. It's just vacant."

Marcus pulled me in arms and I felt his hands rub up and down my back. "I'm glad it's gone Nic. I don't think I could look at the place where you were..."

I pulled away and looked into Marcus' eyes that were now watery like my own. I wasn't the only one hurt that night. I wasn't the only one that had things changed that night. "Have I ever thank you for saving me that night. For saving my life."

"I just wished over and over that I could have made it here sooner. If I hadn't left the house so late and then had that flat tire I could have been here and that bastard never would have laid his hands on you. I should have been here baby, I'm sorry. I'm so sorry."

I watched as his eyes misted up and then kissed his cheek.

"Marcus, you were here. You saved my life!"

"I'll do anything for you, Nic. Anything! I mean that more today than yesterday."

Marcus looked all through me as he spoke and then he brought his lips to mine and my mouth instinctively opened and welcomes his kiss.

Through teary eyes, I kissed him back following the need I had inside me and the need I felt from him. His arms came around me and pulled me closer to his warmth and I let myself dive inside him holding back nothing. And then in seconds it seemed as if all the anger, all the pain and hatred that had lived inside me for so long just went away. Our kiss deepened and intensified with a passion that seemed to release me from every bad thing that ever happened in my life. I was in Marcus' arms and I was free.

We pulled apart and I looked at him not knowing what to say or what to do. I just knew I was okay. I felt it down to my toes. Everything was okay. He brushed his fingertips across my lips, kissed my hand and then turned and started the car. I turned and face forward as we drove to go get Michael.

I was so stuffed I couldn't hardly move. I felt like a turkey on the Thanksgiving table oozing out dressing from the seams. Michael had been home from the hospital for just under three weeks and said he needed to get back in the swing of things. He had spent most of the day in the backyard cooking and fixed his famous grilled salmon and twice-baked potatoes and made a mean seafood salad. Michael and Marcus were now downstairs in the basement with Timothy, Gary and the kids, while the ladies, meaning Marcus' sisters, me, Lisa and Crystal cleaned the kitchen. Mr. and Mrs. Washington had decided after dinner to take a much-needed getaway together and informed everyone that they would see us on Sunday.

"Girl, if I don't see one more plate or fork in this lifetime it will not be too soon," Ashley said, wiping the counter.

"I know what you mean. I love it when we all get together, but I tell you clean up is a bugger," April added on.

Ashley took a seat at the table and let out a deep sigh. "And why is it that the guys always get to go sit on their rear ends when it comes time for cleanup."

I finished wiping the stove and sat across from her at the table. My flat feet were hurting from being on them over an hour.

"You two don't know anything. Why don't you try picking up after three half grown boys day after day. They don't do nothing but leave their dirty socks and big long shoes in the middle of the floor. I swear I come home from work and I know exactly where to find them by following their trail," Anita said going to the refrigerator and pulling out a bottle of juice.

"All of you guys need to quit. You forget I got five plus the big grown one I'm married to. Bathroom duty you don't understand," Lisa said shaking her head.

All of us looked at her and gave her much deserved praise.

"Girl my hats off to you," April said. "Gary's bathroom habits scare the hell out me with all that hair everywhere. I swear I don't if I married a monkey or a man sometime."

We all fell out laughing.

"See that's why I adopted a girl," Angela stated.

"And that's why I'm staying single," Ashley added.

"I don't know Ash." Anita began. "There are a lot of times that I wished that Ricky and I could have worked things out."

"Yeah being single ain't all that it's cracked up to be," Crystal spoke up and Angela seconded her with an Amen of her own.

"Crystal I am surprised you never married," Lisa said.

"I got sidetracked with my career and besides one bad apple kind of left a bad taste in my mouth. I don't know if I could trust a man, love and all of that."

"Well it seems to me that you starting to trust something the way you're making eyes with our cousin," April said.

Crystal blushed and lowered her head. "Michael's a nice man and not bad on the eyes."

"Um, huh," April said and then the both of them started laughing.

"I don't know what it is. It's just that the moment I laid eyes on him we had some sort of connection. I can't explain it," Crystal said looking dreamy eyed.

"It's called love, silly. Wake up. You've fallen for him," Lisa said.

"But what kind of sense does that make, when I've only known him for what a month. I don't even know what kind of man he is. I mean he's a singer and what does that tell you."

I turned to Crystal. "That he shoots from the heart and he's not about games. He's very real, very sincere and very honest and is definitely looking for a woman, not a woman or two, but a woman. He wants commitment, loyalty, family, the house, kids and the dog."

"Wow, you know him pretty well."

"Let's just say that for over seventeen years, Michael and I have spent a lot of time talking. I have mad respect for him and besides him being the best damn singer slash musician LA has ever had he is the best friend a girl could have."

"Kind of like the Badman, uh."

"Yeah kind of."

"Oh come on, Michael and Junior are nothing alike," Ashley commented.

"No, I wouldn't say that Ashley. Your brother and Michael are definitely different but they have a lot of similarities. You can tell they come from the same stalk."

"Except Junior no doubt is probably running around with everything in a skirt," Angela said.

"He's a little selective," I said in Marcus' defense.

"Oh, I don't know Nicole. If he's not with you, he's with everybody. At least that's the way he was when he was here," April joked.

"Girl we would come home from school and see some of everybody creeping out the backdoor or hiding in the basement," Ashley added. "But when you two hooked up all that changed."

"Then it was just Nicole running out the backdoor," Lisa said punching me on the arm.

Crystal jumped in. "And you know it girl. Cause Lord knows she stopped hanging with us and spending all of her time with her A.M. There's no telling what those two were doing."

"Now hold on you two it wasn't even like that," I said.

"Now come on Nicole, you two were crazy about each other and you going to tell me you two didn't do the do," Lisa butted in.

"Come on Nicki, we all grown now, tell it like was. You know you let the Badman talked you out of those panties a time or two," Crystal joked.

"Or three or four," Lisa laughed too.

I stood up laughing myself. "Now hold up. What we had back then was sweet."

"Sweet," Lisa said in her thick accent. "I bet he was."

"Marcus treated me with respect, Lisa and you know that. He genuinely cared about me. It was nice."

"Okay, ladies. This conversation is getting a little too deep. I'm going to go grab my bunch and head on home. It's getting late," Anita said smiling and then came and hugged me. "Bye little sister."

"Hold on Nita, I'm right behind you," Angela added. One by one all of Marcus' sisters said their good-byes.

"Yeah we better go too," Lisa said suddenly. "Timothy's mother is sweet for taking care of my rugrats but I don't like to take advantage you know."

"Can you wait a minute Lisa?" I asked. Suddenly I felt the need to talk to my girls like I used to. "I need to tell you guys something. I didn't mean to hide it, it's just the way things happen you know."

"This sounds serious Nicole, what is it?" Crystal asked.

I looked at the two of them and asked them both to sit back down with me at the table. "I was raped," I blurted out.

"What!" Lisa exclaimed.

"The night Marcus and I left. The night Emily died, I was raped. Marcus found me and his family helped me leave town. That's why we left."

"Oh my God, Nicole. What happened?" Crystal asked with tears starting to form in her eyes.

I took a deep breath and closed my eyes a second pushing back the memories of that most frightful night. "Chris, without going into details I will just say that, it was the most horrible experience I have ever lived through. But I lived and I'm okay. I'm okay because of Marcus and his grandmother. She took me in and took care of me. And Marcus, he was always there. Even when I pushed him away," I said with all honesty feeling tears well up in my eyes. He was always there, just like he is today.

"I never would have guessed. I always hoped that you and Marcus left here to elope or something. I mean we knew how crazy you two were about each other. I'm so sorry, girl. So sorry," Lisa said hugging me.

I met Lisa's eyes. "Hey, I'm okay now. I've been to hell and back a couple of times in my lifetime but I'm okay. I still got my health and once again I got you guys. And I don't care if I move to Timbuktu I going to keep in touch this time," I smiled.

"You better!" Crystal said coming into my arms. I squeezed her back and silently thank God for letting me find them again, then hit Lisa on the arm.

"Girl, you got five boys! Guess you never took those birth control pills, did you?

"Shut up!" Lisa said, hitting me back.

MARCUS

40

It was three o'clock in the morning and once again I couldn't sleep. So many things were going in my head. I was happy. Happy than I had been in a long time and I know that's due to being with my family again. How I'm going to be able to go back to LA next week, I don't know. My life there doesn't even compare to here. There my life exists in the fast lane, fast money, fast women and fast cars. Here I just live and enjoy every moment of it.

And even though the past month here has been filled with ups and downs I'm grateful to be here. I'm grateful to be home. Grateful that my father is going to be able to live his life like he always has. I'm grateful for a lot of things it's just that coming back here has made realize that there is something else I want, something else I need. And that something, that somebody is Nicole. I can't get her out of mind or out of my heart. She's in my blood.

I love her so much it scares the hell out of me!

And I don't understand it. I thought I let it go. Let it go a long time ago. Six months ago I was minding my own business; making money and tasting whatever honeys that caught my attention. Then my girl needs me and I can't say no. I can't turn my back and before I know it I find myself lost in those brown eyes again. What does she have on me? Why can't I shake her? No scratch that, why can't I have her like I need her for life.

I rose out of bed and eased downstairs and then into the basement. Once in the den I turned on the black light that I put in a couple of days ago and then went through some of my sister's old records. I pulled out an old Levert album and placed it on the stereo. As the needle scratch it's way across the first cut, I went to the bar and poured myself a glass of brandy, sipping on it with memories of the night Nicole and I spent together running through my mind.

I remembered the way her hair felt as I wrapped it around my fingers. Remembered the look of her eyes just before they closed as I pulled her face closer to mine. Remembered the softness of her lips, the taste of her tongue, the smell of her neck, the sound of her moans.

Everything about that night is embedded deeply inside me because I swear I never thought it would happen. As much as I wanted it, I thought it was too late. Too much time had passed, too much water was under the bridge, too many meaningless others and maybe even too much friendship to be more than friends. But none of that mattered when I held her. None of that crossed my mind when I kissed her. I just wanted her. Wanted her so bad that everything inside me...

"Marcus?"

I looked up at the sound of Nicole's voice as she stood in the doorway wondering how long she had been standing there. Wondered if she could tell that I was thinking about that night.

"Hey, did I wake you?"

"No. I couldn't sleep so I went to your room to look for you," Nicole said coming into the den.

She was wearing a purple tee shirt with matching boxer shorts. A cute, tomboyish, look that looked sexy as hell on her. I made my eyes divert back to her face as she made her way to where I was standing taking a moment to thumb through some of the records. Her eyes were unreadable. It was almost as if she was sad but then again, I wasn't quite sure.

"Well you found me. You need something?"

"I was kind of hoping for a hug," she said looking up at me.

I placed my glass down on the bar slowly. Took a deep breath. "I think I can manage that."

I reached for her and she fell into my open arms. At contact, the heat of her body sent my blood racing through my veins. She felt so good. So damn good.

"Are you okay, did you have a bad dream or something?"

"No, actually I had a good dream."

"Oh, really?"

"Yeah."

"You want to tell me about it?"

"Not right now. I just want you to hold me."

"Okay," I said pulling her closer in my arms just as the music changed.

Our hug slowly turned into a dance as we both fell into the rhythm of the song. I closed my eyes and guided Nicole in a slow circle as I listened to the words of the song that was saying everything I was thinking.

It's been so long
Since I've had somebody close to me
Can't you feel my body tremble?
The closer I get to you, I want you so bad.

"This is nice," Nicole said bringing me out of my daze.

I shook my head and looked down into her beautiful face. "Yeah?"

"Dancing with you used to be one of my favorite things."

I smiled down at her. "Is that right?"

"Yes. You were a good dancer for the most part."

"And for the other part?"

"Truth?"

"Yeah."

Nicole looked away a moment and then looked back in my eyes, smiled or was that a blush. "I miss being close to you like this."

"Yeah?"

"Yeah." She licked her lips and I almost lost it. I pulled her close and her head rested on my shoulders as my mind wondered back to the night we spent together. And the song, this damn song was not helping a damn bit!

See there's so many things that I dream
That I can do to you
Can't you feel me shaking
The anticipation is getting the best of me.

"Marcus?"

"Yeah?"

"I can't stop thinking about us?"

For a second I couldn't respond. "Us?"

"The way we used to be."

I tried to swallow the lump in my throat.

"What about you?" she asked quietly.

"What?"

"Do you think about us?" she asked looking up at me.

Does night and day count? "Yeah, sometimes."

"That's what I dreamed about."

"About the past?"

"No I don't think so. I mean I just dreamed we were together."

I looked down in her face again. "Is that a good thing?" I asked holding my breath.

"I don't know what do you think?" she asked as her eyes pierced through me making me lose my train of thought.

"What do I think?" I glanced down at her enticing lips and then back into her captivating eyes. *Put pride aside, Junior.* "I think I'm slow dancing in the very spot that I first kissed you to a very suggestive song while you're wearing nothing but a tee shirt and boxers at three o'clock in the morning telling me some things I like hearing. I think I'm either losing my mind, dreaming or being seduced by you very meticulously. And you are definitely working me."

Nicole slid out of my arms and stepped away. "So you're onto me, huh?"

I looked her square in the eye without comment.

"Well, I'm onto you too," she said not backing down from my gaze with a slight smile on her face. "I'm not deaf you know."

"Meaning?" I asked.

"Your music selection, Marcus. You know, Ohio Players' 'Let's Love', Marvin Gaye's 'I want you', and now Levert's 'I've Been Waiting'. A girl might think she was being seduced," Nicole said turning her back to me and slowly walking toward the window.

I couldn't stop the smile from forming on my face. "And if a girl was being seduced, what would she do?"

"Anxiously anticipate the seduction," she whispered turning her body slightly at an angle as her last words dangled in front of me like a piece of candy in front of a child. And I was hungry. Hell I was starving! I took several steps and got as closed as I dared without letting my body come in contact with hers.

The room was filled with sexual undertones. Her voice was laced with sensuality as her silhouette glowed under the moonlight that kissed her face. And the music, the lyrics of the song made me want to sing, cause damn it I wanted her. I wanted to hold her so bad. But I couldn't. If I held her I wouldn't be able to hold back. If I held her, I wouldn't want to let go.

My eyes traveled down the length of her body and then back into those brown eyes that made my knees weaken. She brought one fingertip to my lips and I couldn't stop myself from kissing it.

"Make love to me Marcus," she said with such intensity that I promised to God, she rocked me.

I looked back into her eyes and barely stopped myself from letting the truth roll off my tongue. For seconds I got lost in her words and in the desire that shown in her eyes. I wanted to take her in my arms so bad. But pieces of a conversation played in my head. The words that were said on a morning we never once brought up again. Her hands came up to my face. I covered them with mine and then shook my head.

Her eyes silently questioned mine.

I took a deep breath. "Nic, please don't... don't ask me to hold you in my arms again if you're going to regret it as soon as the sunlight hits that window. Let's not make the same mistake twice." I looked down into her beautiful brown eyes one last time and then did the hardest thing I ever done in my life.

Walked away.

I know what I said was cruel. I threw exactly what she told me back in her face. Even though weeks have passed since that morning and we have somehow come closer than we have been in a long time I had to put it out there. I had to put the ball in her court. I made the first move last time. I had taken the first step, put myself out a limb, and dangled my heart only to get it thrown back in my face. This time, if there is going to be a this time it's all on her. I don't care what Mike says. Hell I can't reach for her. I can't pull her in if she doesn't want to come. She has to come to me, on my terms.

I went to the stereo, took the needle off the record found the power button and turned it off. And I didn't look at her. Even though as I slowly made my way across the room from the stereo to the door I could tell she was standing in a trance, her body trembling, her eyes filling with water, I didn't look at her. I kept walking. I was determined to walk out the door come hell or high water without looking at her or wiping the tears from her eyes or without taking her in my arms. I kept walking even though I felt like I was about to double over in pain if I didn't touch her lips with mine at that damn second. I kept walking. I wasn't backing down. A man's got to do what a man's got do. Forget what my dad said. I can't put aside my pride. Not this time.

"Marcus?"

I stopped on a dime and made change. "Yeah."

She took about six paces until she was directly in the compounds of my personal territorial boundaries. Taking up even my breathing space. We made eye contact, serious eye contact. The kind of contact that went straight through that brick wall I was trying to build up between us and went right inside my chest and stopped the very beat out of my heart.

She momentarily looked away and then back up into my eyes. I watched her lips move in search of words and for the first time in a long time I could tell she was struggling to speak to me. I didn't want her to tell me what she thought I wanted to hear. I wanted her to tell me how she felt.

"Nic, I..."

She put her hand up to stop me and then a slight smile touched her eyes before she spoke. "You know coming back here to this city, being in this room, has made me realize what it was like to have you love me. In this room, I found so much happiness and if I close my eyes I can even feel the first time you kissed me. I never have been as happy in my life as I was when I had your love."

She stopped and took a deep breath as I literally held onto her every word and as her eyes never left mine. She continued, "But my biggest mistake Marcus, my only regret in my life was letting your love go. I pushed you away. And I didn't mean it. All of those times that I told you to go away and leave me alone... what I really wanted was for you to hold me and to tell me you still loved me like you used to and that it didn't matter that I was raped."

I stood perfectly still stunned by her words and hypnotically watched as a single tear rolled down her face. I was more than speechless I was immobilized. I felt like someone had just dropped kicked me back into the past as I stood face to face and toe to toe with the pain of that night. I was totally taken off guard and felt numb inside. I couldn't even react.

"I wanted to be special to you. I loved you so much Marcus and I wanted to show you in every way that I loved you. But after the rape I didn't feel special, I didn't feel good about anything about me. And I didn't feel you could love me anymore."

"Nic...."

"Let me finish. I spent years acting off of my feelings and what I thought was true. But you know rape in itself is just a lie. It's not even about sex. It's about control. And I let my rape control my life. I shut down. I closed the door on our past and our future. I minimized the relationship we had and belittled it because I couldn't see it Marcus. I didn't know what love looked like anymore. I didn't know what us look like anymore.

"But the night when we made love, the moment you kissed me, every thought, every feeling, every moment we ever shared together came crashing down on me at once. I was so overwhelmed because everything felt so right and so good. I knew what we looked like again. I knew how good we felt. And I got scared. I got scared because I... I didn't see it coming. I didn't expect my feelings for you to so strong. I didn't realize how hard I had been fighting the way I feel about you. I didn't realize how much I...I still love you."

"Come here," I said pulling her in my arms and covering her mouth with mine and kissing her until I was breathless. I didn't need to hear her next word. I needed her. Her dark brown eyes looked into mine and I felt totally lost to my surroundings. Nothing mattered to me but this woman that I had only hoped to hold like this again. I closed my eyes, kissed her again. Wrapped my arms totally around her. Pulled her closer to me and lost my damn heart. Completely.

I ran my fingers through her hair and kissed her over and over and then finally just looked down into those deep beautiful brown eyes of hers. "I love you. God help me. I love you so much."

"I love you too, Marcus and I'm so sorry for walking away from you, from us. I should have never let anything come between us."

"Nothing has Nic. Nothing has," I said wiping away the tears that were forming in her eyes. "I'm here baby. I'm here. And I promise you I'm never leaving your side again. Never."

I lowered my mouth to hers, kissing softly the lips that I have craved to touch for so long. She brought her hands up around my neck and I pulled her body closer to me. She felt so good in my arms. I kissed her over and over unable to control my swelling desire. She was so sweet. Her lips were like nectar and her warm body literally set mine on fire. She moved her hands from around my neck and began to run her fingers along side of my face and ears as we continued to kiss. Her touch was so soft and I was slowly but surely loosing control.

I slid my hands around her waist and then let them travel under her shirt and in one movement I had that shirt over her head and on the floor. Her hands were on my chest pulling at my own shirt and I didn't care if she ripped it off, I wanted her skin next to mine so bad. I pulled away from her and then we both started pulling my shirt over my head. She returned back to my arms kissed my neck and chest, held me literally and emotionally.

We moved across the den in a heated embrace: lips touching, hands rubbing, bodies colliding. Heavy breathing deep moans and whimpered cries. The sound of us filled the room like music. I pinned her against the wall, our fingers interlocked. My heart was racing. Then in a matter of seconds we helped each other out of our clothes and our bodies became one.

I looked into her face. She looked into my eyes and began to kiss me wildly slipping that sweet tongue of hers in and out of my mouth. She held me tight. Match my every movement with hers. She lay her head on my shoulder. Her fingernails were digging into my back. She started calling out my name continuously like a song. I held her and rocked her to my beat. Rocked her slow hard and then faster and harder until I was drenched with sweat. She brought her eyes to mine. Looked at me with those beautiful browns. Said words that no woman has ever made me feel.

Somehow we ended up on the couch, she on top of me. I pulled her toward me. Kissed her deeply, passionately. Sounds come out of my mouth. Sounds not words because now I was incoherent. I couldn't think. All I could do was feel. And she felt so good I never wanted to let her go.

I pulled her body to mine and rolled on top of her. Her eyes looked up into mine made my heart smile. We restarted our dance, a slow rhythm with a pulsating beat that grew, expanded and then became bigger than the both of us. We danced and danced until our love mixed and collided and then we held onto each other until the earth stopped shaking.

"Nic. Are you sleep?"

"No."

"Are you sure?"

"Yeah, I'm up."

We were lying in my bed after our all night love session that had started downstairs. We had crept upstairs weak, laughing and in each other's arms only to start up again once we reached my bedroom. I glanced over at her as she lay with her eyes closed. Her hair was tossed wildly all over her head from our throws of passion. Her skin glowed under the pre dawn sky that seeped through my bedroom window. I glanced at the clock. It was ten to six.

"I have something to tell you."

"What is it?" she asked sleepily.

"I love you."

She smiled lightly, her eyes still close. "I kind of got that impression a couple of hours ago."

"Nic look at me."

She turned her head and faced me.

"Can I ask you something?"

She laughed. "What you trying to do make up for lost time?"

"Something like that," I said honestly.

She looked closer at me. "You sound serious, what is it?"

"Do you trust me?"

"Why would you ask me that?"

"Can you answer my question without a question? Yes or no, do you trust me?"

"With my life," she said.

That was one point. "Are you happy?"

"You mean at this moment?" she smiled.

I turned on my side and faced her. "Nic, stop questioning the questions and just answer, okay. Are you happy?"

I watched her take a deep breath and then exhale slowly. "Extremely."

Two points. Now it was my turn to take a deep breath. "Do you need me?"

"In what sense?" she asked and I raised my eyebrow at her. "Okay, okay. I'm sorry. The answer to your question is yes. I can't imagine my life without you. I love you Marcus, deeply, and without question or doubt," she said earnestly taking me by surprise. God she made me so happy. I couldn't stop myself from smiling.

"Okay, do you..."

"Stop."

"What?"

"With all the questions. What do you really want to know?"

"What I want to know is what I'm asking you about?"

"Come on Marcus. I know you better than that. You're leading up to something. What is it?"

"Okay, you're right I am. But you got to let me ask you one more question."

"One?"

"Just one."

"Okay, last one Marcus."

"Will you marry me, Nic?" I handed her the velvet box. The one I bought years ago and found last week in the back of my closet under some more of my old things. The one I had pulled out from under the mattress and held in my hand as we made love the second time.

"Marcus..." Nicole whispered as tears slowly traveled down the side of her face.

I opened the box and took the small diamond solitaire out with shaking fingers. I slid out the bed and got on my knees in front her. "The moment I first looked into your eyes something happened to me that even after all of these years I still can't explain. I don't know if you stopped my heart or started it. I just know that I love you and that I have never stopped loving you and there's no one in this world that I want to love but you. There's no way that I can. You're all I want. You're all that I've ever wanted, all that I ever needed."

I felt a lump form in my throat and had to take a deep breath to continue. "I know I'm not perfect. There are some things in my life that I wish I could change some things that I regret. But loving you is not one of them. You are my heart, my joy. I want to share my life with you, totally and completely and I promise to be by your side no matter what and to love you no matter what. I bought this ring a long time ago and I wanted to give it to you that night...that everything went crazy. I knew then that I wanted you to be my wife. Nothing's changed. Will you be my forever, my always. Will you be my wife?"

I watched silently through watery eyes, as tears instantly filled her eyes and a slow smile fought its way across her beautiful lips as she said one word. "Yes!"

I wiped her tears. She wiped mine. We both looked down at the ring and I took her hand and tried to guide the ring onto her finger but it wouldn't go on. We both laughed.

"I guess we're going to have to go shopping this morning," I said.

"Here, put it on this finger," Nicole said holding out her baby finger. I slid it on. "Perfect fit," she said looking down at ring and then back at me.

"We certainly are."

I slid back in the bed, laid next to her, looked into her brown eyes found her delicious lips and preceded to once again make love to my fiancée. We had a lot of catching up to do.

NICOLE

41

"Say man, you're not going to bel..." Michael started as he bolted through the bedroom door without knocking. I rose up and he looked at me and then at Marcus, grinned and quietly closed the door. Marcus moved closer to me, got all up in my space and I loved every bit of it.

"Was that Mike?" Marcus said sleepily as his hand stroked my back.

"Yeah," I purred back.

"Is he just now getting home?"

I glanced at the clock. It was nine-fifteen. Come to think about it, he was wearing the same clothes he had on the night before. "I guess so." I sat up in the bed. "Where has he been with my girl all night long!"

"What are you fussing about?" Marcus said turning over.

"Mike and Crystal! They left together last night and he's just now getting here. Basic math, Marcus, put two and two together!"

"For what? They've been making eyes at each other from the start. I'm glad the brother got his own business."

"What business does he have with Crystal?" I asked looking over at him.

"The same business I have with you. Why you tripping, you know you're happy about it."

"I am it's just that, I didn't think they would hook up so quickly."

"Mike's my cuz. He knows what he wants. Just like I know what I want. And right now I want my fiancée to come here and..." he started nibbling on my ear and kissing my neck very softly. I slowly eased back down in the bed and into his arms. His warm mouth found mine and he gave me tender kisses.

"Oh baby, you are so warm and so soft," Marcus murmured as he lips continually kissed me as his hands caressed me all over making my body screamed. "You're so beautiful, sexy and um you know I want you girl.."

I laughed and kissed him lightly on the lips. "I bet you have said that to all the ladies in your life."

"You are the only lady that has ever been in my life, Nic."

"Is that right? Just how many women have you slept with?"

I felt Marcus body tense up.

"Without a condom?" I added.

His eyes met mine. "Including you, one. You see what you do to me. Make me break all of my rules," he answered seriously.

"What other rules have I made you break?"

"Never use the 'L' word. Never let a woman knows she has my heart. Never let a woman know she is my joy."

"Well, since I'm such a bad influence on you, what are you going to do about it?"

"This," he said and kissed my lips again and then moved down back to my neck. I pulled him closer to me and then raised my leg to cross his body, felt a sudden tightness.

"Ooh!"

"You like that uh," Marcus said kissing me some more.

"No!"

Marcus rose up and looked down at me. "You don't like that?"

"No, that's not what I mean. My legs are sore. I feel like I been in a round or two with Mike Tyson."

"Oh, I see. Well I can't have my baby hurting. Come here and let me rub you down," Marcus said reaching for me.

"Uh, uh. Keep your hands to yourself. That's what started this in the first place," I smiled at him. "Come on we better get out of this bed. There's no telling what Michael is thinking about us lying around way after nine o'clock in the morning."

"Maybe Mike's thinking that it's about time you and I got our wires together."

"Is that right."

"He's been reading me like a book for months."

"What are you talking about?"

"The way I feel about you. Cuz knows there ain't no shame in my game."

I crinkled my nose as I thought about that, the little stink. So that's why he wanted to know what happened between Marcus and I the night I saw him at the club. I looked down at the ring on my left pinky and twisted it around. "Marcus did you really want to marry me back then."

Marcus smiled up at me. "Most definitely, woman! I wanted to run away to Vegas and do it that very night."

"You are crazy."

"About you, yes!"

I kissed him and then slowly got out of the bed. "I'm hungry. You need to feed your woman."

"Say, I've been thinking," Michael began as he sat down at the kitchen table looking fresh from his shower. Marcus and I had showered earlier together and cooked breakfast together. Okay, I only scrambled the eggs while he did everything else. But my eggs were slamming.

"What are you thinking about, Negro?" Marcus asked him as he spooned some grits on his plate and began putting extra butter on them.

"I'm thinking of making a move. You know leave LA."

Marcus and I both looked at him and then at each other. I poured some juice in my glass curious about Marcus' response.

"Where you thinking about moving to?" Marcus asked.

"Here. I like this town. It's a lot happening here. I want to explore it a little longer. See what pans out for me."

"Or maybe there's a certain someone here you want to explore." They shared a look and then Michael reached for a piece of sausage and then looked over at me with a goofy expression on his face.

I ate some more of my eggs. I was happy if he was happy. I truly was. But what if he looked down the road in a couple of years and wished he hadn't left LA. "What about your career Michael? Before we left LA you were on the verge of becoming the next household name."

"I don't have to be in LA to be a singer. Sure that's where everything happens but if I'm as good as you tell me I'm going to blow up anyway, right."

I smiled and nodded my head and looked over at Marcus who was suddenly eating like there was no tomorrow. "So I see you got everything planned out."

"No I don't. And that's what's so great! For the first time in my life I'm winging it. I'm following my heart, going with the flow, letting it all hang out!"

"Marcus, you sure Michael didn't give your daddy his brain instead of his kidney."

Marcus laughed. "He's alright, Nic."

"No he's not if he's thinking about moving here without a plan."

"I was thinking about it too," Marcus said looking up at me as he drank the last of his juice and put his glass down.

"Thinking about what?" I asked cautiously.

"About moving back here. This is home. I didn't realize how much I missed it until we came back. We have family here, friends here and now Mike. What do you say; can you make this your home again? With me?"

I felt the tears form in my eyes as I looked into his. "Anywhere you are is home to me, Marcus."

"Well, isn't that sweet," Michael said.

Marcus leaned over in his chair and kissed me fully and I placed my arms around his neck pulling him closer. Marcus eyes stayed on mine.

"Okay, so it's settled Nic. We go back to LA next week, tie up all our loose ends and come back here and pick up where we left off seventeen years ago."

"Together," I whispered.

"As husband and wife," Marcus kissed me again.

"What!" Michael exclaimed. Did I miss something last night?"

Marcus and I turned our attention to him and I smiled my biggest smile. "We're getting married!" I wiggled my pinky finger in front of his face.

"As soon as we get back here," Marcus added.

I looked back at him. "As soon as we get off that plane."

Saying goodbye was hard. Even though I knew it was temporary, it was still hard to do. But at least this time I got to say goodbye to Lisa and Crystal. Lisa prepared lunch for Crystal and I at her house on the Thursday before we left. This time when we arrived she took me on a tour of her beautiful two-story home. My favorite room was her spacious kitchen that had every appliance imaginable. We sat and ate on the deck off the kitchen that overlooked Lake Washington and the floating bridge. The view was breathtaking. The September weather was perfect and all the trees were so green and Lisa had a garden filled with colorful tulips and irises that she swears she takes care of herself. She served us grilled chicken, pasta, fresh salad, assorted fruits and ice-cold lemonade. For the first half hour we ate and reminisced about our past and laughed about all the silly things we did. Then next we played catch up when Lisa brought out frozen margaritas. After about our second glass, Lisa had enlightened me on her wedding day and about the birth of all five of her boys. Told me more than I wanted to know, but hey, that's Lisa and I love her anyway.

Crystal shared with me her woes with the different men in her life who she said all sizzled out in grand fashion saying she was too much woman for them because of her career. But she loved her job. She made a difference. She saved lives. I told her my hat was off to her and the hell to any man that thought otherwise! Then it was my turn to speak my piece. To catch my girls up on what was kicking off in my life. I did it with the wave of my hand. Crystal and Lisa both stared at my three-karat princess cut diamond platinum ring that my baby just put on me last night with wide eyes and opened mouths. I got teary eyed and told them how Marcus had proposed with the smaller diamond that I now wear on my right pinky that he bought all those years ago. They both cried and we all laughed and hugged. Then I told them my other news. We were coming home to stay, moving here and making our lives here where it all started. Lisa screamed with joy and hugged me so tight I couldn't breathe. I hugged her back and then gave Crystal a hug and whispered in her ear that Michael was moving here too. She straight up blushed.

On Friday we had a big barbecue at Marcus' parents house. We had already told them they we were getting married and were moving back here and they insisted that we celebrate. By two that afternoon, the huge backyard was filled with all of Marcus' family and of course Crystal and Lisa came with all of her boys and Timothy. Tim and the boys started a football game with Anita's three boys and poor Tasha was left looking on the side.

I looked at the guys and marched into Tim's huddle and grabbed the ball and tossed it over to Tasha. "Here girl, get in there. They're nothing but a bunch of boys. Don't be scared. Take their ball and kick their butts."

She smiled and ran toward Tim. He patted her on the head like he did his own boys and she bent over and listened in on the game plan.

"Look at you getting stuff started," Marcus said walking over to me.

"A girl's got to make her way in the world," I said watching as Tasha put a hit on Q that made him fall back.

Marcus laughed. "You want to play don't you?"

"Hell yeah."

"Go on then. I got your back."

"Yeah, but whose got my legs and my arms tomorrow when I won't be able to move them?"

"I got all that too."

I looked his way. "You got a lot things baby."

I leaned up and kissed him lightly. He pulled me in his arms and our kiss deepened.

"Hey, hey, hey you two. That's a violation," Michael said. "No kissing on the football field.

Marcus grabbed my hand and led me back toward the grown ups at the picnic tables. I took a seat across from his parents while Marcus went to fix him another plate.

"I can't tell you how happy I am that the two of you are getting married and moving back here," Mrs. Washington said.

"I'm pretty excited too. I love it here. I'm so at peace here. Everything is just right."

"I'm glad to hear that daughter in law. You guys have any idea where you're going to find a house?"

"We were thinking about living with you two," Marcus said taking a seat next to me with his plate.

"Excuse me," his dad spoke turning his attention from the football game.

"Yeah dad. You and mom are in this big old house by yourselves. Nicki and I should start our lives and our family right here with you two."

"Think again, Junior. Your mom and I have been alone in this house for over fourteen years. We're just now breaking it in. And now I got the kidney of a thirty-two year old, my Annie's going to have to watch out now. You heard me!"

"Anthony!" Mrs. Washington exclaimed hitting her husband on the arm. Everybody broke out in laughter.

"Oh it's like that dad," Marcus said.

"If you don't know, you better ask somebody, son."

"Say Marc your dad got a little lingo with that kidney, you think," Michael stated.

341

"Yeah, I got a little something, something already." Mr. Washington said moving his head side to side like he was in the middle of a Master P video.

"Uh, uh. Dad quit. Mama, do something with him," Ashley pleaded trying to hold back her laughter.

"Girl, I ain't mad at him," Mrs. Washington said and turned and gave her husband some dap.

We all laughed at the two of them. "There ought to be a law," April said.

"I will look in my legal books first thing Monday morning, okay," Ashley informed her.

"Thank you little sister. Now back to where you guys are going to live. Any ideas?" April asked.

"I personally like that mountain. What's that called again?" Michael asked.

"Mt. Rainier and it's too cold and too far, Mike. Not good," Marcus told him.

"Okay, what about downtown. I would like to get a spot near the Space Needle and be in the middle of everything."

"Crystal, don't you have a condo near downtown?" Anita asked.

She looked up at the mention of her name and shyly answered yes and turned her attention toward the kids. And I didn't miss Michael reaching for her hand and taking it in his.

"So, what about you two?" Anita asked refocusing her attention on Marcus and I.

"Well you know me. Anywhere near the water is fine with me," I said.

"Baby, I was thinking about some land. You know about three or four acres. Get a couple of horses, cows, chickens maybe," Marcus said and I knew he just lost his mind.

"In what lifetime sweetie?" I asked turning to face him.

"Okay, lets compromise. You know like Utah."

I nodded my head cautiously remembering how Jessie Jr. had explained to us how his parents had decided to move on top of a mountain in the middle of nowhere.

Marcus took my hand. "See baby, you want the beach, I want some land, at least one or two acres and two horses tops."

"Uh huh. And we're going to find this place, where?"

"Whidby Island."

"Oh it's gorgeous up there. You should see it now, Junior. Gary and I are thinking about buying some property up there," April said excitedly.

"Yeah, Gary told me about the beachfront properties on at least two acres of land. It's not to far, less than an hour away including the ferry ride. My parents still go up there every weekend. It's private, secluded and even romantic. What you say baby? Can't you see us riding our horses watching the sunrise every morning?"

"Okay, but I have one condition."

"Anything."

"I am not going hiking on any mountains, big hills or little hills. Understood?"

Marcus laughed and kissed my forehead. "No hiking."

"Then it sounds perfect. And I can't wait."

"Me either." Marcus said squeezing me.

"Say, Uncle Junior," Quinton called out.

Marcus let go of me and turned around. "What's up, Q man."

"There's someone here to see you."

Marcus kissed me again. "Hold on to that for me," he said standing up.

I looked into his eyes. "I'll never it let go."

MARCUS

42

Nicole was fast asleep before the plane left Sea-Tac. I looked behind me. Mike was a row over talking to the young lady who sat next to him. They shared a laugh about something and Mike threw his head back and for a second his eyes met mine. I nodded in response and watched as Mike turned his attention back to the woman. I glanced again at Nicole and then out the window. We were probably thirty minutes from landing. I eased my arm from around her and pulled out an envelope from my jacket pocket. I opened it slowly taking a deep breath. I looked at the pictures twice then once again my eyes were on Nicole as she slept. A sudden chill skated across my body. I put the envelope back in my pocket and then placed my arms back around her. She was my world and I loved her more than my life.

DEREK

43

Derek placed the binoculars down on the dashboard of the van and rubbed his tired and red eyes. He glanced at his watch and then at Steve, a DEA detective from the 46th Precinct. Steve was following a lead on a drug bust that might possibly be connected to the Fulton murder case. After months of investigation the police finally linked a name with a picture of a woman who was seen with Fulton on several occasions. Her name was Sheila Larson, the niece of an alleged drug dealer, John Slaughter.

Six days ago, Derek and Steve staked out in front of her condo in an unmarked van, after placing a video-cam in her living room, a tap on her phones and a listening device in every room only to come up with nothing. She barely came home and hardly ever got visitors. Earlier tonight Steve changed the game plan. Around seven thirty Sheila came home left her car parked and unlocked outside of her condo. Steve crawled over to it put a tracking device under it and a listening device on her a pair of glasses that were left in the car. Since her uncle didn't come to her Steve assumed she went to him and he was going to be there when she did.

Derek had no choice but to wait it out. He had nothing but time anyway. More than anything he wanted to prove that there was no way possible that Nicole could have killed Fulton if to no one but himself. He rubbed his eyes again trying to clear the vision of her face from behind his lids. She captivated him. He was fascinated about everything about her.

And he missed her. Missed the touch of her skin. Missed the feel of her lips the sound of her voice. She was like no other woman he had ever met. His brother was right. He was head over heels in love with her. And he was going to prove her innocence and clear her name for good if it was the last thing he did.

"Say, Derek wake up. We got a little action."

Derek looked at Steve and then out the window. Two slim brothers both with bald domes wearing designer clothes knocked on Sheila's door. Derek made them to be eighteen, nineteen or maybe twenty at the most. Sheila stepped outside of her door and closed it behind her and gave her full attention to the two guys.

"Damn, she must be onto the bugs. You see how she closed the door." Derek said.

"Either that or she doesn't trust the two thugs she hired." Steve added looking on.

"Hired?"

"Yeah, she's up to something."

The three spoke for about a minute and then Derek and Steve watched as they strutted away from the door and got back in their convertible mustang pumping up the sounds of some rap song and drove off. No sooner after they drove off the front door opened again.

"Say Steve, there she goes." Derek asked sitting up and grabbing his binoculars.

Steve picked up his and watched as Sheila headed for her car. "Time to put a move on. Keep your eye on that monitor." Steve said to Derek starting the van up after Sheila pulled off and was at least three car links ahead of him.

"Now remember hotshot, you are here for the ride only. This is a drug case and we are going to do things my way. I've been waiting too long on this and you're not going to botch this up. Something's getting ready to go down. I can feel it. So just sit tight and keep your ears and your eyes open! Alright?"

Derek looked at the monitor as it beeped then over at Steve "I hear you man, this is your show."

A cell phone rang.

"Is that yours?" Steve asked Derek.

"No, mine's off."

Steve sped up and got just one car link behind Sheila. "It's hers. Turn the mic up on the bug for the cell phone."

"I can't do that Tre," Sheila was saying in the phone as she pushed her glasses on her face.

"Whose Tre?" Derek asked.

"Keep quiet!" Steve said under his breath.

"What do you mean you can't Sheila? That's a damn order."

Sheila laughed into the phone. "Nigga pleaze. You ain't nobody to be giving orders, alright. Check yourself."

"Alright I will and you will see what Slaughter has to say about it."

"Whatever, Tre I got to go."

"Be at the spot, Sheila."

"I said no, Tre, damn!" Sheila screamed in the phone, pushed her glasses on her face and continued to drive all at the same time. "I got to go Tre."

"Sheila!" Tre yelled. The phone went dead.

Derek adjusted the volume back down. "I wondered what that was about."

"Don't know. Let's just don't lose that car." Steve said putting more distance between the van and Sheila's car.

For the next forty-five minutes Steve drove while Derek watched the tracking monitor. Derek was so engrossed with the monitor that he hadn't been paying attention to where they were headed and was surprised when he felt the car slow down in a residential area. He looked out the darkened windows. "Where the hell are we?"

"Carson," Steve answered.

"You think she's going to see Slaughter out here."

"I don't know, maybe. But it doesn't fit. I've been told that he's a player that doesn't like to leave home plate, and in his case, that's South Central. Look out now. She's pulling over."

Derek and Steve watched as Sheila parked her car and then got out and started walking on foot.

Steve turned to Derek. "Let's see where she goes and then park later."

"I hear ya."

Steve followed at a safe distance as Sheila walked down the block and over to the next street.

"Oh yeah, she is definitely up to something." Steve said under his breath as they watched Sheila stop at the third house from the corner and pull out her cell phone. Derek adjusted the volume on the monitor.

"Nat, I'm here at the gate. What's the code?"

"5678," a male voice answered.

"What about the door?"

"I left it open. You're good to go."

"Where's my package?"

"The main closet off the foyer. Can't miss it. Peace."

"Thanks, Nat. I owe you." Sheila hung up, placed the phone in her pocket and then pulled it back out. "I better turn this thing off before Tre's stupid ass calls me again," she mumbled to herself and then walked to the eight-foot tall black iron gate.

Steve slowed the car to a stop and got out. "Okay, counselor. Take this puppy and park it somewhere behind her car and meet me back here. I'm going on in behind her and around to the back. I'll try to leave the gate open but remember the code just in case. Grab the ear pieces."

Within minutes Derek parked the car and headed back on foot to the turquoise blue colored house. When he got there he pushed the gate. It was opened. He made sure he locked back behind him and then headed toward the back and found Steve knelt down below a window placing the monitor that was connected to Sheila phone in his pocket. Derek threw him one of the earpieces that monitored Sheila's glasses and placed the other one in his ear.

Derek got behind a bush that was close to Steve and looked at the windows. "The windows are tinted."

"Tell me about it. Whoever lives here don't want to be seen. But that's okay. We got ears."

"Yeah, but is that enough," Derek wondered aloud.

"Shh," Steve said touching his ear. Derek stilled and listened.

"Hey, baby. Glad to see me?" Sheila said in a seductive voice.

"Who is she talking too?" Steve said to himself.

"Did you see somebody go in?" Derek asked only to have Steve wave him off.

"How did you get in here," a male voice spoke.

"Like you, I have my ways," Sheila said. "Didn't you miss me?"

"What do you want Sheila?"

"Only what you can give me."

"Don't play games with me. I'm not in the mood."

"Why baby? Why come you're never in the mood to play. You are always so serious, so in a hurry. Slow down and the smell the roses."

"How did you find me?"

"A girl never tells her secrets."

"Then just tell me what the hell you want and get out of my face."

"Ooh baby I like it when you get hostile, such a turn on."

Derek and Steve heard movement in the house and both wondered what was going on. Derek moved to the side of the house in search of a clear window. Bingo. The window on the front door was clear. He called Steve on his two-way and told him to stay low and to come to the front. He looked behind him. They would be sitting ducks out here if someone came up on them, but it was the only clear window. Steve made it around just as the man grabs Sheila by the arm.

"Don't mess with me Sheila. State your business or get the hell up out of here."

Sheila pulled her arm away from his grasp. "You have the perfect name you cold blooded bastard!"

"Get out!"

"NO! I'm not leaving until I get what I came for!" Sheila yelled pulling at his arm.

He grabbed her again and pulled her arms behind her back. "You know better than to step to me like that. I could drop you before you take your next breath."

"And you just made my panties all wet," Sheila laughed wickedly and kissed him on the cheek and then walked the length of the room.

He pulled his coat back on his shoulder and then looked at Sheila. "You're uncle needs to put you on a leash. You're way out of control."

"Man, I wish I could see in there better," Steve said.

"Shouldn't we call for backup?" Derek asked not liking the feel of this.

"Sit tight counselor. This is just some kinky-gangsta mess. Ain't nobody hurt," Steve said squatting down lower to the ground.

"Why did you leave, Ice?" Sheila asked.

"It was time."

"What about my uncle?"

"What about him?"

"He hasn't been the same since you left."

"That's not my problem."

"What the hell is your problem Ice? You think you too good for us now just because you're living all out here in suburbia!" Sheila yelled so loud that Derek and Steve both adjusted their earpieces.

"So did your uncle put you up to this."

"Put me up to what?"

"Finding me."

"Uncle don't control me just like he don't control you."

He stepped toward the front door and Derek and Steve both held their breath. "Well finally we agree on something."

"But he is family. Closest thing I ever had to a father. Just like you're the closest thing I ever had to a man."

He looked at her a moment and let out a slight laugh. "I am not now nor was I ever your man."

"Why you got a girl?"

"Don't worry about what I got."

"Why don't you want to be with me?"

"Why don't you understand that what I want has nothing to do with you?"

"You know nobody just walks away," Sheila said looking around nervously.

"I already did."

"No, you only think you did!" Sheila shouted suddenly and held a gun toward him.

He looked at her from the corner of his eye and slowly turned around looking her up and down with a smirk on his face. "Damn, girl. If I hadn't got with you myself I'd swear you had balls."

She stared coldly back into his eyes. "You didn't actually think I would let you walk away from me after all of these years without paying."

"Paying for what. I don't owe you a damn thing."

"You HURT ME!"

"Well hell I'm sorry! Whatever I did to hurt you, I apologize from the bottom of my damn heart!"

"You don't have a heart, Ice!"

"Well, hell, Sheila I apologize for that too. You happy?"

"Ice why you got to be like this? Why are you so cold?"

"I'm real okay! In case you haven't noticed, this is a cold ass world and Ice is down for Ice."

"And to hell with anybody else?"

"Whatever it takes Sheila is what I got to do. Now why don't you put down the gun, little girl?"

"I'm not a little girl and you know it!" Sheila yelled at him.

"Then why are you acting like one!" he yelled back.

"Because I know that's what you like," Sheila said holding her gun higher toward his face with both hands. "You like your women to be poor defenseless, helpless little girls so you can save them."

"Go to hell Sheila!"

"But I'm not like that. In fact I'm just the opposite. I'm like you. I know how to make my own way. I know how to take what I have to take to get what I need. By any means necessary."

"Okay then little Ms. X, what are you going to do, shoot me?" Derek and Steve watched as he grabbed her hand and helped her hold the gun right between his eyes. "Go ahead. Pull the damn trigger Sheila! Pull it!"

For seconds they both stood holding the gun. Derek shook his head. This fool was crazy. Sheila finally lowered her gun. "Damn it Ice, I love you."

"You got me confused with that pipe baby."

"Shut up Ice!" Sheila said raising the gun back to his face.

"Do what you got to do!"

"Ice let me stay with you, please." Sheila begged suddenly.

"You're crazy Sheila."

"How am I supposed to live without you?"

"How am I supposed to live with you? Don't you get it Sheila I'm through with this life! I'm through with you and your Uncle. I'm tired of this shit! And I'm tired of you. So very tired! You need to leave my house."

"I can't believe you're doing this. I can't believe you're throwing everything away for this..." She stopped in mid sentence and moved toward a closet and opened the door. Immediately Steve and Derek saw someone gagged, blindfolded and tied to a chair.

"What the hell..." Steve murmured as him and Derek watched in amazement.

"...for this bitch!" Sheila screamed as she went over to the chair and pushed it until it hit floor and then went and stood over it. She reached down and pulled the blindfold off.

"Oh, come on now Ice, you look surprised. You didn't actually think I didn't know what's up, did you?"

His mouth suddenly dropped.

"What's wrong? You seemed to be lost for words Ice. Oh, I'm sorry. She calls you uh...*Marcus* right?"

"Oh my God," Derek said pulling the earpiece from his ear and headed for the door.

"Derek, what the hell are you doing?" Steve said sternly.

"That's Nicole Williams! Call for back up!" Derek said excitedly grabbing his own gun and moving closer to the door.

"Shit!" Steve said under his breath and then got on the radio.

Derek squatted in front of door and watched as Sheila waved her gun in Nicole's face.

"Don't you have anything to say for yourself, baby?" Sheila asked.

"You sent that package to me didn't you."

"What package?"

"Don't play stupid with me Sheila!"

"Oh, you're talking about those pictures of that dead body and that gun that I sent to Seattle. Uncle Johnny gave me those a long time ago. Said they might come in handy one day. It's a good thing I listen to him. I learned a lot from him you know."

"Including blackmail."

"It's not worse than murder," Sheila said nonchalantly.

"Get that gun out of her face."

"Not until you tell her."

"Tell her what?"

"About us."

"There is no us!"

"Come on Ice, it's okay," Sheila said as she moved closer to Nicole and placed her gun next to her head and then reached down and removed the gag from her mouth.

"Get... that... gun... out... of... her... face!"

"What's wrong Ice. You're still afraid for your girl to know the real you. Come on now, don't' keep her in the dark. Tell her about the dead body in the picture. Tell her about my uncle, the drug deals, the drive-bys, and the pickups. Tell her about the money, the crack, cocaine, heroin, the pills, the marijuana, the parties, the corners, the alleys, and the trips. Come on Ice! Share your world. See if she loves you as much as you love her! See if she still want to wear that stupid ring!"

"Go to hell!"

Sheila laughed. "Why do you care about her, Ice. Do you know what this bitch did to me, to us? She played us both. All of those years she spent with James do you think she was thinking about you or, or thinking about me. Hell no, this selfish bitch was doing nothing but standing in my way while James strung me along."

"James. What the hell does this have to do with him?"

"James was everything to me!" Sheila shouted. "He was my world until this bitch came along. Then next thing I knew she was writing for him and he was singing on tours and just like that he was gone. Nothing matter to him anymore but his music! For years he promised me that we would get together again, that he would get rid of her. He promised me he wasn't going to marry her. Guess he stuck to that. But he never left her! At least not the way he wanted to."

"You killed James?" Nicole asked weakly.

Sheila looked at her. "Yeah I killed him and then sat back and watched that bastard bleed to death. And now it's your turn. I can't let you have Ice."

She started to pull the trigger back on the gun but before she could Ice reached in his pocket and pulled out his gun and pointed it right between her eyes before she could blink.

"You touch her and I'll kill you! I SWEAR I WILL!"

She stared back at him and her hand came down and she hit the wall as her twisted smile returned. "That's the Ice I know and love! You see that Ms. Thang? Ice is hard! Hell, he's hard as a rock."

"Shut the hell up Sheila!" he shouted still holding the gun in her face.

"Why are you protecting her? She can't love you, Ice." Sheila said calmly.

"Go to hell Sheila! " he shouted looking down at Nicole and then slowly eased the gun down from Sheila's face.

"You know I'm the only woman that can love you Ice," Sheila uttered all of a sudden. "You think she's going to understand why you have to leave town for days and weeks at a time. Will she get why you sleep with a gun under your bed for immediate access or why you don't even sleep at all? She can't go to the places that you go. She can't see the things you see. She can't love you, Ice!"

"You bitch!" Nicole screamed suddenly kicking Sheila over and knocking her gun across the room. Derek and Steve burst through the front door with guns in hand just as more police officers came through the back. Within seconds police both inside and out swarmed the house. Ice froze in his tracks, dropped his gun and placed his hands in the air. Steve placed his gun to his head while another officer handcuffed him and read him his rights.

For seconds Derek stood in disbelief and then went and untied Nicole. Behind him the police wrestled with Sheila and then a single gunshot echoed throughout the room. Derek looked back and saw blood oozing from Sheila's head. Then he looked at Ice whose eyes hadn't left Nicole's since they came into the room.

Derek watched as Steve pushed Anthony Marcus Washington, Jr. in a chair in the interrogation room of the 46th Precinct with his hands in handcuffs behind him from behind the two-way mirror. It took everything inside him not to go in and put his fist in his deceitful face.

She had a gun in her face! A gun! With everything she's been through this past year now this. All because of him! Derek glared into the room as he listened to Steve play pieces of the conversation that was recorded. Marcus didn't blink. He just sat there as heartless and cold as his namesake. Ice!

"We got you man and you're going to give us John Slaughter," Steve said turning off the tape.

Marcus gave no response as he stared into Steve's eyes. His demeanor remained cool as a summer breeze.

"You're in enough hot water to melt Ice. I know you don't want to do time for him too. Where is he?"

Marcus sat perfectly still giving up nothing.

"Look why don't you make this easy on yourself, maybe we can work out a deal with the D.A, uh? I can tell them that hey you just got caught up in some shit behind Sheila. I could loose this tape. All you go to do is give me John Slaughter."

He still gave no response.

"Okay you want to play hard then we'll play hard ball." Steve stood up and looked into the two-way mirror and Derek eased his way toward the door and put his hand on the handle.

"You don't want to give up John than that's fine, be loyal. But what about Nicole I guess you don't give a damn if she goes down with you."

Steve turned around at Marcus' quick movement as he stood up knocking over the chair that he was sitting in. Within seconds Marcus was standing inches from Steve.

"You can't touch her and you know it!" Marcus uttered tightly, anger brimming in his eyes.

Steve smiled into Marcus' face. "You never know. There are all kinds of evidence that can incriminate her at least as an accessory."

Marcus rammed his head into Steve's and instantly blood seeped out of Steve's nose.

"You bastard!" Steve yelled wiping the blood from his nose.

Derek came blaring in the room grabbing Marcus by the collar of his shirt and throwing him against the wall.

"You think you're one cold ass don't you! Not only do you deal drugs and God knows what else right under your family and friends' nose, now you think you can beat up on cops. I'm going to bury you so deep that it will take years for anybody to know what the hell happened to you!"

"It's okay, Derek. I got this," Steve said wiping the rest of the blood from his nose with a handkerchief.

Marcus gawked at Derek. "Derek. As in Assistant D.A, Derek Alexander, the bastard that save Nicole's life one minute and then took advantage of her in the next!"

The two men stared into each other's eyes both not backing down. Derek was filled with contempt. He finally let go of Marcus' collar and walked around the length of the room.

"Steve leave us alone," Derek said after a moment.

"This is my case man."

"Leave!" Derek said louder.

Steve looked at the two of them and left the room. Derek went to the falling chair and picked it up and nodded his head for Marcus' to sit down, but he declined. Derek stood still, his feet apart, fist clinched.

"What happened between Nicole and I that night has nothing to do with this."

"Nicole has everything to do with this!" Marcus yelled.

"And that's on you. Because of you she was kidnapped and held in a closet tied up for hours. Her life was threatened and gun was held to her head. She could have been killed!" Derek shouted and then stopped suddenly as he realized that he was shaking with anger. He ran his hand across his face and then pointed at Marcus. "That's all on you."

Marcus turned his back away from Derek toward the two-way mirror. Derek looked at his reflection. No wonder Marcus could do what he did. At one glance one would never know that he was a drug dealer. He dressed nice, but wasn't flashy. His only piece of jewelry was a nice but understated Rolex. His hair was cut short, his beard and mustache neat. He appeared to be the average everyday, intelligent, confident businessman that he pretended to be.

Had Derek ever met him under any other circumstances he would probably strike up a conversation with him about any of number of things from the stock market to a Lakers' game. But now looking at him, Derek is sure all that laid back persona of his is just a facade to cover the real low life murdering drug dealer that he is. And Derek couldn't put a hand on him.

The tape was nothing but of Sheila spitting out accusations. No judge in the county is going to let that tape in without more evidence and there was none. No money, no drugs nothing was found in the house, Sheila's condo, on Marcus or his car. The police even went to his dealership and came up empty. His tracks were covered. The only way to get him down is getting John Slaughter or a confession from the man himself.

"So what does Nicole think of your lifestyle or did she even know before today that you are the damn scum of the earth?" Derek asked.

Marcus turned around slowly his nostrils flaring. "Don't you dare say her name!"

Derek stood still staring back at Marcus noting the pure anger in his eyes and then let a smile cross his own lips.

"We had a nice time together you know. She's very sweet, very sweet. Leaves a brother breathless, literally, you know. Just the kind of lady I've been looking for all of my life."

Derek paced around the room and watched as Marcus' whole body tensed up, his eyes wide and wild looking. His handcuff hands clinched tightly in a fist.

"Come on think about it Mr. Washington. The truth is out brother. You're a drug dealer, Ice! Whatever you two had is over. You think she's still going to want to be you? I'll be willing to bet that she'll be more than happy to finish what we started the night we met." Derek smiled.

Within seconds Marcus moved so close to Derek that he felt the hairs on the back of his neck stand at attention. His cold steel like eyes glared down at him so hard that for seconds Derek felt trapped in his own skin. He stole a quick glance at the double mirror window and wondered if Steve was behind it and then slowly took several steps away from the infamous Ice and grabbed the door handle.

"The reason why Nicole's going to want me instead of you is because I can walk out of this door. But you never will again."

MARCUS

44

I'm bad down to the bone.
I'm cold to my very core;
Some say I have ice water in my veins.
I'd lie if I had to steal.
I'd cheat if it came down to the kill
all in the name and in the defense of my reign.
But on the lighter side of darkness is my heart;
which when touched
can fill with-overwhelming,
overbearing, raw emotion- that strips me naked;
unmasking my vulnerabilities, controlling my senses,
and revealing my cowardice-to a feeling
that is stronger than I.

I did what I did not because I wanted to or like to but because I had to. I had to do it in order to protect those I cared about. I had to do it in order to save myself. For seventeen years I lived a lie with the truth hanging over my head. I lived two different and separate lives but somewhere in between I got caught up in my own deceitfulness. Ice was my street name, my code. I never meant to become him. But Ice seen too much and was in too deep. He had to fight to survive and took on his own identity. But in truth Ice was born a long time ago.

Glen Hall beat and raped Nicole and stripped her of her innocence and now years later I know he did the same to me. I lost everything that night, my heart, my soul and my damn mind.

When I found Nicole balled up in a corner trying to hang onto life I felt a pain I never knew before and tasted a fear I had never tasted. As I held her in my arms and looked down in her face I could see and feel her slipping away. She looked in my eyes one time and then closed them and immediately felt so lifeless. The tears that were sliding from her swollen eyes dropped on my arm and my heart dropped with it. My soul literally started dying and I cried like I never cried in my life. At that moment I didn't know that some kind of way Nicole was going to pull through. I didn't know that she would somehow find a way to live her life with this horrible night in her past. At that moment I only realize that she was gone, ripped away from me and I knew I would never be the same without her.

By the time I reached my house Nicole had briefly opened her eyes and I dared myself to hope as I screamed for my parents help. My mother came in assessed everything in the blink of an eye and took control. I ran to Baker's house, pounded on his door and finally threw a brick in his window before I saw a light come on inside his house. When we made it back to my house I heard Nicole say one word and to this day I still find it hard to explain what happened to me next. It was at that moment I lost my mind. I left my home my family and my girl with every intention of making Glen Hall regret the day he ever looked at Nicole.

I don't remember looking for him. I remember finding him. Seeing him watching television in the back room of Swann's place. I ran to him pulled him out the chair threw him against the wall and swung at him over and over. Somehow we ended up outside exchanging blow for blow in the pouring down rain. But I didn't feel his blows. He couldn't hurt me more than I already was. He had already destroyed the best part of me. Before that night I had never known such anger, rage and pure unadulterated hatred.

Glen reached in his pocket and pulled out a knife. The same knife he pulled on me in school. I looked down at the six-inch blade gleaming in his hand and I immediately imagined him slicing Nicole with it. Tears of rage filled my eyes and I charged toward him like a bull seeing red and threw him against the gate. He dropped the knife, cursed and crawled until he found it again and this time stood up and pointed the knife toward my side. Out of nowhere Swann was beside me and placed a cold steal object in my hand. I didn't need to look at it to know what it was. I raised my right hand up pointed it directly at him and for a half of second I thought about walking away. Then the sky lit up as lighting shot across it. Glen jumped toward me and the gleam of the knife caught my eye and I could feel Nicole's pain, see her bruised face and without hesitating I fired the gun.

The next thing I truly remember was standing at the airport. Nicole and I said goodbye to my family and the life we once knew and boarded a plane in search of survival. I sat on the plane not thinking of what I did to Glen but of what he did to her. Each time she moved she winced in pain and everything inside me hurt on top of her hurt. I was going to see her through this I swore I was. I was going to stand by her side every step of the way. But what I didn't know was that night changed who I was forever.

Six days after we got to LA I got a phone call. I had been sitting at Nicole's door on the floor as she lay in the bed fighting off nightmares in search of sleep. I stood up at the sound of my grandmother's voice and went down the hall and down stairs to get the phone from her. She briefly touched my cheek with her soft hands before handing me the phone and then walked away. I put the phone to my ear. Swann's voice was crystal clear. I owed him. He delivered Glen and now I owed him my life.

He gave me a name and a phone number. I was to call John Slaughter and work with him immediately. I turned and looked around and saw my cousin coming in the house carrying a basketball and then head upstairs just as Swann reminded me that I could go to jail if he decided to tell the police about Glen and he had proof that I killed him. Angrily I called his bluff and whispered under my breath my own obscenities.

Swann's voice crackled in the phone with laughter and then just as suddenly his tone became very harsh as he cursed me and informed me that every second of every day he was watching me, Nicole and my family back home. Everyone would pay, even my cousin and my grandmother. And then the phone went dead. I stood there in shock and nervously hung up the phone. Two seconds later it rang again and it was John Slaughter. I listened and an hour later I descended into a life that I would never escape.

There have been times that I have wondered if I had it do over again, would I really do it again. Would I take the same route and more times than none the answer is the same because if I'm nothing else I'm true to myself. I know me. I might have been able to walk around for years and hide things from everybody else but I couldn't hide from myself. Ice was my nemesis. I slipped into a dark world that I couldn't run from. I didn't want to live the life I lived but I chose it in a blind rage and I know if faced with the same situation I would do things exactly the same. It's not right by means it's just who I am.

I turned my head toward the bars that I have spent the last nine hundred and fifteen days locked behind and then looked back at the corner of the left wall just above my bed. In block large letters the word CONSEQUENCES stared back at me. A constant reminder left by someone before me as to why I am here. This cell is the culmination and end result of the life I lived for seventeen years but it does not define me. It took my cousin to make me realize that.

Mike and Nicole came to see me as soon I was charged but I refused to see them. My parents and sisters came and I couldn't face them. I couldn't face anybody. At the time anger was set deep in my bones and disgust drew blood under my skin as my whole body felt like it was on fire and I could do nothing but loathe myself and everything I ever did in my whole life. For thirty days I refuse to see everybody, my sisters, my parents. I just wanted to sit and smell my own funky shit. Lay in it roll around in it and wait to die cause I truly believe nobody could pull me out of it.

Nicole wrote to me but I sent the letters back unopened unable to read them, afraid at what they might say. The mere thought of being without her made everything inside me hurt. I wanted someone to reach inside me cut my heart out and throw it away so I couldn't feel the pain of losing her again. How was I going to face her! How was she ever going to believe that I ever loved her when all I have ever done was lie to her!

During my two-day trial they were all in the courtroom but I never turned to face them as they listened to the prosecutions evidence against me. Derek led the three ring circus telling of the sting operation that led to my capture. Slaughter and his boys were dead. They went out fighting when the police finally caught up with them. I was the only one left. I had to pay. The jury found me guilty. The judge held my fate in his hands.

When I stood in that courtroom after hearing my sentencing Mike's face was the first I saw. Our same shaped eyes met and then I looked away. I had betrayed him. I had lied and hid from my family everyday. I misused Mike's trust and belief in me. What he thought was loyalty to him was nothing more than my need to work his gigs. While he was performing I was there dealing to his undying fans.

Before I was transferred, I wrote Mike twice. I mailed the first one asking only that he come to see me. When he came I handed him the second one. In that letter I told him every single detail of my life that he didn't know about: Swann, Slaughter, Sheila, the rape, Glen everything. I even told him how to get my money to give to Nicole. I owed her that much.

He sat across from me opened the letter and read it word for word. His face expressed all that I expected him to feel; disgust, anguish even horror, all of it was in his eyes. He would read a sentence look up into my eyes without a word and then back down at the paper that was nothing but my ugly truth staring him in the face. He finished the letter, folded it up and put it in his pocket without looking at me. It was in that moment that I realized how close we were and how much I had let him down. He saved my father's life and I lied to him. For seventeen years I lied to him everyday.

The guard came over and informed us that the visiting hours were over and I stood to walk back to my cell when Mike called my name. I turned around slowly facing him as he stood up and walked over to me. We stood for seconds eye to eye in total silence my frame slightly taller than his and then he surprised me by pulling me in arms and telling me one thing. The things I've done, does not in any way change who I am.

When I was transferred to the state penitentiary there was a letter waiting on me from Nicole. The guard thrust the already opened letter in my face and pushed me in my new home. I sat on the bed and I don't know how long I sat there holding the letter just staring down at Nicole's handwriting on the envelope. I finally put the letter down on the floor next to the bed and fell asleep without reading it. The next day another one came and the next day another one and I still hadn't had the courage to read the first. By the time I was there ten days I had ten letters and I still couldn't bring myself to open them.

LOVE AND CONSEQUENCES

Then I received a letter from Mike. I sat down and took a deep breath and opened the pages of Mike's letter and immediately my heart jumped out of my skin. There was the picture of Nicole and I taken in my family's backyard at the barbecue. I gazed down at us in each other's arms as we shared a kiss. I looked down at the pages and instead of Mike's handwriting it was Nicole's.

Dear Marcus,

I keep telling myself that you're reading my letters even though
I haven't heard from you. I miss you so much. I miss your voice,
your smile, your light brown eyes, and mostly your love.

As I read the first two sentences my hands began to shake so badly I had to stop and place the paper flat against my legs so I could continue.

I look back in my life and all I see is you.
Every good and miserable moment I went through
you were right by my side. You were always
there to make everything right for me. And
more than anything I need you to believe that
I'm here for you now. I don't care about what
you did Marcus because I know your heart. I know
what it's like to have your love. Baby, please
write back to me. Don't give up on us because I
refuse to. I know you Marcus. I know you're a
man of your word. And when you put this ring
on my finger you promised to stick by my side
no matter what. No matter what Marcus you
promised me forever.
I love you, Nic.

The pages suddenly became blurry and I strained to read the words over and only when I wiped my eyes did I realize I had tears in them. I placed the now wet pages down on the bed next to the picture of me and the woman I have loved all of my life and for seconds the tears kept falling and then seconds later my heart felt lighter than it had in months. I found the other letters and pulled the pages of each of them out and read them all.

In the first letter she told me how Michael had showed her the letter I wrote to him and how she cried for five days straight afterwards because of everything I went through. She talked about the rape and how Glen ripped her soul from her that night and how hard it was for her to struggle to overcome it and the worst part of it all was seeing in my eyes that I blamed myself. She wrote: I remember the nights when you thought I was asleep how you cried and blamed yourself for getting there late and for having that fight with Glen. What happened to me wasn't your fault and I didn't know how to make you see that.

Within an hour I read the other letters. Each one told me she loved me, missed me and forgave me. Each one had blank pieces of paper and a stamped envelope waiting on me to write back to her. And I had ignored her. I had been so afraid of feeling her rejection that I in turned rejected her.

I called out to a guard and asked for a pen and then gather all of the blank pages and began to write. I wrote page after page pouring out my heart to her and telling how sorry I was for what Sheila put her through. I never wanted that part of my life to touch her and I tried so hard to keep it all away from her. I just wanted to love her. Pure and simple that's all I ever wanted from the moment I first met her.

Her letters come almost every day giving me a source of hope for a life outside of this cage and makes me remember the last morning we spent together.

We had breakfast. I squeezed her fresh orange juice and she had scrambled eggs for me and we both had sipped on hazelnut coffee while barely able to keep our hands off each other.

Every two seconds I was touching her hair, holding her hands or rubbing her legs. She had fed me my eggs and kissed me in between bites while rubbing her feet up against me. We didn't have words of conversation but body language that said we were comfortable and happy. And now as uneventful as it all seemed it's what I have to hold onto until I see her again.

NICOLE

45

*If it was easy
it wouldn't be appreciated.
If it was a game
it wouldn't be complicated.
If it wasn't meant to be
it wouldn't hurt when we touch.
If it wasn't worth it
it wouldn't cost us so much.
If didn't mean anything
it wouldn't be nothing to feel.
If it wasn't hard
it wouldn't be real.*

I wrote these words the morning after. Before I understood how or why these words came to me. Making me realize that when it's all said and done the only thing that mattered to me was our love. It may sound crazy to some but it was what I believe and what I felt. I couldn't explain it. I didn't know why. It just was. Like the sky is blue and the ocean is deep, it just was. I loved Marcus and I couldn't let go of that one simple fact.

When Derek came to me and reaffirmed that Marcus had done everything that Sheila said he had done I couldn't focus on it. It all seemed so unreal. I remember him taking my hands in his and telling me of Marcus' crime and I just couldn't let it sink in. I just kept seeing Marcus' eyes and the way they looked at me as they took him away. They were so clear and revealing. It was like looking through a window that had been opened for the first time after a turbulent storm. When he looked at me he didn't try to deny, justify or explain anything. It was so clear that the raging storm that had tossed his life and almost thrown him overboard was over and his soul was now calm.

But I wasn't ready or prepared for his refusal to see me. I didn't understand then, that was the only way he could save himself. I wanted to see him talk to him to reassure him that I would be with him all the way. All through the trial he wouldn't look my way and it hurt. Then Michael explained it so simple. Marcus was turning away because he didn't want to lie anymore.

When I read Marcus' letter to Michael, a damn burst inside of me and I felt pure horror. The nightmares came back and I relived the pain of that awful night. Night after night I woke up screaming, shaking and terrified. I had tried so hard to erase, cover up and run from my past while Marcus lived with that night everyday and I didn't see it because I was so busy thinking that what happened to me only happened to me. I pushed him away, convinced myself that we couldn't be together anymore, that our love had died. But I was wrong, so very wrong. After all of these years it was the furthest thing from the truth.

He finally wrote me back and tears of joy spilled from my heart. He told me how grateful he was to have my love and my understanding and forgiveness. I immediately wrote him back telling him that I was so glad to have his and that I was counting every second of everyday until I was with him again.

I looked outside the kitchen window. It was a clear day. The sky was picture perfect with cotton shaped clouds. I took a deep breath and picked up my pad and pen and then got comfortable on the couch. I began this letter like all the rest but this one would be different in so many ways.

In nine hundred and twenty two days I've seen him only once. He doesn't want me to see him behind bars and I understand and respect that. We had been writing each other every day and I was grateful for that connection but just once I had to see him. What I had to say I couldn't put in a letter.

I walked nervously through the damp like halls and waited in a room filled with strangers for him to join me. He walked in and I had to catch my breath. It had already been two months since I saw him and over three months since I last touched him and it seemed like a million years. He walked over to me, smiled and greeted me with a kiss on the cheek. I pulled him in my arms and for seconds we held each other and then awkwardly pulled away. He took my hand and found us a table away from the others. I sat down and he sat right next to me still holding my hand.

I started doing what I said I wouldn't do. But I couldn't help it. I was so happy just to see him that the tears flowed freely. His smile lightened my heart and then we shared a brief laugh. He asked me what was so important to make me come all the way here instead of writing him. I looked down at the table and then placed his other hand inside mine and then looked into his light eyes. I told him he was going to be a father. I was pregnant with twins.

I watched as his eyes filled with surprise and then happiness as that big smile of his formed on his face exposing his deep dimples. He whispered you're going to have a baby. I shook my head. We're going to have babies, I corrected. He leaned his face into mine and I still can't explain the joy I felt being that close to him again.

LOVE AND CONSEQUENCES

I left that day hopeful. Marcus was sentenced to four years but could get out in less than three with time served and good behavior. I went there that day to let him know I needed him to hurry home to me. In each letter I gave him a progress report on my pregnancy. I was getting big as a house in no time flat and Michael was only too happy to snap pictures of my enlarging stomach.

I told him about each doctor's visit, what vitamins I was taking, about my morning sickness, my cravings and late night snack binges. My feet and hands swelled and I had to take my ring off and wore it around my neck on a chain. I moved into Devon's room downstairs because I couldn't walk up the stairs anymore without getting tired. And then we moved home. I was in my seventh month, Michael had finished his CD and was getting antsy missing Crystal like crazy and Marcus wrote me and told me that he wanted me to be with his family. He wanted us all to be together when he comes home.

Seeing his parents and sisters and being in Seattle, was like being with him. He was everywhere and I felt like I could touch him even though we were hundreds of miles away from each other. When the twins were born I sent him picture after picture of them and videotaped everything they did so he wouldn't miss anything about their life. I took pictures of them eating, sleeping, bathing, their first tooth, of them crawling across the floor and of outfits I bought them. I taped my daughter, Aniya's first steps, and my son, Anthony's first haircut. I even recorded their voices so he could know what they sounded like when they laughed, cried and coed and talked.

Shortly after the twins were born I started on the plans for our house. I wanted Marcus to come home to our home, to his family. I picked out a lot on Whidby Island. With the help of April and Anita I met with architects, builders and contractors to build our dream home. And when things were finally in mo-tion I sent pictures of paint, carpet, cabinets everything that had to be decided on I put in his hands to reinforce that it was his home. Everyday I was out there on our land taking pictures of each stage, the survey, the foundation, and the frame to send to him.

Now the result was our beautiful two-story home that overlooked the ocean and sat on three acres that had plenty of trees in the back. I didn't get the horses, my hands are full enough with the twins and besides I don't know the first thing about horses. The only thing left for me to do now is to plan our wedding, which is going to be small and quaint and the minute Marcus steps off that plane.

I walked upstairs to check on Aniya and Anthony, III. They were fast asleep so I went back downstairs. I took my pad and pen to the terrace and sat out in the ocean air. A breeze gently caressed my face and reminded me of the way Marcus looks at me. I closed my eyes and remembered our first kiss. Could almost feel it. And tears came to my eyes as I thought about how I almost lost him forever. I wiped them away and began to write.

LaTANYA WHITMORE

Love is our one and only everlasting emotion
but so many of us take it for granted
not realizing it's worth or it's value.
We spend so much time searching for it
and then once found think it will always be there
not realizing how special it is
like that precious jewel
that should be kept under lock and key.
But what do we do?
as humans we make mistakes
and hurt the ones that should never be hurt
and abuse the ones that we should cherish.
Never considering ourselves
to be blessed to know
the pure essence of a feeling
and realize that love is...
The most natural thing about us
our basic instinct-
our pure nakedness stripped down to the bone
where there's no false pretense
because it's all that you are and all that you know.
Where there is no room for the superficial
or any kind of hype
cause it's not a game
with rules to follow
or any guidelines to go by
or even a guarantee that you will win.
It's just a chance you take in its simplest form
being careful not to become complacent
as you try to hold on to the best thing that
has ever happened in your life.

I put down my pen went inside the house and into the study and placed it on the desk. I wasn't going to mail it. He was going to get this one in person when he comes home next week. Just as I exited the study I heard Aniya on the baby monitor, calling me. I went up the stairs two at a time and scooped up Marcus' daughter in my arms before she woke up her brother. She placed her little arm around my neck and I kissed her cheek.

As I headed back downstairs the doorbell rang. I glanced through the window and saw a shadow. Aniya was still in my arms.

"Doorbell mommy, doorbell."

I smiled down at her two year old face. "That's right baby, doorbell," I said kissing her again and she then wiggled out of my arms and went toward the Legos she had been playing with earlier in the middle of the floor. I went to the door with the smile for my daughter still on my lips as I turned the handle of the door and pulled it open.

Time stood still, the earth stopped moving, my heart stopped beating and tears instantly filled my eyes. I couldn't move. For months I have been dreaming about this moment. Waiting and anticipating this moment and it was here and I couldn't move.

The storm door opened and I watched as he came closer to me his eyes looking directly into my eyes and something so incredible happened. I couldn't see nothing but what was in front of me. I didn't know if it was daylight or night-time, raining or snowing, summer or fall. All I could see was my Morning's eyes that seemed to be filled with the exact same thing that was in my heart. It was like looking in a mirror.

His arms came around me. I never felt so much warmth, protection and yes oh God yes love. My body trembled as I held him with everything inside of me and cried a million tears. I kissed the side of his bearded face and tasted his tears as he squeezed me tighter in his embrace.

I tried to speak but a thousand words got choked up inside of me and none stumbled out. All I could do was hold him and pray that I never had to let him go again.

I pulled just inches away from him so I could look in his face and into his eyes. "Welcome home baby."

His eyes filled with more tears as his hands gently began to caress my hair and my face. "Oh God, baby. I missed you so much. I love so much Nic."

His lips came to mine touched them tenderly and then I complete lost myself cause I swear nothing as ever felt so good before. Through our tears we kissed over and over and over again and it was as if nothing had ever changed between us.

"I'm so glad to see you, to hold you. You have no idea how much I've prayed to see this beautiful face, your beautiful brown eyes," Marcus deep voice whispered.

"I've missed you like crazy too. I dreamed of you everyday. I wake up in the middle of the night wanting to feel you, to hold..." My tears stopped my words.

"It's okay baby, I'm here. I'm never going to leave you again. Never. I've waited all of my life to love you Nic."

"I love you Anthony Marcus."

"Then marry me, tomorrow."

I smiled up into his eyes. "Try to stop me."

Marcus' lips came closer to mine and again kiss me so sweetly and tenderly that it felt like the first time.

"Mommy, mommy, little brotha up."

Marcus and I both turned toward Aniya. His eyes shone. "She's beautiful baby. Oh God, she's so beautiful."

"Aniya baby come here," I said holding out my arms. She looked at us both and then ran to my arms. I picked her up and then we both looked at Marcus. "Do you know who this is? Remember what I told you."

She nodded her head.

"Can you say hi and give him a hug."

She looked at Marcus a moment like she was thinking real hard and then slowly reached out to him and hugged him. "Hi daddy."

Marcus' face beamed. "Hi baby. Oh sweetie, hi." He leaned over and kissed me as he held her and I couldn't tell who was crying more.

I then went upstairs to get Anthony, III. I came back down and hurriedly placed my son in his father's arms. I watched as Marcus looked at his son and words cannot explain the happiness I felt inside. He looked at me with his tear filled eyes and dimpled smile.

"Little brotha, daddy home," Aniya said to her brother.

Marcus held both of his children and kissed them over and over. For moments I stood and watched as the twins asked him a thousand questions and the three of them fell to the floor. A huge smile was on his face as they jumped on him and tickled him and for the first time Marcus' laughter filled this house. Once again tears came to my eyes. I went and closed the door on our past. Right here and right now is where our life together was going to begin and never end. It was a long journey with many twist and turns but here we are exactly where we always wanted to be, a family. Finally.